FEATURES THESE BES̲... ...NTRIBUTORS

STEPHEN BAXTER, Philip K. Dick and BSFA Award-winning author of the *Destiny's Children* series . . . **MIKE CAREY,** Acclaimed writer for *Lucifer* and *The Unwritten* from DC/Vertigo . . . **PAUL CORNELL,** Two-time Hugo Award nominee for his work on *Doctor Who,* and a writer for the Marvel Comics series *Young Avengers,* and *Captain Britain and MI-13* . . . **PETER DAVID,** *New York Times* bestselling author known for his work on Marvel comics like *Spider-Man,* and *The Incredible Hulk* and DC Comics' *Aquaman* . . . **MARJORIE M. LIU,** *New York Times* bestselling author, and the writer of Marvel Comics' *Black Widow, Dark Wolverine,* and *NYX* . . . **IAN McDONALD,** Hugo and BSFA Award–winning author of *River of Gods* and *Brasyl* . . . **CHRIS ROBERSON,** Award-winning science fiction author, and the writer of DC/Vertigo's *Cinderella: From Fabletown with Love* and *I, Zombie* . . . **GAIL SIMONE,** acclaimed writer of DC Comics' *Wonder Woman, Superman,* and *Birds of Prey* . . . **MATTHEW STURGES,** fantasy novelist and a writer for DC/Vertigo's *Jack of Fables* and DC's *JSA All Stars* . . . **BILL WILLINGHAM,** Creator and writer of the DC/Vertigo smash hits *Fables* and *Jack of Fables.*

☆   ★   ☆

Praise for editor Lou Anders

"Lou Anders is an accomplished anthologist, adept at choosing themes likely to encourage originality of concept from his writers."
—*Locus*

This title is also available as an eBook

MASKED

EDITED BY LOU ANDERS

GALLERY BOOKS

new york   london   toronto   sydney

Gallery Books
A Division of Simon & Schuster, Inc.
1230 Avenue of the Americas
New York, NY 10020

First Gallery Books trade paperback edition July 2010

GALLERY BOOKS and colophon are trademarks of Simon & Schuster, Inc.

For information about special discounts for bulk purchases, please contact Simon & Schuster Special Sales at 1-866-506-1949 or business@simonandschuster.com.

The Simon & Schuster Speakers Bureau can bring authors to your live event. For more information or to book an event contact the Simon & Schuster Speakers Bureau at 1-866-248-3049 or visit our website at www.simonspeakers.com.

Designed by Davina Mock-Maniscalco

Manufactured in the United States of America

10 9 8 7 6 5 4 3 2 1

Library of Congress Cataloging-in-Publication Data
Masked / edited by Lou Anders.—1st Gallery Books trade paperback ed.
    p. cm.
1. Fantasy fiction, American. 2. Superheroes—Fiction. 3. Fantasy fiction, English,
I. Anders, Lou.
PS648.F3W58 2010
813'.0876608—dc22

2010003536

ISBN 978-1-4391-6882-0
ISBN 978-1-4391-6883-7 (ebook)

For My Little Superheroes, Arthur and Alex,
Who Stormed the Fortress and Banished the Solitude

Acknowledgments

As with any anthology project, thanks are due to many people. This time out, copious appreciation is due to my friends George Mann, Mark C. Newton, and Christian Dunn, who had a hand in this anthology's genesis. Thanks also to my editor at Gallery, the incomparable Jennifer Heddle, who, incidentally, also bought my very first professional anthology *Live Without a Net* way back when (and thus had a major hand in launching my publishing career). It's wonderful to be working with her again. Thanks are certainly due to the marvelous Trevor Hairsine for a fabulous cover, and to the very dear Paul Cornell, who, apart from his own wonderful contribution, generously helped with facilitating introductions to some of the comic book scribes herein. Finally, and as always, thanks to my wonderful wife, Xin, for her superheroic levels of love and support.

Contents

Introduction: The Golden Age   LOU ANDERS   xi

Cleansed and Set in Gold   MATTHEW STURGES   1

Where Their Worm Dieth Not   JAMES MAXEY   31

Secret Identity   PAUL CORNELL   53

The Non-Event   MIKE CAREY   71

Avatar   MIKE BARON   89

Message from the Bubblegum Factory   DARYL GREGORY   105

Thug   GAIL SIMONE   135

Vacuum Lad   STEPHEN BAXTER   151

A Knight of Ghosts and Shadows   CHRIS ROBERSON   173

Head Cases   PETER DAVID AND KATHLEEN DAVID   207

Downfall   JOSEPH MALLOZZI   227

By My Works You Shall Know Me   MARK CHADBOURN   283

Call Her Savage   MARJORIE M. LIU   305

Tonight We Fly   IAN MCDONALD   333

A to Z in the Ultimate Big Company
    Superhero Universe (Villains Too)   BILL WILLINGHAM   351

About the Editor   400

The Golden Age

"And the other fields I've worked in—Fantasy, or Children's Fiction, or Horror—tend to be critically looked down on as gutter literature by a certain sort of reader (comics weren't even in the gutter when I started writing them. We were some kind of sub-drain. You looked up to the gutter)."

—Neil Gaiman

Superheroes and superheroines have come a long way since Jerry Siegel and Joe Shuster created the Man of Steel back in 1938. From the prototypical archetypes of Superman and Batman (themselves direct descendants of the pulp fiction heroes Doc Savage and the Shadow), a whole multiverse of costumed crusaders has evolved. Seventy-two years later, and every shape and size of superhuman vigilante has been explored. They may come by their powers naturally or as the result of exposure to some scientific accident. They may rely on a technological arsenal of their own creation or have been bequeathed their abilities by a mentor. They may be caped or cowled, though plenty are neither. They usually have a secret identity, though some forgo privacy in favor of a public life. They may have a cave deep under the ground, a laboratory high above the city, a base at the North Pole, or even a headquarters on the moon. They serve as a shining example or dish out a rough justice. And whoever they are, they all battle colorful rogues' galleries of the worst villains imaginable, from mad scientists to alien monsters, harmless pranksters to homicidal maniacs.

These days, the so-named "golden age" of the comic book field is three-quarters of a century behind us, during which time comic books have grown and evolved a considerable degree. Decades have passed since the first time the lid was lifted on dealing with social issues in a metaphorical context, and after a long struggle, so called "comic books" have found their way into mainstream acceptance as legitimate, sophisticated entertainment.

What's more, the comic book superhero has been a staple of television animation and live-action filmmaking since its inception, so much so that we find ourselves in 2010 with a rich canon of superhero film adaptation. When *Superman: The Movie* debuted in 1978, exactly four decades after Superman's initial comic book incarnation, it set a new standard for excellence in portraying costumed crime fighters in a sophisticated context, a standard exceeded many times over by such films as *Iron Man*, *Watchmen*, and *The Dark Knight* (which was nominated for eight Academy Awards and won two—one for Best Supporting Actor, no less). These days, superhero films are among the most anticipated of Hollywood offerings and the hottest of video games.

The San Diego Comic-Con is now a respected entertainment industry event, covered in major newspapers and staked out by marketing professionals eager to get on the radar of its core demographic, with attendance levels well over 100,000 each year. And years have even passed since works like Michael Chabon's *The Amazing Adventures of Kavalier & Clay*, Jonathan Lethem's *Fortress of Solitude*, and Austin Grossman's *Soon I Will Be Invincible* brought the superhero (or supervillain) to mainstream "literary" respectability. Meanwhile, the Wild Cards books, created and edited by George R. R. Martin in 1987, are once again back on shelves, delighting new audiences with their shared universe of superheroics, and the character of the Escapist, created by the fictional Golden Age writer and illustrator protagonists of Chabon's Pulitzer Prize–winning 2000 novel, was himself adapted into an actual comic book series published by Dark Horse Comics. And recently, *Time* magazine selected Alan Moore's landmark 1986 graphic novel, *Watchmen*, as one of the "100 best English-language novels from 1923 to the present."

But we knew that already. After all, the start of the "Modern Age" of comics dates from 1986, with the publication of Moore's *Watchmen* and Frank Miller's *Batman: The Dark Knight Returns*, seminal works that established the potential of the comics medium for powerful, adult storytelling. Works that we grew up reading.

Perhaps that is why now is the true "golden age" of comics, the best time to appreciate their wonders. All the history, and diversity, that has come before gives us such a rich playground now, a cornucopia of narrative choices, along with an informed and sophisticated audience ready to receive it. The modern comic scribes work with the confidence of knowing that the best of their offerings will be appreciated in and out of the field. Now is a time where everything is possible; there are no limits. After all, seven decades of storytelling has taken us to this point.

The superhero has come into its own, a powerfully pervasive meme threaded through every aspect of our lives, from toys, to games, to graphic novels, to television and film. It enjoys commercial success and mainstream respectability. There has never been a more exciting time to don spandex and a cape, and exploring this phenomenon in prose is a no-brainer that even the worst supervillain couldn't begrudge us.

The anthology you have before you is just that—an attempt to explore the superhero genre in prose form; not as a pastiche or a parody, or a bunch of writers slumming it and having a lark at the genre's expense; but an honest exploration, with the integrity and level of storytelling that contemporary readers of comic books and graphic novels, as well as fans of films like *Iron Man* and *The Dark Knight*, appreciate and demand. You know, "real" superheroes.

What follows are fourteen tales, the majority by actual masters of the comic book form, the rest by some of the most exciting writers of contemporary science fiction and fantasy working today. The results are exceptional. So what are we waiting for? If a nod to our camp past can be excused as we fly into our sophisticated future, then set your atomic batteries to power, your turbines to speed, and let's up, up and away . . .

Lou Anders
From His Secret Headquarters (aka "his office")

☆ ★ ☆

Matthew Sturges has worked on such DC and Vertigo titles as *Shadowpact*, *Countdown to Mystery*, *Salvation Run*, *House of Mystery*, *Justice Society of America*, *Blue Beetle*, and *Final Crisis Aftermath: Run!* With Bill Willingham, he is the coauthor of the Eisner award–nominated *Jack of Fables*, chosen by *Time* magazine as number 5 in their Top 10 Graphic Novels of 2007. In the world of prose-without-pictures, he is the author of the novels *Midwinter* and *The Office of Shadow*, which mix espionage and magic in stories amid a cold war in the realm of faery. One of the hottest writers in the comics field today, Sturges possesses a genius that is evident in the story that follows, a wonderful introduction to his world, and to this anthology.

Cleansed and Set in Gold

MATTHEW STURGES

I'm on the ground, trying to breathe through a chest full of broken ribs. The only reason I'm still alive is because I happen to be invisible at the moment. Verlaine is dead. His body is twitching, trying to patch itself up, but the thing that killed him is chewing on his heart, its long tongue flicking. I can hear Verlaine's fingernails scratching against the rocks.

We all thought Verlaine was immortal. He wasn't.

☆　★　☆

Some low-level administrative assistant from the League of Heroes is trying to take a statement from me in my hospital bed. I'm sort of trying to comply, but each time I breathe it's like someone's sticking a giant fork in my chest. So I'm not as cooperative as I could be.

"How big was this thing?" he asks.

"Biggest one I've ever seen," I whisper, carefully mouthing the words.

"But still a Ghoul? Same physiognomy?"

"His 'physiognomy' is his face. You mean 'morphology.'"

The lackey scowls at me. "Sorry," he says.

"If you don't know what a word means," I say, "don't use it. Then you won't have to apologize."

He shifts uncomfortably in his seat, looking around the ICU ward, maybe hoping that there's some more desirable Leaguer that he can pester. But there isn't.

"Anyway, to answer your question, no. He wasn't like the others. He was bigger. He . . . his fist was like . . ." I hold up my fist and five needles of pain lace across my chest. I notice that the nail on my left index finger is bent backward, nearly disconnected. They've put a bandage on it. This bothers me more than the ribs for some reason.

"His fist was the size of your head," I finally say. "He put it through Verlaine's chest like Verlaine was as mortal as you."

The lackey puts his minirecorder on the table by my bed. His hand is shaking. "How many of them were there? This new variety."

"I just saw the one. He was leading the others, though. Can you imagine that? A leader. A Ghoul King."

The next day, the headlines read GHOUL KING KILLS RUSSELL VERLAINE. I can imagine the League's PR people going back and forth on this. "Is it worse if we admit that there's some kind of new mutant giant Ghoul running around, or if we imply that Russell Fucking Verlaine was murdered by some *regular* Ghoul?" I don't envy them.

☆   ★   ☆

After I leave the hospital—against medical advice; which, whatever— I take a taxi back to my apartment. A few unpleasant bites choked down and a potent healing factor kicks in, spreading warmth throughout my battered bones and knitting everything together in seconds. Oh, God. Yes.

☆　★　☆

I decide that it's best not to appear too healthy at Verlaine's funeral, so I take care to walk slowly and gasp for breath every few paces. I've even gone so far as to put on fresh bandages around my chest. In case someone uses their X-ray vision to look under my shirt, I guess. Although if they could do that, they could see that my bones aren't actually broken anymore. It doesn't matter, though, because all of the people who're capable of doing so wouldn't care. And anyway, one of them is lying dead in a box in front of me.

I'm sitting on a cold metal folding chair, pretending to be hurt, watching them lower Verlaine into the ground. It turns out that they need a special crane and a steel-reinforced casket for all of this, because Verlaine's body is so dense that he weighs just over three tons. The news media are fascinated. Jesus, Russell Verlaine makes good TV, even dead.

When you think "hero," you think Russell Verlaine. You don't think of me. I'm not particularly good-looking, I don't have a fascinating origin story, and I don't even have a constant set of powers that you can put on a trading card. "David Caulfield, The Wildcard. Powers: variable" is what the League Reserves card they did for me reads. You can buy it for a penny on eBay. Shit, I don't even wear a costume. I go around fighting criminals and monsters in jeans and an AC/DC concert tee. I am nobody's favorite hero.

I don't mind, really. The last thing I need is intense media scrutiny. The less they know about me, the better.

☆　★　☆

I stay until the coffin is in the ground and the bulldozers have filled in the earth. I'm the only one left except for Jeanie Verlaine, who's sitting on the ground in front of her husband's grave. The last thing I'm going to do is go try to comfort her or something, so I whisper my last respects to Russell from my seat and then I get up and try to walk away without Jeanie hearing me.

At the entrance to the cemetery is a woman I vaguely recognize as a reporter for one of the wire services. She's standing by the gate, smoking, trying to look casual.

"Hey," I say. "If you're waiting for Jeanie to come out so you can ambush her, forget it. That's the last thing she needs right now."

"Hi, David," she says, as if I hadn't spoken. "I'm Toni Evins, from Reuters."

She intercepts me before I can cross the street. "I'm not here to ambush Jeanie Verlaine," she says. "Give me some credit."

"I don't care what you do," I say. Why am I being such an ass-hole? This right here is why they don't like me.

Toni pretends not to be annoyed. "I'm actually here to talk to you. I heard you were there when it happened."

"Yeah," I say. I try to come up with something to follow that with, but I have nothing.

"If you're interested, I'd like to do an interview with you—get your first-hand impressions, that sort of thing." She smiles gamely.

I close my eyes, shrug. "I don't know. I don't do very well with interviews. I always say the wrong thing. I'll have to pass."

The smile fades. Toni levels her gaze at me. Kate Frost looks at things the same way just before she shreds them with her eye-beams.

"Actually, there's something else I wanted to talk to you about," she says. "Aside from the Verlaine article, I mean."

"I really don't think I'd be interested," I say, and go to push past her.

She puts her hand on my arm, and her grip is surprisingly strong, however mortal. "Terri Day had invisibility powers, cor-rect?"

"Yeah? So? Terri's dead."

"And when you and Verlaine were fighting the Ghoul King, you were invisible. Also correct?"

"I have all kinds of powers. You know: *variable*."

Toni's grip tightens on my arm. "And King Stryker had those green energy blasts. He died, too. About six months ago."

Oh, shit.

I swallow, trying not to look nervous. "It's been a tough year for the League."

"You were sporting some very similar-looking green energy blasts when you and the League were taking out that Ghoul redoubt north of Chicago. I've seen video."

"So?"

"So, I guess I'm wondering exactly *how* you got their powers."

I shrug, a practiced shrug if ever there was one. "A guy at UNC did his doctoral thesis on my powers," I say. "His conclusion was that I absorb them through etheric proximity or something. It's way too technical for me, to be honest."

Toni nods. "Yeah, I read that. Chad Lowenstein. The physics are . . . speculative. And he completely ignores what to me is the most fascinating thing about your powers."

"And what's that?"

"That you only get them from dead people."

There's a pause as Toni and I size each other up.

"You want the interview about Russell, come to my apartment tomorrow and I'll tell you all about it. Whatever sordid little details you want. Fair enough?"

She smiles, and I do not like that smile even a little.

"Sounds good," she says. She turns to go.

"Don't you want to know where I live?" I ask.

"I already know," she says.

☆　★　☆

At home there are a few messages. One from League HQ asking me how I'm doing, which is code for when am I coming back to work. One from Jeanie Verlaine, thanking me for coming to the funeral, asking me to return her call. Surprising, that. The last is from Captain Salem, who wants to go over every second of the battle with the Ghoul King. With Verlaine gone, Salem is probably the only Leaguer that I actually get along with. He understands why we do what we do. He also understands that this is not a perfect world. I think Captain Salem has his secrets, just like Verlaine probably did. Maybe not secrets like mine, but still.

At least Verlaine got to take whatever dirty little secrets he had to his grave. I think about Toni Evins and there's a ball of dread in my stomach telling me that I won't be so lucky.

The League communicator bleeps and out of nowhere all sorts of tactical information starts pouring directly into my visual cortex. The Ghoul King and his . . . minions, I guess you'd call them . . . are attacking Chicago.

☆ ★ ☆

We're lined up on an el track overlooking Grant Park. It's apparently cold outside. I can see Captain Salem shivering a little, even with his big blue-and-white cape wrapped around him. I, however, have come prepared; I have the Human Shield's invulnerability crackling around me, keeping everything in the world at a remove. At home I wavered between Human Shield and the Rock, whose skin is even tougher. But the Rock's appearance is distinctive, to say the least, and with Toni Evins poking around, the last thing I need is for people to draw any more comparisons than they already have.

As a Reservist, I'm only supposed to get called up for League duty during an emergency, but everything's been an emergency lately, so here I am.

The Ghouls are approaching our position in a line. Even the small ones are ten feet high. Their arms hang down to the ground and then some, black (metal?) claws dragging along the streets, kicking up sparks. Mostly hidden beneath their matted white fur are those dead eyes that have thrown the entire Midwest into a panic. Some photographer from *Time* magazine got right up in one's face last month and took the cover photo that scared the bejesus out of America. The fact that he was eviscerated by the thing five seconds later didn't help matters.

More worrisome, however, is the Ghoul King, the impressive

fellow that dropped Verlaine. His fists are clenched and dyed rust brown with what I assume is dried blood.

"Wait until they clear the buildings," says Captain Salem, who's leading the show. "We want as little collateral damage as possible." Personally, I'm more worried about the noncollateral damage, i.e., the damage to my person. But I don't say that.

Everyone else on the bridge splits their attention between Captain S. and the Ghouls' approach. The Captain is an unlikely leader. He's fat, for one thing, and yet still insists on wearing his form-fitting blue-and-white costume. He's also balding and not particularly handsome. But he's smart and he's confident, and that makes up for a lot. Of all the remaining members of the League, he's the only one I'd follow willingly into battle. Apparently the same can be said of Kate Frost, Pickle, and the Lyme Twins, because they show no hesitation whatsoever.

"So, what do you make of this Ghoul King?" Kate asks me, really just making conversation. If we're being totally honest, Kate is good for looking at and for shredding things with rays from her eyes, and not much else. She clearly could care less what I make of the Ghoul King, and I don't even bother to answer her.

Captain Salem is the default expert on all things Ghoul, since he's the one who discovered their origin. When they first appeared six months ago, nobody had any idea where they came from or what they wanted. What they wanted became eminently clear almost immediately: they wanted to kill things and eat them, particularly human beings. Everyone had a theory about them, but it was Captain S. who took the time to study them up close, scanning their cracked-open eggs with some device he'd invented and doing sciencey things with the results.

His conclusion was that the Ghouls are a gift from the seventy-second century, sent back in time by some enterprising villain to plague the twenty-first. Maybe this villain's goal was to murder Verlaine to keep him from stopping a clone of Hitler from taking over the colonies on Mars six years from now. Who can say? For all we know, whatever fiendish plan he's cooked up has already succeeded and the timeline has been altered beyond repair and we're all totally fucked.

☆　★　☆

The Ghouls hit hard and fast. These are not the disorganized hairy zombies we've come to expect. They used to come straight at us, fast and furious, with no regard for their own safety. That made it a lot easier to pick them off. Now they've got a general and he's made them more cautious. Captain Salem quickly adjusts tactics, speaking over the radio implants in our skulls. "I'll take point," he shouts over the din of the Ghouls' screams. "David, you cover for Kate."

Kate, though deadly with her eyes, has no natural defenses, and thus can't be left to fend for herself in combat. Furthermore, she's only lethal against the tough-skinned Ghouls in close quarters; no more than ten or twenty feet. So it's my job to block for her, going in front and keeping her safe so she can do her thing. Since Kate isn't the brightest girl, nor the most composed under pressure, there's the added element of fear that she might, in the heat of the moment, turn my skull into pulp. I don't know if Human Shield's force field is proof against her, and I don't really want to find out.

Pickle is an asshole, but he's good to have in a fight. He bounces around the park, imparting strange momentum to everything he touches, sending Ghouls flying off in all directions, priceless looks of dumb surprise on their faces. One of them impales itself on a light post. When I look back a minute or two later, it's still squirming like a bug, fruitlessly trying to free itself.

The Lyme Twins are fast, tough, and, most important, capable of beating the shit out of Ghouls as long as they remain within six feet of each other. The Ghouls have yet to figure that out, and when they do, I don't guess the Lyme Twins will last very long. I want them to survive—they're good guys, and anyway, I don't think their powers would do me any good.

I'm doing a fine job blocking for Kate, who's doing an even better job taking out Ghouls. I count quietly to myself; a nine-second stare from Kate is what it takes to puree a Ghoul's face. So far, so good.

From my left, I hear Captain Salem shriek in pain. *Shriek*. I've never heard him let loose with so much as an "ouch" the entire time I've known him. I sneak a glance in his direction, and I can see him trading blows with the Ghoul King. First of all, this thing is about twenty feet tall, giving it a serious tactical advantage, and second, it appears to be more or less impervious to Salem's mighty left fist. A fist I've seen punch through solid steel. A fist that made Russell Verlaine himself wince during a charity arm-wrestling tournament.

The Ghoul King is making a low, guttural sound. Jesus, is it laughing? Let's say for the sake of my sanity that it's growling in pain.

I've been distracted for too long, and one of the Ghouls has sneaked past me and taken a swipe at Kate. She's down on the ground, kicking and scratching. The Ghoul stands over her, swiping with its black claws, eager to disembowel her. If it does, it will lean down into her and slurp her entrails right out of her abdomen.

I leap and catch it off guard. I grab its midsection and we go sprawling down into the grass, still wet with dew. I smell earth. The Ghoul is going wild, trying to spin around in my grasp and claw at my belly. I'm not sure how much longer I can hold it. It wrenches its head around, its neck more flexible than a human's, and reaches its yellow teeth toward my throat. Its breath is cold, stinking, fetid. A bottomless cave. The teeth sink into my skin and push hard. The force field that surrounds me bends but does not break. I can feel my larynx being compressed and I can't breathe. Things start to go gray around the edges. Then the Ghoul's eyes go pink and vanish in a spray of blood. The skin is flayed from its face by an invisible whip. The skull shatters into flinders and the brain melts into gray sludge. Its claws disengage and it falls down hard.

I look up and there's Kate, pissed off. "You were supposed to be blocking for me, David." She hits me with a millisecond's worth of her powers and it's like being hit in the face with a porcupine.

I stand up, still groggy, and I see why Kate has the luxury of berating me. The Army has shown up and is lobbing mortars at the Ghouls, who now beat feet into Lake Michigan. The Ghoul King shrugs Captain Salem off and follows suit, sweeping his gaze across us good guys. The gaze says, "Next time." And then he's gone.

I help Captain Salem up from the ground. He looks like hell. His face is bleeding; one of his ears is practically torn from his head. He says, "One more minute and I would have had him, Dave."

He goes heavy in my arms without warning and I stumble. He's unconscious before we hit the ground.

☆   ★   ☆

I'm at my apartment watching TV with the sound off when Toni Evins rings the bell. The ticker running beneath the footage of yesterday's antics in Chicago reads CAPTAIN SALEM FIGHTS GHOUL KING TO STALEMATE. That's a pretty generous assessment of events as I witnessed them, but we need all the moral support we can get. The alternative headline, CAPTAIN SALEM NEARLY GUTTED BY GHOUL KING, doesn't have the proper optimistic tone.

Toni Evins is wearing a suit that would be conservative if the skirt were a little longer. She's wearing makeup, her hair pulled back nicely. She wants to make sure I know how pretty she is. This is supposed to disarm me. It does.

"Nice work yesterday, by the way," she says, sitting gingerly on my sofa. The place is a bit of a mess, and in a brief fit of passive-aggressiveness, I failed to clean it on purpose. "You paid eight to five in Vegas with six kills."

"Well, it's nice to know that I'm exceeding expectations," I say. I feel like I'm supposed to say something else, but I've got nothing. I wonder if this is a journalistic trick, a deliberate silence on her part to keep me talking.

She puts a recorder on the table and the interview begins in earnest. She starts with a few questions about Verlaine's death. What was it like? How did it make me feel? Describe what you saw, and leave nothing out. This is the sort of interview I've done after more than one battle, and the rhythm of it lulls me into a false sense of security.

"You and Russell Verlaine were close, right? In an interview last year, in fact, you referred to him as your 'best friend.'"

"I don't remember saying that, but yes. We were close."

"And it didn't bother you that Verlaine chose Captain Salem to be his best man?" She pauses, looking me in the eye. "I wonder if maybe you weren't *his* best friend."

"Russ had a lot of friends," I say. I believe I could come to despise Toni Evins. This is another one of those tricks, I suppose. Catch you off guard; get you to say something incendiary.

Then she goes for the throat. "So, David, how long do you think it'll be before you show up at some battle with *Verlaine's* powers?"

Before she arrived, I felt a little guilty about what I'm about to do to her. But all of my reservations instantly melt away.

"You clearly have some kind of theory about me that you'd like to discuss, Ms. Evins," I say, with a bit of calculated outrage. "So let's hear it."

She stares at me silently for a moment, her gaze flowing over me and through me. More alpha-dog reporter bullshit, I guess.

"Well, the conventional wisdom about you is that you possess an array of powers, and that you can only use one of them at a time."

"That is what they say."

"I'm not sure exactly *what* it is that you do," she says. "What I do know is that I've researched you fairly thoroughly and I've noticed a very disturbing pattern."

I lean back on the sofa, trying to look casual, prolonging the moment for as long as possible. "Which is?"

"That in each instance that you've displayed any kind of extranormal aspect, you appear to have inherited it from a recently deceased hero." Again the alpha-dog gaze. "Or villain."

"And?" I say.

"I have two main questions. First, do you kill them, or do you wait for them to die?"

She pauses again, waits for a response, and when she gets none, plows ahead. "Second, what do you *do* to them?"

I can't resist smiling just a little. Then I choke down the smile and put my hands up in mock surrender.

"Okay, Toni. You got me. You got me dead to rights."

I stand up from the couch and start to pace the living room. "I'll tell you everything. But on one condition."

She perks up. "Which is?"

"That after I tell you, you agree to give me two days to leave the country before you print my story. That's all I ask."

Now I've hit her where she lives. There's no way she'll say no. "Well?" I ask, giving her my own practiced gaze. "What do you say?"

She stands. "I'd say you've got yourself a deal."

☆　★　☆

Toni's impressed by the false wall at the back of my closet, and the secret, silent elevator that takes us down to the basement of my building. When the elevator door slides open, the chill of the refrigeration units hits her and she flinches.

"Oh . . . my . . . God," she says.

There are five tables lined up in the room. A few bare light fixtures illuminate the concrete floors and walls with a harsh, unforgiving light. On each table is a body covered in a sheet. Each body was placed there on purpose this morning, each occupant chosen for the fullest effect. On the far side of the room is a set of freezers with glass fronts, each holding several shelves of plastic containers, clearly labeled.

"What is this?" she says, and for the first time her composure slips. She's forgotten her alpha-dog moves.

"You wanted to know the truth, and here it is," I say.

I lift the sheet from the body closest to us. His skin is pale and wan in the harsh light. I put his helmet on earlier to make sure that he'd be instantly recognizable. "The Human Shield," I say.

I pull the sheet down from the next table. "Terri Day. The See-Through Girl."

Another sheet. "King Stryker."

Toni Evins backs away from me, her head cocked to one side. "What . . . what do you *do* down here?"

I take a step toward her, smiling what I hope is a wicked smile. "I eat them, Toni."

I take another step and she flinches back. "I eat the flesh right off their dead bones. That's how I get my powers."

"You're lying. You're just screwing with me."

I pull the sheet entirely away from the Human Shield's body, pointing to the neatly carved-out sections of his thighs. "Sorry. No."

Toni struggles to regain her composure. "How . . . how do you live with yourself?" she asks.

I can't hold the act any longer. I shove the sheet back over Human Shield's naked body. "Do you think I *like* this?" I shout. "Do you think this is what I *wanted*?"

I shove Human Shield's gurney and it rolls a few feet, tapping against the one holding Terri Day. "I am disgusted by myself. Every time I get a call from the League I have to force myself to come down here. I gag every single time I put a piece of them in my mouth. Can you imagine the horror of this? The horror of being me?"

Toni comes a bit unglued. "Then why do you do it?" she asks.

"I ask myself that question every single day," I say. "But then I see some pregnant mother get shot by a bad guy in pink tights, or some Ghoul tear apart a bus full of kids and . . . what would you have me do?"

I get right up in her face. "What would *you* do?"

Toni walks the length of the room, reaching out to touch each gurney in turn, but finding herself unable. "You realize that I can't keep something like this to myself." She looks back and forth, from the bodies to me. "The world needs to know about this."

It's time for this to end. I walk to the far end of the room, to the one body that I haven't yet uncovered.

I pull the sheet back, gently. Donna Porter's world-weary face looks blankly up at nothing. "Do you recognize her?" I ask.

"No," says Toni, forcing herself to look.

"No, of course you don't. Donna wasn't much of a hero. She was terrified of fighting, couldn't stand the sight of blood. Her power was a curse to her. She hated using it, and I think—and this is just a theory, okay?—I think she let herself get killed."

I pull the sheet down from her, exposing her nakedness, her total vulnerability. "You know what Donna's power was?" I ask.

Toni shakes her head, unable to speak.

I pick up a scalpel and carefully cut away a square of Donna Porter's leg. I hold the morsel up for Toni to see.

I pop the bit of meat into my mouth, chew slowly, swallow, making sure that Toni watches it all. Not for her sake, but for mine. "Donna's power was mind control."

Toni's eyes widen. She steps back from the table, stumbling over her own feet.

"Donna could have ruled the world with her power," I say. "But it disgusted her, just like mine disgusts me. The difference, though, is that I keep doing it, despite how much I hate myself."

I can feel Donna's power rushing into me. I can feel Toni's mind in my mind. It's like an intricate web, constantly in motion. The tendrils of that web are clearly outlined in my mind, each strand representing a thought or a memory. I can feel the currents in her mind: the disgust, the fear, the nausea. I can sense her decision to turn and run.

"Stop," I say, feeling the nerve impulse rush down to her feet and stopping it. Toni freezes, wavering.

"Here's what's going to happen," I say. "You're going to take your little recorder and you're going to erase any evidence of your time here today. Then you're going to go back to your office and destroy any notes you may have about me."

I take her by the chin, gently, forcing her to look at me. "Are we clear so far?"

I allow her to nod.

"If you've discussed your suspicions about me with anybody—an editor, say—and they ask you about me, you just tell them that there's no story there. Tell them that the UNC student's dissertation turns out to be right on the money.

"And then you forget all about this. Whenever you think of me in the future, you'll think about how uninteresting I am. Thinking about me at all will make you feel bored." I'm saying all this aloud, but the words aren't really necessary. I'm rearranging the web of thoughts in her mind, putting all of this information directly into her cerebrum.

"You're going to leave here now, and you're going to forget you were ever here. By the time you get back to your apartment, you'll already be thinking about other things. Nice things.

"And you'll feel good about yourself. You'll think of things that you always wanted to do and you'll make plans to do them. You'll let yourself love freely. You'll forgive yourself for everything you've ever done that you regret.

"Do you understand all of that?"

Toni nods and I let go of her.

"Let's go, then." I lead her gently by the elbow back to the elevator.

At the door to my apartment, I kiss her on the cheek. "I'm sorry about this," I say. "I really am. But I've reached a point where one more immoral act barely weighs in the balance. And I don't think you'll suffer for it."

"You had it all worked out," she says, her voice weak. I admire her willpower. Speaking at all under Donna Porter's spell must be nearly impossible.

"You're not the first reporter who's asked those questions," I say.

After she leaves, I sit down on the couch and try not to throw up. I give myself five minutes to despise myself, and then I put it out of my mind and move on. I have to.

Someday I really need to send that bastard at UNC a thank-you note.

☆   ★   ☆

On the machine there's another voice mail from the widow Verlaine. I delete it without listening to it. Then there's one from Captain Salem asking me to come see him at League HQ. My stomach clenches into a knot. My first thought is: He knows.

Of course, that's what I always think.

☆   ★   ☆

As League Chairman, Captain Salem gets a nice cozy office on the top floor of the building. Said building, I learn from a sign in the lobby, is being renamed Verlaine Tower. Captain Salem waves me in and shuts the door, sits me down in a comfy chair, and then just stares at me from across his desk.

"What's up?" I say.

In response, he opens a desk drawer and takes out a gold pin, pushes it across the desktop toward me.

"Welcome to the League, David," he says. "Lifetime member, as of today. No more of this Reservist bullshit."

This is the moment that any B-list hero dreams of, being pinned and getting your code name etched onto the granite block outside and getting your own chair at the big table. I feel like a fraud. But I take the pin anyway.

"We would have had a proper ceremony," he says, "but with the whole Verlaine thing it just seemed . . ."

"No, I understand," I say. I don't have to tell him that I don't want any ceremony; he knows me well enough to figure that out on his own.

"Verlaine always told me that I'd be a lifer over his dead body," I say.

For a second I think the Captain is going to jump over the desk and throttle me with his massive fists. But he laughs, louder and longer than is really necessary over such a tasteless and untimely joke.

"He really liked you, you know," says Captain Salem. "He said you were the real deal."

"What's that supposed to mean?"

"Don't be a dipshit, David. You know exactly what it means." He stands and tugs down on his costume front, but it does his profile no good. "Russell Verlaine saw more than the rest of us. You know what I mean."

"Yeah," I say. He's not talking about the X-ray vision.

"I miss him," I add.

"Me too."

Captain Salem walks around the desk and lays a giant hand on each of my shoulders. "Welcome to the club, Wildcard. I wish it was under better circumstances."

There's nothing really to say to that.

"Oh yeah," he says, clouting me on the back, knocking the wind out of me, "Analytica's satellite intelligence thinks it knows where the Ghoul King's going to strike next. As a full member, you get to be one of the first in line to have your ass handed to you by the thing."

He stops me by the door on my way out. "If you've been saving some really fantastic power for a special occasion, David, now would be the time to debut it."

☆   ★   ☆

Operation Interceptor is planned for 0600. I spend the night before in the basement, looking at the dead bodies laid out in my own lair. "Who's it going to be?" I ask them. "Which one of you stands the best chance in this thing?"

It occurs to me for the first time that everyone here is dead for a *reason*. Whatever powers they had, it wasn't enough to keep any of them alive.

After hours of deliberation, Human Shield gets the dubious

honor. I slice a chunk the size of a sugar cube from his left buttock and choke it down. Fifteen seconds later I punch the concrete wall and don't feel a thing.

☆ ★ ☆

At 0540 I'm standing on a beach in Wisconsin in cutoffs and flip-flops with nine other Leaguers. It's cold and the capes are snapping in the wind. Spandall keeps out the cold fairly well, but only if it actually covers your body. It's clear that Kate Frost and the Muse are freezing their asses off in their skimpy little outfits. Kate hasn't said a word to me since Chicago, which is fine with me.

Analytica's satellite intelligence has given us an 89.4 percent probability that the Ghoul King and his minions will show up to ravage downtown Milwaukee sometime between now and noon. The Army and National Guard are on standby—in monster situations the League always gets the first crack. The government likes it that way because it doesn't cost them anything, and the Leaguers like it because it gets them on TV more often.

At 0725 or thereabouts, Captain Salem and Power Pat are taking turns seeing who can pound the biggest hole in the sand when it happens. There's an explosion of spray and the Ghoul King erupts from the water, surrounded by roughly sixteen billion of his Ghoul friends. The actual number, I will learn later, is more like six hundred, but still more than we've ever seen in one place. Hell, it's more than we even knew *existed*.

Captain Salem waves us forward, himself in the lead, heading straight for the King. Over the comm he's alerting the military to what they've already figured out, which is that this has suddenly become a weapons-free, all-hands-on-deck, get-the-fuck-out-here-now situation. All hell then promptly breaks loose.

☆ ★ ☆

What not even Analytica has predicted is that the Ghoul King has given his army the ability to fly. We discover this when the first Air Force jets hiss low over the beach to strafe the enemy, only to find the enemy leaping up into the sky and tearing their wings off as if the planes were giant houseflies.

Kate Frost is the first to die. I watch a Ghoul literally tear her head from her shoulders. It makes a wet sucking sound.

He grabs me next and tries the same trick, but because I'm surrounded by Human Shield's force field, he's unable. In what I assume is frustration, he leaps up into the air and hurls me down onto the beach from a height of about a hundred feet. The impact takes my breath away and makes my ears ring, but through some miracle of physics doesn't pulverize my bones. For a solid minute, all I can do is lie on my back and watch the bloodbath going on around me. Automatic weapons fire sizzles over my head; mortars concuss in the water. I can hear the sonic booms of Power Pat and Captain Salem's punches. I feel the ground vibrate as Muse unleashes her subsonic growl at some nearby Ghoul, and then hear the sound of its bones snapping to shards in response.

☆　★　☆

I pick myself up and stagger around for a second, trying to get my bearings, but bearings elude me. Ghouls are everywhere, in the sky, on the ground, in the water. They're clawing and biting at anything they come near. One of the Lyme Twins is lying bloodied on the beach, thus rendering the other one both terrified and powerless. Power Pat is either unconscious or dead, on her back in the surf, the waves rolling over her massive biceps. To the good guys' credit, the beach is also practically carpeted with Ghoul corpses, and the sulfuric smell of their blood is nearly overpowering.

A hundred feet or so, down the beach, Captain Salem is duking it out with the Ghoul King. The King has a distinct height advantage, but the Captain moves incredibly quickly for such a fatass. The famous fists are pummeling the King pretty badly, but the Ghoul King gives the impression that he could do this all day, whereas Captain Salem is already starting to flag.

My head clears and I'm running across the beach to help the Captain, dodging downed Ghouls and soldiers alike. I get tripped up a couple of times, and I'm swiped and bitten at more times than I can count, but the Human Shield has yet to fail me.

I get within striking distance of the Ghoul King just in time to see him take Captain Salem's right fist in his own and crush it. The Captain, for all his machismo, screams like a baby, and I don't blame him. He pulls back a bloody lump of flesh, his eyes wide. The Ghoul King pauses, as if giving the Captain a moment to realize how dead he is before the Ghoul King finishes the job. Then the monster seems to lose interest in him and just tosses him aside. The Captain hits the ground with a soft thud, still more or less alive.

☆   ★   ☆

I check my back pocket, and my emergency rations are still there. I take out the baggie and grab the hunk of raw meat that was once part of the Nightingale's shoulder. In the heat of the battle I barely even notice the taste. I count to fifteen, then crouch down and leap into the air with all the strength I have left. Whatever crazy shit it is that resides in the Nightingale's cells that allowed him to fly kicks in and I'm airborne. Ten seconds later I'm halfway across Lake Michigan, but the acrid smell of dead Ghouls doesn't leave until I'm almost over New York.

☆   ★   ☆

I've crossed so many lines in my life that I didn't think there were any more left to cross. But it turns out there's one more.

I fly home for some supplies, and then to the cemetery, where I touch down on the ground in front of Verlaine's grave. I sit down and look at the fresh earth, sifting it in my hands, knowing I've got to hurry and not wanting to. I've got a bit of Digger Jakes wrapped in cellophane and I'm unwrapping it when I hear footsteps behind me.

It's Jeanie Verlaine, bringing flowers to her dead husband's grave. She doesn't seem surprised to see me.

"Hello, David," she says, forcing a smile. "I was wondering if I'd see you here. I've been watching you guys on the TV all morning. I saw you fly away."

"Yeah," I say. "I . . ." I trail off.

Jeanie sits down next to me and places the flowers on the fresh dirt. They're daisies. For a second, neither one of us says anything.

"I know why you're here," she finally says.

"What do you mean?"

She looks at me, forces me to look at her. "David, Russ had powers nobody knew about. He could look at someone's DNA, just standing in front of them, and know how a particular gene would be expressed. He understood people; he could see right into their hearts. You know, their secret hearts."

I look away.

"No, David, listen. Russ always knew how you got your powers. He knew it five minutes after meeting you. But don't worry; I'm the only person he ever told about it."

"I'm not sure what to say."

"Russ knew that someday you might need him. You know, that you might need *his* powers. Especially if . . . you know."

"If someone killed him, you mean."

"Right." She takes a deep breath. "He knew that if he ever got killed, then you might need to . . ."

"I would have to *eat* a piece of him, Jeanie." I'm sweating and I feel cold at the same time. "I would have to dig him up and cut off a piece of him and *eat* it. Don't tell me that doesn't revolt you."

She stands up, holding her hands to her head. "Of course it *revolts* me. I think it's disgusting!" She turns away. "I'm not Russ."

She sniffs and wipes her nose with the back of her hand. "But it doesn't matter what I think. Russell knew and it didn't bother him at all. He pitied you."

"I don't want his pity!" I bark.

"Yes, you do. You want *his* pity. He was a better person than us. He had a perfect moral worldview, can you imagine that? He just *knew* right from wrong. He never felt jealousy, never felt sorry for himself, and he never condescended to anyone. He knew how *hard* it must be to be you. He knew how much you hated yourself for doing it, and he knew that you did it anyway because you were willing to sacrifice your own self-worth in order to do the right thing.

"Don't you get it? He loved you for that. He said that it made you a better person than him, because he never had to make the choice that you did."

As usual, I can't think of anything to say.

"Look," she finally whispers. "We're wasting time. We both know what you need to do here. I can't watch you do it, so I'm going to leave. But I needed you to know that you had Russ's permission. You had his blessing."

She turns to go, then says, "He figured you probably couldn't bring yourself to do it otherwise."

"He was right," I say.

I wait for her to go. She hurries along the path and disappears from view. I choke down Digger Jakes and start clawing at the dirt. I can feel the grit sinking into my fingernails, cold and eternal. Then Digger's power kicks in and the hole opens wide. In less than a minute I'm in a dank hole, standing over the coffin of my best friend, looking down at his face. Even in death, his body refused to be tarnished. The hole in his chest has sealed itself, leaving him perfectly whole in his spotless gold Spandall costume.

Before I even touch him, I realize my stupid mistake. Verlaine's body is virtually indestructible. I have no idea how I'm going to eat it.

☆　★　☆

I've got just enough Nightingale left to fly myself home, praying that nobody comes across Verlaine's open grave in my absence. I rifle through the basement, thinking furiously. What am I going to do? I go through about a dozen of the containers in the freezer, tossing them aside one by one, before I remember the Rock.

The Rock was known as the Indestructible Man until a chemist with a grudge found a way to destruct him. Then the Rock was just known as "deceased." Rock's been sitting on a gurney in the freezer for months. It took weeks to plan and execute the removal of his two-ton body from Highland Cemetery, where he's still believed to be buried, just a couple rows down from Verlaine. Now his dead eyes are staring up at me from inside their granite-like lids. His skin feels like polished marble; he is all over a dark green speckled with silver veins. His particular mutation left him without genitalia, so he never bothered to wear a costume. He just went around naked, wearing nothing but a fanny pack to keep his keys and wallet in. Aside from the fact that I'm certain to take on his very distinctive appearance if I eat him, the lack of genitals is another big reason why I've never done it.

There's nothing to do about that now. I get a fresh scalpel and look down into the wound in Rock's chest where the mad scientist hit him with his chemical spray. Though unfortunate for the Rock, the hole is a godsend to me, because I couldn't bite through Rock's skin any more than I could bite through Verlaine's. But inside the hole, his guts are just as soft and pink as anybody's. I slice out something that might be a bit of lung and pop it into my mouth.

It's not something you get used to.

When Rock's power suffuses through me I suddenly feel heavy and cold, and every part of me aches. God, is this how Rock felt all the time? I never heard him complain about it, not once. He was actually one of the most upbeat guys you ever met. For my own sake, I tell myself that this pain is just a side effect of the admixture of Nightingale and Digger Jakes and everybody else I've been snacking on the past few days. I've learned the hard way that a mixed diet is fraught with peril.

☆   ★   ☆

Now that I'm the Rock, I realize that I weigh about a million pounds, and I'm not sure if my car will even support my weight. So I steal my neighbor's Hummer, holding my breath as I settle down into the seat. The thing protests, the frame groaning miserably, but goddamn if that machine isn't worth the price tag and the lousy mileage.

By the grace of God, when I pull up next to Verlaine's grave, it's just as I left it. I jump down into the hole without thinking and fall right onto Verlaine's chest with a heavy thud. To his credit, and to the point of this whole enterprise, his ribs don't even bend.

I kneel down in the grave, leaning awkwardly over the open coffin. I tear the Spandall from his right arm and hold the arm up in front of me. The musculature is perfect, the skin unblemished. I feel like I'm defacing an idol.

I bite down. Nothing. It's like biting steel. I bite again, harder this time, and I can feel the skin give way, just a little, but my Rock teeth sing with a queer pain, like I'm biting down on electrified tinfoil.

I bite down as hard as I can, clamping my jaw on Verlaine's forearm like an attack dog. I can feel the teeth beginning to crack in my mouth. The pain, my God the pain is unbelievable. Just when I think I can't take another second of this, Verlaine's skin parts and his flesh pours into my mouth, soft and clean, filet mignon.

The transformation is mind-blowing. Verlaine blasts through my system, ejecting the Rock without a moment's notice, totally taking me over. I feel him surge into my bones and muscles, bubble up into my brain. My teeth begin to heal. My body balances and relaxes, poised and graceful. My mind reels; I'm dizzy with the potency of it. Then Verlaine seeps into my consciousness and I feel a sense of clarity like nothing I've ever experienced. I'm gasping, trying to control my thoughts. Everything is so *obvious*. Verlaine, who he was. Me, who I am. I see the way Verlaine saw, not just with my eyes, though this too is astonishing and I find myself drinking in even the tiniest aspect of the visual world. But I feel his goodness and wisdom as well. I reflect on myself. I see and understand David Caulfield: Wildcard in a way that I've never, ever known myself, and I realize that this is how Verlaine always knew me.

I know that Verlaine, though he would never have told anyone, apparently not even Jeanie, actually held one small, petty jealousy.

It was of me.

Flying with Verlaine's power is nothing like flying on Nightingale Air. The wind doesn't fight against me—it becomes my ally. The Universe lifts me and carries me where I want to go. I can sense the globe underneath me; I can feel the vibrations of the cities. I can smell the Ghoul King and his children ahead of me while I'm still over Pennsylvania.

I see him the instant he clears the horizon, my vision cutting through clouds and air pollution. I can see him like he's right in front of my face. I feel invincible.

Oh my sweet fucking Christ. This is exactly how Verlaine must have felt flying toward the thing on the day he died.

Verlaine wasn't invincible. He wasn't immortal. My skin crawls and even that sensation is multiplied a hundredfold by my enhanced awareness. What chance do *I* have?

It's too late, though. The Ghoul King has put down everyone who's stood against him. It's been almost three hours since I left the fight and the King and what remain of his minions are having the city of Milwaukee for brunch. I see him right in front of me. I'm flying at around six hundred miles an hour. Somehow he senses me coming and turns to meet me. Unable to pull back in time, I accelerate directly into his lashed-out fist at the speed of sound.

☆　★　☆

To Verlaine, pain is a sensation that, like all sensations, can be savored by his heightened consciousness. My own way of thinking about pain—i.e., that it hurts—vies with Verlaine's and it's like I'm seeing double, but with my mind instead of my eyes. The pain separates what is quintessentially me from what is quintessentially Verlaine, and the comparison in no way flatters me.

It takes a second for me to realize that I'm on the ground and that the Ghoul King is standing above me, shrieking. His right hand is hanging at an odd angle and I realize, peering through his rocky exterior with X-ray vision, that my impact on him broke two bones in his wrist. All *I* broke was my nose. Take *that*, asshole.

My mind gets caught up in the many nonvisible spectra for a

second, and when I switch back to plain old light, I note that in
the Ghoul King's left hand he is holding a minivan. I don't need
Verlaine's insight to realize that the King's plan is to brain me with
the minivan, so I pivot and stand, gracefully pirouetting my body
in the air. My God, how this body moves. That sense of total invulnerability rises up in me again, and I remind myself that this very
feeling is probably what got Verlaine killed in the first place. If I
have any advantage over my old friend, it's that I understand the
concept of limitations.

I've got two good fists, so I go in swinging, pounding at the
Ghoul King with everything I've got. He's covered with stinking fur, but the skin beneath the fur is unlike other Ghoul skin.
It's like shale, sharp and grating. I can feel my knuckles scraping
against it.

The King's still got one good hand, and when he gut-punches
me with it, I am forcefully hurtled backward like a cartoon character. I arc over the bloody beach, remembering just before I slam
against the sand that I can fly. Instead of slamming into the beach,
I sort of skim across it, creating a rill of glass from the heat of the
friction of the sand. I'm down again.

Clarity again, like pure water, overcomes me. I can hear the
waves and the Ghouls rampaging down State Street. I can hear the
whipping of the news helicopters' rotors and I can see and hear
their newsfeeds, translating the satellite transmissions into sight
and sound in my mind. Everyone is watching me. All eyes are on
David Caulfield. The Wildcard.

I sing to gravity and I'm buoyed up and again I rush the Ghoul
King, looking for a vulnerability that neither Verlaine nor Captain
Salem was able to find. Somewhere to the left of me I can hear the
Captain's ragged breathing; he's still alive.

I strike over and over, pounding the monster with fists made of
pure momentum, and if he slows at all I can't sense it. He's swiping
at me with those black claws but I'm able to stay just ahead of him.
I'm learning his rhythms. I can see him as a collection of atoms, as
a coherent energy system, as an expression of artificial DNA. All

kinds of stuff. These perceptions keep me alive, but don't give me any more advantage than that.

We slug it out for long minutes; I can count the exact ticks of a watch on the wrist of a dead soldier. I hit the beach thirty-seven minutes and nine, ten, eleven seconds ago. I'm finding it difficult to concentrate—the everythingness of Verlaine is draining me.

No, wait. It's something else. I'm scanning my own body chemistry and I don't like what I see. The RNA in my cells is beginning to revert to David Caulfield standard. Any minute now, Verlaine's power will start to drain from me, and I'll be dead. I'll be a sidebar in a magazine article about the Milwaukee Massacre, which is what CNN is apparently already calling it.

Move, dodge, punch, retreat. We've fallen into a rhythm. We're up in the air now, I realize, a hundred feet above the beach. The Ghoul King flies with dire purpose, pushing off hard against air. I can't keep this up. Gravity is tickling at my body now. I pull back and lurch downward, losing my grip on the sky for a moment. He kicks me in the face and I feel my occipital bone crack. Verlaine's now-sluggish healing factor grudgingly repairs it.

I am going to fall.

The Ghoul King grabs me by the neck and squeezes. I manage to wrench my fingers beneath his, just enough strength remaining in me to keep my head from popping off, but I can no longer breathe and the world is going black. The Universe in all its manifold glory recedes and regular reality returns in muddled sounds, the smell of blood, and pain, pain, pain.

The Ghoul King smells victory. He lifts me up to stare directly into my eyes, to show me the bleak, relentless intelligence behind his own. He opens his mouth and shrieks in victory.

I stretch out my neck and bite off his tongue.

In wild rage, he flings me away. I'm sailing through the air, swallowing living meat that tastes like rubber and acid. I'm a slave to physics now; with the last shreds of Verlaine's clarity of thought, I plot the parabolic trajectory of my fall to earth. I tumble over and I can see the sand rushing up toward me. The last Verlainesque sensation is the fading voice of a reporter shouting, "Jesus Christ, he just bit off that thing's *tongue!*"

I hit the earth hard and roll, wet sand clinging to my fur. My rough skin and claws kick up gouts of sand. Hunger swells up in me. Raw hunger, desperate hunger, and hatred. Nothing has ever felt as good or as satisfying as this. I stand, turn, and regard myself above me, floating downward, sensing my own confusion.

The Ghoul King snaps into place inside me and I know that I'm me and that he's him, but I don't think that he understands that. He's reaching out toward me, recognizing me, wanting me. I think maybe the Ghoul King is actually a Ghoul Queen. There's something motherly in its gaze. No, yes, I am female. I am reaching out.

I jump off the ground toward her. We connect and I slash with my claws with every ounce of strength I possess. There's an infinite well of potential energy behind my motions, powered by hunger and hate. I catch my self/enemy by surprise. She is reaching out to embrace me and her blood spills out and turns to spray in the wind.

She is cunning and bold. She is brilliant. She somehow intuits what has happened, that she has been copied. She swipes at me with a look of purest rage, but her strength has already begun to fade. I'm digging, digging inside her exposed abdomen, slicing up everything I can touch. She becomes deadweight in my arms and we fall together in a tangle. The fall is so slow—her sense of time is not human; we seem to be falling forever together. The two seconds of our descent are smeared out over what feels like minutes.

I turn my head to look down and the soldiers and reporters and bystanders and the few remaining Leaguers are all looking back at me with varying degrees of mixed hope and horror. They know. The smarter ones are putting it together already. The Wildcard, his powers, dead heroes, a bitten-off tongue. Maybe somebody's already dispatched a camera crew to Verlaine's grave, where Jeanie may still be waiting. I have no idea what she'll tell them. It doesn't really seem to matter.

Lights pop. The whole world flares up. Flashbulbs and impact. Time returns.

The ground rises to meet me for what feels like the hundredth time. A dragon is dead in my arms and I have become it and I have slain it.

James Maxey is the author of the Dragon Age fantasy series: *Bitterwood*, *Dragonforge*, and *Dragonseed*. A graduate of the Odyssey Fantasy Writers Workshop and Orson Scott Card's Writers Boot Camp, in 2002 he won a Phobos Award for his short story "Empire of Dreams and Miracles," and has since published numerous short stories in *Asimov's Science Fiction* and elsewhere. His first novel was the cult-classic superhero tale *Nobody Gets the Girl*, which was ahead of the current curve when it comes to superheroes rendered in prose tales, so it shouldn't come as any surprise that he knocked this story out of the park.

Where Their Worm Dieth Not

JAMES MAXEY

Atomahawk took a pack of unfiltered Camels from his utility belt and popped a fresh cigarette between his lips. His fingertip glowed like a miniature sun as he lit it. Acrid smoke curled toward Retaliator.

Retaliator, squatting on the edge of the roof of the long-vacated factory, said nothing as he continued to stare down at the docks of the darkened warehouse. It was two in the morning; it had been at least twenty minutes since the last goon had furtively slipped inside. Despite Retaliator's focused silence, something in his posture must have changed imperceptibly.

"What?" said Atomahawk, sounding defensive.

"What what?" Retaliator answered, keeping his voice gravelly and neutral, still not looking at his long-time ally.

"You flinched when I lit up," said Atomahawk. "You've got a problem with my smoking."

"I'm not here to pass judgment," said Retaliator, who recognized the irony of the statement. The whole reason he was a crime fighter was that he was willing to judge people. This was why he spent nights skulking dark alleys in dangerous parts of town rather than drinking brandy by the fireplace in his fifty-room mansion. He was well-known for his ability to see things clearly, in black and white, cutting through the haze of gray fog that afflicted so many of his fellow men. He sighed.

"A: Lighting your cigarette with your powers is about as stealthy as waving around a road flare. B: Kids look up to the Law Legion and you're its most powerful member. If they see you smoking, they'll think it's okay. C: You're my friend, John. You deserve a better death than lung cancer."

Atomahawk nodded as he hovered closer to the roof's edge. John Naiche was a full-blooded Apache who looked quite striking in his bright-red plastisteel armor. His long black hair flowed like a cape down his back. He'd been a founding member of the Law Legion along with Retaliator, Arc, She-Devil, and Tempo. The big Apache took a long draw on the cigarette, then flicked it away.

He crossed his arms and said, "You know I took it up again right after your last funeral."

"Again?" asked Retaliator.

Atomahawk furrowed his brow, puzzled by the query. Unlike Retaliator, he wore no mask to hide his features, only war paint that looked like swept-back hawk's wings.

"You said 'again,'" said Retaliator. "It implies you used to smoke before."

"Oh," said Atomahawk. "Yeah. When I was in high school. I quit when I joined the Marines. But for the last ten years, any time I get stressed out, I can't help but think about putting a cigarette in my mouth. The last time Prime Mover killed you, I bummed one from a teenager outside the funeral home. I haven't been able to stop. Honestly, why should I worry? My blood is more radioactive than uranium. I have to bury my feces in lead jars because they'd kill any ordinary man that got near them. Cancer's coming, probably, but it's the radiation that will do me in, not cigarettes."

Retaliator struggled not to roll his eyes. He'd heard Atomahawk's my-power-is-my-curse shtick often enough that he could recite it by rote.

A long moment of silence passed as they both stared at the warehouse.

Atomahawk said, "Anyway, I'm not the most powerful Legionnaire anymore. She-Devil's scary now that she's eaten Satan's heart. And Golden Victory could probably take me in a fight, if it came to it."

"I could take you in a fight," said Retaliator. "It doesn't change the fact that kids look up to you."

"You dress like a refugee from a bondage flick," said Atomahawk. "Don't lecture me about corrupting children. How's Nubile doing, by the way?"

Retaliator pressed his lips together tightly. "She's off the respirator," he said softly, losing the deep raspy baritone he normally affected. "The doctor's say . . . they say she might recover more brain function in time. It's still too early to know."

"That's good," said Atomahawk, in a tone that really said, "That sucks."

Retaliator stood up, stretching his back. He tugged up his pants, which had slipped down a bit. Perhaps he did look a bit like a bondage fanatic in his black leather pants, knee-high boots with about a hundred silver buckles, leather gloves that laced up his forearms, and a black mask that concealed all his features save for zippered slits at the eyes, mouth, and nostrils. His shaved chest was completely bare, showing off the hundreds of scars he'd acquired over twenty years of crime-fighting. His skin wasn't bulletproof, but his entire cardiovascular system was composed of high-tech bioplastics from the twenty-eighth century that few twenty-first-century weapons could damage.

His outfit, he knew, made some people uncomfortable. But they'd been the clothes his father, Reinhart Gray, former chief justice of the Supreme Court, had been found dead in. Police had ruled his death accidental, saying he was the victim of autoerotic asphyxiation. Eric Gray had become the Retaliator in order to solve the mystery of his father's murder, a quest for justice that still drove him twenty years later. Wearing his father's clothes wasn't a sexual statement. It was, instead, a warning to the unknown murderer, a reminder that there was one man, at least, who still remembered his crime.

"Here comes Casper," said Atomahawk.

"Don't call him that," growled Retaliator.

The ethereal form of Witness floated toward the roof. Witness was really Chang Williams, the ghost of a twelve-year-old conjoined twin whose now-separated brother was currently in a coma. Chang's spirit was trapped on earth, unseen by all save for the few souls who'd been to the other side and returned. Since nearly all the members of the Law Legion had died at one point or another, they had recently adopted the ghost-child and given him a new life as Witness, an invisible, intangible spy who could gather information in the most dangerous environments without risk to himself.

Witness floated before them, completely naked, since souls have no need for clothes. It was politically incorrect to call conjoined twins Siamese, yet Chang was, in fact, from Thailand, formerly known as Siam, though he'd been raised in America. He was thin, almost girlish, having died before puberty, with skin the color of a walnut shell; his dark eyes had no irises as he stared at Retaliator and said, "There are a dozen men inside. They frighten me. I can't touch them."

"You can't touch anybody," said Atomahawk.

Witness reached out and placed his skinny fingers onto the Apache's boot. The big man gave a small yelp and jerked his foot away. "What the hell was that?"

"You should read the dossiers. Witness has a graveyard touch," growled Retaliator. "He can brush against anyone's soul and make them feel the mortal chill of their own guilt."

"So, what, the men in that warehouse have no souls?" asked Atomahawk.

"They've signed Prime Mover's contract," said Retaliator, with a sigh. "Another dozen lost to the God Clock."

"They're well armed," said Witness. "Assault rifles and fancy-looking pistols. They've got cases of C4 in the back of the warehouse. Also, five or six small helicopters. At least I think they're helicopters; they don't have rotors attached. They're planning to blow something up, but no one said what."

"The Supreme Court," said Retaliator.

"Is this anything more than a guess?" said Atomahawk.

"Tomorrow is when they're hearing arguments on Prime Mover's appeals. They're being asked to decide if a murder conviction can stand if the victim is later restored to life by a time-travel paradox."

"Even if he gets off on that technicality, he's guilty of hundreds of other murders," said Atomahawk. "He's not going to walk. Also, why blow up a hearing that might lead to a ruling in his favor?"

"It's too big a coincidence that his goons are stocking up on explosives. Security is going to be high tomorrow. He would blow the place up just to prove he still runs the world even from a prison cell."

"Is he that crazy?"

"Maybe," said Retaliator. "Or maybe the guy rotting in prison isn't the real Prime Mover. When they put him in jail, Prime Mover claimed he was a cop named Jason Reid who'd somehow been put into Prime Mover's body. An hour later, though, he was back to normal. Assuming 'normal' is the right word for a man who believes he's God."

"You're taking the idea he can swap his soul into other bodies seriously?" asked Atomahawk.

"I'm talking to the ghost of a Siamese twin and an Indian with a fusion reactor where his heart should be," said Retaliator. "I'm not in a position to dismiss anything as impossible."

Atomahawk nodded toward the warehouse. "We going to do this thing?"

"Go," said Retaliator. "Make it loud."

Retaliator jumped onto his zip line and slid down to the Dumpster behind the warehouse as Atomahawk blazed through the night sky like a comet. He landed on the trash bin as a thunderous crack came from the front of the warehouse. The ground shook as the steel door near the Dumpster blew from its hinges, a victim of the rapid change in air pressure inside the building as Atomahawk blasted through the front doors.

Retaliator's muscles tensed. He toyed with the closed switchblade in his palm. Any second, at least one of the goons would make the sensible decision to flee. That would be Retaliator's cue to drag him into the Dumpster and have a few private moments during which he would make the goon tell everything he knew about Prime Mover's plans.

The seconds passed in odd silence. Normally by now hired muscle would be shooting at Atomahawk, not believing in his well-documented invulnerability. Nothing short of an antispace grenade was going to hurt Atomahawk, and Retaliator had secured the last of the five prototypes.

A full minute went by. At last, someone stuck his head out of the door. It was Atomahawk.

"You should probably take a look at this," he said.

Retaliator jumped from the Dumpster and looked into the warehouse.

The vast space was well lit by a few atomaflares drifting in the air. The warehouse was completely empty. There weren't even any cobwebs.

"I've scanned all spectrums. Nothing is hiding invisibly. There's chaotic heat residue from people who were here, but I'm afraid I wiped out any useful IR information with the blast that took out the front doors."

"I swear they were here two minutes ago," said Witness, who'd joined them.

Retaliator sighed as he rubbed the bridge of his nose through his mask. "Prime Mover must have activated another power of the God Clock. Teleportation? Time Travel?"

"She-Devil might know the next power," said Atomahawk.

"After all, she was around when they built the Antikythera mechanism."

"Go to DC," said Retaliator. "Keep an eye on the courthouse."

"They aren't going to let me anywhere near the building," said Atomahawk.

"That's why you have a secret identity," said Retaliator.

"I'm six-foot-five, I don't wear a mask, and I set off Geiger counters from twenty feet away," said Atomahawk. "My secret identity isn't as useful as yours, rich boy."

"Figure out something," said Retaliator.

Witness said, "It's no problem for me to get in. I'll contact you the second I spot anything suspicious." He faded from sight, back into the ghoststream.

Atomahawk lifted into the air. "It might not be him," he said.

"It's always him," said Retaliator. "Every time I think Prime Mover is finished, he comes back stronger than ever."

"Lucky thing for the world you're always waiting for him," said Atomahawk.

"Yeah," said Retaliator, his shoulders sagging, as leaned against the Dumpster.

"What?" asked Atomahawk, pausing twenty feet up.

"What what?" asked Retaliator.

"You look so down. This isn't like you."

Retaliator reached back and unzipped his mask. He tugged it off, letting the chill November night cool his sweaty hair. "How do you know it's not like me? What makes you think you know anything about me?"

"I've watched you die three times and seen you get married twice," said Atomahawk with a wry smile. "I've literally been to hell and back with you, man. If I don't know you, who does?"

Retaliator scratched the callus on his neck left by the mask. "So what was it about my last funeral?"

"That made me start smoking again?" said Atomahawk.

"Yeah."

He shrugged. "The first time we thought you were dead, it was right after the Snarthling invasion. Half of the Law Legion still had alien duplicates running around, so it wasn't a big surprise when we pulled the real you out of the goo-coffin on that captured saucer. The second time, of course, we both died when Dr. Novy blasted us with the antispace grenades, and we were too busy fighting our way out of hell for me to get stressed out. But the third time you died . . . I thought it had really happened. We didn't know you'd been pulled into the twenty-eighth century by Fan Boy, and that the corpse we buried was only a matter-balancing time-echo. It felt final. I should have known it wasn't. We Law Legionnaires never stay dead."

"Or the villains," said Retaliator, shaking his head wearily. "I've seen Prime Mover get torn apart by alligators. I've watched him fall from planes, get run over by a tank, get shot by his own henchman, and decapitated by a helicopter. I get a few months of something almost like peace . . . then he's back again. It never ends."

"People come back," said Atomahawk. "It's a crazy world."

"My father didn't come back," said Retaliator. "Amelia didn't come back."

Atomahawk's face fell. He said, apologetically, "I didn't mention the weddings to—"

"Torture me?" said Retaliator. Not a day went by when thoughts of his shattered lovers didn't haunt him. His first wife, Amelia, had taken too many sleeping pills; she'd found out the truth of his second life and never learned to cope with the stress of knowing where her husband really spent his nights. His second wife had known the truth, of course. When Nubile had joined the Law Legion, she told everyone she was nineteen, although, in truth, she was fourteen, exactly half Retaliator's age at the time. She'd passed as older due to her shape-shifting. Fortunately, the first four years they'd fought side-by-side, their relationship had never advanced past teasing flirtation. When they'd finally taken off their masks and progressed to the next phase, Retaliator was no longer technically a pedophile.

"I'm not trying to torture anyone," said Atomahawk. "Don't let events bring you down, is all I'm saying. We're fighting the good fight. A war can't be judged by a single battle."

"Get to DC," said Retaliator, pulling his mask back on. "We've got work to do. I'm going to talk to She-Devil."

☆ ★ ☆

As Atomahawk vanished into the night sky, Retaliator walked to the nearest manhole cover. "Going to talk to She-Devil" was both the easiest and the hardest thing in the world. She-Devil claimed to be Uruk, a five-thousand-year-old woman who'd met Satan in Mesopotamia and broken his heart after a torrid love affair. As a result, he'd cursed her with eternal life and his own duty of punishing the souls of the wicked. But, save for her inability to die, he hadn't given her any special powers to carry out her mission. Thus, she'd started her career constantly drawn to confront the wickedest men on earth utterly without the power to harm them. Her first thousand years had been hellish, as she'd fallen again and again into the hands of men so vile and depraved they made Ghengis Khan look well-adjusted. Unfortunately for Satan, he'd underestimated the human ability to adapt. Angels and demons were created knowing everything they would ever know. They had little capacity to learn. Humans, on the other hand, improved with age. As the centuries went by, Uruk became nearly unbeatable in hand-to-hand combat, and eventually mastered the mystic arts as well.

Arc and Tempo had a conspiracy theory that She-Devil had formed the Law Legion specifically so that they could all be killed by Dr. Novy and sent to hell to serve as allies in her final battle with Satan. It was too much for Retaliator to think about, to be honest. Before the Law Legion, his career had consisted of beating up muggers and drug dealers. It was easy to make the judgment that a man peddling junk to school kids deserved to have his teeth pounded from his mouth. Moral clarity became more difficult when he was called upon to judge alien bureaucrats, time-traveling machine men, and antimatter refugees from the seventh dimension.

Retaliator rolled aside the manhole cover and beamed his flashlight down into the darkness. Below him was nothing but the muck of a storm drain. He leapt, pulling his arms in as he dropped through the hole. He landed, not in knee-deep water, but in a large cavern lit by the reddish glow of the lava river that bisected it. This was the Devil Cave, filled with memorabilia gathered over five millennia of adventures. The place looked like a graveyard for props from a thousand B-movies. He jumped across the lava river and approached the golden throne. Supposedly, Midas himself had used this chair.

"I know you're here," said Retaliator. "I couldn't be here if you weren't."

"I was just waiting for you to say hello," a woman's voice answered behind him.

"Hello," he said, turning around.

Retaliator was a tall man at six foot three, but She-Devil was at least a head taller, and taller still if you counted the long black horns curving up from her brow. Her skin was red; not American flag–stripe red like Atomahawk's armor, but blood-red. A pair of leathery wings jutted from her shoulders. She wore armor made from black scales of the dragon she'd slain when they'd escaped hell together.

"What brings you here, Eric?" Her voice was disturbingly normal coming from a black-lipped mouth with white fangs flashing within. She sounded like a gray-haired librarian from Kansas, not an immortal vanquisher of evil. She was also the only one of the Law Legion to ever call him by his first name.

"I need you to tell me what you know about the Antikythera Mechanism."

"Which one?" she asked.

"There's more than one?"

"Of course. There's the original that was pulled out of its watery grave as little more than a slab, and the new one built by the Red Alchemist from the gamma-ray analysis of the old one, then stolen by Prime Mover."

"That's the one. The God Clock. The last time Prime Mover had it in his possession, he fed it one hundred souls to move the Heaven Wheel and it gave him the power of invisibility. What's the next power on the wheel?"

"What does it matter?" asked She-Devil. "The God Clock is safely locked away in the pit of souls."

"Is it?"

She frowned. "I know that Prime Mover keeps getting trickier, but, really, he's only a delusional old man once you strip away his gizmos. There's no way he could have stolen the mechanism."

"What's the next power?"

"Soul walking, but—"

"Soul walking?"

"It would allow him to exchange his mind and soul with that of another person for a one-hour period."

"So the man in prison—"

"No," said She-Devil. "It's him. A body swap could only last an hour. Even if he had the power, he's been in prison for months."

"Would his victims recall what had happened during that hour?"

She shrugged. "These things don't really come with instruction manuals."

"What's next on the wheel? After soul-walking?"

"Extradimensional portals. You could use the wheel to create an unseen gate into a hidden dimension. Sort of like my Devil Cave, or the pit of souls, which is a hidden dimension inside a hidden dimension."

"Show me the mechanism," he said.

She rolled her eyes, in a fashion that reminded him of Amelia when she was exasperated. "Fine," she said, taking a seat on the throne. She used her long black fingernail to trace a circle in the air. Then, she poked the circle in the center, as if the air was a sheet of glass that she'd just cut a hole into. The air fell away in a jumble of sharp-edged fragments, leaving a perfect black circle behind.

A chill wind cut through the Devil Cave, moaning like lost souls. She reached her hand into the hole. Her lips pressed together as her eyes narrowed.

"It's gone, isn't it?" said Retaliator.

She gave him a look that chilled his bones. In the many years he'd fought by her side, never once had he seen her eyes filled with fear.

"He possessed you," said Retaliator. "He'd already activated the soul-walking before we captured him. He possessed you and retrieved the God Clock. When the hour was up, you didn't remember."

"That's not—"

"Don't you dare say that's not possible!" snapped Retaliator. "It's the only thing that makes sense!"

Her red cheeks turned pink as the blood drained from her face. She closed the portal as she slumped into her chair.

"There . . . there was a day, back in August, when I woke up in my mortal form of Eula Leahy and I had no memory of what I'd done the night before."

"You didn't find this unusual? You didn't think this might be worth mentioning to your teammates? You're the most powerful woman in the world. You skewered Satan with his own sword! Don't you think it might be important to keep track of where you are and what you're doing at all times?"

"Don't judge me, Eric," she said, her voice little more than a whisper. "You haven't lived my life. You've never seen the horrors I've seen. Sometimes . . . sometimes in order to get to sleep, I have a drink or two or three. It's something . . . it's something I'm in control of . . . most of the time."

Retaliator took a long, slow breath. Sometimes it was difficult to remember that underneath all the magic, She-Devil was only a woman doing a job she didn't want to do.

"Look," he said. "The next time you feel like your only hope of getting some peace is a bottle, give me a call. We're teammates, Eula. I'll drop whatever I'm doing and talk you through the darkness."

She responded with a dry chuckle. "For the sake of the world, let's hope that my mood is never so dark that I need to turn to the Retaliator for a pep talk. Leave here, Eric. I need to do further research. There will be forces at play in this cave which no mere mortal can witness and hope to retain his sanity."

"Fine," said Retaliator, "but—"

But he was talking to a wall. He was back in Gray Manor in his own bedroom, facing the Annie Leibovitz portrait of himself and Nubile on their wedding day. It's funny; he knew Sarah first as Nubile, and even now thought of her by that name, even though she would never fight crime again after Prime Mover had put three bullets into the base of her skull. Without her powers, she'd likely be dead. As it was, she was merely an empty shell who didn't understand what people were saying to her in the few moments a day she drifted into wakefulness. She would never be Nubile again. She might never be Sarah again.

He sat on the edge of the bed and pulled off his mask as tears rolled down his cheeks. He lived in a world where a select subgroup of people never really died. He'd cheated death three times, Atomahawk had been dead twice, and Reset's whole power was resurrecting himself; he sometimes died two or three times a day.

He knew, he knew, he knew that these were the exceptions, that every single day thousands of ordinary people died, and stayed dead. It made his pain so much sharper to know that he was alive while his father was still dead from strangulation, that he was alive while his mother was still dead from cancer, that he was alive after Amelia swallowed all those pills and choked on her own vomit. And Sarah, poor Sarah—why was she a vegetable while he was walking around healthier than ever thanks to a heart from the future?

He wiped his cheeks and sucked up the pain, turning the leather mask in his hands, until his true face stared up at him, judging, the empty eye slots full of scorn.

He rose, pulled on a robe that hung down to his ankles, and walked down the hall. He squinted as he stepped through the door at the end, moving from lamp light into overly bright fluorescent whiteness. The last three rooms of the wing had been transformed into a private hospital. On the other side of the glass, a doctor looked up at him, then turned away.

He went to her room.

Sarah Kontis Gray was sleeping in her white hospital bed. The room was oddly silent now that the respirator had been removed.

The nurse by the bedside, a thin black woman with streaks of gray in her hair, rose as he entered.

"She's been sleeping well," she whispered.

He nodded. In truth, though, he didn't believe the words. In the three years they'd been together, he'd never seen Nubile sleep on her back. She always slept on her side, with her head pressed up against his shoulder. She looked so wrong on her back, with every muscle slack. The crisp white linens lay neatly across her. Normally when she slept, she was murder on blankets, tugging and tucking and stuffing them under body parts until everything was just right.

"Thank you," Eric whispered as he turned away.

If he wanted to find comfort for his aching soul, this was not the place to look for it. He walked to the library, activated the hidden elevator, and rode down to the quiet room. He tossed the robe aside and pulled on his mask. The door slid open on the stone-lined chamber.

Lawrence David Rambo was slumped on the stone floor, snoring. His ankle was red and raw where the iron manacle held it. He was naked save for the leather bands around his neck and wrists. His body was covered with welts and purple bruises haloed in yellow.

Lawrence David Rambo wasn't a supervillain. He was a petty scoundrel, seventeen years old, from a suburb near Baltimore. He'd discovered it was easy money to wave a gun around in small mom-and-pop stores out in the boonies, where he'd get away with a hundred bucks if he was lucky, a case of beer, maybe a roll of scratch-off lottery tickets. He'd never shot anyone, but he'd pistol-whipped a sixty-year-old woman who hadn't been moving fast enough, and had once pointed his gun at an eight-year-old boy who'd been coming out of the restroom, forcing him to lie down and count to a hundred, shouting that if he stopped counting he'd die.

Lawrence David Rambo was white. His parents were middle-class. He'd been arrested twice for trivial crimes, but never even spent a full night in jail. He was the sort of kid the broken justice system would allow to slip through the cracks until he killed someone.

Retaliator doused him with a bucket of cold water.

The young man gasped awake, trembling.

"Ohgoddon't," he whimpered as he curled into a fetal position. "Ohpleaseohpleasedon't."

Retaliator looked down through his zippered eye-slits at the very worst of humanity. When other men thought of evil, they thought of villains like Hitler, or Osama bin Laden, or Prime Mover. But Retaliator saw the truth. The true evil of the world was insidious in its smallness, the petty, pointless meanness that would pistol-whip a grandmother or badger a crying child. The big evils of the world were easy to manage. Armies were sent after men like bin Laden. But the same governments that raised the armies would provide lawyers to men like Rambo, subhuman scum who had hurt people not for any grand plan of world conquest, but simply because it was easy to bully those weaker than him.

Save for his rebuilt heart, Retaliator possessed no superpowers. What he did possess that allowed him to stand beside demigods like Atomahawk was clarity of vision. He could see through the veil of excuses and justifications that society wove to hide the reality of the evil in their midst.

Eric Gray's great power was his ability to see the world in black and white.

He selected a bullwhip from the wall, its tip studded with shards of broken glass.

His prisoner released a series of incoherent whimpers that Retaliator recognized as pleas for mercy.

Retaliator dropped his voice to a cold bass rumble. "Begging will only make me beat you harder."

The young man slowly stilled his voice in a series of choked sobs.

"Or perhaps it's silence that will infuriate me," said Retaliator, raising the whip, knowing, in truth, nothing the boy did mattered anymore. He would never leave this room alive.

☆　★　☆

As Eric Gray, it was simple enough to obtain a seat in the gallery of the Supreme Court, even at the last second. She-Devil was in her human identity of Eula Leahy and accompanied him as his guest.

Ordinarily if he was seen around town in the company of a woman, it would be fodder for the tabloids, but Eula was a small-town librarian from Kansas who looked to be in her mid-sixties. In her gray pantsuit, she was nearly invisible in her normalness.

"Where's Atomahawk?" she whispered as they took their seats.

"Fifty miles straight up," Eric whispered back. "He can be here inside of five seconds once Prime Mover's thugs show."

"If they come," said Eula. "Prime Mover stands a good chance of prevailing. Why would he pull something big like this?"

Retaliator didn't answer her question before the bailiff called the room to silence and ordered everyone to rise. The nine judges filed into the room. Eric felt a stirring of sadness as he watched their black robes sway. He remembered his father's robes from long ago.

Eight of the judges sat.

The chief justice, Lucas Shoen, remained standing. With a swift motion, a silver revolver dropped into his hand from his black sleeve. He placed the gun against his temple.

"Bring me the Law Legion," he said, in a crisp British accent that Eric recognized immediately. There was a flurry of confusion as the guards stationed around the rooms drew their guns. Eric grabbed Eula and pushed her to the floor, hiding behind the benches.

"How could he soul-swap with Schoen?" Eula whispered. "When would they ever make eye contact? Prime Mover's still in jail! I checked the magic mirror before I came here."

Eric instantly saw the only possible answer. "The power must work no matter what body he's in. He could jump from person to person for months, swapping every hour, until he arrived in the body he wanted . . . to . . ." His voice trailed off. "You have to leave," he said.

Eula nodded, understanding. There was circumstantial evidence he'd possessed her once. She was among the most difficult of the Law Legion to track down; this whole event could have been staged just for the chance to possess her again.

In the time it took Eric to blink, Eula had vanished, slipping back into the Devil Cave.

Eric reached under the bench and grabbed his utility belt. There had been no way to get through security while wearing it, which is why he'd had Tempo time-walk into the building at five in the morning to plant it. He crushed a sleeping-gas pellet between his fingers. The people immediately around him fell like flies. Seconds later, people cried out in panic as the gas spread, incapacitating everyone. Retaliator pulled on his mask and sprinkled his five-thousand-dollar suit with the nanites he'd taken from Mothmaster. Instantly the wool fell to dust, revealing his costume. He fastened his utility belt as he stood, palming a concussion grenade.

Nearly everyone in the room had fallen now, save for the chief justice, who was held conscious by the full power of Prime Mover's nearly matchless will.

"Hello, Eric," said Prime Mover.

Retaliator didn't blink.

"Surprised that I know your secret?" Prime Mover taunted.

"You were inside She-Devil for at least an hour," said Retaliator. "I could uncover every secret of the Law Legion if I had ten unguarded minutes with the central computer. I imagine it might have taken you twenty."

"Where are your friends, Eric?" said Prime Mover, pressing the pistol more tightly to his temple.

"It's just you and me this time," said Retaliator.

The chief justice's left eye twitched. While his expression of satisfied smugness didn't change, Retaliator knew that Prime Mover had to be disappointed by this news. No doubt he hoped to possess a more powerful hero, someone like—

A concentrated burst of energy flashed above them, leaving a perfect circle in the ceiling. The bright red form of Atomahawk streaked down from the sky, landing in the middle of the room, his fists wreathed with balls of white plasma. He stood with his back to Retaliator, facing the chief justice.

Retaliator started to scream a warning.

He got out the word "close" when the gun at the chief justice's temple disintegrated as Atomahawk's atomavision ripped it apart at a subatomic level.

The word "your" ripped from his throat as the chief justice smiled.

The word, "eyes" crossed his lips as Atomahawk whirled around, now wearing the very same smile.

"Shit," said Retaliator.

"Language," said Prime Mover as he floated into the air, flexing Atomahawk's fingers as if testing to see how well they fit.

Retaliator reached for the antispace grenade, a small box the size of a deck of cards that could destroy all matter within a three-foot sphere by creating a pocket of alternate physics where the Higgs boson had no mass.

His fingers never reached his belt before Atomahawk's impossibly hot fingers closed around his throat and jerked him from his feet.

"This is more like it," Prime Mover giggled. "The power of a living sun at my command! I'm going to kill a lot of people in the next sixty minutes, Eric. You, however, will not be one of them. You've humiliated me so often, Eric, that I don't want your misery to ever end, Eric, Eric, Eric! When you learn what I've done to—"

Suddenly Atomahawk jerked backward, gasping as if he'd been stabbed. Retaliator fell from his slack grasp, landing, appropriately enough, on the prone form of Vance Davis, the attorney who'd been prepared to argue Prime Mover's case.

Witness floated behind Atomahawk, his ghostly forearm reaching into the radioactive Indian's back. Retaliator could tell from the position of the boy's arm that his fingers were closed around Atomahawk's heart. Prime Mover was getting a full dose of the graveyard touch.

If Witness could distract Atomahawk for another thirty seconds . . .

It took only three seconds for Atomahawk's reddish skin to flash through every color of the spectrum, then beyond. His skin turned clear as glass. Sparks leapt from the silver buckles on Retaliator's boots. Witness wailed, then disappeared.

Atomahawk fell to his knees as his skin returned to its normal hue. He chuckled breathlessly for a few seconds. "I always . . . suspected . . . there was an electromagnetic frequency . . . that could reach the bloody ghoststream," Prime Mover said, wiping his lips.

"You sound winded," said Retaliator.

"Perhaps I'll massage your heart and see how you sound," Prime Mover grumbled.

"I was going to blame the smoking," said Retaliator, holding up the pack of unfiltered Camels he'd swapped on Atomahawk's utility belt. In his mind, he counted down six, five, four, . . .

"I'm so sorry, John," he said, despite the lump in his throat.

"What are you—"

Prime Mover never finished his sentence. There was a silent flash. In the aftermath, there was a perfectly concave indention in the marble floor where Atomahawk had knelt.

He'd just killed his worst enemy and best friend with a single act, but he had no time to contemplate what had happened. The goons in the warehouse, with the helicopters and the high explosives—this had never been their target. In the pit of his stomach, he knew where Prime Mover had sent them.

☆　★　☆

Eric Gray, the man who saw things in black and white, sat amid the mound of black cinders that had once been his mansion as pure white clouds the shape of comic book thought balloons drifted in the November sky. He had his mask wadded into a ball in his left hand; the island was completely silent. While the place was technically a crime scene, he had enough pull to allow him these few precious, private moments alone in the remains of the house he'd grown up in.

Only, as an even darker shadow fell across the charcoal that had once been the hardwood of his living room floor, he realized that this was no longer a private moment.

"I'm sorry about Nubile," said She-Devil. "Also . . . well . . . you know."

"She'll be back," he whispered, through a voice wet with tears. "John, too."

"I understand it's hard to let go," said She-Devil. The outline of her wings and horns were sharply defined as they stretched out before him.

"She's not dead," he said, shaking his head. "We thought she was dead when she was shot. But she was alive, even if her mind was gone. Now her body's gone. You've played this game long enough. No body, no death. That's how I know Atomahawk will be back, with a story of how he got shunted into another dimension, or backward in time, or whatever. We never stay dead."

She-Devil's shadow horns shook slowly.

"Eric, there's a time when hope is healthy, and a point where it's just a form of self-torture."

Retaliator nodded. "I know a thing or two about torture. There's a pain you can create with despair. And there's a deeper, darker, more desperate pain you can fuel with hope."

Black ash swirled in the chill breeze.

"Things look bleak now," said She-Devil. "You paid a high price. But you won. You finally stopped Prime Mover. He's in hell now. Find comfort in that, if you can."

"You know a lot about hell," said Retaliator.

She-Devil's shadow shrugged. He didn't have the strength to turn his head to face her.

"So you know the myth of Sisyphus."

She-Devil said nothing.

"Condemned to eternally push a rock up a hill. Every time he reaches the top, the stone rolls right back to the bottom."

"I've heard the myth," she said.

"We go out every week and fight bad guys and save the world," said Retaliator. "We die. They die. We all come back. We thwart their plans and lock them in prison cells and two months later they're standing on the Eiffel Tower waving around the latest and greatest doomsday ray and shouting demands. It never ends. It never ends. We get the rock to the top of the hill, and have to watch it roll back to the bottom."

"You're understandably depressed, Eric. You've lost your wife and home. You've lost your best friend. And now the police are hunting Retaliator for the murder of Atomahawk. But you'll bounce back. You'll make it to the top of the hill again. You always do. Maybe this time, the rock will stay put."

Eric rolled his mask into a cylinder and kneaded it back and forth in his fists. He swallowed his tears, then said, "You told us that you'd been tasked by Satan to find the most wicked men who ever lived and punish them."

She-Devil's shadow froze.

His voice dropped to a near whisper as he asked the question that terrified him most. "Is this . . . is this hell? Am I Sisyphus? Is this how you've chosen to punish me?"

He turned to see her face.

She was no longer there.

He dropped his mask, as tears streamed down his cheeks. His hands shook as he unsnapped the pouch on the front of his belt. The pouch held an antique, ivory-handled derringer that had belonged to his great-grandfather. Atomahawk had teased him about keeping it in his belt along with all his high-tech toys and gizmos. If he had to carry a gun, certainly Retaliator could have afforded something with a bit more heft.

But it doesn't require that much force to drive a lead slug through the roof of one's mouth. The steel barrel was cold as ice against his lips, and brought forth the most exquisite and terrifying sense of déjà vu.

He wondered, when this all began again, if he would remember pulling the trigger.

The writer of such Marvel comics titles as *Wisdom*, *Captain Britain and MI-13*, *Dark Reign: Young Avengers*, and *Black Widow: Deadly Origin*, Paul Cornell is perhaps best known for his work on the BBC's new *Doctor Who* series, for which he has twice been nominated for the prestigious Hugo Award. He is also the author of the novels *Something More* and *British Summertime*, and the creator of Bernice Summerfield, a *Doctor Who* companion who has gone on to spawn her own series of books, short story anthologies, and audio dramas. A fantastic writer in any form, Cornell gives us a tale that pushes the limits of double identities.

Secret Identity

PAUL CORNELL

Jim Ashton heard the magic explosion. So could all of Mantos. He tried to look surprised. He put down his pint, spun around, looking out across the canal. Pretending he didn't know what that was.

"Look at Lois Lane," said Hugh, sitting beside him. He, typically, hadn't flinched at the noise.

"What?" Jim turned back from the window, annoyed at the other man's grin.

"Is Chris really going to come out of the loo and sit back down here? Come on. It's all right. If anyone can keep a secret, this lot can."

"You reckon? And," he quickly added, "I don't know what you're on about."

Hugh lowered his voice. "Chris is the Manchester Guardian. Everyone knows they're the same bloke."

Jim found himself wearing a sad smile as the sound of another explosion echoed over the water. "Do they?"

☆   ★   ☆

The Guardian caught the second of the Top Hat's magic spikes a nanosecond after he'd thrown it, clenched his fist on it, and dumped the energy into the atomic void in his palm. This magic villain really could do anything: change time and space. The first throw had caught him off guard, spun him round in a whiplash of colors. But now he was closing on his opponent, flashing through the air toward him as their enhanced senses calculated the impact—

He had a second to see the shocked expression on the Top Hat's face—

He was there faster.

His senses were better.

He deflected the bolt intended for his head up into the sky. He wouldn't let it hit Canal Street.

Enough of this! He broke through the Top Hat's magical shields with one punch.

He grabbed the magician by the collar and slapped the hat off his head.

It went spiraling down into the lights of the bars and restaurants along the canal.

The Top Hat tried to say something, his hands flailing, his expression demanding mercy now that he was powerless. He knew where the Guardian would send him. His eyes reflected the moon.

The Guardian grabbed him with both hands and spun three times, until he was at maximum magical velocity—

He released the magician. Straight at the moon.

The Top Hat blazed a sudden bright line into the stratosphere. A reverse meteor. Faster than escape velocity.

He'd hit the lunar surface in about three days.

Without his hat to grant the wishes that gave him his powers, this time it might actually take him a while to escape.

The Guardian glanced down and used his magical vision to find the hat. A group of students had grabbed it, were laughing about it, trying it on. Gay lads from the Uni, a couple of fag hags with them. They'd been queuing outside one of the bars while watching the battle. The people of Manchester had always watched the magic "hero fights" in their skies, treating them like the weather.

The group of straight sightseers in front of them had also been watching, but now they'd gone back to arguing with the doormen. That bar had a door policy of quizzing people who wanted to get in, trying to enforce gays only.

The Guardian didn't understand how people could be like that.

With a thought and a rainbow blur, he was there.

He took the hat from the kid who was holding it. "Dangerous magic. Would you please let me deal with that, sir?"

"Sure, sorry." The kids were beaming at him. "Bloody hell, it's you!"

"It is!"

"He'll tell you!" one of the girls from the party by the door called out. "We're mates of his!" She gestured over her shoulder at the party of grinning straight lads with her. "Tell him we're all very very gay!"

The kid who'd given the Guardian the hat looked at him with a twinkle in his eye. *Go on!*

The Guardian turned to Tall Ben, who was the one who stood at the door of this place on busy nights now, asking the embarrassing questions, with a hefty bouncer on either side of him. Ben met his gaze. The Guardian had never liked Ben, even before Ben had license to not just tell people they weren't gay, but that they weren't gay *enough*.

"What can I do for you, hero of all gay people?" Tall Ben asked.

The Guardian gestured to the girl and her boozed-up mates. "You've humiliated them enough."

"No, mate, I've just started. That lot just want to have a look at what they'll never have. They want to point and laugh."

The Guardian frowned the frown of a man impatient with debate.

Ben's clothes were suddenly ruffled by a blur of air. And there was the concussive noise of the door opening and closing too fast to see—

And the group of kids had vanished inside.

And the Guardian was back, his hands behind his back, whistling nonchalantly.

The kids from the Uni tried to hide that they were laughing.

Ben looked at the bouncers, and they tiredly headed inside to find the straight boys. "Guardian, or should I say Chris Rackham—"

The Guardian found himself taking a step toward the man, provoked despite himself. "I am not—"

"Oh, right, it's different when it's *you* being pointed at. Whatever. You do that again and you're barred. Whatever you're calling yourself." And he let the party from the Uni in, just to show he was on the side of good.

The Guardian stood sizing the man up, feeling lost in a way that didn't suit the costume he wore.

It was then he heard the noise.

The applause his magic hearing had picked up came from the tower of the old Refuge Assurance building.

It was the sound, across the city, of one woman clapping.

☆   ★   ☆

"Well done! Bravo!" she had placed her ivory staff to jut out from a ledge on the tower, and was standing on it like a gymnast, one foot in front of the other. She was wearing her long white coat and mask, her form-fitting white costume under it, black hair tumbling down her back. Very red lipstick and nails. Her voice was upper-class, unashamed, committed.

The Guardian grasped all this in one magic glance.

And then he was standing in the air in front of her, his arms folded, aware of every car and individual on the street below, every face looking out of every hotel room window. Aware of them in a distant way. Much more aware of her.

"Bravo," she said. "Well handled, there."

The White Candle was a thief who stole art, mostly from gay men's houses (probably more because of her area of operations than anything else) through magical means. She imagined herself to be doing nothing particularly wrong. The Guardian disagreed. They'd crossed paths three times before. She'd somehow avoided capture every time.

"This is daring," he said. "Even for you."

"I couldn't help but applaud your part in that little confrontation," she said. "I can tell, you see. With my magic gaydar."

"What?"

"Whatever that rainbow costume of yours says . . . you're one of *us*, darling."

The Guardian raised an eyebrow and stepped forward to confront her.

☆ ★ ☆

Jim woke up at the sound of the curtain being pushed back, the familiar slide of the window closing in the spare room. The soft concussion of air that marked the change.

Chris went to the bathroom, then came into the bedroom. He looked thinner than ever. Jim was sure he'd dropped half a stone in the last three weeks. Ever since this nonsense had started. It was all the Mighty Sphinx's fault. If he hadn't come out as really being that tiny librarian, maybe nobody would have started linking Chris, a man with a runner's physique, with the insanely muscled Guardian.

The shape of their faces was different, even, because of the muscles. But if you had the thought in your head, and you got a good look . . . and of course the Guardian would never wear a mask . . .

Chris was still wearing his suit because they'd gone for a pint after work, before that bloke with the hat had popped up again. He took off the jacket and plonked it on the hanger, tried to smooth out the creases.

"How did it go?"

"Bang, zoom, to the moon. As bloody usual. I got the hat this time." He held it up, and put it down on the side table.

"That's what people were saying. It sounds like you were hard on Ben."

"Yeah. S'pose I was. Couldn't help it."

"I see why that place does it. I'd feel the same if a bunch of twats came in and started taking the piss."

"Me too." Chris had finished undressing, and now he got into bed. "I kind of agree with it, even. I was chosen to be the Guardian by the Coven because I'm all about . . . well, letting people be who they are. But the Guardian takes that right up to eleven. He's very focused. More—"

"Straightforward."

"Yeah."

"I mean, he doesn't really *do* complexity."

"Right."

Jim let himself lie with his head on Chris's chest, like always. But it didn't feel good now. He wanted to get to the point. "So then what did you do? After Tall Ben? I was kind of thinking you'd be here when I got back." Benefit of the doubt. He wasn't going to be the jealous one. The thought crossed his mind that he was being cruel anyway, that it would have been easier on Chris to yell at him. "Did summat else happen?"

"Kind of."

"What?"

A long silence. Oh God. Jim found himself controlling his breathing. It's just time, just move on through time, get to the tough bit, you're strong enough to deal, you know you are.

"White Candle—"

Jim closed his eyes. "Again."

☆ ★ ☆

The Guardian had stepped onto the roof and moved carefully closer to her. He could smell her perfume. It was trying to intoxicate him, to suggest all kinds of drama and exoticism about her, to mentally take him to the bedroom mirror where she put it on—

He stopped himself. Yes, it was indeed just perfume.

What was wrong with him? He couldn't sense any magic making him look into her face, making him concentrate on her eyes and mouth, making him consider how soft her hair was. Making his eyes glimpse her breasts and the shape of her pelvis.

There was no such magic coming from her. There hadn't been the last time they'd met either.

He knew what was wrong with him.

And it was very wrong.

He knew everything was simple, when you took away the evasions and lies that made life complicated.

But he was not what he was supposed to be.

He felt like punching her into the next building for making him feel like this.

But that would be wrong too.

"How about you don't run away, for once?" he asked. "How about you really take me on?"

"I could say the same." Her voice was brittle. He could imagine the noises she'd make. He killed the thought.

And she'd suddenly laughed and thrown herself off the building.

He sped after her.

She danced across the rooftops, throwing glamours and dazzles and feints expertly behind her, some of which he walked through, some of which he had to smash aside, some of which he had to suddenly duck because otherwise they'd have had him.

A clever pattern of harmlessness, then punch, varying always, uncertainly deadly.

He ducked ducked ducked, chose a moment when she'd stopped throwing and had to leap, was in midair—

And flashed past her.

He pulled the air carpet from under her and heard the fragments of the levitation spell fall singing into the void over Oxford Road.

Crowds were rushing onto the pavement from the Cornerhouse bar and the BBC and the hotels—

He caught her before she hit the ground.

She lay there in the crook of his arm, curled like a pussycat, an unperturbed smile on her big mouth. "If I've done something wrong," she said, "then you should punish me."

And then she kissed him.

And he let her.

☆ ★ ☆

"Oh, stop, stop right there!" Jim was sitting up, the quilt pulled defensively around him. "Did she really say that?! I mean, that's the sort of thing you like, is it?! Or are these your smutty fantasies?!"

"Not *mine*—"

"Bollocks! If it's not *you*, how come I recognized you, three years back? That's why we're together, remember, because I saw through your clever disguise of a pair of glasses!"

"But—"

"You're saying *he's* not *you*. Even though he looks just like you in a Charles Atlas Before and After. How come you remember everything he does, then? How come you can do a little bit of detective work as you, and then change into him and—?"

"I don't know! I've got different . . . opinions than him—"

"If you act different when you're him, maybe that's just 'cause you with muscles knows he can finally get the *girl*, while mildmannered you has to settle for—"

"Because the gays are *so* much less about the body beautiful than girls are!"

"Well tell me then! Tell me how you in a costume and muscles is different from you now, to the extent where it's okay if—"

"I didn't *say* it was *okay*! Even *he* doesn't think it's okay!"

"You don't normally say you and him. Up until now it was all 'I saved him' and 'I fought that villain!'"

"Because I was proud of it up until now!" And that was a bellow.

Jim found himself silent in the face of that.

He didn't want to lose himself by matching that anger. He didn't want to lose . . . this.

That was why this was so terrible.

But damn it, he needed something. Something to balance this huge gaping harm that, in that calm, laid-back voice of his, Chris had just . . .

"Beer," he said. "Now."

☆　★　☆

They went into the kitchen and sat down with a beer each and didn't say anything until they'd each thrown it back and got another.

Chris tried again. Carefully. "It's . . . like some sort of . . . drug."

"The power, you mean?"

"No. I mean . . . all the muscles—"

"What?! Being macho means you go straight? My own research would seem to indicate—"

"I *mean* maybe there's summat chemical that goes with these *particular* muscles! They're not just my arms pumped up, they . . . replace my arms. When I change."

"Your eyes are the same. Your teeth and hair are the same. Well, maybe your teeth are straighter. And it seems that's not the only thing."

"They only *look* the same. The eyes can do all the magic stuff. The teeth and hair are *bulletproof.* Until now, I always thought it was the same brain in here, but—"

"Oh, what? You're saying being gay . . . or not being gay . . . is a *brain* thing?"

"Well . . . since *everything* about a person is a 'brain thing'—"

"I mean, not a mind thing, but something to do with the physical . . . brain! You're saying being gay is about your glands, a pituitary condition! So, you're the same mind, the same bloke, but when that mind is in the Guardian's body, with a healthy pituitary gland, all thoughts of faggotry—"

"I didn't say anything like that!"

"Well, good, because I have never heard anything so homophobic in my life."

"Whether it is or not, it might just be *true*, like."

"Well even if it is, how does this scientific explanation help?"

"This *magical* explanation. If you want science heroes—"

"I want London, I know. I wonder if their queero—queer hero, see what I did there?—I wonder if he has these problems. Shall we call the Ravenphone and ask?"

"You said homophobic," said Chris suddenly. "Oh. What if that's deliberate?"

"I'm not past you shagging a woman on the roof of the Arndale Centre, so don't talk like we're into postmatch analysis now."

"No, listen, I change into the Guardian by saying a magic word. We know the spell was created back in the eighteenth century. What if whoever started this put in . . . design limitations?"

"Oh, right. Because good magic is about natural things, noble things, heroic things, and not a bunch of fags like us, and that this is just you reverting to that—"

"Oh, don't be—"

"What? My boyfriend tells me that, for the first time in—"

"Ever. I've never fancied women. I started looking at blokes when I was nine. Everything I do as the Guardian, when I look back on it, feels like a dream I had. In this particular dream, it's like I was . . . eating something I'd normally hate, like broccoli, only in the dream I'm really enjoying it."

"I don't want to hear about whatever it was you ate. I'm thinking of packing my bags. I really am. Because we can't go on like this, Chris. This hurts too bloody much." He got up and walked around the kitchen a bit. And managed, after a swig of beer and a deep breath, to get to the point. "All right. When you're him . . . do you still fancy me?"

Chris closed his eyes. A very long silence. To the point where Jim was about to interrupt by thumping him—

"No. No, I don't think he does."

Jim was about to . . . he didn't know what he was about to do, but Chris got up and stopped him doing it. Put his hands to Jim's face.

"I didn't know that, okay? Not until just that second, when I thought about it. Because in all this time I've only been him for a few minutes here and there, saving people and fighting villains and stuff—"

"And you haven't really had much time for dating?"

"Listen to me! *I* still fancy you! I *love* you—!"

Jim couldn't answer.

"I don't want to do anything to hurt you—"

"Chris, everyone will have seen. And everyone already bloody knows you're him! What happens the next time you become him, and she turns up? Because I suppose you let her go—"

"She slipped out of his . . . out of my clutches—"

"What happens?"

"Well, he's a very moral person. He doesn't want to see you hurt either. He just . . . can't be anything he's not. He doesn't do shades of gray."

"So he'll try to be . . . not faithful, 'cause he doesn't want me, but . . . celibate . . ."

"And eventually . . . he'll fail." There was such quiet loss in his voice as he said it.

"So what you're saying is, you're going to turn into him next time, *knowing* that sooner or later you're going to be unfaithful to me."

Chris was silent. Looking away.

"It's like you . . . get drunk on a regular basis, and every time you say it's not *me* who's doing this woman, it's not *me* who's driving this car . . ."

"You're right. You're right!" Chris threw his arms in the air, admitting defeat.

He slumped against the wall and looked out the window into the night.

Then he looked back at Jim. "Okay. So I'll stop."

"What?"

"I'll stop being him. I'll pass the magic word onto someone else."

Jim felt suddenly more loved than he'd ever been in his life. And more guilty. At the same time. He rubbed his fist into his brow. "You'd really do that?"

"Yeah." And the look on Chris's face said he meant it.

"Okay. Great. Do that."

Chris nodded, started moving, decisive as always. "I'll call the Coven, tell them to get the ceremony ready and start searching for someone worthy—"

Jim grabbed his arm. "Don't."

They sat back down together, looking at each other, silent.

"I love you," Chris said again. Meaning that he really would do this.

"And I love you." They snogged for a bit. Found great relief in holding each other, knowing they were going to stay together. "But, Chris, are you sure about this? It's not just us, is it? You're very good at being the Manchester Guardian. Any new guy . . . it'd take him ages to get it together. It took you ages, didn't it? And in the meantime, who knows what'd happen? Who knows who'd come after Canal Street? Especially with all this publicity. It'd be a hell of a risk for you to do this now."

"None of that is more important than me and you. And besides, what choice do we have?"

Jim didn't know.

☆ ★ ☆

They went back to Canal Street the next night. Putting on a brave front.

It wasn't quite like that Welsh village where they'd flounced through the door of a pub and then, under the influence of a lounge bar of stares, marched to the bar like navvies.

But it was close.

Everyone was looking at Chris. Betrayed.

Jim wanted to say to them that the very same night their representative hero had been with a woman, he'd also saved the whole street from a villain who'd never cared what damage he did to the people and property who suffered in his endless vendetta against Chris.

And it wasn't as if this lot had unreservedly loved the Guardian lately, was it?

They went into Mantos. Jim thought for a moment that the barman wasn't going to serve them, but he finally did. So this was what it had come down to, feeling that old nervousness about whether or not people were looking, in one of their own bars, on their own street.

They found Hugh and sat with him. After a moment of awkwardness, offset by the sheer theatricality of how he played that awkwardness, he let them. "So," he said, "Chris. How *was* last night?"

"The Guardian," Jim found himself suddenly saying, "never *said* he was gay. He looks like he is, with all the rainbow flag stuff, but he never said it. Isn't it enough that he protects our lot?" He raised his voice, so that everyone looking could hear. "What, were any of you lot hoping to shag him?"

He would have gone on. But Chris put his hand on his and stopped him with a look.

He might have said something else anyway . . .

But from outside there came the sound of magic power crackling through the air.

Chris looked like he might make an effort and stay put.

But Jim gave him a shove. Go on.

Chris didn't bother trying to be stealthy this time. He just got up, without a look at anyone else in the bar, and headed out the door.

Jim could feel people leaning over, craning to look out the door, hoping to see the change.

"Don't wait up for him, like," someone said.

Jim closed his eyes and felt pride rather than pain. He was making a sacrifice. And he absolutely knew that Chris was too.

Chris walked out to the water's edge, aware of everyone on Canal Street looking at him. Waiting to see if he was going to change. And probably then shag a woman immediately.

He looked up in the air, and there he was. Jumping Jack. He was stepping from sparkling magic disc to sparkling magic disc, throwing lightning randomly down into the streets, calling the Guardian out.

Not the murderous sort, this one. The fun kind of magic villain that the people of Manchester most enjoyed. His lightning just gave you a bit of a jolt.

Lives were not at stake. Not this time.

He didn't have to change if he didn't want to.

But where would he draw the line? He'd vowed to meet every threat to this little community, vowed to stop every single affront, nasty or sporting equally, as the Guardian.

The Guardian would do his absolute best to not be seduced. He'd probably succeed, now he'd realized his true nature and wasn't being taken by surprise by a secret shame. That innocence of his was shored up now, prepared.

But that meant that his other half shouldn't be his whole self. That he should deny an aspect of what he was. And wasn't that what he was all about defending?

Chris kept watching Jumping Jack as his silhouette sailed past the moon.

And then an intense expression came over his face.

And he started to run in the direction of the house he shared with Jim.

That night, all of Canal Street looked up from their pints to hear a very solid impact of magic villain with water, and a subsequent yelling as magic lightning shorted out in contact with said water. And lots of huffing and puffing as said magic villain was dragged up onto the side of the canal and sent packing.

And then there was a long wait after the battle was obviously over, and Jim Ashton felt everyone looking at him, with pity and contempt.

☆ ★ ☆

Across the city, a pair of handcuffs closed onto the wrists of a surprised White Candle, who'd been only just about to leave through her own bedroom window. "I can get out of these in seconds," she said, "unless you don't want me to."

"I *don't* want you to," said the Guardian, gently landing her on the pavement in front of a waiting van from the Manchester Constabulary's Magic Division, "and so you'll find, those being solid silver, that you can't."

"That was almost a joke. That's unlike you."

"Well, making jokes is one of the things I'm looking forward to doing a little more."

She tutted at him as she stepped into the van, like she was stepping into a limo. "And I thought we'd shared something important!"

"We did," he said. "Which gave me intimate knowledge of you. Enough to follow your perfume home." He took her aside from the police officer in the back of the van for a moment. "Once you've served your time, hey, I'd really like to take you out to dinner."

She looked boggled at him.

He gave her a wink and hopped out of the van.

He watched it drive away with slight regret in his new heart.

☆ ★ ☆

Late that night, Chris Rackham showed up at the door of that bar down the street that had Tall Ben standing there judging people.

"Astonishingly brave of you to even try," he said. "But no. Of course not. We all know about your alter ego."

Jim arrived and joined him. They stood there, holding hands. Together.

"It doesn't matter," said Ben. "What matters is what you're *really* like, Chris. When you're not lying to us."

The Guardian landed beside them.

Tall Ben looked between them. "Oh very clever," he said. "Magic trick, is it?"

"It's the truth," said Chris. "And we're going to go in now." And he led Jim into the bar.

Tall Ben considered for a moment and then didn't stop them. "Well then," he said to the Guardian. "Do you want in and all?"

"No," said the magic hero. "I came to let you know you can still call on me for help. I'm straight. But I'm still the protector of this area, and everyone in it."

Ben sized him up for a moment, and then nodded. "I s'pose it'll have to do."

The Guardian raised an eyebrow at him. And flew off into the night.

☆ ★ ☆

"What's the Guardian going to *do* all day?" said Jim, when they got home.

"Explore space, he says." Chris took the top hat from the kitchen table, where he'd left it after using it the other night, and hid it in the bottom of the wardrobe. "And get a girlfriend, I should think. He's all excited. He says it's like being alive for the first time. He says he always wanted not to change back, but thought it'd be oppressing me to even ask."

"Won't the Top Hat be able to reverse the spell, if he ever gets back from the moon?"

"I s'pose that'll be summat else for him and the Guardian to fight about. And if he puts us back together, I'll just beat him again and use the hat to split us apart again."

Jim brushed his teeth and got into bed, and relaxed, properly relaxed, for the first time in ages, as Chris lay against him. "And you aren't going to resent me for this?" he said. "Long-term, I mean. Not being able to fly anymore and that?"

"It was always like a dream," said Chris, pulling him into an embrace. "And we all get to fly in our dreams. This way I get to be myself, all the time."

And from outside they heard the sound of magic explosions.

And they smiled.

☆　★　☆

Mike Carey's considerable talents have been on display in such comic titles as DC Vertigo's *Lucifer*: *Hellblazer*, *The Sandman Presents*, and *The Unwritten*, and Marvel's *X-Men: Legacy*, *Ultimate X-Men*, and *Secret Invasion*, and many, many more. He is also the author of the five Felix Castor novels: *The Devil You Know*, *Vicious Circle*, *Dead Men's Boots*, *Thicker Than Water*, and *The Naming of the Beasts*. A power writing about powers, Carey gives us a tale that is anything but what its title implies.

The Non-Event

MIKE CAREY

Ptah! **Pfff! Kah!**

Nice to have that gag out of my mouth. Got anything to take the taste away? Water, you say? Well, if it's all you've got, I'll take it. But it's your choice: I'll sing a lot louder and clearer if you give me whiskey.

So you want me to talk about Gallo. Sure you do. And you want to hear about how he came to be lying there, with no head on his shoulders, and if I feel any remorse about killing him.

Well, you know, I don't feel much about it one way or the other. The man was an idiot, and worse than that, an idiot who spat when he talked. A pornography addict who liked to talk about his hobby; a man who fell for pyramid selling schemes and wanted all his acquaintances to join the club; a serial drinker of cheap supermarket beer that made him so flatulent birds fell out of the sky wherever he walked.

But nothing in his life became him like the leaving of it. Gallo died classy. I'll give him that. That's why I agreed to come here. I'm making this statement. I'm cooperating with your dumbfuck investigation, even though I know the conviction is a lead-pipe certainty whether I talk or not.

I'll tell you the whole story about Gallo's death. I just feel like somebody should. The rest—the confession and everything—yeah, you can have that too. Take it and choke on it, you fuckers.

So to start with, it was Pete's idea. Pete Vessell, this is, aka Hyperlink. Not Pete Haig, who is Vessell's brother-in-law. Haig's deal is converting base metal into live frogs, which as you'd imagine is not a power that's in great demand anywhere sane people gather. Vessell has teleportation powers, and even though they're not as good as the teleportation powers Mass Transit has, say, or even those of Doctor Phase or Little Johnny Blink, they still raise some interesting and suggestive possibilities.

Let me spell it out. Vessell's deal is that he can instantaneously appear anywhere his name is written down. I know, I know, it's like a bad joke. You blink out of reality and reappear inside a fucking mailbox, right? Great party trick. And then you stay there for a good half hour, because that's how long it takes Vessell to recharge. Before he came up with that Hyperlink name, I suggested Return to Sender and Eponymous Boy. He didn't laugh.

Anyway, Vessell brought me in, because I do the whole talking-to-locks thing. I suggested Naseem Hadid, who goes by Perspective, and George Gruber, the Tin of Rin Tin Skin. Then Naseem brought in Cindy Fellows, aka Guesswork, who I think was her girlfriend at the time. It was a good balance of powers, all things considered. But everything depends on the context, of course. Everything depends on the actual job.

The job in this case was a bank vault: DeJong's, on Aldwych. It's technically Dutch soil, by means of some obscure legal switcheroo, so the filthy rich use it as a left-luggage locker for all the stuff they don't want to pay UK tax on: their Krugerrands and their diamond necklaces, their Fabergé eggs and their bearer bonds. There's a nice concentration of obscene and highly portable wealth, and Vessell—who used to be a banker himself before the endoclasm—had scoped it out pretty well.

We met up in his basement—which he's done up okay, but which still smells of sour milk no matter how many potpourris he puts down there—to go over the logistics and sniff each other's dog tags. The basement was a necessary part of the equation because it's lined with lead, which means nobody is going to be reading your lips from five miles off using their X-ray vision. Lead is a nostrum that seems to work against a whole range of superpowers, for reasons nobody has ever been able to explain; but Vessell is friends with Timeslide and Granite Phantom, too, so he'd managed to get the room time-proofed and phase-sealed. Or at least he said he had. You never know how much is bullshit with him.

He'd made an effort, I'll say that for him. There was wine and beer, and a party plate from Marks and Sparks with little sausage rolls and vol-au-vents on it: everything except massage chairs. Vessell seemed to want to make the planning of the robbery a festive occasion, whereas mostly they tend to be fairly task-centered affairs.

So there was a good atmosphere, as far as that went. But when we ran through the plan, it was obvious it still had a serious flaw. Probably more than one, if the truth be told, but certainly one that kind of jumped up, grabbed you by the collar, and screamed "serious fucking flaw!"

We could get into the building at night when it was empty. We could break the vault and get our hands on a good proportion of what was in it. With Naseem on board, we could even stow the goods where they couldn't be found until the heat died down and it was safe to sell them on.

But we didn't have a strong guy. None of us, not even George, had the serious offensive capability that would allow us to walk away after the job through the shitstorm of superpowered cops who would come down on us out of a clear sky, bringing to bear such a ridiculous variety of powers that our feet would not touch the fucking ground. We needed at the very least the Rainbow Bandit or Ultravox, and preferably one or more of the four Apocalypse Boys. Otherwise there was no way we were getting out of that vault in units of more than one molecule across.

I should say here that this stuff hurts me. It hurts me in my heart. I was a career criminal back in the old days, before all this bullshit, when all you needed was a crowbar and a hopeful disposition. These days, you can't even knock over a post office without Doctor Doom, Lex Luthor, and the marching band of the radioactive zombie death-ray commandos on your team. And even then, it's ten to one that one of the really big hitters like Saint Seraph or the Epitome will amble along and you'll go to the wall anyway.

It's not the endoclasm that's the problem, you know? It's human nature. The endoclasm gave about one in ten people superhuman powers, but most people are scared shitless when microwaves shoot out of their arses or their chins sprout adamantium bristles or they wake up one morning lying upside down on the ceiling. They fall apart quickly, burn out in some really nasty superpowered suicide, or else repress their abilities so deeply they effectively depower themselves: psychic castration, the experts call it. Two kinds of personality ride the crisis out okay: the deeply criminal and the deeply moral, or, as you might say, the walking ids and the walking superegos. And those law-and-order bastards seem to outnumber us enhanced villains by about a hundred to one.

I don't mean supervillains, you understand: I mean good, old-fashioned burglars, bank robbers, and stick-up merchants who just happen to have picked up powers during the endoclasm. We're not interested in ruling the world, or destroying it, or having a big, pointless punch-up with a bunch of twats in tights. We just ply our trade, when we're allowed to, do the job, and then clock off.

So yeah, anyway, we're contemplating the ruin of Vessell's plan, and we're thinking too bad, because it's a nice bank vault full of all kinds of good stuff, and it would be a pleasant thing indeed to get in there and have a rummage around. Then Vessell said, "In case you're wondering about the getaway, I'm thinking we'll use Gallo."

There was a blank silence. It was just amazement at first, but then I went right on through to being angry. Seems I was wrong about why Vessell had brought me in: it wasn't because I'm Lockjaw, it was just because I used to be friends with Gallo.

"Gallo?" Gruber echoed. He's not good with civilian names.

"He means the Non-Event," Naseem said. "And he's out of his bloody mind."

"I agree," I said, getting up. "Thanks for the vol-au-vents, Vessell, but fuck you very much for the rest of it. I'm not galloping into town with Rizzo Gallo on the next horse, that's for friggin' sure. Good luck with that."

Vessell jumped up hastily, making calming downward movements with his hands so he looked like a chicken that was having trouble taking off. "No, listen, Davey," he said. "I'm serious. I've thought it through and it's going to be fine. Really. Just hear me out. If you don't think it will work, then you can walk."

"I can walk now," I pointed out, demonstrating.

"But what do you lose by staying one more minute?" Vessell insisted, stepping into my way. He was sounding kind of whiny now, and I started to remember all over again some of the reasons I didn't like him. "You listen, you make up your mind, if it doesn't work for you, you're gone. Come on, you owe me that much."

I didn't owe him a thing, if the truth be told, and we both knew it. He's brought me in on a job or two, sure, and I've always carried my weight. But that's the sort of fruitless argument where once you get into it you can end up ripping out each other's teeth with pliers. I prefer to keep the moral high ground if I can help it. I shrugged, remained on my feet, but stopped heading for the door. Folding my arms, I adopted a "so convince me" stance.

And he did. He convinced me. As he explained his plan, by some fluke or intuition he met all my objections in the order they came to me. By the time he was done, I was thinking—very much to my surprise—that this thing might actually have a chance of working.

"Well, I'll talk to Gallo," I said, grudgingly. "No harm in that, anyway."

Sure. No harm at all. God likes a good laugh now and again, doesn't he? That's what irony is for.

☆   ★   ☆

Gallo was living all on his own in a rat's-ass workman's cottage just outside Luton—the only inhabited building on a condemned row that was short but not sweet. I mean, someone would have had to drop serious money on the place to bring it up to the point where you could describe it as a slum. Right then it was just four walls and—intermittently—a roof.

Gallo didn't mind much. His needs were modest, and he enjoyed his own company. More to the point, he was scared shitless of anybody else's. The Extra-Normal Affairs people were talking back in the day about giving him a pension to stay away from major population centers, but then the Tories got in again and the mood swung. They left Gallo to starve on his own time.

And that gave me my in, as it were. I pointed out to him that this job would set him up for the rest of his life. He could buy a place in the country, a thousand miles from anywhere. Buy a tent and live on top of a mountain in Tibet, or out in the Kalahari, I don't know. Anywhere except the ragged edge of fucking Luton: even a dog deserves better than that.

Gallo shook his head slowly, clearly not liking the idea. "I don't know, Davey," he mumbled in that singsong way of his. "I mean I really don't know. I'm doing all right here."

I looked around his living room, staring in turn at the two cracked teacups, the sway-backed Formica table, the ancient portable TV zebra-striped on top with cigarette burns. I didn't need to say anything: Gallo knew what I was thinking.

"But it's all right for me," he said, throwing out his arms in what was either a shrug or a plea. "I don't miss anything very much. And at least—out here—I can't hurt anyone. That's the most important thing. There's nothing much to upset me, but if I do get upset, then nobody gets hurt." Both times he said the word *hurt* he lingered on it, almost making it into two syllables. I knew where he was coming from, and I even agreed with him up to a point: there are two kinds of bad jobs, the screwups and the slaughterhouses. Worst kind of all is the kind that starts off as the one and slides into the other.

"Okay, Rizzo," I allowed. "So you're doing nobody any harm. But fuck, you're not doing a damn bit of good to anyone, either. You're barely living. You've got all that power stored up inside you, enough to bring a whole city to a standstill, and you're living like a cockroach under a brick. You don't think you deserve a little better, maybe? I mean, who dares wins, man. Specifically, who dares wins a ticket out of this shithole into a nicer shithole, with hot water and clean towels, and a well-stocked liquor cabinet."

I mentioned that last point because Gallo used to put it away like a sailor on shore leave, and because despite being pathetically happy to see me he hadn't offered me one of the three cans of lager staying semicool in a red plastic bucket full of water on the floor next to his chair: husbanding his resources, I figured.

Gallo rubbed the bridge of his nose, where he used to wear big bottle-glass spectacles before he gave up the unequal race against his birth defects. He made a noncommittal sound. "I thought you didn't do this stuff anymore," he hedged. "Since . . . you know . . . what happened to Kim."

It was a low blow, in a way: Gallo breaking the established ground rules to fend me off. I don't talk about my kid, and what happened to her when she lost control of her phasing powers. I'd even trained myself out of thinking about it. That turned out to be a dumb move, though: one time when I opened the wrong drawer and got hit by a photo of her, aged 9, blowing out her birthday candles, it took me a second even to remember who she was. I'd gotten that good at editing out my own memories, my own feelings. I'd cauterized Kim right out of my fucking mind.

"Yeah," I said. "Thanks for bringing that up, Gallo. You're right. I got out of the blagging habit for a while. Then I got back in again. What the hell, you know? It passes the time." By which I meant it's better than sitting at home with two bottles of whiskey and seeing how far you make it into the second one before you pass out.

"I don't know," Gallo said again.

"You don't know what?" I demanded, a little testy now.

"Well, I might let you down, is one thing. I'm not . . . you know . . ." He shrugged again. "I can't control it. When it happens, it happens. But I can't *make* it happen."

Part of me wanted to walk away from this, but the other part—the part that had swallowed Vessell's line and was already figuring out how to spend all that money—was bigger and stronger and a whole lot more devious.

"Rizzo," I said, "your powers kick in whenever you get upset or scared or nervous or even just surprised. I think I can guarantee that if you go into that bank next Tuesday, one or more or possibly all of those things is going to happen. You don't need to do a thing except turn up. And the beauty of it is, even if they nail the rest of us you're in the clear. Nobody will ever be able to prove you had a thing to do with it."

Gallo seemed to like that part. "They won't clock me for the inside man?" he asked, wanting to hear me say it again.

"No reason why they should," I said. "Psi-screening is illegal in the EU, so the only people who can finger you are you and us. We'll be in Jamaica, where extradition is just a bunch of sounds you can limbo to, and you'll get a big, fat, freshly laundered check in the post three days later. Or more likely, the key to a safe deposit box in Switzerland where your share will be waiting for you to claim it whenever you want to."

Gallo's eyes misted up. He was thinking of colonnades of cheap beer, enchanted caverns of porn—his usual low-rent pursuits writ large and glorious. I felt like a shit pulling this number on him, but in my own defense I meant every word. I really didn't have the slightest inkling of how things were going to go.

I had to hang around a while longer, but I didn't really have to work at it anymore: Gallo was talking himself around now, without any help from me. I let him do it, shook his unpleasantly moist hand, and hit the road.

Three days to make it happen. Then the rest of my life to lie back at my ease in some place where rain never falls, and tell the story to eager, admiring women with California tans and Garden of Eden wardrobes.

Three days wasn't long enough, as it turned out. As soon as he heard that Gallo was on board, Vessell got retrospectively serious about the reconnaissance. He decided he wanted to know which supernormal security firms DeJong's had on retainer, as well as the shift rotas at New Scotland Yard. It was good to know who might be coming to the party, and how long it might take them to get there. He wanted to leave as little as possible to chance—a sentiment I could very much get behind.

So we ended up switching the target date from Tuesday to Wednesday, which sounds like nothing much but actually contributed significantly to our downfall. Am I talking too fast for you, flatfoot? I said "contributed significantly"—the word you wrote there looks like it has at most six letters. I'm not signing a précis, you understand me?

The other change, which made a whole lot of sense in the context of Vessell's master plan, was that we were going to do the job right in the middle of the day, rather than at night. That felt weird, I have to admit. As Lockjaw, I usually prefer to have my conversations with deadlocks, bolts, and security systems in the peace and quiet of 2:00 a.m., when you're generally guaranteed a little privacy. This was going to be a different kind of operation, but I felt like I could handle it. We all felt like we could handle it.

Naseem went in at 10:00 a.m. She'd already opened an account the day before, and paid the first quarter's rental on a safe deposit box. She went to the desk now and asked if she could get access to the box and drop off a few items. She held up a little lead-lined case that looked as though it might contain jewelry.

They took her down to the vault, where a superpowered security guard (it was Tom Tiptree—Telltale) scanned her for weapons or suspicious items, finding nothing at all. The little case was full of necklaces and trinkets: maybe a little cheap for this place, but what does a cop know about jewelry? They let her through. Telltale and another guard, the Iron Maiden, went in with her and stood at a discreet distance while she went to her safe deposit box and opened it.

There was nothing inside the safe deposit box except the documents Naseem had left there the day before. One of them was a legal-looking letter signed by one Peter H. Vessell.

There was a blinding flash and a whiff of ozone as Hyperlink—right on cue—zeroed in on his name and teleported in. He had a bulky rucksack on his back, and his hands were open in front of him as though he was making an offering: Tin and me were sitting on his right and left palms respectively, having been shrunk by Perspective an hour before to about half an inch in height. She restored us to normal size in front of the astonished faces of the guards, and I punched Telltale out before he'd even got done saying "What the fuck?" Tin had a harder time of it with Iron Maiden, who quite frankly outclassed him in the smarts department and fought like a gleaming, rust-free ninja. In the end he won on mass, ramping up the density of his metal body until his feet were sinking into the concrete when he moved and his punch was like a slap in the head from a wrecking ball. The Maiden went down with serious dents in her chassis.

We checked our watches. 10:07, which meant we were well within the margin of error. Vessell got to work, hauling out the other safe deposit boxes and piling them up in front of Naseem. She shrank them in batches of a dozen or so, turning each big, heavy steel container into a dinky little thing about the size of a thumbnail. Into her jewel case they went, in clattering handfuls.

Meanwhile I sweet-talked the door to the secondary vault, which Vessell's sources said was full of bullion. My power is a little weird, if the truth be told: a little . . . well, analogue. Soft around the edges. I talk to locks, and they instinctively like and trust me. I can't give them orders, but I can usually persuade them. A little bit of flattery goes a long way, and tone of voice is just as important as what I say.

It took me three minutes to coax the vault door to open. It was a time lock, so it had a lot of inhibitions about opening up in the middle of the day, so far off the normal schedule. I reassured it that I'd still respect it in the morning, told it all the usual things a lock likes to hear about the quality of its build and the fine balance of its tumblers, and finally there was a slo-mo *click-cluck* sound as it opened up for me.

By this time, Naseem had finished with the deposit boxes. She zapped the bullion bags, of which there were fewer, and piled them in on top until the case was brimming. Then she miniaturized the contents by another fifty percent or so and piled in some more. Finally she closed the case, locked it, checked the seal—which had to be perfect—and gave us the nod.

"Okay," Vessell said tersely. "Ten-fifteen. Let's go."

In a perfect world, of course, we could all have gone back the way we'd come, by means of Vessell's Hyperlink powers. But there's that half-hour downtime to factor in, and the near-certainty that we'd be followed all the way to Hell and back by whatever super-goons the bank and the Met put on our tails.

But the plan had allowed for all this.

I chatted up the main door of the vault and it sprung very readily: in my opinion, it had probably been sprung before. We stepped out and headed on up the stairs. There was another guard at the top, but he had a brute force power of some kind and Tin walked right over him just as he was starting to Hulk up.

A clatter from behind us made us all spin around, Tin already pulling back his fist for another juggernaut punch: but it was only Perspective. She'd tripped over a mop and bucket that were just lying there on the stairs, dropping the jewel case, which made a deafening clatter as it bounced back down two or three steps. She retrieved it, gave it a cursory check, and hurried back up to join us.

Wednesday. The cleaner was halfway through her shift, and she left that stuff right where she was going to need it again after her break. That was all it took. Funny, huh? How you can be dead and buried and still keep right on walking, not knowing you took the hit.

We walked into the bank proper, where the ultrarich citizenry were conducting their everyday transactions—taking out another million in small change to see them through the weekend, making a down payment on a Caribbean island, stuff like that.

"This is a robbery," Vessell said commandingly. "Nobody move."

A mother with two twin girls shrieked and clutched them to her bosom. A fat man gave a strangled sob of terror. An A-list celebrity forgot for a moment that this was real life and stepped out of line to confront us, then caught a warning glance from Tin and stepped right back again.

Of course, there were digital sound pickups all over the room that would respond immediately to the word *robbery*: also, despite the stern tone, we weren't doing anything to stop the tellers from punching their panic buttons, so there were silent alarms going off all around us. Obligingly, we walked out into the center of the room, well away from the innocent bystanders. All except for Vessell. He went right up to the nearest line of people, unshipped his rucksack, and took a machine rifle out of it. It was, to be honest, the scariest thing I'd ever seen. It looked like it had been drawn by Rob Liefeld.

By the miracle of superspeed, teleportation, time manipulation, and dimension-jumping, we were suddenly surrounded by heroes. We were expecting them, of course, but Altered State, Beast Man, Telstar, Green Glow and Razor Wire, Cy-Bug and the Zen-tity make a pretty impressive entrance. If the truth be told, I pissed my pants. Only slightly, but credit where it's due: these guys were ready to kick our arses all the way to Land's End, and they looked like they could do it without even getting an elevated heart rate.

Vessell took them in his stride, though. He just jabbed backward with the butt of the gun and broke Gallo's elbow with it.

That part wasn't in the plan, and it probably wasn't even necessary. Gallo had been standing in line since 10:10 a.m., waiting for us to come up the stairs and the whole thing to kick off. He'd probably been fighting off panic for much of that time, so the likelihood is that his powers would have manifested as soon as he got a good look at the opposition. But Vessell wasn't leaving anything to chance.

Gallo howled and crashed to his knees, clutching his injured arm. Then the howl modulated into something else: something that wasn't sound or sight or fish or fowl or anything human beings have a name for—an invisible energy that curdled the air and rippled outward from Gallo (if invisible things can do that) to saturate the room in an instant and permeate through its walls into the wider world.

For a mile or more on all sides of us, things stopped happening. Car engines misfired. Phone calls got disconnected. Card readers on ATM machines became dyslexic. BIC lighters refused to spark. Even the wind died.

But these were just side effects. The full brunt of the Non-Event's terrible power was felt by those of us belonging to the super-normal persuasion. Tin lost two-thirds of his body mass between one moment and the next: he staggered and almost fell as he changed back into flesh, screaming out a breath that was now too big for his altered lungs. The Zen-tity crashed even more painfully into reality, his liminal forms coalescing into one with a sound like a flag cracking in the wind. He groaned and crumpled to the ground in a heap. Green Glow's flames guttered and died; Beast Man shed all his fur in a second and stood before us stark naked, conclusively answering that question about his sexual equipment; Altered State turned from cobalt blue to ordinary flesh tones, made a sound like a hamster being stepped on, and fell neatly on top of the Zen-tity.

All of which left Pete Vessell holding the only gun in the room, and facing a clutch of heroes who were suddenly powerless.

This is how it should have gone, then. We should have corralled the impotent fuckers into a corner of the room, backed out through the door where Guesswork was waiting with a van, and vanished into the sunset to the tune of a humorously twanging banjo.

What we'd lost sight of in all this, of course, was Perspective. Gallo's ripple wave went through her, too, and while we were all

watching the heroes dropping like autumn leaves, she lost control
of the contents of the jewel case. Sure, it was lead-lined, and therefore impermeable to Gallo's null-wave; but the lining had broken
open in one corner when she dropped it on the stairs: just a tiny
crack, but it was enough.

Fifty bags of bullion and close to four hundred steel deposit boxes expanded to full size in half a heartbeat. It was like a
fountain—except that a fountain doesn't weigh two and a half tons,
and it doesn't explode outward at mach two in big, hard, sharp-
edged pieces.

Naseem caught one of the boxes in the face as it sprang back to
full size: it punched her off her feet and she hit the floor hard, her
head hitting the tiles with a sickening crack.

The mother with the twins went down under the bullion bags,
still trying to shield them with her own body. It was impossible to
tell how much weight landed on top of them: they just disappeared
from sight in an avalanche of glittering gold.

The fat man got a deposit box slammed into his chest, and fell
backward, pole-axed. The movie star was pulped by a cascade of the
damn things, and got a death scene more visually impressive than
anything he'd ever managed onscreen.

It was all over in a second, and we were left staring open-
mouthed at the carnage. There was an appalled silence that was
absolute except for a patter of blood on stone from away to my left:
I resolutely didn't turn my head to look. Then the screams and the
sobs started up from all around.

"Okay," Vessell said, in a strangled voice. "Nobody make a—"

Razor Wire gave a wordless yell and threw himself at Vessell.
More by instinct than anything else, Vessell pressed down on the
trigger and the gun spat staccato fire. Razor Wire was chopped to
pieces in midair.

"Nobody move!" Vessell bellowed, more authoritatively. "Nobody fucking move!" He looked around at us wildly, desperately.
"Davey, Naseem, Gruber, pick up those bags and drag them out to
the car."

None of us made a move: Naseem because she was unconscious on the floor with blood pooling underneath her fractured skull, George and me because we couldn't have made our legs work right then if God himself had leaned down out of heaven and given us the order to quick-march.

"Vessell," George said inanely. "Oh my God, Vessell. Look what happened!" He was staring at Naseem, and I saw tears running down his cheeks.

"The job's not finished yet," Vessell spat. "Let's go, let's go!"

There was a distant wail of sirens.

"I don't think we're going anywhere," I said. A great weight of exhaustion and misery hit me like a bag of bullion to the back of the head. It was the kids: I think it was, anyway. On Tuesday they wouldn't have been there, and I wouldn't have seen them get buried. Something inside me wouldn't let go of that image, as much as I wanted to. "I don't think we're going anywhere, Vessell."

"Drop the gun," said Telstar, grimly, "and give yourselves up. One of Zen-tity's other selves has healing powers. You have to let him work."

She had a point, as far as that went. But it was going to take a lot more than throwing our hands in the air and saying "Kamarade!" I held out my hand to Vessell.

"Give me the gun, Pete," I said.

He pointed it at me instead. "The job's not over," he repeated, his eyes wild and his teeth bared in a snarl. "We're walking out that door, with as many bags as we can—"

Tin slammed a deposit box into the side of Vessell's head and dropped him. Telstar went for the gun at the same time as I did, but I got to it first and she skidded to a dead stop as I swung it up to cover the heroes.

"Easy," I said. "You just stay back there. There's something I've got to do."

I found Gallo among the wreckage, half buried. His breathing was loud and harsh, like a broken bellows. There was blood trickling out of his nose and the side of his mouth.

"Davey," he quavered, his voice weak and ragged. "Did anyone get hurt?"

I nodded solemnly. "A lot of people got hurt, Rizzo. Kids and all. A lot of people. You think you can turn your powers off?"

His face took on a distant look for a moment or two as he concentrated. Then he shook his head. "No," he said. "Too scared. And it hurts too much. I have to be quiet, by myself, to make it stop."

He noticed the gun in my hands for the first time. He stared at it in total mystification for a moment, as though it was a copy of *The Sound of Music* he'd inexplicably found in his porn stash. Then he looked up at me, and we sort of understood each other.

"Oh," Gallo said. "Oh."

"I'm really sorry, Rizzo," I said. "I shouldn't have dragged you into this."

He shook his head wordlessly. I don't know if he was disagreeing, or if he just meant it wasn't worth talking about. I started to explain about Zen-tity and the healing thing, but I think he got the broad idea without needing to know the details.

"I'm scared," he said. "I'm really scared. I don't want to see it coming."

"Close your eyes," I said. He closed his eyes.

"Now count backward from a hundred."

"A—a hundred—"

The gun was on full automatic. At that distance, it turned his head and shoulders and upper torso to paste.

That's the meat and potatoes, isn't it? Armed robbery. Assault. Murder. Anything else you want, feel free to add it on: it won't make any difference at this stage.

We worked with the heroes to excavate the survivors from under the bullion bags and deposit boxes. Zen-tity did his miraculous thing, and most of them were okay again: the woman with the twins, the fat man, even Naseem. The movie star stayed dead, though, and so did Gallo: even miracles have limits. And it turned out the guard on the stairs, who Tin had trampled down, was dead too. So there you go. Even if everything had gone according to plan, we'd still have had blood on our hands.

Look at us, eh? The endoclasm turned us into gods, and all we do is play cowboys and fucking Indians. I reckon we deserve what we get. Most of us, anyway. I feel a little bit sorry for the likes of Gallo, who don't want to play but get sucked in anyway.

That's all I've got to say. You'd better put the gag back on, now, and lock it tight. Otherwise I'm going to start sweet-talking these manacles, and you'll have a jail-break on your hands.

This the transcript? Okay, somebody give me a pen.

I'm all yours, fuckers.

Best known as the creator of *Nexus* (with artist Steve Rude), multiple Eisner Award–winning author Mike Baron is also the cocreator of *Badger, Feud,* and *Spyke,* and has written for such mainstream comics as Marvel's *The Punisher* and DC's *The Flash* and *Batman*. In addition to his Eisner Awards, he is a multiple nominee for Best Writer in the Kirby, Harvey, and (additional) Eisner awards. A longtime martial artist, he applies this knowledge to what might happen if a "superhero" ever arose in our own world.

Avatar

MIKE BARON

Hoyt Beryl, tall and gangly, flowed through the intricate precision of *Bo Sai* like water flowing downhill. He'd been testing for three hours, but if he was fatigued he didn't show it. Finishing the form with a flourish, he snapped into the ready position and bowed toward a table where three men sat: head instructor James Gilfoyle, Gilfoyle's master Sun Pak Kim, and Filipino Eskrima master Fenton Garcia.

When Hoyt finished there was a moment of silence. Then the applause began, led by Garcia. The whole school, plus friends and family, had gathered for the test, four men and one woman earning their black belts. Hoyt had no friends except for those he made at karate. Hoyt's father had been an alcoholic cocaine abuser who'd bugged out when Hoyt was five.

Hoyt's mother, Ashley, was in Blackhawk gambling with her new, younger boyfriend. Hoyt was on his own, as he had been through most of his life. His decision four years ago to step inside the storefront dojo had marked a precipitous change in direction and had probably saved his life. He'd slept many a night on Gilfoyle's sofa, gone to school with Gilfoyle's son Charlie, currently a Marine in Fallujah, and trained every day at Gilfoyle's Karate.

After the belt presentation they posed for pictures. Fellow classmates slapped Hoyt on the back and Gilfoyle said, "Come on, kid. I'll buy you dinner and a root beer."

"No, thank you, sir," Hoyt replied. He'd learned to use the honorarium in karate. His mother would have been shocked, if she were capable of shock.

"You're not going home to an empty house, are you?" Gilfoyle asked.

"No, sir," Hoyt lied. "My mom's taking me out for dinner."

"When am I going to meet your mother, Hoyt? You've only been with me for four years."

Hoyt shrugged, smiled. "She's a busy woman, sir, what with her two jobs and all."

"Well, she must be some kind of saint to raise a kid like you while holding down two jobs. Say hello to her for me and let's see if we can't get together next week sometime."

"Yes, sir."

Hoyt hit the showers, changed into his civvies, and left the storefront dojo on West Colfax in Denver. He was stoked. He was pumped. He was fifteen. He'd wanted to be a martial artist since seeing *Enter the Dragon* on a friend's DVD player. It was a warm June night, perfect for what Hoyt had in mind. He ran, leaping over parking meters, cutting through an alley where a cat squalled in protest, over a fence, off a Dumpster onto the roof of a commercial mall like a chimp launched from a catapult, down again onto a concrete landing on all four limbs like a cat, past the scary apartment building where the gangs hung out to a shabby two-bedroom wood-frame house in a largely Latino neighborhood south of Colfax. The dirt yard served as a comfort station for dogs.

A light had been left on in the living room to discourage burglars, not that Hoyt or his mother had anything worth stealing. It was their third dwelling in three years, all in the neighborhood, all obtained through desperate pleas and federal assistance. Like they were some kind of white trash.

Well, we are white trash, Hoyt thought as he slipped silently into the kitchen through the back door. The first time he and Ashley had moved it was because a pair of tweakers broke into their apartment, trashed everything, tipped the refrigerator over, shit on the dining room table, pissed on the beds, and stole twenty-three dollars and Hoyt's *Street Fighter IV.* He'd play that sucker for hours, losing himself in his avatar, Thunderhawk. It was make-believe, and the robbers took it away.

Hoyt had suffered nightmares for months afterward. All his life he'd been kicked around like a soccer ball. When they'd first moved to Denver from Cheyenne, Hoyt had been easy pickings for the neighborhood bullies. The karate studio had sucked him in like the gaping maw of a jet engine and had yet to spit him out. During the interim he had grown six inches and packed on forty pounds of muscle.

It was "Uncle" James who marched down to the local school and helped Hoyt enroll, forging Ashley's signature on the application. It was Gilfoyle who'd partnered Hoyt with his son Charlie, who tutored him in math and history.

It was Gilfoyle who gave Hoyt his First Dan in Tae Kwon Do.

Had Gilfoyle known what Hoyt planned to do with it, he might have taken it back.

Each class began with three oaths.

"I promise to develop myself in body, mind, and spirit, and avoid anything that would limit my mental growth or physical health.

"I promise to develop self-discipline, to bring out the best in me and those around me.

"I promise to use the skills I learn in class constructively and defensively, to never be abusive or offensive."

Hoyt was about to break the third oath. He had waited many

years for this night, postponing gratification until he was ready, living deep within himself, content with being ostracized, and then as he grew in prowess, size, and grace, content to distance himself from other students who, cognizant of his change, made overtures. Including girls.

Hoyt was ready. He'd been waiting his whole life for this moment, this brief window of opportunity that opened between the wildass dreams of youth and the wisdom and hindsight of maturity.

Hoyt turned on the light in his bedroom. His tightly made bed, a mattress with hospital corners, lay on the floor next to obsessively neat stacks of books and comics. Tolkien, Jack London, Mark Twain, Marc Olden. Batman, Spider-Man, The Badger. The stacks were tightly squared away with no overlap or spillage. A rickety wooden desk held a used PC that one of the black belts who worked at Hewlett-Packard had given him and helped him set up.

Posters of Bruce Lee, Barb Wire, John Elway, the Watchmen, and Carmelo Anthony were thumbtacked to the shabby plaster wall. Hoyt slid the vinyl accordion closet door to one side with an arid squeak. He gathered the black BKs, the loose-fitting black cotton trousers from Asian World of Martial Arts, a black sweatshirt, the black leather gloves, and lastly, the sheer black mask that covered his head completely but allowed full vision due to its diaphanous nature. Like Rorschach.

Hoyt understood the difference between comic book heroes and real life. He understood physics. He wore a cup. He didn't kid himself that he could fly or burn holes through walls.

But Hoyt was confident he could kick the shit out of anyone who wasn't a professional fighter. For the last three years no one had messed with him. The last person who tried ended up with a broken wrist and Hoyt ducking suspension because his assailant had been a well-known troublemaker.

Hoyt's heroes were Batman, the Punisher, Rorschach, and especially Badger, a deranged war veteran who identified with animals.

Hoyt had a puppy for two weeks before his mother accidentally left the gate open. A day later, Hoyt found the puppy burnt and disemboweled behind an upholstery shop. Someone told him the Alameda Posse had done it for shits and grins. Their tags were all over the neighborhood. Some merchants didn't even bother to remove them until the city bitched.

Hoyt had made good money every summer cleaning the graffiti off local businesses. Peers sneered and jeered. Hoyt didn't care. He earned the money he needed to (a) keep the house and (b) fund the Project.

The Project that began tonight.

Project Tagger.

Hoyt stood in front of the mirror and pulled the mask over his head. Like a condom. Protecting him from viral evil. A stylized letter *T* leaped from its black background like a hungry face hugger. Tagger turned off the light. In shadow he was darker than the devil's asshole.

He hefted the 'chuks in one hand, the sai in another. Carry them or not? He replaced them in their canvas bag and took an iron device that looked like the sign for pi and fit in the hand like brass knuckles. Two of the points protruded between the fingers. Finally he took the aerosol can of red paint. A powerful magnet clung to the base, holding the interior rattle in place so that it wouldn't make a sound when he moved. He slipped the punch and the paint into a black fanny pack.

"I am nothing," he swore in the darkness. "I am nothing if I am not helping people."

Hoyt had learned by age six that self-pity did no good. He'd learned that all things were relative, that his own misery was nothing compared to some of the kids he'd seen on the street, feral kids whose parents were crack whores and syphilitic losers.

He had his youth. He had his skills. He had direction and the will to back it up.

Look out, Denver.

Tagger flowed soundlessly from his house, a black snake in a gutter. He moved in the shadows, hugging walls and climbing buildings. Ahead lay the Carlton Arms, a rundown four-story apartment block, the last outpost of civilization before Rock Creek Park, a serpent winding its way through Denver's tenderloin, a conduit for rapists, murderers, and thieves.

Tagger hunkered in the shadow of an ancient cottonwood twenty feet from the rear of the Carlton. An iron fire escape hung ten feet over the alley. The fire escape went all the way to the roof.

The French art of *parkour* consists of moving swiftly and gracefully from object to object, using the full range of human motion. It was specifically designed to deal with obstacles by turning them into advantages. Those who practice the art are known as *traceurs*.

Tagger took off running and leaped, his gloved hands clamping securely to the frame of the fire escape without touching the ladder. No sound betrayed him as he effortlessly chinned himself, gripped the top of the rail and pulled himself up and over.

He ascended the iron stairs, stepping close to the side to avoid the slightest squeak. Gangsta rap belched from an open window. Christina Aguilera from another. Tagger hoisted himself onto the roof. He wasn't even breathing hard. He'd been running five miles a night for the past two years.

Tagger had the roof to himself. Empty beer bottles and smashed crack vials littered the black-topped surface. A few dead plants sprouted from desiccated pots, a gardening project long since abandoned. As Tagger flowed to the opposite side of the building, the only sounds were the tell-tale crunch of broken glass beneath his feet and the wail of sirens, like crazed banshees, crisscrossing the city. Tagger crouched on the parapet above a sheer eighty-foot drop and gazed into the heart of darkness. Rock Creek Park lay across the street, an urban jungle watered by snow melt from the nearby Rockies. Even on the hottest days the water ran dark and cold.

The air smelled of garbage, pine, honeysuckle, and diesel.

Tagger listened, cupping his ears with his hands. Sounds of the jungle began to emerge. A cat's scream. Barking dogs. A vulgarity hurled into the night. Booming bass in a tricked-out Honda. Tires squealing.

Tagger knew he would find what he sought in Rock Creek Park. It was time.

He walked to the roof entrance and pulled the broken door open with a shriek of protesting metal and crunching glass. The interior was unlit and stank of piss and disinfectant. The bulbs had given out long ago and no one had replaced them. No maintenance man entered the stairwells. Faint light from the landings showed the walls covered with graffiti.

Two gangbangers were smoking crack on the third landing. Hoyt ran at them two steps at a time. The gangbangers, tribal tats peeking out of their gray wifebeaters, looked up. Their hair had razor cuts and highlights. Eighty bucks of haircuts each.

"What the fuck—" one said before Hoyt's heel smashed into his face, bouncing his head off the cinderblock wall with a moist thunk. The other gangbanger instinctively reached for something in his pocket as Hoyt spun expertly, lashing out with a reverse back-kick that slammed the banger's head off the wall like a squash ball.

The first banger moaned and held his hands to the back of his head. Blood poured down his back onto the wall. He looked up. Hoyt grabbed his ears and zoomed in six inches from the banger's face. Three-D effect. He jammed the banger's Adam's apple with a leopard claw strike, reached down and yanked loose the big Harley wallet attached to the banger's belt by a chain.

Forty bucks. The other banger was coming around.

Hoyt withdrew the small aerosol can from his belt pouch, yanked the banger's head upright by his oily black and purple hair, and painted a red *T* down the middle of his face while the man gasped and spat.

"Tell them Tagger was here," he hissed, and *bam*, he was outta there.

The first blow had been struck. The first chord of fear had sounded. Project Tagger had begun.

It had been so easy—so easy to overwhelm the crack-addled

gangbangers in the stairwell. It didn't seem real, like playing a video game. He was his own avatar. Like he was hovering somewhere up above the action and could see himself. Down the staircase on spring-green legs, into the stinking lobby awash in garbage, crushed crack vials and empty wine bottles, out the door onto the stoop, past the five bangers intimidating pedestrians, past them so fast they shut up for a second in amazement.

As Hoyt disappeared into the dark he heard one of them say, "What the fuck? Was that a vampire?"

"No, man, it was a zombie, dude. Dint you see *28 Days After*?"

The spruce and cottonwoods swallowed Tagger whole as he headed south, adjacent to but not on the concrete path. He'd read the police reports off the computer. A gang had been haunting the park, stealing bikes by whacking riders in the back of the head as they rode by. Four rapes in two months. Stabbings, drug deals, murder. Rock Creek had it all.

Tagger was more likely to make noise stepping on crack vials than grass. The banks of Rock Creek, which could change overnight from a sleepy sewer into a raging river, were covered with rock and devoid of grass. Buffalo grass grew in the shade of the cottonwoods, and the Parks Department had planted thousands of blue spruce and Douglas fir to create a green belt that wound through Denver, past Invesco Field, underneath the Interstate, by the state capitol, and on into the arid plains of the east.

Tagger moved silently but swiftly, alert to any sign of criminal activity. He startled a coyote, which lifted its snout from its business, leaped the creek in one bound, and was gone. Most of the path lamps overlooking the concrete trail had been shot out by gangbangers.

Tagger stopped. There was something not right about a cluster of bushes fifty feet ahead. Tagger went into a crouch. He looked and listened. The dark bulk of the shadow shifted itself to get more comfortable, inadvertently displaying an aluminum baseball bat. It was a bicycle batter in the warm-up bin. Tagger tensed, sensing he was about to go into battle. He willfully relaxed his abdominal muscles, seeking a calm cool spot in the middle of his gut. Hysterical glee nibbled at the edge of his consciousness, as it had the first time he'd won a fight. His blood hummed. But from which direction would the victim come? Should Tagger sneak up on the dude and take him out? Was it right to take preventive action before a crime had occurred? What did Gilfoyle call it, "prior restraint"?

I ain't no cop, Tagger thought. *I am the dark conscience of the city, the embodiment of its victims' prayers and a summons for others to follow.*

Still he waited, weighing his options. He was confident he could sneak up on the bike batter unseen and unheard. Slap a rear naked choke on him and leave him tied up for the cops like the Batman. Tagger knew that realistically, he would just as likely leave enough clues for the cops to find him. He didn't need to advertise himself. The criminal scum on whom he preyed would do that for him.

A faint light appeared intermittently a hundred yards down the path. A bicyclist headed their way, leg lamp describing an oncoming spiral. The rider would reach the bike batter before he came to Tagger, unless Tagger acted fast. Seeing and feeling the batter tense up and concentrate his attention on the approaching cyclist, Tagger took off in full sprint, landing on the balls of his feet, making no sound on the arid, sandy earth. The bicyclist was ten feet from the bushes as the batter tensed, bat behind his head in the classic stance, ready to spring.

Tagger sprung first. Four feet from the bike batter, he threw himself into the air, turned sideways and lashed out with a flying sidekick that struck the aluminum bat, slamming it into the side of the batter's head with a slight bong. The batter said, "Oof."

The cyclist, wearing a streamlined helmet and a little dentist mirror, glanced once in their direction and took off with renewed vigor, ass pumping up and down as he put his full weight into it.

Tagger landed and rolled, rising instantly to his feet. The bike batter retained his grip on the bat, put a hand to his head, and gaped in astonishment at the lump. His beady, bloodshot eyes focused on Tagger.

"You fuckin' with the wrong dude, man." He came forward, swinging the bat before him in furious arcs.

Tagger timed it, sprang forward inside the swing and smashed his forehead into the batter's nose. Tagger grabbed the batter by the shoulders and jammed his knee into the batter's gonads.

The batter dropped, groaning and cursing, to the ground, knees drawn up. "Ahmina fuck you up, man . . . You know 'bout MS 13? We gonna bleed you for days, man . . ."

Tagger seized the bat, holding it casually for a minute while the batter looked up through pain-glazed eyes and saw, for the first time, his antagonist.

"What the fuck are you, man?"

Wham! Tagger brought the bat down with the full force of his body onto the batter's knee. He felt bone and cartilage tear through the bat. The batter would never again play baseball. The batter screamed high and piercing like a girl or an alley cat. Tagger removed the spray paint from his fanny pack, took off the magnet, shook it and painted a red *T* on the batter's face.

He leaned in, inches from the groaning batter's ear. "Tell them Tagger was here."

He was outta there.

Tagger was so stoked by his mission he'd forgotten to search the batter for money. Oh well. It was his first night and thus far it had been spectacular. Two for two.

He was an avatar operating in a three-dimensional game with simultaneous players. First Person Shooter. Only he did no shooting.

Like the Badger, Tagger eschewed guns. He'd been lucky so far. He hadn't thought about ballistic armor, but why not? Batman had it. You could buy the stuff online from cheaperthandirt.com. Or anywhere.

He'd considered calling himself Avatar, but he didn't want the DC Legal Department on his ass. He would have enough trouble as it was.

Two for two and it seemed unreal. Tagger had never felt more alive, his senses magnified a thousandfold, like a dog's, or a bat's, or an eagle's. He could smell juniper and pine and garbage. He could hear the burble of the river, an owl's call, the traffic on nearby Allen Street, a police siren halfway across the city. He could see the stars through the trees, the distant twinkle of condos and the downtown skyscrapers, fast-food wrappers thrown to the ground.

And most of all, he could *do*.

Do the things that others only dreamed about. Do them because he was fifteen and crazier than a shithouse rat. Fifteen with a nascent conscience and character not yet touched by mortality. Capable of astonishing feats.

A woman's shout briefly pierced the velvet night, abruptly cut off. Sounds of a struggle coming through the buffalo grass. Tagger had his work cut out for him. Even as he flowed through the thorns and saguaro, Tagger wondered why no one had done it before, gone on patrol, opened a can of vigilante whup-ass.

Everybody knew the cops only came round after the blood had soaked into the ground. Every kid Hoyt knew carried some kind of weapon. There were tough men, capable men in the city, men who could go into a mob and single-handedly stop it dead. Why hadn't they taken up the mantle?

Tagger hoped he would be the tipping point, opening the flood gates to dozens of other heroes. As Chairman Mao said, "Let a thousand blossoms bloom."

Tagger reached the scene in seconds. Two men held a woman down in a copse of trees. Tagger could see the flash of her leg as she struggled. The men grunted and snickered.

"Hold her, you asshole!" one said.

"Shut up, bitch!" said the other, smashing the woman across the mouth.

Tagger took the iron punch from his fanny pack and gripped it in his left hand. He walked up to the closest assailant, not bothering to conceal himself but not announcing himself either. The men were bloodlust oblivious, their attention riveted on the woman they intended to violate.

"Hey, fuckwad," Tagger said in a conversational voice.

The dude jerked around so fast it was funny. That's when Tagger slammed him in the jaw with all his strength.

The man shrieked and fell back with his hands to his face. When he pulled them back, Tagger could see the jawbone exposed in bloody grooves of flesh. The other rapist sprang to his feet and whipped out a straight razor, which he held with the blade bent back over his knuckles.

"What the fuck are you," he raged. "Some kind of half-assed superhero?"

The woman scrabbled backward into the brush. Razor man advanced, holding the blade in front of him like a lantern. "You wanna fuck with us? Zat it? Okay, motherfucker. Let's do it."

Tagger watched the man carefully, planning his move.

That's when the first man grabbed him around his ankles and brought him down. Grunting and cursing, the man reached for Tagger's genitals. Only the fact he was wearing a cup saved him. Even so, the rapist punched his cup hard enough to make him see stars and his eyes water. The man was big—much bigger than Tagger, as he pulled himself up and began to rain blows down on Tagger's head.

Tagger turned away, trying to ward off the blows with his arms, when he felt an explosive impact in his side, driving out all the air, letting in all the pain. A rib cracked. The razor man kicked him with size-14 Doc Martens. The razor flicked down. Tagger barely had time to jam his shoe at it, saving himself from being ripped open like a slaughtered pig.

Still gripping the iron jabs, Tagger hammered away at the first guy's head, each blow sending a thunderbolt of pain through Tagger's ribs. Blood and drool flowed freely from his assailant's shattered jaw. One of Tagger's wild blows struck the man on the chin, and with a squeal of pain he fell sideways.

Razor man swung his razor hand, cutting through Tagger's black sweatshirt and opening a long shallow cut on his upper arm. Tagger struck out with one leg, catching razor man in the knee, stopping him cold. Razor man's square face went white. He had a little pencil mustache and blue-gray flames flickering up through his collar.

Tagger staggered to his feet, shuffling toward razor man with his left hand leading.

Control the knife hand.

Tagger wished he'd brought the nunchuks. Or a club. Sensing Shatterjaw about to come at him again, Tagger struck out with a spinning backkick that caught the man square on the solar plexus, causing him to collapse like a tent in a tornado and fall to the ground with a dull thump.

Tagger looked around. The girl had fled. So far so good.

Razor man was breathing hard now, nothing left for threats or curses, stalking Tagger in a workmanlike manner, razor held low before him. They circled, Tagger acutely aware of the life of the city rising all around them: the honk of horns, the shouts, the airplanes, the dogs. His opponent had a massive occipital brow and was built like a linebacker.

Razor man rushed. Tagger spun, lashing out with a reverse backkick that struck razor man square in the gut. Razor man grunted and grabbed Tagger's ankle, quicker than he thought possible. They went to the ground. Tagger focused on the knife hand, working that wrist while his bigger, heavier assailant tried to use his weight to pin Tagger to the dirt.

Tagger smashed the man's hand with his iron points, receiving a nasty cut across three fingers. Razor man dropped the razor. Tagger went to work with a vengeance, flailing upward with the device as blood flew.

"Fuck this shit!" the razorless man declared, abruptly getting to his feet and lumbering off into the woods. Tagger lay on the ground, breath rasping in and out like an anchor chain. The pain in his throat and lungs was intense. Slowly, ever so slowly, he got to his hands and knees. Nausea washed over him like a riptide, and he barely had time to rip off his mask before he vomited, the sour smell filling the copse. Blood from his forearm and his nose flowed freely into the dirt. He couldn't remember being hit in the face.

He stayed that way for long minutes while he struggled to regain his breath and listened to the city. There were no screams. Tagger looked around. The dude whose jaw he'd broken lay on his back at an awkward angle, his thick, tattooed arms splayed. Tagger crept over and pulled out the man's wallet.

Fourteen dollars and a photo of the man smiling with a plump wife and two little girls.

Tagger slapped the man's grooved cheek. "Hey. Hey, wake up."

He felt for a pulse along the carotid artery. Zippo. The dude was dead. Croaked. Worm food.

Suddenly it all seemed very real.

☆　　★　　☆

Daryl Gregory's debut novel, *Pandemonium*, won the 2009 Crawford Award, and was short-listed for the World Fantasy Award, the Shirley Jackson Award for best dark fantasy or horror novel, the Locus Award for best first novel, and the Mythopoeic Award, for best adult fantasy novel. *Pandemonium* was followed by *The Devil's Alphabet*, a tale of quantum physics and murder in a mountain town. Gregory has been published in *Asimov's Science Fiction*, *The Magazine of Fantasy and Science Fiction*, *Alfred Hitchcock's Mystery Magazine*, and elsewhere, and has been reprinted in numerous Year's Best anthologies. *Pandemonium* mixes demonic possession with golden age comic books, so it's no wonder that Gregory's short fiction often ventures into superhero territory as well. I can't imagine it will be long before we see him writing comics as well; the following tale attests to his ability.

Message from the Bubblegum Factory

DARYL GREGORY

The guards, Dear Reader, are kicking the shit out of me.

The first few steps of my plan for breaking into the Ant Hill were simple: Drive through the outer gate in my rented Land Rover, brake to a halt well short of the second gate, and then step out of the car. I thought that once I'd assumed the posture of absolute surrender—prone, hands on the back of my head, stillness personified—they wouldn't feel the need to stomp me like a bug.

Unfortunately, no.

The subsequent intake process, however, is everything you'd expect of the world's only Ultra-Super-Max prison. They carry me under a half-lowered blast shield that looks nuke-proof, then through a vault door, and finally into a series of cold, concrete rooms where I am fingerprinted and photographed, palpated and probed, swabbed, scanned, and scrubbed, deloused and depilated. They keep me naked. My head throbs from the pounding I took at the gate, and my stomach feels like it's been turned inside out.

The paperwork is stunning. They even make me sign for the lime green jumper they throw at me.

The warden comes in as I step into it. Judging by the demeanor of the guards and the way one of them cracks me in the ribs when I don't zip up fast enough, this is an honor of some kind. One millionth customer, maybe.

The warden looks like a . . . Does it matter? He is the warden. Supply your own visual.

He frowns at me. "You're the mascot."

"That's kind of offensive."

"The sidekick, then. The nut job who went crazy on TV last year."

"Now you're just being mean."

He looks me up and down, taking in my skinny arms, my puffy eye, my pot belly. He shakes his head in bewilderment. "How the hell did you think you would get in here, much less out again? Look at you. You're out of shape, you have no weapons, no powers—" He gives me a hard look. "Do you?"

"Not really," I say. "Well, one."

The four guards in the room suddenly tense. I hear a subtle but bracing sound: the double creak of leather gloves pulling back metal triggers.

"I can't be killed," I say.

I smile. "I mean, not because of anything *I* can do. It's just— Look. When I was hanging out with Soliton and the Protectors, I must have been kidnapped once a month. Held hostage, used as bait, snared in death traps. They especially liked to dangle me."

"What?"

"Over tubs of acid, piranhas, lava pits, you name it—villains are very big on dangling. Twenty years of this, ever since I was a kid. You wouldn't believe the number of times I've been shot at, blown up, tossed into rivers, knifed, pummeled, thrown off buildings and bridges—"

"You don't say."

"Oh yeah, half a dozen times at least. My right ear drum's still perforated from being chucked out of a plane." I lean forward, and the guard puts a hand on my chest. I ignore him. "See, here's the thing. I should be dead a hundred times over. But the rules of the universe don't allow it. I'm not bragging—that just seems to be the way it works."

The warden smiles coldly. "Cold" is the only form available to him, the sole version taught in Sadistic Warden School. "That's not a superpower, Mr. King. That's a delusion. One shared by every teenager who doesn't wear a seat belt."

The guards' guns are still aimed at me, but I no longer seem to be in imminent danger. The warden opens a manila folder. "You went missing from St. Adolphus Psychiatric Hospital in Modesto, California, six months ago. No one's seen you since."

I shrug.

He flips through more papers. "Where have you been, Mr. King?"

"Does it matter?" I say. I wait for him to look up. "Really. Are you at all interested? Will it make a difference?"

He considers this. "No, as a matter of fact." He closes the folder. "I've already called for a helicopter to take you out of here and back to your doctors in California. This is not a hospital."

"I've heard that."

"People like you, even famous people, are not in my remit. You are not what this institution is for."

"But what about my crime? Don't you want to punish me?"

"What crime is that?"

"Assaulting a federal officer." And then I kick him in the nuts.

I'll give the warden this: He doesn't go down. He staggers back, red-faced and wincing. He gets his breath back while the guards whack me like a piñata until the candy comes out. And by candy, I mean, not candy.

After a while the warden kneels and lifts my head off the floor. "You win, Mr. King. You get an overnight stay." He taps my forehead. "You're going to talk to my men, and you're going to tell them everything—your deepest fear, your favorite color, your grandmother's social security number. You're going to tell us where you've been for six months, why you're here now, and what you thought you would accomplish. Everything."

I make a sound that ends in a question mark.

"Yes," he says. "Everything."

☆   ★   ☆

Picture it from above, Dear Reader, say from a huge, invisible eyeball floating above the plains. From ten thousand feet, the Ant Hill is just a gray dot in the middle of a huge blank square on the North Dakota map, a cement speck surrounded by half a million acres of treeless prairie. Drop a few thousand feet. You make out a single road heading toward the heart of the Ant Hill. And then you make out concentric rings that the road pierces: the outermost ring is just a chain-link fence, easy enough to drive through, but the next two inner rings are taller, reinforced, with sturdy gates. The road ends at the innermost ring, a cement wall twenty feet tall. Inside the ring is an oval of cobalt blue, a manmade lake. Beside the lake is a gray cooling tower like a funeral urn, then the cement dome of the reactor building, and half a dozen shorter buildings huddling close. The familiar shapes of the tower and dome, repeated in nuclear power plants across the globe, have always put me in mind of mosques.

The Antioch Federal Nuclear Facility was built in the '80s, designed to manufacture weapons-grade plutonium for the hungry guts of America's ICBMs. A few months after Soliton's arrival, however, a freak accident shut the plant down. (Freak accidents became a lot more common after the Big S touched down, and we would have had to stop referring to them by that name if they hadn't created so many freaks.) Before the plant could reopen, Soliton's adventures had (a) ended the Cold War, and (b) provided a need for a new kind of jail.

So they renovated. You couldn't see much of the work on the surface. But that's the thing about ant hills.

The guards drag me through approximately three thousand miles of tunnels. I could be wrong—they smacked me around quite a bit. I'm just happy that I haven't blacked out or thrown up.

They toss me into the cell. I'm expecting a sarcastic line from the guards—"Welcome to the Ant Hill," perhaps—but they disappoint me by merely slamming the door.

I pull myself up onto the bunk and lay there for a while. There's a toilet, a sink, and a cardboard box holding a roll of toilet paper. There don't seem to be any cameras in the cement ceiling—I'm too low a threat for the expensive rooms.

My stomach rumbles.

"Jesus, hold on a minute," I say.

I pull myself into a sitting position, put my hands on my knees, and take a deep breath. "Okay," I say. "One, two—"

My stomach lurches, and a ball of peach-colored goo flies out of my mouth and splats against the floor. It looks like Silly Putty, but it gleams with silvery veins like snail tracks. It's still connected to my gullet by a long, shiny tail, and I can feel the stuff shifting in my belly. "Gahh!" I say. Which means, roughly, Hurry the hell up.

The long stream of putty reels out of my stomach and out my throat like a magician's scarf trick. The glob on the floor grows as it absorbs mass, becoming a sphere about ten inches in diameter. With a final, discomfiting *fwip!* the last of it snaps free from my throat. The sphere starts to quiver like a wet dog, flinging silvery flecks in all directions.

I fall back against the cot.

A tiny, warbling voice says, "Just for the record? I am never doing that again."

A tiny hand appears beside my head, and then a doll-size thing climbs onto the cot next to my head. It looks like a miniature Michelin Man, all peachy beige, including round white eyes and a

Kermit the Frog mouth. "What the hell took you so long?" he says. "The gel was starting to burn off, I was in there so long. You know what it smells like in there? Exactly what you think it smells like."

"I wasn't enjoying it either, Plex."

He squints at my face. "You provoked them, didn't you? I couldn't make out what the hell you did to the warden."

I sit up. "He was going to send me back to the hospital. Now at least we get to stay the night." I nod toward the door. "You think you can get through it?"

"Please," he says, and rolls his Ping Pong ball eyes. "Take this." He holds up a three-fingered hand. The middle finger bulges, becomes a sphere, and then falls off with a wet pop.

I pick up the blob, mush it a bit between thumb and index finger, and press it into my ear. It's uncomfortably warm, like fresh-chewed gum. "Match the skin tone, okay?" I tell him. "I don't need to look like I've got a wad of white boy in my ear. Okay, give me a test."

Check one, check two. Sibilance. Sibilance. The voice is loud in my ear. The vibration tickles.

"Don't scream or you'll blow out another ear drum," I say.

You know, he says in a confidential voice. *If I go up any more of your orifices, we're registering for place settings.*

"Just get going. I'll wait here for you." I fall back against the cot. No pillow, but I don't think it's going to interrupt my sleep.

Guards come for me hours later. I assume it's morning. They put shackles on my wrists and legs, then frog-march me to an elevator. According to my research there are fifteen levels in the Ant Hill. We start on Level 5 and then go up to Level 1. The administration offices are just a short walk from there.

The warden looks upset. He tells the guards to secure me to the guest chair and then get out. Then he picks up a sheaf of papers, glances at them, and looks at me with an expression of fresh disgust. "What's the matter with you?"

"You're going to have to be more specific."

"This nonsense about wanting to tell me Soliton's true identity."

You told them that? Plex says in my ear.

"I didn't think you'd want me to tell your employees."

"You're lying."

"Warden, I was a member of the Protectors—sorry, 'Soliton and the Protectors.'" The big guy always insisted we say it that way: He Gladys, we Pips.

"You weren't one of them. You just followed them around."

"Again with the demeaning statements. Just because I wasn't one of the people in capes didn't mean I wasn't part of the team. I was the first member, if you want to know. I was there on Day One. If you look at the first pictures of when he landed—"

"I've seen them. You're the boy dressed up in the baseball suit."

"I wasn't *dressed up*, I was the bat boy. That was an official Cubs uniform."

I loved that suit. Loved everything about that job, but especially hanging out with the players, chewing gum in the dugout while they chewed tobacco. A guy in my small group at the hospital said it proved I had an early tendency toward hero worship. Another patient said I had a costume fetish. I'm not saying they're wrong.

I was standing in the bullpen when somebody shouted and there he was, a man in T-shirt and jeans tumbling out of the empty sky like a shot bird. At first I thought a drunk had jumped from the upper deck. But no, the angle was all wrong, he was directly over center field and falling at tremendous speed. He hit and the turf exploded and the stadium went silent. Everyone just stood there. I don't know why I moved first.

"I was the first one to help him out of the crater," I tell the warden. "The first person he spoke to on the planet. He took off his glasses, shook my hand, and said, 'Thanks, Eddie.'"

"He knew your name?"

"Spooky, huh? I didn't think much of it at the time. But later—

twenty years later, embarrassingly enough—I realized that was the first clue. The first bit of evidence telling me what he was. Have you have ever read the Gnostic Gospels, Warden? No, of course not. But maybe you've heard of them. *National Geographic* ran a translation of the Gospel of Judas a few years ago that suggested that the man had no choice but to—"

"Stop babbling. You're not making any sense."

"Fine, let me bring it down to your level. How about Bazooka Joe comics?"

"What do you *want*, Mr. King?"

Well, I tried. "I want to talk to Ray Wisnewski," I say.

He pauses half a second too long. "Who?"

Eddie, is it part of the plan to tell them the plan?

"Come on," I say to the warden. "Ray Wisnewski—WarHead? The man who killed two million people in Chicago?"

"I don't know what—"

"The glowing guy in your basement. I know he's here. All I need is a half-hour conversation. See, I'm doing a kind of informal deposition. I'm putting together a case against Soliton."

"You really are insane."

"No, you're supposed to say, 'Case against Soliton? He's a hero, what did he ever do?' And then I tell you that he's responsible for the deaths of millions, not to mention everyone on the planet who's been injured, widowed, made into an orphan, generally had their lives destroyed every time Soliton and the Protectors went toe-to-toe with some—"

"You're blaming *him* for Chicago? He didn't set off War-Head—that was the Headhunter."

"Ah. Let's talk about the late Dr. Hunter. Did you know that Soliton captured him not two months before Chicago? And then he was sent here, to your prison. Even though he'd escaped from the Ant Hill four times before."

"You think *I'm* responsible?"

"I think you're incompetent, but no, not responsible. You're just a cog—a malfunctioning cog, maybe, with a couple teeth missing, whose very flaws may be necessary to the continued running of the system—but not the prime mover. Not by a long shot. Soliton is the one responsible. Not just for Chicago—for *everything*." I can see he's too angry to listen properly. "So how about it? You walk me down to wherever you're keeping WarHead—"

"Absolutely not! You can't come in here trying to sell a hero's secrets to get some—"

"Warden, I'm not selling secrets, I'm selling silence." He still doesn't understand. "If you let me talk to Ray," I say slowly, "I promise *not* to tell the world Soliton's real name."

"You're bluffing."

"That I know his name? Sure I do, it's D—"

"Don't say it!"

"Why not? You afraid he'll hear you?"

It's not an unreasonable fear. As far as anyone knows, Soliton doesn't possess superhearing, but he has a tendency to develop new powers whenever he gets bored.

"You can't do that." He grimaces. "You can't just . . . give away a hero's secret identity."

Funny, they didn't have a problem outing Teresa at her trial. "How about this." I lean forward. "I'll just whisper a clue."

"You'll do no such—"

"*He's my dad.*"

That shuts him up.

"Well, not biologically," I say. "You may have noticed that Soliton's white. Though I guess that could be one of his superpowers." I lean back in my chair. "Anyway, I was twelve years old the day he fell—that kind of rules out paternity at the chronological level. No, I mean, legally. He became my guardian after my parents were killed when I was fifteen—by two different supervillains, by the way. My backstory's a little complicated. But basically, he's my father."

He said he wanted everything, Plex says.

The warden stares at me. It's too late for him now; the idea is in his head and he can't get it out. He knows he can look up my record, find out who my guardian used to be. He doesn't know

Soliton's name yet, but forever after he will know that he *can* know it. Every day he'll have to decide whether or not to act on that knowledge.

Also, he can't get rid of me. "So. Do we have a deal?"

☆　★　☆

The trip down to my new cell in the ultra max wing—an upgrade that I consider quite the compliment for a person with no powers— is a brisk affair. We ride the elevator down many floors below my original cell, and then the four guards hoist me by each limb and carry me like a battering ram, stomach-side down, at trotting speed through the corridors. I don't have much opportunity to look around, but the cell doors have small windows, some of them with familiar faces pressed close to the glass. Reptilian faces, deathly pale faces, faces with elaborate tattoos. If my mouth wasn't taped shut, I would point out to the guards which of these residents I helped put in here.

My new cell is identical to the old one, except for the lenses set into the ceiling. For the next several hours I lie still on the bed, breathing through my nose. I know I'm on Prison TV, but I'm intent on becoming the most boring channel imaginable, the C-SPAN of inmates.

I should have explained myself better to the warden. Dear Reader, do they have Bazooka Bubblegum in your world? Every piece has a tiny Bazooka Joe comic strip wrapped around the pink gum, and at the bottom of every strip is a fortune. The summer Dad fell to earth, I opened one while I was in the dugout and the fortune said, "Help, I'm trapped in a bubblegum factory." I thought that was hilarious. I was too young to recognize an old joke.

The older I get, the more I realize that there are no new jokes. There are only minor variations and endless repetition.

I wake up when the door makes a sound like a shotgun racking a shell. My stomach thinks of lunch. Then the door swings open and a guard stumbles in, holding his face. Except he has no face, only a blank patch of skin covering his eyes and nose and mouth. He stumbles blindly, then abruptly kneels down.

I told him I'd open an air hole if he cooperated, Plex says in my ear. *Could you knock him out, please?*

I glance up at the lenses in the ceiling. There's no way to tell if they've been blinded, but I have to trust Plex.

There's a truncheon strapped to the guard's belt. They don't carry guns on the floor, for good reason, but I know from recent personal experience that these guys *love* to use their truncheons. I pull it free, step behind the man, and take a batter's stance, aiming carefully at the back of his head.

I know how it must sound to you, Dear Reader. You're thinking, a blow like that could kill the man. Paralyze him, perhaps. Would it reassure you to know that I've been hit from behind like this more times than I can count? In any reasonable world, my brain should be hamburger by now. I should be dead or gibbering in the corner of a state hospital.

Yet I live on. I persist. And this man will live on, not because of who he is, but because of what he is. Yes, he is a minion whose real face is as blank as the Plexo-covered one, but he is a minion working for the U.S. of A., a good-hearted lawman trying to do his part in the war on crime. At this moment, in this circumstance, he is as invulnerable to permanent harm as I am. And when he wakes up in the morning, perhaps with a headache and a nasty bruise, he will not even wonder at his good fortune. For men like him, the rules of this world prevent even the self-reflection that would expose its irrationality.

I swing, and the baton makes a sickening sound against the back of his skull. He pitches forward.

"Eddie? Hey, Eddie?" I get the impression Plex has been calling my name for a while. He's slipped free of the man's face and formed into a thin little figure, a doughboy after a fight with the rolling pin. "You okay?" he asks.

"I'm fine." I toss the truncheon onto the bed and start stripping the guard of his clothes. "I take it you found the control room."

"I'm in about twenty pieces, crawling through the electrical panels. So far they haven't figured out why the cameras are out on this cell, but they're sending a couple guys to investigate. They'll be here in about two minutes, Naked Man."

I toss the jumper across the room.

"By the way," he says, "do you know they have Icer in here?" He's trying to sound casual.

"We don't have time for vendettas, Plex."

"What? I thought that was the whole point."

"Just tell me if you found out where they're keeping Teresa."

"Same floor as this one. They've got her knocked out, hooked up to some kinda I.V."

Not good news. My main plan, such as it is, depends on her being awake, mobile, and pissed off. "Okay, you go try to wake her up."

"Where are you—? Wait, not Ray."

"How many floors down is he from here?"

"You told me Ray was optional."

"He's still our best chance of getting out of here." I button my new black Ant Hill security shirt. As for the pants, the legs are too short and the waist too wide. At least the shoes fit. "Plus, I owe it to him."

"He's a crybaby! A boy scout crybaby, which is the worse kind." Several of him sigh. "Okay, fine. Though I have to tell you, he's halfway to China. Take the elevator down until you smell magma."

In the hallway we split up: I go right, and Plex goes left and up the wall to the ceiling. We haven't really separated, however—Plex is in my ear whispering directions like a GPS. I tuck in the back of my shirt and hustle toward the elevators, head down. Unfortunately, the staff dress code doesn't include face-covering helmets, so my disguise will be useless if I come face-to-face with anyone; I just hope it fools the people behind the cameras.

The elevator is waiting for me, the door thoughtfully held open by whatever chip off the ol' Plexo has gained access to the Hill's control systems. I step in just as the two guards come around the corner. The door slides shut.

"Thanks, man," I say.

De nada.

☆   ★   ☆

The ride seems to take forever, though mostly that's nerves. The LED numbers go up as I go down, and at Level 13 Plex directs me down another hallway to a huge freight elevator. That one is supposed to take me the rest of the way down, though the gap between 14 and 15 is half a minute long. Finally the carriage jolts to a stop and the door opens on a cool, dimly lit room. Opposite is a huge door like a submarine hatch. It's pasted with yellow and black radiation warnings.

Two Demron radiation suits hang on hooks next to a rack of oxygen bottles. I pull on one of the suits even though I know it'll be useless at the kind of levels Ray is capable of putting out. I decide to skip the SCBA and just go with the hood. Before I zip up I scoop Plex out of my ear and paste him to the wall. He squeaks in protest.

"You don't need to pick up any more REMs," I say. "Look what happened last time."

I walk stiffly up to the door. There's no doorbell. I knock, and when there's no answer, I start cranking. I immediately break into a sweat and the mask fogs.

After two minutes of work the hatch opens and I step into a cavern.

Sodium vapor lights hang from the high ceiling. The space is huge, but crowded: Yellow and blue barrels stretch into the dark, around piles of rusted scaffolding, stacks of construction equipment, even vehicles—all the irradiated garbage of Antioch. I may be imagining it, but my fillings seem to tingle.

There's a path through the barrels. As I walk I become aware of the thump of music coming from distant speakers. I circle around a yellow backhoe on deflated tires and see an open space decorated like the set for a high school play: A couch, several chairs, a kitchen table, bookshelves. Huge black rectangles are set up along the back of the space on makeshift easels. Ray stands in front of one with a paint brush, layering more black onto black.

He's a big man, almost seven feet tall, but he's hard to see clearly through the yellow haze surrounding him.

I don't want to get close when he's throwing off MeVs like this. I shout, but he doesn't hear me over the huge stereo. I find a length of rebar, bang it against a steel drum: nothing. Finally I cock my arm and heave the rebar into his living room.

He turns, looks at the bar on the floor, then looks around until he sees me. He squints. I can almost feel the x-rays through my hood. He says, "Ed?!"

He starts toward me, arms open, then pauses when I take a step back. "Oh, sorry," he says. He concentrates, and the light show around his skin fades.

I take off my hood. "Just keep sucking in those neutrinos, okay?"

He grabs me in a bear hug. "I can't believe it! I heard you were in the hospital! What are you doing here?"

"Breaking you out, of course." He frowns and releases me. "Unless you don't want to."

He decides I'm joking. "Come on and sit down," he says, and leads me to the couch. "You want a beer? No, second thought, better not. You should keep the suit on, too." He walks to a stereo sitting on a bookshelf and silences it.

"So, Ray. What's up with the paintings?"

"I dunno. Just something I've always wanted to do." He nods at the canvas in front of me. "That one's called *Girls at the Circus.*"

"They're very, uh . . ."

He looks at me expectantly.

". . . dark?"

He laughs. "To you, maybe."

I shake my head. "Listen, I came to ask you something, and I don't have much time."

He sits down on the couch. "You really did break in here. Just to see me."

"You, and Teresa."

"She's *here*?"

"Where else would they keep her? They've got her drugged up and locked down. I thought I would . . ." I smile, feeling embarrassed. I've only shared the plan with Plexo before now, and he's not quite a critical audience. "I'm putting the band back together, Ray."

He laughs. "I thought you were just the roadie." I give him my wounded look and he laughs harder. "Besides, Soliton and Gazelle already did that, didn't they?"

"Fuck the New Protectors. I'm talking about the real Protectors: You, me, Lady Justice, the Dead Detective, Plexo—"

"Flexo? He's alive?"

"He goes by Plexo now—the Multiplex Man. He's not just rubber anymore. After Chicago he became sort of . . . It's hard to explain."

Ray shakes his head. "He was always such a pain in the ass. But I'm glad he's alive. That makes me . . ." He purses his lips, controlling some emotion. "I'm glad."

"Chicago wasn't your fault, Ray."

He doesn't bother to answer.

"Ray, you know whose fault it is."

"I know what you're trying to do, Eddie, but when the Headhunter did that to me, it's because there was something in me that—"

"That's bullshit. It wasn't you, it wasn't even the fucking Headhunter! We have to go back to first causes, Ray. Before Soliton, we didn't have telepathic masterminds trying to turn you into a bomb. Yes, there were problems before Dad landed—wars, disease, regular crime. But we didn't have *supervillains*. When somebody got dropped into a vat of chemicals, they *died*, they didn't turn into fucking Johann the Lizard Man."

"Or me," Ray says.

"Or you." He was just a janitor, a poor schmuck caught in the tunnels when 3,000 degrees of radioactive steam hit him. In any sane universe he would have been instantly transformed into a

broiled corpse. "Sometimes one of the good guys gets lucky," I say.
"But the point is, we wouldn't *need* heroes like you if our world
hadn't taken a left turn. Chicago was . . . unspeakable. But it wasn't
the start of it and it sure ain't the end. How many innocent bystanders are still getting killed each year from all this brawling?"

"Soliton saves people every day."

"Mostly from other superfreaks! Think about all those city
blocks destroyed, governments toppled—"

"Evil governments."

"Do you think America is *supposed* to be occupying all those
countries he overthrew? Iraq, Iran, Afghanistan, Trovenia,
Ukraine—what the fuck are we doing there? Our soldiers are getting blown up because he can't be everywhere at once. Thanks to
him, the entire world *hates* us."

"Eddie, is this about Jackie?"

"What? No. This has nothing to do with her.'"

"She didn't just join the team, she married him. That makes her
your stepmom, kind of."

"You can shut up now."

"It's just, you seem to hate him so much, Eddie, and you two
used to be so close. When you talk like this . . . It's like that night
on the TV. You sound crazy."

"Someone had to speak up," I say. "Teresa didn't deserve to go
to jail, not when it wasn't her fault."

"Eddie, she cut off Hunter's head."

"So, extra points for irony. She only corrected the problem
Soliton refused to solve."

Ray looks sad. "You can talk that way in front of me, maybe.
You can say that to other people in the Protectors. But not in front
of the public, Eddie. They look up to us."

"They shouldn't be looking up to superheroes, Ray. They
should be looking up to themselves. Okay, that didn't come out
right, but you know what I mean." I stand up. "I just came to tell
you, I'm getting Teresa out of here, and you're welcome to come
with me."

Escape Plan A: Ray realizes that yes, Eddie was right all along, and leads us through the very steam tunnels that created him, absorbing deadly residual radiation, until we reach the coolant tower and our magic carriage swoops down to take us away.

Ray stares at his feet.

"Don't worry about it," I say. "Really. But you should know that in the next few months, well, people will probably be saying lots of bad things about us. They're going to call us criminals. I just wanted you to hear from me first, so you'd know why I was doing it."

He looks up. "Doing what? What are you planning?"

"What we should have been doing all along. Saving the world."

☆   ★   ☆

After I've stripped off the Demron suit and mopped the sweat from my ears, I pop Plexo back in.

Plan B? he says. I can hear the eagerness in his voice. Plan B is chaos. And I don't have a Plan C.

"Call the television stations," I say. "And release the cyber-yetis."

He whoops in joy. Probably several of him do.

They aren't real yetis, of course, just genetically engineered gibbon/human/Linux hybrids, but they're eight feet tall, quick, and bitey. It would take pages to detail their origin and complicated history. Suffice it to say that Dad's fought them half a dozen times and had a hell of a good time on each occasion, because they kept coming back with upgrades and novel tweaks. Also, he likes monkeys.

I contracted anonymously with their creator to have a score of the Version 8.0's released in an abandoned amusement park in Newark, New Jersey, booted up in Rage Mode. All we had to do was make sure that Dad knew they were on the loose—the equivalent of showing a toddler a shiny object. That's always been his Achilles heel: Super A.D.D. Anything interesting, he has to chase after it, then punch it.

Dialing now, Plex says. Most of his mass is hovering high above the Dakota plains, surrounded by bizarro-tech equipment. *Oh, wait, almost forgot. There's a problem with Teresa. I've unplugged her, but she won't wake up.*

"Heading your way," I say.

I'm out of the elevator and hustling down the hallway when I see guards crowding around my most recent cell; they've found the man we knocked out. I turn and start back the way I'd come. "Plex, I need an alternate route, pronto."

Go right at the next hallway, then right again. It's a big square.

I turn the corner, and nearly slam into the warden himself, leading a trio of guards toting scatter guns. I duck my head and step aside. He glances at me, then shouts, "King!"

I've spent a lot of my career running, and I used to be pretty good at it. I knock aside the nearest guard and sprint for the next corner. I swing around that, into a long straight corridor.

"You're supposed to be guiding me!" I yell.

Don't get snappy. I'm spread a little thin, you know. WNET has me on hold—plus, Teresa just threw up on me.

That seems like a good sign. At least she's awake. "Go to phase four!"

I love it when you talk all mastermind-y.

The patch of wall next to my head explodes; shrapnel peppers the side of my face. I slow to a stop and put up my hands. Before I can turn around, a guard crashes into me and pins me to the floor. Two other guards pile on. It's all very reminiscent of my first hour in the Ant Hill.

They roll me over. We're next to a cell door, and a long pale face looks down at me through the door's thick glass. It's Frank McCandless, or, as he likes to refer to himself, The Hemo-Goblin. (Not even his friends could talk him out of it.) He smiles, showing his fangs.

The warden gets my attention with a poke of a gun. The double barrels are aimed at my nostrils. "I have half a mind to test that superpower of yours," he says.

He won't pull the trigger, of course. It would be cold-blooded murder, and he's not that type. But even if he was Lord Grimm himself, he wouldn't do it. They never do. They all want to talk first. Then move on to the dangling.

"Did you enjoy your conversation with Mr. Wisnewski?"

"I did, actually."

"But you didn't come here just to talk to him, did you? You're here for her."

I smile my aw-shucks smile. "You got me there."

He presses the barrels to my forehead. "She's a convicted murderer, Mr. King. You're not leaving with her. I've already—"

The lights snap off, throwing us into pitch darkness. "What the hell?" the warden says. A few seconds later the yellow emergency lights come on. Alarms blare.

I haven't moved a muscle—not with a gun to my head. While I have complete confidence that the universe is bound by the rules I've outlined, I don't believe in *taunting* it.

"What did you do, King?" the warden asks. Plaintively, it seems to me.

The cell door next to me makes a familiar shotgun-loading noise. The warden frowns. The next door clacks, and the next one. Up and down and across the Ant Hill, three hundred and five cells unlock.

The phrase "And then all hell broke loose" is probably as overused in your world as in mine. But basically, yes.

☆   ★   ☆

By the time I make it to Teresa Panagakos's cell, she's sitting upright on a hospital bed, eyelids at half mast—though with her that could mean anything. Plex stands on the pillow beside her, a hand patting her cheek. He's stretched himself into a stick figure with a lollipop head. He sees me come in and does a double-take, corkscrewing his neck.

I guess I look pretty bad. I shut the door on the zot and screech and roar of supercriminals having their way with their oppressors and sit down on a corner of the bed. Plex hands me a corner of the sheet and I wipe the blood out of my eyes. I'm not sure whose blood it is.

"How's she doing?" I ask.

Teresa mumbles something in reply. She doesn't look much like Lady Justice. Her face has no color, and her gray hair is long and straggly. The arms and legs poking out of the hospital gown are almost as thin as Plexo's.

"Teresa, it's me, Eddie. Eddie King. We've come to take you out of here, okay?"

"Stop," she says.

"Stop what, hon?"

"Talking to me. Like a baby." Her milk-white eyes fasten on mine. "Blindfold," she says.

"Oh please," Plexo says. "We're pausing to put on *uniforms?*" But he makes a spike of his hand, pokes through the sheet, and tears off a clean strip. Teresa leans into me as I knot it behind her head.

"I'm going to pick you up now, Teresa. Ready?" I put one of her arms over my shoulders and hold tight to her waist. "Here we go."

She's light as foam, but her legs barely take her weight. It takes us half a minute to cross the room. We're not going to get anywhere at this rate. Plexo's at the door, tapping his stick foot.

"I'm going to have to carry you," I tell Teresa. She makes a disgusted noise, but she doesn't fight me when I scoop her up.

At the cell door we pause for a moment to allow a huge armored form to charge past, then step into the hallway.

"Which way?" I ask Plex.

"How should I know? I fried every camera I could get my hands on."

"Plex . . ."

"Go right—that'll take us to the central stairwells and the elevators."

I shake my head. "That's where metal guy and everybody else will be going. I think there's another stairwell to our left."

"Why did you even ask me then?"

The corridor is surprisingly clear; the fighting has already moved past us to the floors above. With Teresa in my arms, I can't manage more than a trot. Plex scampers ahead, and by the time I reach the end of the hallway he's holding open the stairwell door.

We start up. Shouts echo down from the floors above, but the way immediately ahead seems clear. After two flights I'm drenched in sweat and my back is killing me. I lower Teresa to the floor.

"You run like a chain-smoking baby," Plex says.

"Shut," I say to Plex, and take a breath. "Up."

He sighs, a neat trick in a body that seems to have no lungs. "I'm going to go scout ahead," he says. "You two take your time."

Plex bounces up the stairs. I try to get my breath back.

Teresa looks up at me through the blindfold. "I always knew you'd turn to a life of crime," she says. I can't tell if she's joking. I never could tell with her. We've known each other for twenty years, but I was just a kid when I met her, and I've never completely shaken off that first dose of hero worship.

"Do you wear your bow tie anymore?" she says.

That used to be my signature look: suit jacket, good shoes, and bow tie. "I gave it up," I say. "Everybody thought I was in the Nation of Islam. You think you can hold onto my back?"

I hoist her up and she fastens her arms around my neck. I walk bent over, pulling myself up the rails with both hands. "Why are you doing this?" she says into my ear. My non-Plex-filled ear as it turns out.

"Guilt?" I say. "Sense of duty?"

"I don't think so."

But that *is* why I'm rescuing her. At least partly. "It's complicated," I say. "I need your help with something."

"You want to kill him."

I miss a step and grip the rail harder to keep my balance. "It's not like it sounds," I say. "Soliton has—"

"I'm in."

I stop. I can't see her face, but I can hear her breathing. "Really?"

"Really. Keep moving, please."

"I never could hide anything from you," I say, and then I stop talking because Plexo has just said, *Uh oh.*

"What?"

It's your super ex-girlfriend.

"Can't be. She's in New Jersey. They're all supposed to be in New Jersey."

"Are you talking to Flexo?" Teresa says.

I tap my ear and nod.

Well, there's a plume of dust coming at the Ant Hill at, like, eight hundred miles per hour.

"But the alarm just went off!" I say. "Even at her top speed she couldn't have—"

Oh. The warden. He must have called them. Maybe even before I went down to see Ray.

Teresa says, "You have a radio?"

"Kind of. Any sign of the big guy?"

Not yet.

I lock my arms under Teresa's butt and start double-timing up the stairs. Teresa's a bag of bones jouncing on my back. "They're coming for us," she says.

"So far just the Gazelle." But we both know that anywhere the Gazelle goes, hubby and the New Protectors won't be far behind.

"I can't hurt him, you know," she says. "The sword can't even touch him."

"Yeah," I say. Meaning, Yeah, I noticed that when you tried to chop him in half—but I don't have the breath for that. I was with Soliton when he went after Teresa a few weeks after Chicago. I was still on his side, then. Still a believer. We'd just discovered what she'd done to Dr. Hunter, and I went along to try to get her to surrender peacefully.

Yes, I was an idiot.

She was waiting for us in the Utah desert, a hundred miles from the nearest town, so that they wouldn't kill anyone when they went at it. Until that day I'd thought that Lady Justice was Soliton's match—the check to his nearly unlimited power—but no. That's not the way this world works. Soliton will have no other heroes before him.

We reach the landing at Level 1 and Plexo's yelling in my ear: *She just ran past me. And me! Down the central stairs. She's checking the stairwells, man. Move!* Somewhere below, a sound like the roll of thunder: titanium boots hammering concrete, fast as machine-gun fire.

I yank open the door and stumble through into a long hallway hazed with smoke: the row of intake rooms where they processed me. The old woman on my back feels like a cast-iron stove. I drop to my knees, and Teresa slides off and thumps to the ground. I manage a "Sorry."

Dim figures wrestle in the distance. Voices shout. I get to my feet, turn toward the stairs, braced for her.

I'm wrong again. She comes at me from behind, through the smoke.

The Gazelle, fastest animal on any number of feet, skids to a stop with a scrape and shriek. I wheel to face her.

God, she's beautiful. The costume looks like it's been redesigned by Jean-Paul Gaultier, but she's kept the thigh-high golden boots. They still knock me out.

"Hey, Jackie."

Her voice comes out in a squeal—she does that when she's revved up—but then she concentrates and brings down the speed. "—combing this place for you, Eddie. No, I've been looking for you for months. What the hell are you up to? What are you doing with *her*?"

I think it's pretty obvious, but I want to be helpful. "I'm kind of . . ." I take a breath, and then cough in the smoke. "I'm in the middle of a jail break."

"Oh, Ed. You were doing so well." I frown. I don't think I was doing well *at all*. She says, "Listen to me. I'm going to round up the escapees, so why don't you get out of the crossfire, and afterward—"

"You're using that mom voice again."

"Dammit, I don't have time to argue you with you. Take Teresa into a cell and wait for me to come back."

I glance back. Teresa's on the ground behind me, propped up on her elbows. I say to Jackie, "If you're trying to talk me into turning myself in again, that only works once." I cough again. "I will say this, though, you were right about the quality of that hospital. Great doctors, professional staff, decent food. Except for the forced meds, it was—duck."

She becomes a blur, and a big green arm swings down through the space where she'd been standing. Her leg comes up in a round-house—two loud *thwacks* as she spins and connects twice before the man can even recoil—and Johann the Lizard Man hits the floor.

"You still trust me," I say.

"I heard him coming." But there's a smile in her voice.

"You know what diagnosis they gave me?" I say. "Adjustment disorder. I'm not much for psychological mumbo jumbo, but I had to admit that that one was dead on."

"Eddie—"

"You ever read the Gnostic gospels, Jackie?"

She stares at me.

"It's like they're talking about Dad. An insane, capricious god messing with us for his own amusement. That's when I realized, if God is insane, how can there possibly be a cure for an *adjustment* disorder?"

"Ed, your jailbreak is over. The only question is—"

"Over? Before Dad gets here? He'll hate that. He loves chasing down bad guys—he's like a fucking Labrador retriever shagging Frisbees." I take a step forward. "Jackie, you know how bored he gets when there's no one to fight. He hates it. And the past few years, he's been getting bored more and more easily. The usual shit isn't doing it for him anymore. You can see it in his eyes."

"What? I see no such thing."

"We're not *real* to him. Not like the people back on his home Earth."

"Don't start this again," she says.

"Listen to his voice when he talks about the people he used to work with at that lab. Or Jesus, that fucking Mustang he used to drive. *That's* the real world to him. This is just . . ." I stop, see how still she's gotten. "He's never talked about his home world with you?"

"We talk about everything."

She's lying. "Then he told you how he didn't have powers there? No one did. It's like our world used to be. Like it's supposed to be."

Her hips shift in a familiar way. At any moment she'll put the left side of one golden hoof across the right side of my head, and there's not a damn thing I can do about it.

"Jackie, wait. He doesn't love you. And you don't love him, not really. See, he's got to have a girlfriend—that's in the script. That's what he wanted, and so that's what happened. He's *making* you love him, just like he made those supervillains hate him. But you can fight this, Jackie. You can join us."

"This conversation's over, Eddie."

And then, heat. A jet of flame whooshes between my legs. Jackie becomes a human torch, whirling around in circles. She doesn't scream, but I do. I jump sideways.

A few feet behind where I'd just been standing, Teresa's on her stomach, aiming a sword of flame where my crotch used to be. I'd forgotten she was back there. "Take her down!" she yells.

I step up to Jackie, clench a fist. "Hit her!" Teresa yells. "Hit her!"

Then Jackie's gone, disappeared into the smoke—probably to find a fire extinguisher. Or the lake.

She'll be okay, I tell myself. She's a fast healer.

"Are you kidding me?" Teresa says. The sword disappears and her hand unclenches. "*Join* us?"

I don't want to talk about it. I extend a hand, figuring Teresa's has cooled off by now. "Can you walk?"

She can, sort of. She looks stronger than she did five minutes ago. I put an arm around her and we limp through the smoke.

Prisoners come up from behind, push past us. Some are winged or clawed or bulging with muscles, but most of them look like ordinary men and women in cheap coveralls, unremarkable and indistinguishable without their costumes. They don't seem to recognize us in the mad rush for the exit.

The vault door has been torn from its hinges. Teresa and I shuffle through, and then we're in the no-man's-land between the vault door and the blast shield. The shield has been stopped just a few feet above the floor; prisoners slide and skitter under it like roaches.

I manage to direct Teresa through the gap, and when I scramble after her I'm blinded by golden light. I shade my eyes and squint, heart hammering. But it's not Soliton—it's just the afternoon sunlight streaming through shattered windows. The floor is a glittering beach of broken glass.

Outside, the guards are taking their last stand. They're firing down into the yard from towers and administration buildings. A few of the prisoners, the berserkers with more testosterone than sense, are throwing themselves against the buildings and crawling up the towers, but most are running for the fences. The flyers and other fast movers are already gone.

"Plex," I say. "Where the hell are you?"

Little busy! he yells in my ear.

"Please tell me you've got a way out of here," Teresa says.

And then I see Plexo. A dozen pint-size blobs are swarming a red-haired prisoner, tearing into him like a gang of ninja gingerbread men. I don't recognize the man he's attacking until I see that one of his hands is made of crystal. He grabs the neck of one of the little Plexos, and the miniature turns white and shatters into a puff of flakes.

Plex screams, *You want a piece of me? Huh? You want a piece of me?*

I yelp and grab my ear. The bit of Plex I've been carrying has launched itself from my ear canal toward the fight.

"Jesus, Plex, leave the Icer alone, we've got to—"

I hear a distinctive, whooshing hum. The air above the yard

shimmers like a heat mirage on a desert highway, and a huge black sphere, fifty feet in diameter, abruptly appears, dropping fast.

"That sound," Teresa says. "I know that sound." She looks in my direction. "It's that piece of crap the Magician used to ride around in."

"Please don't call it names when we're inside," I say. "It's sensitive."

Painted on its side is a black *8* in a white circle. Before the sphere can touch down, the circle irises open and a six-by-six slab of Plexo leaps out, flattened like a flying squirrel. The Icer has time to scream before he's enveloped by a blanket of flesh.

I grab Teresa's hand but she shakes me off. We need to run, but she can only move at a walk. A few of the other prisoners are looking at the sphere, dimly realizing that their most likely means of escape has just landed. A steel ramp extends from the base of the door with a rusty shriek but stops a foot short of the ground. I take Teresa's hand again, and before she can pull free, I tell her to step up.

She scowls at me and says, "They're here."

"Who?"

She points over my shoulder at the eastern sky.

From a mile away, the group of flyers are no bigger than specks. The lead figure, however, is unmistakable: that golden glow, that speed, those impossible, inertia-less changes of direction, like the beam of a flashlight flicking across a wall. The laws of physics do not apply to him. He is not in the world, Dear Reader, but projected upon it like a cartoon.

I would like to say that the sight of him doesn't faze me. But Jesus, I've seen the man shrug off an atomic explosion. I'm not ready for him yet.

I shove Teresa's bony butt up and through the door, then scramble in after her. "Eight-Ball!" I yell. "How're the batteries holding up?"

On the main video screen, white text swims to the surface: "Reply hazy, try again."

Shit. I lean out the door. "Plex! Dad's here!"

Below, Plex unwraps himself from the Icer, and the man falls unconscious to the ground. "Now would be good," I yell.

I scan the sky. The flyers are closer, and I can count them. Only three with Soliton. Half the team is probably on the east coast, fighting yetis. Not that it matters. Soliton alone can mop us up.

But then the group dives toward the ground, disappearing from my line of sight. They're rounding up the faster escapees first.

Plex pogos up and through the hatch. I slam a button and the door begins to cinch closed. "Make with the disappearing," I tell the 8-Ball. "And get us to five thousand feet right n—"

Talking becomes impossible as the G's throw me to the floor. Half a minute later I push myself upright and stumble to a screen and toggle to one of the cameras aimed at the ground. The heroes are in the yard now. I make out a couple of blurred forms careening between lime-green dots—Gazelle and Dad, the only two capable of those speeds, having their high-velocity way with the prisoners.

Such fun they must be having.

"Eddie." It's Teresa. "Eddie, look at me."

"When he gets like that you just got to poke him," Plex says.

"Eight-Ball, get us higher," I say. "But not so fast this time. Then head east."

Teresa's gotten to her feet. She says, "Did you really believe what you said to Jackie back there? You think he's a god?" She's adopted the tone of a cop talking down a junkie.

"Don't get him started," Plex says.

"Then you're already screwed, Eddie. If he's scripted Jackie, if he's scripted everything, then the story already includes us. What we're doing now. Everything you're planning."

"Pretty much," I say. I thought this through months ago. "Headhunter's dead. Dad's got to have a nemesis—he wouldn't know what to do without one. Might as well be me. Besides, there's plenty of precedent for sons wanting to kill their fathers—it's not exactly an original plot line." I smile. "The difference is, I believe in my job."

She doesn't say it, but I know what she's thinking. "You don't have to believe me for us to work together, Teresa."

"*I* don't," Plex says.

"We all want the same thing," I say. "We need each other."

"If the sword can't touch him," Teresa says. "Nothing can."

"Nothing in this world," I say.

"So you're going to hurt him how? Harsh words?"

"The sidekick has a plan," Plex says.

She tilts her head. She seems to be staring at me through the blindfold. "No. Now he's the criminal mastermind."

"Excuse me?" I say. "*Insane* criminal mastermind."

Even at this speed it's a long trip to the ruins of Chicago. Plenty of time to explain what I have in mind.

This is my message to you, Dear Reader: We're tired of being trapped in here with your madman, your psychopath playing out his power fantasies with us. Two million people were erased from my city. I lost every relative, every childhood friend, every neighbor and teacher and shop clerk I grew up with. Why? Because it was *interesting*.

No more. We're sending him back to you.

Watch your skies for a man tumbling to earth like a shot bird.

Gail Simone is the acclaimed writer of such DC comics as *Wonder Woman*, *Superman*, *Birds of Prey*, *Villains United*, and *Secret Six* (both the miniseries and the ongoing monthly it spawned). She has also written *Deadpool* for Marvel; *The Simpsons* for Bongo Comics, a creator-owned project, *Welcome to Tranquility*, for Wildstorm; and many other titles. In the world of television, Gail penned the "Double Date" episode of the animated series *Justice League Unlimited* and scripted an episode of GameTap's *Re\Visioned: Tomb Raider Animated Series* entitled "Pre-Teen Raider."

Thug

GAIL SIMONE

hello. my name is alvin becker but i gess you know that al-
redy becuz i am the only one that will read this. my pee oh said
I wasnt learning from my mistakes so i should keep a JOURNAL.
he give me this book and a DICTIONARY to look up the words i
dont know how to spell so good so this is my JOURNAL and my
name is alvin becker but everybuddy just calls me thug.

why thug you are wondering. it is becuz of a time wen i was a
kid and i gave another kid the BUSINESS.

i gess i dont have no use for the female girl types becuz i like to
look at them but they do not like to look at me not even one little
bit. i was big the biggest kid by far at Lu Sutton Elementary School
bigger than some of the teachers even. my second grade teacher
was miss condero and she said i had hands like a rushin wrestler
which i was kinda proud of on account of how she said it nice not
mean. but i never did get any hair on top of my head and my head

was big and I gess my teeth were too and so maybe that made me a monster or someone who looks like a monster becuz like i said the girls. the boys would say bad things they would always call me becker the pecker or peckerface which i new even then was bad becuz I asked my teacher what a pecker was and hoo boy did I get a look!!!

so there have only been two girls what were nice and thats my mom and lynn miller who was in the same grade as me and where i was big she was little like a tiny little bird that you just wanted to look at every day. not touch becuz it was too pretty to touch but just look and look and look and look. that was lynn miller with bows in her hair and pretty yellow dresses and black shiny shoos not even on church days.

the other was my mom who is an angel now so you better not say anything bad abot her i am not kidding. you just think some thing bad abot her and man you are in for a world of my fist in your face and that is some thing you dont want a bit i am telling you!!!

the boys were bad like i said and i did not like them and they did not like me and always the names and sometimes rocks but i did not hit them becuz my mom said one hit from me on those boys and I would go to juvie and juvie was a place where the preverts made you take your pants down and do stuff with your butt. i didnt want to do butt things so i didnt hit even tho i was kind of CURI-OUS abot a place where your butt was such a big deal. she said i was DEVELOPMENTALLY DISABLED which i gess is just a nice way to say dumb. i know im dumb. So what. there are worst things to be and that is what i will tell now.

anyway, the boys were bad bad bad but why i keep saying is becuz the girls were a milyun times worst. a milyun milyun milyun times worse. a boy could say you are a peckerface, alvin pecker and it was just like you did not feel it but if a girl said you was ugly that felt like a burning hammer in my heart and i would think think think abot it for days and nights nights nights and not sleep and not eat and even going to the bath room made me think think think abot ugly and how that was what i am.

but lynn miller was so nice it was almost like she was not female at all. she had a brace on one leg from some bad sick that she had wen she was just a baby and i thot that was a rotten deal how being sick wen you were a baby could follow you around like that forever just a big metal MEMORY on your leg that said you were sick and you were weak wen you were too little to do anything abot it and hey here is a leg brace to remember me by forever howdy do. i did not think it was so ugly but the boys were mean abot it she said and the girls like girls are always a milyun times worst and sometimes she would cry and that was like that hammer in the heart again but this time it also made me mad not just sad.

lynn miller would talk to me at resess and she said that i would grow out of being strange looking she was wrong abot that it got a lot worst but I gess that was just her nice talking and she was always talking nice even abot those stupid girls who called her metal leg and cripple crutch.

they would say that and i would want to hit them but again i would remember what my mom said abot my butt and i would shut up but i would think think think abot hitting them and maybe they might look ugly for a while and lynn miller would be the prettyest girl in Lu Sutton Elementary and then she could make fun of them for that and i would laff and laff.

i asked my mom abot it and she said maybe this lynn girl likes you alvin maybe she wants to be your girlfriend and i just nodded but inside i thot abot how moms love there kids so much they dont know what is real becuz there is no world where even a nice bird girl like lynn miller would want a peckerhead for a boyfriend never no never sorry mom i am sorry mom that world is not a real place anywear.

so one day it was at lunch and i was eating by myself i got so hungry that i had to have two lunch boxes and that was another name for me hungry heffer which i still dont know what that means for sure JOURNAL. but it must be hilaryous becuz the boys would laff and laff. some times i would eat lunch with arnie who was the CUSTODIAN and was big and a little bit slow like me and that was the best becuz no one would talk at all. arnie was cleaning up wear a kid barfed the school lunch corn chip chili basket and so he was not there at first or things would have been different my hole life maybe.

i gess i should say that i had an arch enemy back then who was matt savoy. the girls would talk to matt savoy like he was a movie star and talk abot his icy blue eyes and his famly was rich rich rich but all i saw was his mean. day and night matt savoy was mean. most of the boys were only mean wen other boys were around but matt would be mean even if it was just him and me in the hall way or bath room. he once threw wet toilet paper at me wen I was at the URINAL doing number one and wen i turned around he laffed and said nice pecker becker and i gess that was the funniest thing ever becuz he told the hole school and for a long time everyone said nice pecker becker every time they saw me. nice pecker becker nice pecker becker all day every day for a long long time. and matt savoy laffing like a crazy kid HA HA HA always HA HA HA.

i new that there was bad in the world becuz matt savoy taut me that with his eyes and how he would laff and i did not think he was good looking at all even tho he had icy blue eyes that looked like a blue razberry slushy at the darby street grocery.

i tried not to let matt savoy see anything i liked becuz i new he would destroy it i just new it some how. i acted like my star wars lunch box was stupid becuz i new he would throw it over the fence or in the creek. i used plane markers not the kind that smell like cherry becuz matt savoy kept stealing them and breaking them and hocking loogies on me wen i tried to get them back and one time i pet the class hamster and it was gone the next day and matt savoy told me he flushed it after he wiped with it and I believe him too and even miss condero who is so smart abot everything talks to matt savoy like he is better than anyone and so that is why it is only two good females in the world and not three. i think even lynn miller liked his icy blue eyes but i vowed never to drink a blue razberry slushy and told myself it would taste like poison and one sip would kill me like lava in my throte.

this part is bad so get ready i think its the worst story ever told.

we had monkey bars in our big sandbox at resess they were too short for me so of corse there was a lot of jokes abot me being an ape but so what after a year of nice pecker becker that did not seem so bad. lynn miller was excused from the monkey bars and most of our sports becuz she was cripple crutch the kids said and i gess that was mean but also true and no ones fault not even matt savoy. but one day i saw matt savoy talking to some of the meaner girls like i said i thot the girls were much meaner but maybe i was wrong and they were showing off for matt becuz this is what happened.

some of the girls like tabitha and rachel and emma said lynn should try and use the monkey bars and they would help and they felt bad for being mean and they would help. that is the part that is bad becuz lynn new they were mean but still wanted so bad to be there friend and wanted so bad to be I dont know what the word is but like them a little bit I gess. I dont know why this JOURNAL is supposed to make me feel better becuz i get sick thinking abot it.

i wanted to say don't do it lynn but i wanted to see her smile so i just shut up and ate my sandwich and the three girls helped hoyst her up and they promised to help her down wen she got tired they promised that is the saddest thing the way they promised. so she is hanging there and smiling she didnt weigh anything so she is hanging there and she starts to get scared becuz her leg if she falls will break real easy and she is crying and i am afraid to help becuz all the kids are laffing and they will laff at me too and say i am in love with lynn miller which i was but no one could ever know becuz i wont be able to live if they find that out.

she starts crying and then she is really bawling and what happens but matt savoy with his parents money and his blue razberry eyes comes up from behind and pulls her panties all the way down to her shiny black shoes. she was so surprised she didnt know what to do and even some of the mean girls seemed to gasp and rachel looked like she would cry and maybe there was some thing in there hearts still even though i dowt it. it was windy an her dress wount stay down in the wind. no one said anything for a minit even i was too shocked and i turned away it was horrible horrible.

wen i turned back i saw matt looking at lynn real hard with his slushy eyes. he had a strange look like he wanted to do some thing even more worst but didnt know how. once you pants somebuddy that is about all you can do rite? but he was smiling but it reminded me of a alligator or a snake or some thing. Then he started laffing. Just laffing laffing laffing like a little girl naked and crying was the funnyest thing that ever could be and i new he liked it he liked her crying. HA HA HA says matt savoy.

everyone started laffing. everyone. they crowded around so the teacher mister lutero could not see. and matt savoy with his rich parents and perfect teeth started calling her crutch crotch crutch crotch crutch crotch and she could not take it no more and she dropped she dropped she dropped from the monkey bars and I heared her leg snap like a carrot in a salad from all the way across the sandbox. The sand was little rocks really but rite underneath was hard cement and who thot up that idea I can not imagin.

that is wen I new there was bad in the world and I new I would never get away from matt savoy unless I did some thing abot it. I new that lynn miller would never get away from matt savoy unless I did some thing abot it. nice pecker becker lasted a year but I new crutch crotch would never leave her even if she went to live on gilligans island.

so i dicided to do some thing. i went to lynn miller and I pulled down her dress but her leg was hurt so bad and bent so wrong that she just screamed louder and i dont really remember what happened very well but I do remember that i pulled the metal monkey bar out of the ground cement and all and i gave matt savoy a few wacks with it and i have to say it did make me feel a lot better to see him lose abot haff of those perfect teeth. there was a lot of blood and i almost screamed that i wondered if it smelled like cherry like my markers that he ruined but i was too mad to talk. the teacher started to scream at me and I remember he said stop that stop that you god dam THUG and so i took a wack at him too and didnt feel one bit bad becuz he taught pee ee and wasnt very nice to lynn even before her leg cracked. i didnt care abot juvie or my butt or anything i just was mad.

miss condero came out crying and she asked me to put down the metal toob and she looked really scared and i looked at the end of it and saw some thing that looked like it might be matt savoys nose and i thot that was not very good news for mr slushy eyes matt savoy and maybe the girls will have some funny names to call him like no nose savoy or mr half a face and that did make me feel a lot calmer. i thot if lynn miller could see what he looked like now maybe her leg might hurt a little less and that made going to juvie worth it butt and all.

arnie came and saw what i had done and i think he almost smiled but then he said good god alvin you sure gave this kid the BUSINESS and i said i gess i did and i put down the pipe and waited for them to help lynn I wouldnt let anyone touch her til the AMBULANCE came and then i said i gess its juvie for me and boy was i rite.

im tired and i hate this remember. more abot juvie tomorow JOURNAL.

☆ ★ ☆

the hole butt thing was not true. maybe some of the guys got there butts looked at but no one looked at mine not even in the shower. i would have been in third grade too yung for juvie but i was so big they made a SPECIAL ALLOWANCE. my mom came to see me and she was always bringing cookies a batch for everyone and a batch for me. she said I should pray hard and work with the COUNSELORS which i did but partly it was becuz i wanted them cookies. so in some ways juvie was way better than Lu Sutton Elementary all in all.

there was some gangs that tryed to get me to fight or to join or to cry but i told them i would give them all the BUSINESS and punched a big hole in a brik wall and they backed off. I did get a COUNSELOR and after talking to me one time he said i had LA-

TENT SOCIOPATHIC TENDENCIES so i looked that up in my DICTIONARY and laffed becuz for a smart guy he was awful DEVELOPMENTALLY DISABLED.

one of my bunk mates was a red haired kid called stormy now i dont trust no red haired kids but he was all rite he would stop people making fun of me and he said i was smarter than I thot and dont ever listen to haters. i liked stormy. he was small and got picked on before we came friends but not after i hit that wall. he ran the place pretty much. he could get cigarettes and sometimes apple wine and naked picture books. i didnt look at the naked picture books becuz they made me think of little bird girls crying in the sandbox.

a few things happened. arnie came to visit and he said that they had a new playground all round plastic over a big foam mat and that you could not break a leg on it if you fell from a ZEPPELIN which did not make any sense to me but he laffed so i laffed. miss condero came but she mostly cried and i could tell she was scared so i made like i had the texas trots and left and i think she was glad even tho she new i was lying. my mom every thursday came with cookies cookies cookies.

til one thursday she did not come and the gards told stormy why and stormy told me that she died. the gards were afraid to tell me even with all their guns and riot gear. thats how i new stormy was my friend. he said it was a hit and run driver and she did not feel no pain and she was in heaven now and I asked a lot of questions abot that and stormy anserd them all even tho i had a milyun. he talked abot how my mom was playing the harp and was happy and watching over me and I thot that was weird because my mom could not even sing could not even tap her foot in time but sometimes i sware i thot i heared the harp music. stormy boosted some cookies from a crying fat kid and we ate those and i listened for the harp music all night long.

i had a job and that job was laundry after cleaning some of those shorts I dont know why anyone wants to see anyones butt that is for sure.

abot two years after i got a letter which was weerd becuz i never got mail from anybuddy ever but this letter had my name on it alvin becker in pretty handwriting. i looked at the return address and it said LYNN MILLER and i almost cryed rite there.

i did not open it for two days just kept holding it and looking at it stormy said hey alvin whyncha open that god damn thing already and i said i cant i cant i just cant.

finally i did. it didnt say i hate you alvin and it didnt say i love you alvin. it just said that she was going to a new school now and her leg was the same after some SURGERY but that she would never walk rite after she broke it that one time i told you abot remember? she said she rode a pony on her birthday and that her new apartment had a swimming pool so she could do therapy which is like sports for cripples I gess. she said she had a cat named fancy. every thing she said sounded really nice to me.

she said she thot abot me and she hopes i am well and she is sorry to here abot my mom and then i did cry and stormy yells everyone out of the room god damn it he needs some PRIVACY. i dont read books but i read that letter prolly a milyun times or maybe more. stormy helped me rite back and i said i was fine and my friend stormy was helping and i thot abot her too and i asked how she was and i made stormy underline it like how are you *really???*

i got a letter a few days later and it had a drawing of her walking without a brace in some grass and all she wrote was that she relized there were a lot of matt savoys and they were everywear and you could never escape all the matt savoys of the world.

that did not make sense. stormy tried to explane but i did not understand. there were lots of matt savoys? they were everywear?

i was hopping mad. i had stormy rite a letter. I said she should show me these matt savoys and if they made her cry or even came near her panties i would give them the BUSINESS. i would give every one of them the BUSINESS.

she did not rite back after that so I gess it was rong to say.

stormy said he wanted to help me trane for the future becuz i could not warsh dirty underdrawers my hole life. so i became his ASSOCIATE and we ran the place. if anyone wanted anything we got it for them and if they didnt pay i would snap their fingers or toes. it made me feel bad at first then i thot of matt savoy and it was hard to stop at one finger or one toe. I just wanted to snap and snap and snap.

pretty soon everyone paid.

stormy said we were WEED and SPEED and i was weed and he was speed and we sold those and some other things too and pretty soon i liked to have money and respect and i had lots.

pretty soon i liked snapping fingers too.

wheel of fortune is on. that lady who turns letters on that show is so smart, she always turns the letters without even looking!

☆ ★ ☆

stormy got out two years before me and that was a lonly time. i tried to keep WEED and SPEED going but i found out kwick that i could not do it. i am not smart. i know that.

☆ ★ ☆

stormy rote to me and he said the big money was working with SUPERVILLAINS. he was working for a guy called MISTER METEOR who had the power to call little balls of fire abot the size of the hamster that got flushed in grade number 2. he said there was a job for me wen i got out and i said okay becuz its not like i will be a science guy when I grow up.

i got out wen i was sixteen and stormy picked me up in a van he bot special to fit me becuz now i am almost 8 feet tall. he asked what i wanted first grass or ass and i said neither becuz i wanted a real cheeseburger so we had abot a milyun of those.

wen i showed mister meteor that i could pick up the van he hired me rite away and gave me a mask and a shirt with a big huge fireball on it which i thot was pretty funny. he asked me what my hench name would be and i said thug thinking it was scary. he said it was perfect.

mister meteor was not much of a supervillain. we robbed normal people okay but wen we tryed to rob a bank it was hopeless. first he set off the fire alarms and then one of the tellers a girl even sprayed him with a fire EXTINGUISHER and by the time the cops came he looked like he was already in jail so i grabbed stormy and bashed down a wall and we ran.

i may not be smart but i know wen people are broke and our next couple hench gigs were bad. we did a cuple weeks with the COLOR KING who never seemed to rob anyone just get in fites with SENSATION who is this woman with big bosoms who fights crime in a swimsuit. he would fite with her and we would stand around like we were all DEVELOPMENTALLY DISABLED. there is no money in fiting bosom girls and so no cheeseburgers either so whats the point???

then we got a gig with the AMMONIAZON who wanted to pay us in SEXUAL CONGRESS which i figger is just more naked books but with out the book part and i figger that prolly involves lookin at some ones rear end again and i remembered them shorts in the laundry at the juvie and i didnt want no part of that.

around this time stormy started to think abot how strong i was and he said i should try bein a SUPERVILLAIN myself and he said the ones we was working for didnt have the rite MOTIVATION and i asked what that was and he said REVENGE and i said what did i want REVENGE from and he said SOCIETY and all the best SUPERVILLAINS wanted REVENGE and i reminded him that i sometimes needed help finding my way home from 1 block away and he said that was so and we didnt talk abot that idea no more.

then oh boy did we get a break. one of the smartest SUPERVILLAINS was a guy called MISERY MAN and he said he wanted us to come and work for a REAL master criminal so stormy said that was the big time and that was that.

every thing changed for us then. we got our own fancy cars with rockets. we had cheeseburgers every nite we wanted it and i wanted it every nite. we wore a fancy armor soot I sware he looked like a astro not or some thing. he had a mask that wen you looked at it you did not see his face but your own face stairing back at you like a mirror. stormy said it was scary as well i wont say what stormy said it was as scary as becuz it is a bad word.

he patted me on the back one day and said i was part of his family now and everyone would be scared of us. scared as what stormy said.

and they were. we fought the TITAN TWINS and LEOPARD LASS and CRUSADING SPIRIT and beat them all good. misery man didnt have no powers but he had a lot lot lot of science thinking and money so he had abot every kind of gun and toy. and they were scared. the cops and the bad guys and the good guys and every one.

we hit banks and trains and one time even a cruise ship and i asked stormy how much money did i have now and stormy said it was more than i could count to and i said a milyun and he said yeah. i thot i heared a little harp music rite then i am not lying.

i started to have a real good feeling abot being a hench and one day we were robbing this casino and i was helping myself to the buffet wen i heared a terrible sound and a scream like a friend of mine which was stormy. wen i got to him he had been shot and was a little bit on fire which i patted out but i am afraid i patted too hard becuz i am sure i cracked some of his ribs like the bbq ribs on the buffet. he looked up at me with the saddest eyes and then my only friend was gone. it made me mad so i gave that casino the BUSINESS and i gess some people got hurt which only made me sadder the next day. i dont like to hurt no people that arent bothering me any way.

misery man was very nice abot it he said take the day off alvin becuz you are part of our family now and we lost a family member but i said there was only one thing to make me less sad and that was since he was the smartest man could he find a girl named lynn for me just to see if she is okay and if she is happy and see if she walks in the grass with out no brace like in her drawing back in juvie. he said he would do it and not to worry alvin he would do this for me he would find lynn miller and he was so sad abot stormy. he was so kind abot it that i started to bawl a little then a lot and couldn't stop and he got me a blanket and pillow and i fell asleep rite there in his misery lab which was where he kept his misery sekrets.

i fell asleep while he was writing some notes or some thing and dreamed of cookies and pretty little bird girls and a nasty dream abot the naked picture books woked me rite up. i started to think. I think think thinked hard. i thot stormy and my mom were trying to tell me some thing.

and I thot what it was. i did not tell misery man lynns last name.

so i looked and i found some thing. he had kept a JOURNAL just like mine only his was in perfect riting and I bet the spelling was good too. And oh boy did I find out some things. i opened rite near the end and read it mostly backwords so it was from recent to past.

misery man had killed stormy. not the gards i should have thot of that becuz what casino gard has a gun that shoots fire? he killed him on purpose. my only friend.

back farther. he hired me and stormy and he laffed abot it actually laffed on the page like HA HA HA HA HA HA. why was that so funny???

back farther. he was keeping an eye on stormy and me watching every job we took since i got out of juvie. every bad gig he watched. with laffs HA HA HA HA on the page.

then i fownd the baddest part.

he killed my mom.

he had killed my mom and made it look like a ACCIDENT. he had run her over in the street then run her over again and there were two pages of HA HA HA HA HA HA HA.

i went back to the most newest entry and read carefully tho reading makes my head ache.

kill lynn miller it said. that was it. no HA HA HA. Just kill lynn miller.

☆   ★   ☆

so i went to his quarters in the misery cave to talk to him for a minit.

☆   ★   ☆

and maybe give him the BUSINESS. give him the BUSINESS real good.

☆   ★   ☆

i went into his room i did not try to be quiet. he had a bunch of death traps but i think he did not know how strong i had gotten and they did not slow me down much and the pain helped me focus on what needed to be done. Lynn miller must be my age now but she was still a little girl in the sandbox in my remember.

wen he saw me with his book he started to laff just like on the pages HA HA HA and he shot at me with the gun that he used to kill my only friend in front of the all you can eat bbq bar at the casino. it stung and i heared my skin burn but only a little.

he started to say some thing abot how he was glad he ran over my hore of a mother and thats wen i ripped the mask off his head and saw how many scars he had and how his face barely looked like a human face no more. He did not have a nose for one thing but i still did not think what that meaned.

☆   ★   ☆

i grabbed his arm and twisted it and there was a loud pop sound and he stopped HA HA HA ing pretty quick and i liked that and i grabbed a leg and did the same thing and now it was more like BOO HOO HOO and tears rolling down his ugly ugly scarred face.

tears rolling out of those icy blue razberry slushy eyes. all the best SUPERVILLAINS are abot REVENGE stormy said. misery man said to me nice pecker becker with his ugly ruined mouth and got out one sort of HA but there was blood in his mouth so it didnt bother me so much this time some how.

i saw i could cover up the sound of his bad talk with the sound of snapping so i made more snapping noises. i did not protect lynn miller wen i was a kid and that is why every thing went so rong but this time i would protect her. and make a LOT of snapping sounds.

like a carrot in a salad.

like a MILYUN carrots in a MILYUN salads.

Renowned science fiction author Stephen Baxter has won the Philip K. Dick Award, the John W. Campbell Memorial Award, the British Science Fiction Association Award, the Kurd Lasswitz Award (Germany) and the Seiun Award (Japan), among others, and has been nominated for awards such as the Arthur C. Clarke Award, the Hugo Award, and *Locus* Awards. He is the author of the Destiny's Children series of *Coalescent, Exultant, Transcendent,* and *Resplendent*; the Time's Tapestry series of *Emperor, Conqueror, Navigator,* and *Weaver,* the a Time Odyssey series (written with the late Sir Arthur C. Clarke), and the environmental catastrophe duology of *Flood* and *Ark*. An absolute master of science fiction, here he brings a scientist's eye to the superhero genre.

Vacuum Lad

Stephen Baxter

It was the moment I first glimpsed my own secret origins, and, maybe, my true destiny.

I was sitting in a shuttle, en route to a swank L5 orbital hotel where I was due to start another three-month residency for another seven-figure-euro fee. Of course I was in uniform, my suit and mask black and threaded with silver, a design suggestive of space, the vacuum. The uniform is what people expect. At the moment it happened, I was signing autographs, modestly fending off questions about my heroics during the Hub blowout, and sipping champagne through a straw.

"It" was a scratch on the window. A scratch coming from *outside* a shuttle whizzing through the vacuum of space.

And a face. A human face beyond the window, no pressure suit, nothing. A mumsy middle-aged woman. When I looked, she beckoned and smiled, and mouthed words.

Welcome home, Vacuum Lad.

☆   ★   ☆

The world knows me as Vacuum Lad, the name Professor Stix gave me.

The only other thing the world knows about me, aside from my singular power, is that I'm from Saudi Arabia. That was another suggestion of Professor Stix. She said I should keep my own identity secret, for the sake of my family. But I should reveal my nationality, since wretched Saudi, in these shambolic post-oil days, could use a hero of its own.

Professor Stix designed my costume and had it made up, and did a pretty good job, though it's always chafed at the crotch. She even handles my business affairs. You could say Professor Stix created Vacuum Lad, the image, the commercial enterprise.

But she didn't create me, the boy inside the costume, born Tusun ibn Thunayan in Dhahran twenty-one years ago, in the year 1557, or 2136 as the Christians record the date.

And she didn't give me my power.

It was only an accident that my power was revealed to me, in fact, and an unlikely one. I mean, how many people do you know who've been exposed to space, to the hard vacuum and the invisible sleet of radiation?

When it happened I was just a kid, nineteen years old, on my way to study ecological salvaging in Ottawa, Canada, thanks to a European Union post-dieback Reconstruction scholarship. I think I would have been a poor student, and would pretty soon have been back home in Dhahran, working for my father's struggling business—we turned abandoned oil wells into carbon sequestration sinks by filling them with algae-rich slurry. It would have been a living, but my older brother Muhammad would have gotten the lion's share of the family fortune, such as it was. But I never got to Ottawa.

The shuttle was a Canadaspace suborbit hop from Riyadh to Ottawa. I wasn't sipping champagne or signing autographs then, I can tell you. Crammed in a cattle-class tube with forty-nine other marginally poor, I was squeezed against the wall by the passenger next to me, a jolly lady from Burundi who spoke pleasantly. "You will study? Studying is beautiful. I myself am visiting a great-niece who is studying environmental ethics in Montreal. Do you know Montreal? Montreal is beautiful . . ."

I was polite, but I tuned her out, for I was enjoying my first taste of spaceflight.

From launch the ship sailed over the Gulf where, through the window to my left, I saw vapor feathers gleaming white, artificial cloud created by spray turbines to deflect a little more sunlight from an overheated Earth. The arid plains of the east were chrome-plated with solar-cell farms, and studded with silvered bubbles, lodes of frozen-out carbon dioxide. The Caspian Sea was green-blue, thick with plankton stimulated to grow and draw down carbon from the air. Asia was plunged in night, with little waste light seeping out of the brave new cities of southern Russia and China and India.

The Pacific was vast and darkened too, and it was a relief to reach morning, and to pass over North America. But all too soon we were already starting our descent, banking over the desiccated Midwest. Far below us, tracing a line through the air, I saw the white glint of a sulfur-sprayer plane, topping up faint yellow clouds of sun-shielding sulfur dioxide. And, given the position of the sun, if I had been able to see out to the right, toward space, I might have glimpsed the Stack, a cloud of smart mirrors a hundred thousand kilometers deep, forever poised between Earth and sun to scatter even more of the sunlight. But the right-hand window was eclipsed by the lady from Burundi.

That was when it happened.

The hull failure was caused by a combination of metal fatigue and, it is thought, a ding in the shuttle wall from some particle of orbital debris, maybe a fleck of two-century-old frozen astronaut urine. Spacecraft are pretty safe. It took a compound failure to break through that shuttle's multiply-redundant safety features. And if not for that complicated accident I'd have quietly landed at Ottawa with the rest, and subsided back into anonymity and near poverty, and that would have been that.

But the astronaut piss hit.

A blowout is a bang, an explosive event. At first I thought some terrorist had struck. There are many on Earth who oppose space-flight. But then I felt the gale, heard the howling wind, and saw the space in front of me filled with bits of paper and plastic cups, all whirling toward my right. I started to feel cold immediately, and a pearly fog formed in the air, misting cabin lights that flashed red with alarm.

Decompression. I had paid attention to the safety briefings. I opened my mouth wide, and let the air rush out of my lungs, and from the other end let it all go with the mother of all trumps.

I knew I had only seconds of consciousness. Almost calmly, I wondered what I should do.

But I was trapped in my seat by the lady from Burundi. Dying, she gripped my hand, and I squeezed back. She was trying to hold her breath. I imagined the air trapped in her lungs overexpanding and ripping open lung tissues and capillaries. The pain must have been agonizing. And she was looking at her hands in horror, her bare arms. They were swelling. Soon the hand that held mine was huge, twice its size, comical, monstrous. Yet my hand was normal, almost. I thought I could see a kind of mist venting from my pores, and my skin seemed to be hardening, shrinking back. Not swelling at all.

As her grip relaxed I pulled away.

In the vacuum silence, the passengers around me were con-vulsing or going limp. And then the stewardess, the solitary flight attendant in the cabin, came drifting over our heads, a drinks tray floating beside her, a broken air mask half-fitted over the swollen ruin of a pretty face. There would be no salvation from the crew.

Still I sat in my seat. I was cold. Frost on my lips. Glaze of ice on eyes. Acute pain in my ears, a dry tearing in my throat. All this in mere seconds since the blowout.

Nobody else was moving. Was I the last one conscious?

I broke out of my shock. I punched my seat clasp and wriggled out from behind the bulk of the lady from Burundi. Floating over the heads of the bloated, inert passengers, I saw the hole in the opposite wall for the first time. It was a neat rectangle, less than a half-meter wide, a slab of darkness. It was small.

Smaller, in fact, I saw, than the attendant's drinks tray.

I moved fast. I pushed off from the wall and fielded the tray. It had handles underneath, and a Velcro top to hold the drinks. Dragging it behind me, I squirted my way out of the hole, out into space. Then I turned around and held the tray in the hole, bracing my feet against the soft insulation blanket of the shuttle's outer hull, pulling at the tray's handles with my hands to seal the hole. And through a window I saw mist, the reserve air supply at last having a chance to fill up the cabin.

It was only then that it occurred to me that I'd stranded myself outside the ship.

Well, there was nothing for it but to hang on as long as I could. I didn't feel scared, oddly, of death. I just imagined Muhammad's face when he learned how foolishly I'd met my end. It would have been fitting, given what followed, if at that moment I'd glanced up to see the Stack of Earth-protecting mirrors with my freezing eyes, but I did not. I just laughed, inside, thinking of Muhammad.

In a few minutes the cockpit crew were able to get through to the cabin and start delivering emergency medical aid. About half the passengers survived. Well, half is better than none. It took them fifteen more minutes to mount an operation to retrieve me from my impulsive spacewalk. I was unconscious by then. My flesh wasn't swollen, but my skin was desiccated—the copilot said it was like handling a mummy. I was smiling. My eyes were closed.

And my heart was beating, after fifteen minutes in space.

☆ ★ ☆

My new life went through a series of phases.

First I was a patient. Once on the ground, along with the

other survivors I was whisked into an Ottawan hospital. I'd suffered much less than some of the others. Their tissue swelling went down quickly, but many had ruptured lungs from trying to hold their breaths, and air bubbles in the bloodstream, and brain damage from hypoxia, and so forth. With me it was mainly dehydration. After a couple of days of sleep and a drip in my arm, I was walking around. I appeared to suffer no lasting harm save for a mild blotchiness about my rehydrated skin.

Then I was a media hero, the boy who'd saved the spaceship. Even my shutting myself out of the ship was interpreted as bravery rather than crass stupidity. That was terrific, but it lasted mere hours. The world's gaze moves on quickly. My brother Muhammad said that it would have lasted longer if I'd been better looking. (Later, Professor Stix sent out software agents to minimize search-engine links between my Vacuum Lad incarnation and this first amateur outing. It wasn't hard, she said, which rather disappointed me.)

Then I was a hero at home in Dhahran. Even Muhammad was briefly impressed. But as I anticipated, he was soon tormenting me for my brilliant plan to seal myself outside the spaceship hull. My mother made a fuss of me, however, and we gave thanks to Allah together.

Then I became a medical curiosity. The doctors in Ottawa were unable to figure out how come I was still alive. So they called me back for tests, to which my family agreed after negotiation of a fee and some discussion of medical copyright.

And then I was referred to Professor Stix.

☆   ★   ☆

I was flown to Munich, Germany, at the heart of the European Union. A driver met me at the airport and drove me into the city. I had never been to Europe before. I had never seen such wealth, even in Canada, never seen so much greenness, so much water.

We arrived at an imposing campus-like institute. Here, I met

Professor Stix for the first time. "Welcome," she said, and shook my hand. "I am Professor Maria Stix."

"Hello, Maria."

"You may call me Professor Stix." She led me to her office.

She was perhaps forty. Her figure was sturdy yet voluptuous, her face beautiful but severe, her cheekbones set off by the way she wore her brown hair neatly swept back, her blue eyes if anything enhanced by the spectacles she wore. I lusted after her. I was nineteen years old. I lusted after many women.

In her office, which was equipped like a doctor's surgery, she immediately began a preliminary medical exam. "This is the Max Planck Gesellschaft zur Förderung der Wissenschaften," she said briskly, as she measured my (rising) blood pressure. We spoke in English; her accent was light, not German. "Founded in 1911 as the official scientific research organization of Germany, and funded by the national government and later by the European Union to perform research in areas of particular scientific importance and in highly specialized or interdisciplinary fields."

I stumbled over the words. "And am I an interdisciplinary field?"

She smiled. "Your survival is a puzzle."

"And who's paying to solve that puzzle?" I asked bluntly.

"The European Space Agency. You can see the practicality." She sniffed, elegantly. "I myself am French. The Germans have something of a history in the field of extreme medicine, dating back to experiments performed on prisoners during the Second World War. You may debate the ethics of using such data." She grabbed my testicles. "Cough."

That was the beginning of an extensive survey of my peculiar condition. I was pulled and prodded, scanned and sampled at every level of my being from my genetic composition upward. It was not long before Professor Stix, with my consent, subjected me to further vacuum exposures, in a facility designed to test robotic spacecraft in conditions approaching space, a chamber like a vast steel coffin. My exposure was gradually increased from seconds to minutes, though Professor Stix did not dare take me anywhere close to the fifteen minutes to which I was exposed after the accident on the Canadaspace flight.

After some weeks of this she gave me an informal précis of her results.

"Your recovery times are actually improving," she said.

"Thanks."

"Yet 'recovery' is probably the wrong word. Your body accepts vacuum as an alien yet survivable medium, rather as my own body can survive underwater without ill effects."

I said nothing, imagining the professor's elegant body underwater.

"Your body has a number of mechanisms which enable it to survive. Your lungs and indeed your bowels are unusually efficient at venting air."

I grinned. "I fart well."

"Hmm. And with internal gases removed, other conditions such as a rupture of lung tissues will not follow. In vacuum, most of us suffer ebullism, which is a swelling caused by the evaporation of water in the soft tissues. Your tissues, on the other hand, eject water rapidly through the pores, at least as deep as a few millimeters, and the outer skin collapses down to a tough, leathery integument. Like a natural spacesuit, protecting what lies beneath. There is also a unique film over your eyes, an extra layer which similarly toughens to retain your eyes' moisture, though they are always prone to frosting. Meanwhile the pumping of your heart adjusts, and the balance of venous versus arterial pressure reaches unique levels in your vacuum-exposed body. Oxygen-rich blood actually seems to be trapped in your brain, thus nourishing it beyond normal limits and reducing the risk of hypoxia."

"How long could I survive in vacuum?"

She shrugged. "We could only discover that by testing you to destruction. I would suspect many hours—even days."

The next briefing she gave me, some weeks later, was rather less encouraging.

In her office once more, she opened a drawer in her desk and produced a jar that she set on the table. It contained a kind of grub, dark brown, only a millimeter or two long.

"What is this?"

"A tardigrade. Known in some countries as a water bear. Very common."

"Ugly little thing."

"Tardigrades can survive desiccation. Some have been known to last a decade without moisture. There are other creatures which can survive extreme dryness—rotifers, nematodes, brine shrimp. And this makes them capable of surviving in space, for as long as several days in some flight experiments."

"Like me."

"Yes. You also, it appears, have the capability to recover from moderate doses of radiation better than the average human. You have a mechanism which I suspect is rather like that of the bacterium *Deinococcus radiodurans* with the capability of repairing cellular damage, even recovery of damaged DNA strands. It has always been an open question why such creatures should have facilities to enable them to survive in deep space for extended periods. Perhaps this is a relic of our true origins, if we came here from another planet, wafted as spores across space. These traits may be ancestral."

This sounded fanciful to me. I asked, indicating the tardigrade, "What has this to do with me?"

She said she believed she had discovered the cause of my peculiar abilities. There were traces of viral activity in my DNA, which had modified the genetic information there, leaving sequences which had some correlation with the genes of *Deinococcus* and the tardigrades and so forth. "This appears to be the result of an infection when you were very small. There is no trace of similar modifications in your parents."

"Something in the air."

"Possibly something artificial," she said. "Created and released, perhaps globally. I am speculating. Why would anybody create such an infection?"

I shrugged. "What's next for me?"

This was the bad news. The European Space Agency had hoped to use lessons from my anatomy as part of a conditioning regime for their own astronauts. But because my condition was genetic, and the result of agents Professor Stix had yet to identify, I was of no use.

I was disappointed. "Perhaps I could become an astronaut."

She smiled, not unkindly.

"Then is it over?" I was already forgotten as a space hero. Was I now to be discarded even as a medical specimen? And, worse, was the flow of money from the Planck Institute to my family about to be cut off? Was it back to the slurry wells for me?

Professor Stix seemed on the point of saying yes. But then she pouted, quite prettily. "Not necessarily. Let me give it some thought. In the meantime I will book you more time in the vacuum chamber."

☆　★　☆

Once more I submitted to my ordeal in that metal coffin.

But I noticed a change in the testing regime. The intervals I was exposed to the vacuum were gradually increased. And, rather than lie inert on some bed with wires protruding from my body, now I was asked to perform various physical tasks—to walk around, to move weights, to complete small jobs of more or less complexity.

It was obvious to me, even before Professor Stix admitted it, that this was no longer a medical study. I was being trained.

After a couple more weeks, having thought it through, Professor Stix put her proposal to me.

"It seems a shame to waste your unique abilities. You have already demonstrated your value in an emergency situation. But a tolerance of vacuum is useless at sea level in Saudi Arabia. You have no place in ESA's exploration program, but there are many commercial enterprises operating in near-Earth space—suborbital and orbital flights, hotels, factories, research establishments. At any given moment many hundreds of people are in orbit—and therefore subject to the a risk of blowout."

"What are you suggesting, Professor?"

She smiled. "That we hire you out, to the commercial organizations working in Earth orbit. You would serve as a fail-safe in case of the final catastrophe. Of course, you could only be in one place at a time. But having you on hand, visibly present and ready for disaster, would be a profound psychological comfort for a lay passenger—much more so than theoretical assurances about fault trees and failure modes. You would be a luxury item, you see, in demand by high-paying customers. People fear decompression, however irrationally; people will pay for such comfort. It is very unlikely that you will ever have to face a real emergency again. I've already discussed this in principle with various insurance companies."

I smiled. "I like the idea. Tusun ibn Thunayan, life saver!"

"Oh, that's rather bland." She glanced over my body, evidently sizing me up. "We should think about branding. A costume of some kind. You would be your own walking advertisement."

"A mask! I could wear a mask."

She nodded slowly. "Anonymity. Yes, why not? It might protect your family from ruthless competitors who might seek, in vain, to find another like you among them. You would need a name."

"A name?"

"Such as Rescue Man."

"That sounds rather unspecific," I said.

"Perhaps."

"Blowout Boy!"

"Ugh! That sounds pornographic . . . Vacuum Lad," she said thoughtfully.

I think we both knew immediately that was the one. "I like it! You know, my brother Muhammad has many advantages over me, but not a secret identity."

"Hmm. We will have to consider how to launch you as a commercial proposition. Once the costume is ready, other promotional material, a sound financial base in place, we should mount a demonstration to show your capabilities."

"'We'?"

She smiled, as sweetly as she ever had, at me. "Do you have an agent?"

☆ ★ ☆

The public launch of Vacuum Lad went spectacularly well.

Professor Stix and I ran up a certain amount of debt, for the costume and various marketing materials, and most significantly for the hire of an orbital shuttle from a Britain-based spaceline. Our flight lasted four full orbits, for two of which, in the world's electronic gaze, I cavorted in space for up to ten minutes at a time. I performed simple tasks, demonstrated my lack of any supporting equipment, and, glamorous in my costume of silver and black, I shot through space powered by a small jetpack (with, at Professor Stix's insistence, the backup of an invisible monomolecular tether back to the shuttle).

The orders for my services came pouring in, through our chosen partners in the insurance industry. So did demands for media interviews, carefully filtered by Professor Stix. My family and countrymen rejoiced in my exploits. And then came the usual fringe contacts, from people who wanted to marry me or compete with me or assassinate me. (And that was the first I heard of the Earth First League, who opposed all human presence in space, and, therefore, me.)

Our debts were soon cleared, and we were in business.

Then followed months of a strangely idle, yet strangely exciting, life. I was assigned to flights with various spacelines and stays at orbital hotels, each of whom devised simple but effective failure-mode procedures for me to carry through in the event that my peculiar services should be required. In the uneventful hours I spent in flight, or the weeks I spent in the hotels, I was a celebrity, unmistakeable in my dramatic costume. In return for my enigmatic company I was bought fine meals and wines, laden with gifts I shipped back to Professor Stix—and received offers of companionship, not all of which I turned down. Well, would you? I liked to boast about it to Muhammad. I did, however, often dream of the lovely Professor Stix, rather than focus on whatever vacuously pretty rich girl was in my arms at the time. And I always kept my mask on.

The professor had assured me that I would very likely never have to deal with a genuine disaster again. Yet she was wrong.

☆ ★ ☆

During my stay, the United Nations Hub was still little more than a torus, a tube of corridors and rooms, restaurants and fitness rooms, set slowly spinning about its midpoint to provide a small measure of apparent gravity. Its most spectacular features were big picture windows that looked down on the Earth far below, and on the ongoing construction all around the Hub, and a wheeling panorama of stars.

This was just the start. The Hub was set high above the world in a stationary orbit, turning with the Earth itself. One day it would be linked to the planet by a thread, a space elevator, the fulfilment of an old dream, at which time it would blossom into the most spectacular resort in cislunar space, and a key node for transportation beyond Earth orbit.

And that was why it was attacked by the Earth First League.

This North American terrorist cell publicly expresses fears about the elevator's economic impact on more traditional space industries. This is mere political cover. In fact it opposes all human presence in space for ideological reasons, as an expression of the technocratic thinking that, they say, led to the dieback in the first place. So they tried to destroy the Hub—and they timed their attack for my presence aboard, so they could destroy me, an ultimate human expression of our future in space. It was in this incident that I learned I had a sworn enemy.

They targeted the windows, the beautiful windows. They were of a toughened, thick but very clear plastic, set in robust frames. The designers believed that the Hub itself would have to fall apart before the windows failed. But the saboteurs had infiltrated the construction operation and set strips of explosive around the frames of several windows.

In a blowout you have to act fast. In vacuum, most people lose consciousness in ten seconds or so, and most will be dead in a minute and a half, two minutes. I had my jetpack strapped to my back. I hurled myself through a gaping, ripped-open window frame and for those two minutes retrieved the wriggling, convulsing bodies that had been hurled out into space, one after the other, and zipped them up in emergency pressurisation bags. I saved a dozen.

Then I spent the next several minutes retrieving the bodies of those who had been thrown too far for me to catch in time, a dozen or so more.

The incident cemented my fame. Demands for my services exploded, and my fees sky-rocketed. My life, already good, became better. I admit I felt as if I deserved this good fortune, this attention. Perhaps all nineteen-year-olds feel they are special.

Yet guilt nagged at me, for the dozen I had not saved. What's the point of a hero who can't rescue everybody?

And, in the sometimes lonely hours I spent in my luxury zero-gravity suites, waiting for emergencies that never came, I sometimes wondered if my abilities had been meant for more than this. Even Professor Stix, my one full confidante, could not answer such questions.

Oddly, it never occurred to me to wonder if I was unique. Not until I discovered that I wasn't.

☆ ★ ☆

The contact came at Mumbai spaceport, as I waited to be shipped to an upper-crust L5 orbital hotel for a three-month residency.

And there, in the first-class lounge, I was approached.

"Excuse me. Is this seat free?" He sat down beside me before I had a chance to reply.

The man was older than me, or Professor Stix, perhaps fifty. He was soberly dressed, if a little plainly for the exotic setting of that lounge; he did not look like a first-class passenger. Yet he carried a ticket folder. For my part, I didn't recognize him. At first I thought he was a fan, and fretted vaguely if he was some threat. But from the moment I looked closely at him, I knew why he had approached me. For, under a dark Indian complexion, I could see how his skin was mottled.

He smiled. "You've been enjoying yourself," he said, in clear but accented English. "But most of us prefer to keep a low profile."

My heart beat faster. "You are like me."

"Yes. Once I thought I was unique, too. Then another approached me, as I approach you now. It is not yet time for my ascension, of course. Or yours."

"Ascension? I don't know what you mean."

"All your questions will be answered. Even those," he said a bit sharply, "you have apparently not had the wit to ask. Don't take your Nigeria flight up to the Hilton." He handed me the ticket he was holding. "Take this one."

I glanced at it. "Peru Space." I wasn't happy at the idea of switching. We were getting a kickback from the shuttle company.

"The flight is just as comfortable, and takes off not much later. You'll have to change lounges, though."

"Why this one?"

"Because of the route. This shuttle's track takes you over the subsolar point. That is, you will cross the line between Earth and sun. And on that line, of course, lies the Stack."

"The Stack? The mirrors? What's the Stack got to do with it?"

He stood. "The Damocletian will tell you that."

"What Damocletian?"

"It's best you find out for yourself." He bent down, prised up a corner of my mask, and laughed. " 'Vacuum Lad.' I don't want you to think I'm po-faced, that we all disapprove. Your life does seem rather fun. And useful. You're saving lives; you're not any sort of criminal. But there are other choices. Have a good flight."

Of course curiosity burned. I could hardly refuse to go on the Peruvian flight. Could you?

I cleared it with Professor Stix. I could give her only evasive reasons as to why I wanted to switch. I was uncomfortable lying to her. In my way, you see, I was hopelessly in love with her. And yet, even before I boarded the shuttle, I had the feeling that from now on Professor Stix would play an increasingly diminished role in my life.

And I was right. For it was on that flight, as I sipped champagne and signed autographs, that there came that extraordinary scratch on the window.

☆   ★   ☆

The woman in space gestured, indicating that I should move down the spaceplane to the airlock at the rear. Of course the flight crew were by now aware of the woman's presence. It took me only a moment to persuade them to let me through the lock; their human longing to be present at a historic moment in the career of Vacuum Lad overrode the safety rules.

When the last of the air sighed away, I felt the usual hardening of my skin, the prickly cold around my eyes and mouth, the gush of air from my mouth and belly, the peculiar arrhythmic thumping of my heart. It was no longer painful to me, more a welcome thrill, like a bracing cold shower. I had gone through this experience more than twenty times, including Professor Stix's experimental sessions in the vacuum tank in Munich.

But never before had I swum into vacuum to see another person waiting, like me dressed only in everyday clothes, in her case a tough-looking coverall with soft boots, gloves and tools tucked into her belt. Behind her, at the other end of a trailing tether, was a kind of craft—like a yacht, with a patchy, gossamer sail suspended from a mast. The sail was huge. A man, as naked to vacuum as the woman, clung to the yacht's slim body—and there was a child, I saw, astonished, no more than seven or eight years old, a boy playing restlessly with the rigging attached to the single mast.

The woman smiled at me. I mouthed, as clearly as I could, *How are we to speak?*

She reached for me. Her hands in mine were warm. She pulled me close, opened her mouth, and kissed me. It was an oddly polite, asexual gesture, but as our lips sealed I could feel her tongue, taste the faint spice of her trapped residual breath. And with that trace of trapped air she whispered to me. "If we touch—see, let your teeth touch mine—speech carries through the bone, the skin." Her accent was light American. "My name is Mary Webb. I was born in Iowa. And you, Vacuum Lad?"

Suspended in orbit, my lips locked to this strange woman's, it was not a time for anonymity. I told her my full name.

"I suppose you're wondering why we sent for you."

"You could say that."

"Ask your questions."

"Your yacht," I said impulsively. "Is it a solar sail?"

"Yes. Slow but reliable. Ben loves it. My son, you see him playing there—"

"He was born in space."

"Yes. Yes, he was born in space. But still, most of us are born on Earth and incubate there, as you have, before emerging."

"'Incubate'?"

"You wonder where we live. The yacht is actually part of our home. We inhabit the Stack."

"The Stack. The mirrors?" My lips locked to hers, I rolled my eyes to look up. The Stack was a swarm of mirrors, individually invisible, yet their cumulative effect was a subtle darkening and blurring of the sun.

"Each mirror is about a meter across. They are sheets of a silicon nitride ceramic. There are millions of them, of course. You can see our sail is stitched together from several mirrors. My husband made the sail. He's good with his hands."

The man was grinning at me, across the gulf of space, grinning as I kissed his wife. Beneath me the Earth turned, and passengers and crew goggled at us from the shuttle's windows.

"You live on the Stack."

"That's right. On it, in it, around it. It is why we exist. Why you exist. And why, some day, you will join us."

I didn't like the sound of that. "I don't understand any of this."

"What," she asked, "do you know of the Heroic Solution?"

☆　★　☆

It was all a relic of the very bad days of a hundred years past, when the collapse of the planet's climate was acute. Some feared that the gathering extinction event might soon overwhelm mankind: the dieback. The governments and intergovernmental agencies at last reached for drastic measures.

"This was the Heroic Solution," Mary Webb said. "Geoengineering." Massive human intervention in the processes of nature, everything from seeding the sea with iron to make it flourish to building giant engines to draw down carbon dioxide from the air. "A company called AxysCorp was responsible for the Stack, mirrors at the Lagrange point intended to complement atmospheric systems: sulfur dioxide particles in the stratosphere, and mist thrown up to the troposphere by giant engines patrolling the sea, a multilevel system designed to reduce the sunlight falling on the Earth."

"It worked," I murmured into her mouth. "The Heroic Solution. Didn't it? The climate was stabilized. Billions of lives were saved. The recovery began. That's what I learned at school."

"Yes, that's so. But the Heroic Solution was always controversial, precisely because of all the engineering. What if the Stack, for example, were to fail? If so, the warming it has kept away would befall the planet in one fell swoop—worse than without the Stack in the first place. Can you see?"

"So it cannot be allowed to fail."

"But every engineering system fails in the end. And so the Stack is not so much a shield as a sword of Damocles suspended over the world."

"Ah. And you 'Damocletians'—"

"Are AxysCorp's backup solution."

AxysCorp, I learned now, had seeded the air of Earth with a genetically engineered virus, a virus that created a whole new breed of space-tolerant humans specifically equipped to maintain their giant system. People would persist, the argument went, where machines would fail: people, self-motivating, self-repairing, self-reproducing, the ideal fail-safe system. But people of the right sort had to be engineered themselves.

"The virus is still in the atmosphere. Every year a handful of individuals are infected and modified. Many of them live and die without ever knowing they are potential Damocletians. But if some accident befalls them, an exposure to low pressure or vacuum—"

"As befell me."

"We contact those who become aware of what they are. And we invite them to join us up here, when they are ready."

I felt angry. "I was *meddled* with, my whole life changed, by engineers who were dead long before I was born. What about ethics? What about my rights, my choice?"

Mary sighed, a peculiar noise in the back of her throat. "Actually, this is typical of the Heroic Solution generation's projects. Given immense budgets, huge technical facilities, virtually unlimited power, and negligible political scrutiny, their technicians often experimented. *Played*. Even the Stack was an innovative solution to the problem of building a space shield—innovative compared to the big discs thrown up by the Chinese, for instance. But they often went too far. Some of the Heroic Solution outcomes are effectively crime scenes. *We*, however, have recognition of our status as citizens with full human rights by the UN's Climatic Technology Legacy Oversight Panel."

"But you're forced to live on the Stack."

"Not forced. But it's what we're for. Where we're at home. We have shelters, of course; most of the time we're out of the vacuum. We have factories and workshops. We repair old mirrors and manufacture new ones—no, that's the wrong language, it's more than that, more spiritual. We tend the field of mirrors, as a gardener tends a flower bed. Flowers of light. In Iowa we had a garden. This is the same. It's . . . enriching."

"And that's what you want of me. To come and join you in the endless weeding of your mirror garden, all for the benefit of those down on Earth, who know nothing of you and care less. For that I should leave behind my life—"

"Your identity as Vacuum Lad?"

I blushed behind my horny outer layer of skin.

"You have family?"

"Yes. They would miss me. And I, I would even miss Muhammad. My brother."

"Yet they are not like you. Yet this is your place." She embraced me. "Listen. It's wonderful here. We live as no human has before. And we aren't limited to the Stack. Look again at our yacht. We sail on light, down to the Earth—away to the Moon, where the children play in the craters and kick up the dust. Some of us are talking about an expedition to a comet."

"A comet?"

"Why not? We can live anywhere, anywhere between the planets and the stars." She twisted so she was looking down. "We protect the Earth. That is why we are here. But sometimes the Earth looks very small. It is easy to forget it even exists. Those long-dead geoengineers didn't mean it to be so, but that's the way it worked out.

"Some say that the adaptations of microbes and animals which the geneticists used to manufacture *us* are relics of a dispersal of life across space in the deep past. Now those same adaptations are being used to spread life once more, human life, across the solar system. We are the future, Vacuum Lad. Not those down below."

And she withdrew, breaking her long kiss.

☆　★　☆

I fulfilled my obligations. I returned to the shuttle, and flew on to the Hilton. On a secure link I told Professor Stix of all that had happened to me.

For now my life will go on. I continue to earn. I have my family to think of—even Muhammad. And for now Earth needs Vacuum Lad. That's what the contracts and my agency agreement with Professor Stix say. And it's what I believe, too. It is my duty.

And then there is the Earth First League to be dealt with. My enemies have tried again to assassinate me, more than once. Mary Webb talks of war, war between the Damocletians and the League, between the sky and the ground. A resolution is approaching.

Beyond that I am unsure.

In space, I look down at the comfortable fug of gravity and air where my family lives. But on the ground, I look up to the stars where Mary Webb and her Damocletians swim, and my skin itches to harden, my lungs to empty of stale air.

I often wonder how I will know when it is time for my ascension. Perhaps, as I ride another shuttle on the way to another routine money-spinning job, there will be another scratch on a space shuttle window. *Welcome home, Vacuum Lad.* And then I'll know.

I think I'll keep the costume, however.

Chris Roberson is the author of fourteen novels (and counting), among them *The Dragon's Nine Sons*, *End of the Century*, and *Book of Secrets*, as well as *X-Men: The Return*. For DC Vertigo, he has written the miniseries *Cinderella: From Fabletown with Love*, and is the cocreator of the ongoing monthly title *I, Zombie*. Roberson is also the publisher of MonkeyBrain Books, an independent publishing house specializing in genre fiction and nonfiction genre studies, and he is the editor of the anthology *Adventure Vol. 1*. He has been a finalist for the World Fantasy Award four times—once each for writing and editing, and twice for publishing—twice a finalist for the John W. Campbell Award for Best New Writer, and three times for the Sidewise Award for Best Alternate History Short Form (winning the Short Form in 2004 with his story "O One" and the Long Form in 2008 with his novel *The Dragon's Nine Sons*). Roberson is currently writing the first "authorized prequel" to Philip K. Dick's *Do Androids Dream of Electric Sheep?* for Boom! Studios, a twelve-issue comic book miniseries entitled *Dust to Dust*. A prolific writer across multiple media, Roberson always displays a strong pulp influence and a staggering imagination.

A Knight of Ghosts and Shadows

Chris Roberson

As the chimes of midnight rang out from the tolling bells above, a hail of argent death rained from the twin silver-plated Colt .45s onto the macabre invaders from the Otherworld, and the cathedral echoed with the eerie laughter of that silver-skulled avenger of the night—THE WRAITH.

From the secret journals of Alistair Freeman
Saturday, October 31, 1942.

I dreamt of that day in the Yucatan again last night. Trees turned the color of bone by drought, skies black with the smoke and ash of swidden burning for cultivation, the forest heavy with the smell of death. Cager was with me, still living, but Jules Bonaventure and his father had already fled, though in waking reality they had still been there when the creatures had claimed Cager's life.

As the camazotz came out of the bone forest toward us, their bat-wings stirring vortices in the smoke, I turned to tell my friend not to worry, and that the daykeepers would come to save us with their silvered blades at any moment. But it was no longer Cager beside me, but my sister Mindel, and in the strange logic of dreams we weren't in Mexico of '25 anymore, but on a street in Manhattan's Lower East Side more than a dozen years before. And I realized that the smoke and ash were no longer from forest cover being burned for planting, but from the flames of the Triangle Shirtwaist Factory fire that had ended her young life. "Don Javier will never get here from Mexico in time," I told my sister, as though it made perfect sense, but she just smiled and said, "Don't worry, Alter. This is the road to Xibalba." Then the demons arrived, but instead of claws, they attacked us with the twine-cutting hook-rings of a newsvendor, and we were powerless to stop them.

Charlotte is still out of town visiting her mother and won't be back until tomorrow. When I awoke alone in the darkened room this morning, it took me a moment to recall when and where I was. In no mood to return to unsettling dreams, I rose early and began my day.

I ate alone, coffee and toast, and skimmed the morning papers. News of the Sarah Pennington murder trial again crowded war reports from the front page of the *Recondito Clarion*, and above the fold was a grainy photograph of the two young men, Joe Dominguez and Felix Uresti, who have been charged with the girl's abduction and murder. Had it not been an attractive blonde who'd gone missing, I'm forced to wonder whether the papers would devote quite so many column inches to the story. But then again, there were nearly as many articles this morning on the Sleepy Lagoon murder case just getting under way down in Los Angeles, where seventeen Mexican youths are being tried for the murder of Jose Diaz. Perhaps the attention is more due to the defendants' zoot suits and ducktail combs than to Governor Olson's call to stamp out juvenile delinquency. If the governor had the power simply to round up every pachuco in the state and put them in camps, like Roosevelt has done with the Japanese, I think Olson would exercise the right in a heartbeat.

I didn't fail to notice the item buried in the back pages about the third frozen body found in the city's back alleys in as many nights, but I didn't need any reminder of my failure to locate the latest demon.

But this new interloper from the Otherworld has not come alone. Incursions and possessions have been on the rise in Recondito the last few weeks, and I've been running behind on the latest *Wraith* novel as a result. I spent the day typing, and by the time the last page of "The Return of the Goblin King" came off my Underwood's roller it was late afternoon and time for me to get to work. My *real* work.

As the sun sank over the Pacific, the streets of the Oceanview neighborhood were crowded with pint-sized ghosts and witches, pirates and cowboys. With little care for wars and murder trials, much less the otherworldly threats which lurk unseen in the shadows, the young took to their trick-or-treating with a will. But with sugar rationing limiting their potential haul of treats, I imagine it wasn't long before they turned to tricks, and by tomorrow morning I'm sure the neighborhood will be garlanded with soaped windows and egged cars.

I can only hope that dawn doesn't find another frozen victim of the city's latest invader, too. After my failure tonight, any new blood spilled would be on my hands—and perhaps on the hands of my clowned-up imitator, as well.

The dive bars and diners along Almeria Street were in full swing, and on the street corners out front pachucos in their zoot suits and felt hats strutted like prize cockerels before the girls, as if their pocket chains glinting in the streetlights could lure the ladies to their sides.

On Mission Avenue I passed the theaters and arenas that cater to the city's poorer denizens, plastered with playbills for upcoming touring companies, boxing matches, and musical performances. One poster advertised an exhibition of Mexican wrestling, and featured a crude painting of shirtless behemoths with faces hidden behind leather masks. A few doors down a cinema marquee announced the debut next week of *Road to Morocco*. I remembered my dead sister's words in last night's dream, and entertained the brief fantasy of Hope and Crosby in daykeepers' black robes and silver-skull masks, blustering their way through the five houses of initiation.

The last light of day was fading from the western sky when I reached the cemetery, wreathed in the shadows of Augustus Powell's towering spires atop the Church of the Holy Saint Anthony. A few mourners lingered from the day's funeral services, standing beside freshly filled graves, but otherwise the grounds were empty.

I made my way to the Freeman family crypt and, passing the entrance, continued on to the back, where a copse of trees grow a few feet away from the structure's unbroken rear wall.

As Don Javier had taught me a lifetime ago in the Rattling House, I started towards the wall, and an instant before colliding with it turned aside toward an unseen direction and shadowed my way through to the other side.

Don Mateo was waiting for me within. He'd already changed out of his hearse driver's uniform and had dressed in his customary blue serge suit, western shirt printed with bucking broncos and open at the neck, a red sash of homespun cotton wound around his waist like a cummerbund.

"Little brother," he said, a smile deepening the wrinkles around the corners of his eyes. He raised his shotglass filled to the rim with homemade cane liquor in a kind of salute. "You're just in time."

When Mateo speaks in English, it usually means that he's uncertain about something, but when he gets excited—or angry—he lapses back into Yucatan. Tonight he'd spoken in Spanish, typically a sign his mood was light, and when I greeted him I was happy to do the same.

"To your health," I added in English, and, taking the shotglass from his hands, downed the contents in a single gulp, then spat on the floor a libation to the spirits. Don Javier always insisted that there were beneficent dwellers in the Otherworld, and libations in their honor might win their favor. But while I'd learned in the years I spent living with the two daykeepers, either in their cabin in the forest or in the hidden temples of Xibalba, to honor the customs handed down by their Mayan forebears, and knew that the villains and monsters of their beliefs were all too real, I still have trouble imagining there are any intelligences existing beyond reality's veil that have anything but ill intent for mankind.

When I'd finished my shot, Don Mateo poured another for himself, and drank the contents and spat the libation just as ritual demanded. Then, the necessary business of the greeting concluded, he set the glass and bottle aside and began to shove open the lid of the coffin in which my tools are stored.

"Four nights you've hunted this demon, little brother," he said, lifting out the inky black greatcoat and handing it over. "Perhaps tonight will be the night."

I drew the greatcoat on over my suit. "Three victims already is three too many." Settling the attached short cape over my shoulders, I fastened the buttons. "But what kind of demon freezes its victims to death?"

The old daykeeper treated me to a grin, shrugging. "You are the one with the Sight, not I." His grin began to falter as he handed over the shoulder-holster rig. "Though Don Javier might have known."

I checked the spring releases on both of the silver-plated Colt .45s and then arranged the short cape over my shoulders to conceal them. "Perhaps," I said. But it had been years since the great owl of the old daykeeper had visited us in dreams.

As I slid a half-dozen loaded clips, pouches of salt, a Zippo lighter, and a small collection of crystals into the greatcoat's pockets, Don Mateo held the mask out to me, the light from the bare bulb overhead glinting on the skull's silvered surface.

The metal of the mask, cool against my cheeks and forehead, always reminds me of the weeks and months I spent in the Rattling House, learning to shadow through solid objects, cold patches left behind as I rotated back into the world. I never did master the art of shifting to other branches of the World Tree, though, much to Don Javier's regret.

The slouch hat was last out of the coffin, and when I had settled it on my head, Don Mateo regarded me with something like paternal pride. "I should like to see those upstarts in San Francisco and Chicago cut so fine a figure."

The mask hid my scowl, for which I was grateful.

Since beginning my nocturnal activities in Recondito in '31 I've apparently inspired others to follow suit—the Black Hand in San Francisco, the Scarlet Scarab in New York, the Scorpion in Chicago. Perhaps the pulp magazine's ruse works as intended, and like so many here in the city, they assume the Wraith to be entirely fictional. There are times when I regret the decision to hide in plain sight, fictionalizing accounts of my activities in the pages of *The Wraith Magazine* so that any reports of a silver masked figure seen lurking in the streets of Recondito will be written off as an over-imaginative reader with more costuming skill than sense.

But noisome as such crass imitators are, whether inspired by the reality or the fiction, as I tooled up this evening I never imagined that I'd be forced to contend with one here in my own city.

Don Mateo recited a benediction, invoking the names Dark Jaguar and Macaw House, the first mother-father pair of daykeepers, and of White Sparkstriker, who had brought the knowledge to our branch of the World Tree. He called upon Ah Puch the Fleshless, the patron deity of Xibalba, to guide our hands and expand my sight. Had we still been in the Yucatan, the old daykeeper would have worn his half-mask of jaguar pelt and burned incense as offering to his forebears' gods. Since coming to California, though, he's gradually relaxed his observances, and now the curling smoke of a smoldering Lucky Strike usually suffices.

This demon of cold has struck the days previous without pattern or warning, once each in Northside, Hyde Park, and the waterfront. When Don Mateo and I headed out in the hearse, as a result, we proceeded at random, roaming from neighborhood to neighborhood, the old daykeeper on the lookout for any signs of disturbance, me searching not with my eyes but with my Sight for any intrusion from the Otherworld.

I glimpsed some evidence of incursion near the Pinnacle Tower, but quickly determined it was another of Carmody's damnable "experiments." I've warned Rex before that I won't allow his institute to put the city at risk unnecessarily, but they have proven useful on rare occasions, so I haven't yet taken any serious steps to curtail their activities. I know that his wife agrees with me, though, if only for the sake of their son Jacob.

I caught a glimpse of the cold demon in the Financial District, and I shadowed out of the moving hearse and into the dark alley with a Colt in one hand and a fistful of salt in the other, ready to disrupt the invader's tenuous connection to reality. But I'd not even gotten a good look at the demon when it turned in midair and vanished entirely from view.

The body of the demon's fourth and latest victim lay at my feet. It was an older man, looking like a statue that had been toppled off its base. Arms up in a defensive posture, one foot held aloft to take a step the victim never completed. On the victim's face, hoarfroast riming the line of his jaw, was an expression of shock and terror. But before I had a chance to examine the body further, I heard the sounds of screaming from the next street over.

There is a body, I Sent to Don Mateo's thoughts as I raced down the alleyway to investigate. Had the demon retreated from reality only to reemerge a short distance away?

But it was no denizen of the Otherworld menacing the young woman huddled in the wan pool of the streetlamp's light. Her attackers were of a far more mundane variety—or so I believed. I pocketed the salt and filled both hands with silver-plated steel.

Eleven years writing purple prose for *The Wraith Magazine*, and it creeps even into my private thoughts. Ernest would doubtless consider his point made, if he knew, and that bet made in Paris decades ago finally to be won.

The young woman was Mexican, and from her dress I took her to be a housekeeper, likely returning from a day's work cleaning one of the miniature mansions that lined the avenues of Northside. She was sprawled on the pavement, one shoe off, arms raised to shield her face. Two men stood over her, Caucasians in dungarees, work-shirts, and heavy boots. The older of the two had the faded blue of old tattoos shadowing his forearms, suggesting a previous career in the merchant marine, while the younger had the seedy look of a garden-variety hoodlum. With hands clenched in fists and teeth bared, it was unclear whether they wanted to beat the poor girl or take advantage of her—likely both, and in that order.

The hoodlum reached down and grabbed the woman's arm roughly, and as he attempted to yank her to her feet she looked up and her gaze fell on me. Or rather, her gaze fell on the mask, which in the shadows she might have taken to be a disembodied silver skull floating in the darkness. Already terrified by her attackers, the woman's eyes widened on seeing me, and her shouts for help fell into a hushed, awestruck silence.

The prevention of crime, even acts of violence, is not the Wraith's primary mission, nor did the situation seem at first glance to have any bearing on my quest for vengeance, but still I couldn't stand idly by and see an innocent imperiled. But even before spring-ing into action, my Sight caught a glimpse of the tendril that rose from the shoulders of the tattooed man, disappearing in an unseen direction. No mere sailor down on his luck, the tattooed man was possessed, being "ridden" by an intelligence from beyond space and time. And protecting the people of Recondito from such incursions *is* the mission of the Wraith—and if the Ridden was in league with those whom I suspected, vengeance might be served, as well.

"*Unhand her,*" I said, stepping out of the shadows and into view. I Sent as I spoke, the reverberation of thought and sound having a disorienting effect on the listener that I often used to my advantage. "*Or answer to me.*"

The two men turned, and while the hoodlum snarled at my interruption, there glinted in the eyes of the Ridden a dark glimmer of recognition.

The possessed, or Ridden, can be deterred by running water

and by fire, both of which tend to disorient them, but neither is capable of stopping them altogether. Even killing the Ridden's body is not a permanent solution, since the Otherworldly parasite will continue to move and operate the body even in death. The only way to put a Ridden down is to introduce pure silver into the body, by bullet or by blade, which serves to sever the connection between the parasite and host.

That's where my twin Colts come in.

The hoodlum released his hold on the woman's arm, letting her slump back onto the pavement, as the Ridden turned to face me, his eyes darting to the silver-plated .45s in my fists. I wondered whether the hoodlum knew that his companion was more than he seemed to the naked eye.

Typically the Ridden I encounter in Recondito are lackeys of the Guildhall, working as muscle for a political machine whose methods and reach would have eclipsed Tammany Hall in its heyday; the demon parasites from beyond are offered the chance to experience the sensual joys of reality in exchange for their services, while the hosts are most often thugs for hire who have disappointed their employers once too often. That one of the two attackers was Ridden suggested strongly that these two were Guildhall bruisers enjoying a night away from roughing up the machine's political enemies.

"*Now step away,*" I ordered, aiming a pistol at each of them.

After I recovered Cager's body from the jungle, I took his Colt M1911 and my own and plated them with silver from the daykeeper's secret mine, and cast silver bullets to match. I usually carry a pistol in either hand, but make it a habit never to fire more than one at a time. Despite what the pulp magazines would have readers believe, no one can hit the broad side of a barn firing two guns at once. The first time I tried it, honing my skills in the forest above Xibalba, the recoil drove the pistol in my left hand crashing into the one in my right, with my thumb caught in between, the skin scraped off like cheese through a grater. And though the gloves I wear as the Wraith would save me from another such injury, I've found that the second Colt is much more useful as a ward against attack—the silver serving to keep any Ridden from venturing too close—and then ready with a full magazine to fire if the seven rounds in the other pistol run out before the job is done.

The silver of the Colt in my right hand was enough to make the Ridden think twice about rushing me, while the bullets in the Colt in my left were sufficient to give the hoodlum pause—I wouldn't fire on a man who wasn't possessed unless it was absolutely necessary, but it was clear that *he* didn't know that.

"*Por favor . . .*" the woman said in pleading tones, scuttling back across the pavement from me, seeming as frightened of the Wraith's silver mask as she'd been of her two attackers' fists only moments before. "*Ayuda me . . .*" I knew it wasn't me she was asking for help. But then, who? The shadows?

I intended to end the suffering of the Ridden's host-body, a single silver bullet driving the parasite back to its home beyond the sky, and to chase the hoodlum into the night with enough fear instilled in him that he wouldn't soon menace another girl walking alone by night.

"*Now,*" I said and Sent, gesturing toward the hoodlum with the Colt in my left hand, "*one of you I shall send back to your Guildhall masters with a message . . .*"

The hoodlum began to turn away, shifting his weight as he prepared to take to his heels and flee.

I smiled behind my mask, raising the pistol in my right hand and training it between the eyes of the Ridden. "*. . . and the other shall* be *that message . . .*"

And then, the arrival of my clowned-up imitator made a hash of all my plans.

"No, *malvado,*" came a somewhat muffled voice shouting from the shadows, "you're not going anywhere!"

Before the hoodlum knew what had hit him, a blur of silver and black came rushing out of the shadows, tackling him to the ground. Raining a welter of blows down on the hoodlum's head and shoulders, the newcomer kept his opponent pinned to the ground like a wrestler on a mat. And the impression of a wrestler was only strengthened when he looked up in my direction and I saw the black leather mask he wore—it was of the same type as those worn by the Mexican wrestlers, but this one had a stylized white skull stitched over the face.

The young woman still huddled at the edge of the streetlamp's light, looking in wide-eyed shock at the strange figure dispensing a beating on her erstwhile attacker. She whispered, "*Sepultura*," and I wondered why she spoke of the grave.

"Don't worry, *señorita*," the masked man said, leaping to his feet and striking a faintly ridiculous pose, hands on his hips and arms akimbo. "Sepultura is here to help!"

The masked man—this Sepultura—wore a gray boilersuit, black leather paratrooper boots, and black leather gloves, with an army officer's web belt cinched at his waist with pouches all around. He stood perhaps a few inches shorter than me, and while he was clearly in fighting trim—the moaning hoodlum on the pavement a testament to the strength of his blows—the ill-fitting boilersuit made him look somewhat paunchy.

"*Depart, interloper!*" I took a half-step forward and waved him away with the barrel of the Colt in my left fist. "*This is none of your concern . . .*"

In the confusion created by the arrival of this so-called Sepultura, the Ridden saw the opportunity to escape. And while I warned the masked fool away, the tattooed Ridden spun on his heel and started to run off in the opposite direction.

"Don't worry, *Señor* Wraith," Sepultura said with a jaunty wave, lunging after the fleeing Ridden. "I'll stop him . . ."

The Ridden looked back and glared at the pursuing Sepultura, and the phantasm that clung to the Ridden's shoulders flared bright with hatred, feeding off the emotions of its host body.

At that precise moment Sepultura stumbled, throwing his hands up before him protectively, his eyes widening in surprise visibly behind the eye-slits of his mask.

The Ridden was already several strides away and increasing the distance between us with every footfall. But Sepultura was now directly in my way, and any shot fired might strike him by mistake. Fool that he clearly was, I wasn't about to shoot him down, but at the same time I wasn't going to let the Ridden escape back into the city.

"*Fiend!*" I shouted, Sending out waves of anger to disorient the parasite's senses. I took two steps forward, and before colliding with Sepultura I shadowed, ghosting right through him and only returning fully to reality when I was clear on the other side. "*Give my regards to hell!*"

I fired a single round from the .45 in my right fist, the silver slug catching the Ridden just above his left shoulder blade, driving through his heart, and exiting out the front. As the host body shouted a quick bark of pain, I could See the parasite's tendrils recoiling in aversion to the silver, retreating back beyond the walls of reality. By the time the tattooed form collapsed to the pavement, life slipping away, the parasite was already gone.

I turned, ready to render aid to the young woman, and to Sepultura an admonishment to keep out of my business. But there was no sign of either of them, the moaning form of the hoodlum all that remained in the streetlamp's pool of light.

I rejoined Don Mateo in the hearse and we resumed our rounds of the city's streets, though I didn't catch the slightest glimpse of the cold demon again tonight. It was not until relating to Don Mateo the encounter with the young woman, her attackers, and the masked meddler that I realized that the white skull emblazoned on Sepultura's leather mask must have been inspired by my own silver skull.

Bad enough that I have imitators in San Francisco, Chicago, and New York, but *now* I have to contend with one right here in Recondito?

The crooked police officer turned, a still-smoking revolver in his hands, and froze at the sight of a black-shrouded silver skull emerging from the darkness. "The last innocent has suffered at your hands, recreant," grimly intoned THE WRAITH.

SUNDAY, NOVEMBER 1, 1942.

I awoke well before dawn this morning, my shuttered bedroom drenched in inky darkness. As so often happens when I find myself in dark silence so complete, I fancied that I was still an initiate in the Dark House, learning to expand my senses beyond the mundane five. Could the dozen years since have been one long dream, and at any moment Don Javier might bring a lantern and lead me out into the daylight once more? Or perhaps even Xibalba was a dream, and I am still a child in the Lower East Side, racked with fever and lying in my parents' bed, all alone in our rooms as mother, father, and sister are away at work. If my whole life since then *were* a fever dream, it would explain a great deal. Wartime adventures, European wandering, jungle expeditions, hidden temples, secret orders, invaders from beyond—easily the stuff of a child's fevered imagination.

I sometimes wonder whether the situation isn't even more prosaic than that. How easy it would be to believe that I, a Jew posing as a Gentile, became dissatisfied with too ordinary a life and simply created one more worth the living. Rather than a masked avenger who passes his activities off as fiction, I could be a writer of cheap fictions who imagines himself the heroic figure about whom he writes.

But all too quickly my idle musings in the night can turn darker. I remembered the chill of the Rattling House, and Don Javier's lessons about shadowing and shifting. And though I mastered the art of shadowing through solid objects, my one attempt to shift away from reality entirely ended in disaster, with only the beacon of Don Javier's Sent thoughts to guide me back to the here and now. But for a brief instant I was lost in the Unreal, adrift in that space that is no space, a realm which the mundane senses are completely incapable of perceiving—the only impression I have of unreality is that of unending cold and darkness.

Don Javier had taught me about those who get lost in the midst of shifting, unable ever to return. Some are initiates like I had been, trained in the use of their Talents, but others are merely ordinary men and women who don't realize the skills they possess until it is too late. Most who have the Sight but not the training are driven mad by the voices in the end, and those who shadow without first learning the art can return to the Real with their hearts on the wrong sides of their bodies, or with their internal organs on the outside and their skin and hair buried within.

All over Mexico the story is told of *La Llorona*, the Wailing Woman, but only in Xibalba is it understood that she was an untrained shifter unable to realign with reality, stuck forever between the Real and the Unreal, invisible to all except those who possess the Sight.

When I refused to continue studying the art of shifting, I never admitted that it was because I feared following in the ghostly footsteps of *La Llorona*, feared becoming an insubstantial figure belonging neither to this world nor the next. But considering that Don Javier could peer right into my thoughts, I imagine I didn't have to say a thing.

The latest *Wraith* novel complete, and Charlotte not due to return until later in the day, I rose early, shaved and bathed, and, having dressed in a freshly laundered suit, made my way to the cemetery. Even at that early hour, there were any number of Mexican families already gathering at the gravesides of their loved ones, preparing for *Dia de los Muertos*.

When I shadowed unseen through the rear wall of the crypt, Don Mateo had breakfast waiting for me—hot coffee laced with cinnamon, fresh thick corn tortillas, and meat jerky broiled on an open flame.

The old daykeeper was in a sentimental mood, perhaps inspired by the Day of the Dead celebrations only now getting under way outside, and fell to talking about the Yucatan jungle as we sipped our steaming cups of coffee.

I asked him if he ever regrets coming with me to Recondito, leaving behind the only life and home he'd ever known.

Don Mateo was philosophical about the whole matter. "When the doors to the Unreal began to close in Mexico, the daykeepers gradually lost their purpose. Recondito is now the most active of the true places. Where else should my duty take me but here?"

I realized today that I am now almost as old as Mateo was when he and Don Javier first found me in the jungle, close to death after the attack of the camazotz. Don Mateo had already seemed so old, to be only in his middle forties. But then, when my father was forty-three years old, he'd already been an old man, as well, or had seemed like one in the eyes of his young son. I don't *feel* old—at least, not until a full night's patrol, when my joints ache from the chill of shadowing and my muscles grow as taut as steel knots—but there are lines around the eyes that stare back from my mirror, and the streak of white that's been in my hair since Cager's death is growing steadily larger. I'll eventually have a full head of white hair with a single streak of black, assuming I should live so long.

I stayed and chatted idly with Don Mateo as the morning wore on, as we serviced my tools, casting new bullets out of the lumps of silver ore we'd brought from Xibalba, honing the edges on the silver blades I carry up my sleeves.

When a glance at my wristwatch showed me that noon was approaching, I made my farewells to Don Mateo and arranged to meet him back at the crypt that evening for another patrol. For the moment, though, I intended to head over to Charlotte's place and welcome her home in style.

By the time I left the crypt, Mass had ended at Saint Anthony's, and the Mexican families who'd been just beginning to gather in the early morning were now settling in, decorating the graves of their loved ones with *ofrendas*—golden marigolds to attract the souls of the dead, toys atop the tiny graves of the dearly departed *angelitos*, and bottles of tequila or mezcal for their full-grown relations. Everywhere could be seen *confite, calvera, pan de muerto,* and *calacas*—or candy, sugar skulls, "bread of the dead," and miniature figurines of skeletons dressed in the clothes of the living.

In the stories Cager told me of Recondito, the Oceanview neighborhood was described as the home of Irish sailors and seamstresses who worked hard, drank their fill, and prayed for forgiveness come Sunday morning. When I first moved to the city, having taken my friend's name and identity as my own, I quickly settled on a townhouse in Oceanview, close by the cemetery where Don Mateo had found employment. But while my new Irish neighbors were always quick to complain about the growing number of Mexicans moving into the area, I found that the oldest headstones in the cemetery were inscribed with Spanish surnames, dating back to the time when a Franciscan mission had stood on the ground Saint Anthony's now occupied, back when this part of Recondito was little more than a collection of rude huts housing the new city's principal workforce. Though there are increasing numbers of newcomers immigrating from Mexico to Recondito every day—bringing the zoot-suiter gangs and their violence with them—the Irish didn't make their way to the Hidden City until the turn of the current century, after generations of their Hispanic neighbors had been born, christened in the Church of the Holy Saint Anthony, and buried in old age in the adjacent cemetery.

As I made my way out of the cemetery this morning, I passed a heated argument underway in the shadow of one of the largest and oldest of the headstones, a family marker inscribed simply with the name AGUILAR, with smaller stones placed in front marking individual burial plots. The two men shouting at each other might have been father and son. The older was dressed soberly, having likely just walked out of the morning's church service, but the younger was a pachuco in high-waisted baggy pants held up by suspenders, the legs cuffed over double-soled Florsheim shoes, his hair slicked back with pomade in a ducktail comb.

In a mix of Spanish and English, switching back and forth

sometimes in the span of a single sentence, the two men were heatedly discussing the Sarah Pennington murder trial, the young man apparently taking the position that the defendants had been unfairly accused, the older arguing that the two simply *had* to be mixed up with gangs and violence, or else why would they dress as they did. This led to the young man demanding to know whether the older man was accusing *him* of being in a gang, simply because of his manner of dress, and the older man replying that if the double-soled shoe fit . . .

All of this shot back and forth between the pair before I'd taken six steps past them, when the older man suddenly ended the discussion and my forward motion with a single word: "*Sepultura.*"

I was brought up short, and glanced back over my shoulder at them. It took me a moment to parse out the last sentence I'd heard. The older man had said something like, "Why can't you be more like that Sepultura?"

I wondered for a moment if the older man had simply switched from English to Spanish in mid-sentence again, and had been referring to a "grave" instead of saying the *nom de guerre* of my latest imitator.

But then he went on, saying, "*Sepultura* saved your cousin last night from *violadores*. He is a hero to our people. What are you but *un delincuente juvenil*?"

The young man seemed to deflate, like the fight had gone out of him, and instead of shouting back he covered his mouth, as if concealing his expression. I noted a cross tattooed inexpertly on the fleshy part of his right hand between thumb and forefinger. Most likely a gang sign of some kind, I reasoned.

The older man noticed me looking their way, no doubt seeing the expression of annoyance on my face, and I hastened to look away, continuing out of the cemetery and onto the street. It was several blocks before my fists unclenched at my sides.

How long *has* this Sepultura clown been skulking about the shadows of Recondito without my noticing? Or has he, like the zoot-suiters, come to my city from elsewhere, perhaps arriving from Mexico with the wrestling exhibition? It would explain the leather mask, if so.

I'd forgotten to bring the present I picked up last week for Charlotte, so stopped by my place to get it before heading over to her apartment. But when I got home, I found Charlotte waiting for me there, brewing a fresh pot of coffee and idly paging through a book bound in green leather. In gilt letters on the front cover was the title, *Myths and Legends of Varadeaux.*

"I thought you despised this translation," Charlotte said, without looking up from the pages.

"I do," I answered, draping my suitcoat over a chair and coming to stand beside her. "But I knew you'd love the Xenophon Brade illustrations. Besides, once you take it home I won't have to look at Lovelock's execrable translation anymore, so it hardly matters."

Snapping the book shut, Charlotte looked up at me with eyes widening. "This is for *me*? But, Alter, it must have cost a *fortune.*"

Charlotte is the only person who calls me Alter. But then, she's one of only two people still living who know that it was Alistair Micjah "Cager" Freeman who died in the Yucatan back in '25 and not his former squadmate and traveling companion, Alter Friedman. But then, "Alter" wasn't my name either, not really. My parents had already lost two previous babies when I was born on the ship en route from Romania, with my sister Mindel being their only child to survive to that point. I was sickly and small, and my mother insisted that my given name never be spoken aloud for fear that it would alert the *nit-gute* to my presence. Instead, they'd call me Alter, as if calling me "old man" would foil whatever plans the *malekhamoves* had for me. How surprised my mother would have been to learn that her little baby had grown up to be the Angel of Death himself, in a sense.

"It wasn't cheap," I answered, putting my arm around her shoulders, "but my girl is worth it."

Charlotte leapt to her feet and planted a kiss on my lips, and then spun away with a laugh. "Wait right here, I've got something for you, too."

"What, did Mother McKee knit me another pair of socks?"

She came back with a oversized portfolio in hand and slugged me playfully in the shoulder. "You should be so lucky. It took Ma *years* to knit that last pair."

Untying the stays on the portfolio, Charlotte slid onto the table's surface a canvas mounted on wooden stretchers, twenty-two inches by thirty, and covered in oils.

"It's the cover for *The Hydra Falls*," she said, eyes searching my expression for approval. "What do you think?"

The painting depicts the Wraith on a rooftop with a crescent moon high overhead, muzzle flare lighting up the barrels of both Colt .45s as he fires on a massive nine-headed dragon that is rearing up over the skyline of Recondito.

"It's perfect, Red." And it was . . . even though the real Mr. Hydra stood no taller than six foot three and looked more like George Raft than St. George's Dragon. But the reading public didn't need to know the reality. What mattered to them was the illusion. "And I know that Julie will be glad to have it. Another day and he was going to have to run a stock image, instead."

"Oh, phooey," Charlotte said, waving a hand dismissively. "Bernhardt can go hang. I *told* him I'd finish it when I was away, didn't I?"

I wasn't in any mood to argue about our mutual editor, and let the matter lie, ending the discussion with another kiss.

As Charlotte carefully repackaged the painting, I poured us a pair of coffees. Do any of the faithful readers of *The Wraith Magazine* suspect that the "Chas. A. McKee" who provides the macabre and otherworldly covers and illustrations for the magazine is "Charlotte McKee"? Would they enjoy her work any less if they did?

But if they don't suspect that the illustrator is a Vassar grad and a knockout, they don't even *dream* that the Wraith of the stories might be anything other than a nameless spirit of vengeance, or that there is a living man behind that skull of silver steel.

"I made dinner reservations at that place in Little Canton," I called from the kitchen, and Charlotte replied with a short yelp of delight. Never come between a woman and her dumplings, I have found.

I glanced at a recent issue of *The Wraith* lying on the side table, showing my silver-skulled alter ego in close combat with a brace of demons. Like so many of the other paintings Charlotte had done over the years, this one was drawn from life. She was one of those rare people born with the Sight, able to peer beyond the everyday and see the things that lurk unnoticed in the shadows. That's what brought us together in the first place, years ago, and it's what makes her perfect to illustrate my stories. Even when she exercises a bit of artistic license, as when she imagines Jacob Hydra as an oversized dragon, she draws on her own experiences with invaders from the Otherworld as a model.

"I missed you, Red," I told her as I carried the coffees from the kitchen. She'd only been gone a week, and it had felt like an eternity.

"Come here," she said, taking the cups and setting them on the table next to the book and portfolio, careful not to spill. Then, with the coffee safely out of the way, she grabbed hold of my shirt front and pulled me close, her breath hot on my neck. "*Here's* what you missed, I'll bet."

I'll draw a curtain across the remainder of the day, but suffice it to say that the coffee cooled untouched on the table, and we never did make it to the restaurant for dinner.

Charlotte's asleep now across my bed, and her slight snores are like music to me—will we ever give up the pretense and move her out of her apartment altogether? The moon is rising over the city, and Don Mateo is waiting for me at the crypt. I'll let her sleep. Perhaps tomorrow she and I can discuss our future together for once, instead of always fleeing headlong from our pasts.

"You've worked your employees to their deaths," hissed THE WRAITH, looming over the factory owner who quavered in flickering firelight. The ring of salt the masked avenger had cast on the floor would keep at bay any of the villain's

unearthly minions who had not already been driven beyond reality's veil by the flames, leaving their corpulent master defenseless. Black-gloved hands reached out in claws toward the wretch's plump neck. "Now you shall sample a taste of their pain . . ."

MONDAY, NOVEMBER 2, 1942.

Don Mateo and I found another frozen victim last night, a woman of middle age, this time closer to home at the boundary between the Oceanview and the Ross Village. But we weren't rewarded with another glimpse of the cold demon itself. Five victims so far, at least, and we're no closer to driving the fiend back to the Otherworld.

I slept little after returning home, but well, wrapped in Charlotte's arms, and dozed long after she'd risen in the morning to go deliver the cover painting to Julie. When I finally came to full wakefulness, I remembered that I owed him a delivery, too, and, dressing quickly, set out with the latest *Wraith* manuscript bound up in brown twine under my arm.

Julius Bernhardt looked like a cartoon sitting across the desk, chewing on an unlit cigar with his shirtsleeves rolled up over hairy forearms, already sweating despite the cool November morning. He thumbed through the top few pages of the manuscript, his bushy brows knitted.

"It's another winner, Freeman," he said, slamming his open palm down on the stack of paper. "As soon as that dizzy girlfriend of yours comes through with the next cover, we're set to go. God forbid we have another delay."

I failed to mention that my "dizzy" girl hadn't missed a deadline yet, and that the only delays in *The Wraith*'s publication schedule in years had been when Julie had mismanaged the accounts and left us without the funds to cover the printing costs. If I hadn't stepped in and become a silent partner, Bernhardt would probably have given up shares of the company to the printer and distributor to cover the debts, and the outfit would have ended up a "captive publisher," never able to earn its way out.

There's hardly enough Xibalba silver left to cast bullets these days, though, so I won't be investing in any new publishing schemes anytime soon—not that Julie ever guessed where my funds came from. He's always taken at face value that I'm the heir to the Freeman fortune—and that there *is* a Freeman fortune left to speak of, come to that. When I met Cager, he scarcely had a pot to piss in. The scion of the Freemans, son of one of the oldest and most well-established families in Recondito society, he'd been as dirt poor as me. But while my family never had any fortune to lose, Cager Freeman's fortune in shipping and mining concerns had all been lost after the Guildhall had ruined his father's name and seized his family assets.

"But there's just one thing," Julie said, pulling the soggy stogie from his mouth and gesturing punctuation in the air. "Do you *have* to keep writing stories with crooked cops and politicians as the black hats? Can't you truck out everyday *gangsters* now and again?"

In the trenches of France, Cager had confided to me the strange truth about his father's death, and the unearthly creatures he'd glimpsed that night. It was only later that we made the connection and realized that a secret cabal in Recondito was in league with dark powers, but of course by then it was all too late. Too late for Cager and his family, at least, but not too late for vengeance. That was half the reason I came to Recondito, and my motivation for taking my friend's identity, to knock the Guildhall off their pins with the thought that the son of their rival had returned from exile to haunt them. The fact that the Guildhall was mixed up in so much of the Otherworldly incursion in the city, in one way or another, just meant that my sacred mission as a daykeeper of Xibalba and my quest to avenge the Freeman family could march together hand-in-hand.

"I'll do what I can," I told Julie, lying through my smile.

Pass up the chance to cast as fictional villains the kind of fiends who are really behind so much of the city's evil? Not on your life.

Promising to turn in the next *Wraith* novel in a fortnight, and not a moment later, I left Julie's office and headed up to Little Canton to meet Charlotte for lunch. The dumplings were every bit as good as she'd promised. Leaving the restaurant, we ambled back through the city in no particular hurry rather than hailing a cab: stopping in at the antiquarian bookstore in the Ross Village to rummage for treasures; getting ice cream at the soda fountain in the drugstore on Odessa Avenue, ignoring the youngsters flapping their garishly colored comic books at one another while arguing the relative merits of one tights-wearing buffoon over another. The newsstands are filled with such poorly written and wretchedly illustrated tripe, crowding out the respectable pulps, and seeing the crude cover illustration of a figure in hood and tights swinging on a rope high over a skyline—and swinging from *what*?—I couldn't help but be reminded of my copycat.

But all in all it was a lazy Monday afternoon and a perfect stroll, marred only by a scuffle we encountered outside the bars on Hauser, a fight having broken out between zoot-suiters and a group of servicemen on leave. Charlotte gripped my arm, whispering that I shouldn't get involved, but the police had already arrived to arrest the pachucos, so there wasn't any reason for me to interfere. For a stretch of a few blocks, with the soldiers and policemen out in full force, rounding up the delinquents, it felt for a moment like Recondito was a city under siege, invaded by outside forces. And considering the demons and the zoot-suiters, I suppose it is, in a way.

When we got back to my place, Charlotte couldn't stay, having plans to meet her girlfriends for bridge this afternoon. I'm alone for the moment, the sunlight streaming in through the open window. It's days like this when I wish that my life *was* simply a daydream, and that I was no more and no less than what I pretend to be. A lazy afternoon of dumplings and bookstores and ice-cream sundaes with a pretty girl on my arm? Who *wouldn't* want that life?

☆   ★   ☆

Later.

It's late night—or perhaps already early morning—and I've barely the strength to lift my pen, but I feel it necessary to record my thoughts on the evening's events while they're still fresh in my mind.

I have been wrong about so many things.

The cemetery was crowded with families concluding the *Dia de los Muertos* celebrations, and I was forced to Send distractions into the minds of more than a few to cover my approach to the crypt. No one took any notice of the hearse as Don Mateo steered out of the garage and onto the thoroughfare, though I sat back in the shadows of the passenger seat and tilted down the brim of my slouch hat to conceal the glinting silver of my mask.

Down on Bayfront Drive, Don Mateo noticed the metallic taste and buzzing sound of a demon incarnating before my Sight even caught a glimpse, the foul impression left on mundane senses when a tiny portion of the Otherworld's alien physics intrudes on our world. As I shadowed out of the moving hearse, one hand filled with salt crystals and the other with a loaded .45, I thought for certain that we'd located the elusive cold demon at last. But the creature I found on the dock was only a minor shade, a mindless moving patch of darkness, nothing at all like the demon I'd briefly glimpsed on Saturday night.

I pinned the shade in a ring of salt, the bare handful I carried more than enough for the task. And though Don Mateo had the acetylene torch ready in the hearse, the flame of my Zippo lighter was sufficient to drive the creature back to the Otherworld.

There was no chance that so insignificant a demon could have been responsible for the gruesome freezing deaths of recent days. It was only as we pulled away from the docks, and the foul impressions of the incursion faded, that I recalled that my previous brief encounter with the cold demon had not been accompanied by any such sensations.

We headed down Prospect Avenue, past the Guildhall that looms like a medieval fortress over the surrounding buildings, and I could sense the lingering etheric disturbance of every summoning and incarnation, every binding and compact, that the grim masters of the political machine have performed over the years. Generations of Guildhall leaders have made deals with devils, literally and figuratively, to maintain their grip on Recondito, and so far as I'm concerned everyone in the organization has blood on their hands. And while I've been able to curtail their activities to a large extent since taking up the mantle of the Wraith, I am only one man, and have yet to put an end to their dark deeds altogether. Some day, I know, I'll lose my patience, tire of the long game, and storm that castle with guns blazing—and though such an open assault would doubtless mean my life, I'd at least be able to take with me as many of those overfed bastards as possible. But that would leave Recondito unprotected in my absence, and so I marshal my reserves of patience, and continue to take the Guildhall's pieces off the board one pawn at a time.

We made our way through the Financial District, up through Northside, and down through Hyde Park and Ross Village, all without any sign of the cold demon. We skirted Ross University and turned onto Mission Avenue to cut through Oceanview on our way south, and that's when I saw him. Not the demon of cold we'd been seeking, but that imitator who calls himself Sepultura.

He was lurking in an alleyway, his gray boilersuit and black gloves and boots rendering him almost invisible in the shadows, but the stark white skull sewn onto his mask shone in the dim light like the full moon.

Perhaps it was my mounting frustration over my inability to locate the cold demon, or perhaps I was simply annoyed to be reminded that a copycat was skulking around the streets of *my* city, but as soon as I saw Sepultura in the alley I shadowed through the side of the hearse and dove for him, hands out and grasping. Did I intend to throttle him? To knock some sense into his masked head and drive him out of Recondito? I'm not sure, in retrospect, and now I'll never know.

I regained solidity as soon as I passed through the closed door of the hearse, and was less than an eyeblink away from tackling Sepultura to the ground. But to my astonishment he reacted immediately to my sudden appearance before him, diving to one side as I approached. I sailed past, only narrowly avoiding crashing to the rough pavement of the alleyway, and tucked and rolled my way into a crouch. When I spun around, I saw that Sepultura had dropped into a defensive posture, shoulder to me and hands held loosely before him like a wrestler waiting for his opponent to make the next move.

"You've trained," I said in faint admiration. "Not bad." Then I added an undertone of Sent thought to my spoken words, *"But you're no match for the* Wraith.*"*

I surged forward, my greatcoat swirling around me to conceal my arm motions, and my right fist lashed out like a striking cobra at his head.

Sepultura managed to duck to the side and block the blow with his forearm, but just barely, and the force of the impact sent him sidestepping to retain his balance.

"*Órale!*" he said, and I could almost hear him grinning behind his mask. "You're fast." Lightning quick, he jabbed straight at my neck with his left. "Always talk about yourself in the third person, though?"

I snapped back in time to avoid the jab, and then swept a leg out in a sidekick, catching him with a glancing blow to the hip. "I've heard you do the same, 'Sepultura.'"

He staggered back, gripping his hip and hissing in pain through the mouth-slit of his mask. But he kept on his feet, and after a split second was back in a defensive posture. "Touché."

He'd managed to shrug off the disorienting effects of my Sending, and was holding his own in hand-to-hand. It was clear that my copycat was not to be dismissed lightly.

"Why did you come to my city?" I demanded.

"*Come* here?" Sepultura snarled. "*Pendejo*, I was *born* here."

I was wearying of this game, and eager to get back to the hunt. Bracing myself, I readied to leap forward and shadow straight through Sepultura, intending to solidify as soon as I was past him and then strike a blow from behind before he knew what had happened. But before I could move he suddenly straightened, his gaze trained past my shoulder at something farther up the alleyway.

"Sarah?" he said, arms falling to his sides and shoulders slumping.

I turned, and there before me hovered the demon of cold.

Only it wasn't any demon, whether of cold or any other sort. It was a girl, or rather the ethereal and not-entirely-present specter of a girl. I recognized the murder victim from the front pages of the *Clarion*—Sarah Pennington.

I could feel the waves of cold radiating from her, and my breath fogged in the frigid air as it passed through my skull-mask.

"F-Felix . . . ?" the specter said, in a voice that reverberated strangely with distant echoes.

"No," Sepultura said, and stepped past me, tugging the leather mask from his head. He turned his bare face to the specter above. "It's Beto." He paused, and then said, "Roberto. Roberto Aguilar."

The specter wailed in dismay, and seemed to flicker from view for the briefest of instants.

"Where . . . where is Felix . . . ?" her echoing voice called out.

The unmasked Sepultura was revealed to be a young Mexican man, no more than twenty years old. He was looking right at the apparition of the girl, though mundane vision would see only an empty alley in front of him. That meant that he had the Sight, though he might never have realized it until now.

But though we live in a demon-haunted world, the spirits of the dead never return to visit the living. There is only one way I know for a live person to become a specter such as floated before us.

The echoing voice of Sarah Pennington howled in sorrow and fear once more, and, muttering beneath my breath, I named her. "*La Llorona*." Wailing Woman.

I stepped forward and placed my hand on Sepultura's shoulder. "You know this girl?"

He turned to me with wide eyes, looking as though he'd forgotten I was ever standing there. "I didn't think . . . Felix *couldn't* have hurt her . . . killed her . . ."

"Felix!" the specter of Sarah Pennington wailed.

"No one hurt her, son," I said. "And she isn't dead. She is simply . . . lost."

It was likely the girl hadn't ever imagined that she could shift away from reality. Not until she did it for the first time, and found she couldn't get back.

"She's been seeing my friend Felix," Sepultura finally said. "Felix Uresti. But her dad, he wasn't happy about her dating a Mexican. Said he was going to put an end to it. Joe Dominguez went with Felix to her house, to help her get away from the old man, but Pennington came out with a shotgun. Started shooting in the air like it was the Fourth of July. The way Felix tells it, things went crazy, Sarah came running toward him, then she just . . . vanished."

Typically the untrained shift instinctively in states of agitation and trauma, often fleeing some perceived danger. The poor girl running away from a shotgun-wielding parent would definitely qualify.

"Felix and Joe took off running," Sepultura continued, "and the next day the police came and carted them away, charged with kidnapping and murder."

"Felix!" the specter wailed, perhaps in response. "Where are you?"

The specter drifted a few feet nearer, and waves of freezing cold lapped over us. I thought back to the Rattling House, and the brief moment I'd spent in the Unreal, that unending realm of darkness and cold. I knew now how the victims had come to be frozen; she'd been searching for a way back, and grabbed hold of anyone she could. How was she to know that her very touch would bring cold death?

Was she too far gone now to attempt to grab onto either of

us? Or was the reminder of her lost Felix enough to stop her in her tracks, ignoring us because neither of us were the one she sought? I couldn't say, but knew that we would have to put an end to the danger she presented, and soon.

"But you knew your friends were innocent," I said, looking from the specter to the young man beside me. I recognized him now as the young man from the argument I'd overheard in the cemetery.

He nodded. "That's why . . . well . . ." He paused, and gestured with the skull-faced mask in his hand. "Sepultura."

"You were trying to clear your friends' names."

The young man drew himself up straighter, lifting his chin. "I'd read all about you in the magazines. I figured, if *he* can do it, then why can't I?" He looked back to the specter. "I never believed that Felix killed the girl, but she *couldn't* have just vanished. I figured that she had slipped away in the confusion, and that someone *else* had nabbed her before she could rejoin Felix. So I put on the mask and started searching the streets, looking for the kind of *cabrón* who would snatch pretty girls. But now that we've found her, we can *prove* Felix and Joe didn't kill her." He glanced over to me, his expression hopeful. "Right?"

I tightened my hand on his shoulder, sympathetically. "I'm afraid it won't be so simple."

I released my hold on his shoulder, and pulled pouches of salt out of my greatcoat's pockets in either hand. I passed one of them to the young man, who accepted it with a questioning look.

"We'll do what we can about your friends," I told him, tugging open the drawstring on the pouch. "But there's something we must do, first."

Though one is a lost human being and the other is a fiend of the Otherworld, there was much in common between the specter before us and the shade that I had banished on the dock earlier tonight. Neither of them can conscience crystalline structures of any kind, and the perfectly cubed molecules of everyday salt are particularly anathema. And running water and flames are capable of discomfiting both, and of driving them away from reality.

I motioned the young man to mirror my actions, and began laying down a wide ring of salt on the ground beneath the specter's hovering form.

"I will explain later," I said, not unkindly, when I saw his confused expression.

There is simply no way to end Sarah Pennington's suffering, at least no way that Xibalba ever knew. But it *is* possible to drive her away from reality, pushing her further into the Unreal where she will pose no further risk to the world she's left behind. And God forgive me, I had to do it.

"*Don Mateo*," I Sent to the old daykeeper in the hearse idling a short distance away. "*I'm afraid we will need the acetylene torch.*"

Already the sky outside has begun to lighten, and dawn is not far off. I'm reluctant to sleep, worried that the image of that poor girl will revisit me in my dreams, but I can't keep my eyes open any longer.

The city was safe . . . for now. It was only a matter of time before evil once more imperiled her innocent citizens. But whatever the threat, whether man or monster, from earth or beyond, they would have to contend with the city's ever-vigilant silverskulled sentinel—THE WRAITH.

TUESDAY, NOVEMBER 3, 1942

The papers this morning carried the story of how Joe Dominguez and Felix Uresti escaped from jail in the night. The *Clarion* quoted the Recondito chief of police as insisting that the two young men could not have broken out of their cells on their own, and must have had outside assistance. The *Telegraph*, never shrinking from sensationalism, quoted an unnamed jailer as saying that "only a *ghost* could get through those walls."

Or a Wraith, I'm tempted to point out.

Without a body to produce, living or dead, there was simply no way of proving the innocence of the two men. Even if I *had* been willing to step forward, reveal myself, and testify in court, the account would simply be too fantastic for a jury to accept. But I could not allow two innocent men to go to the gas chamber, not if I had the power to see justice done.

The two were startled when I shadowed through the wall of their cell, to say the least. But when I explained why I had come, and what awaited them if they remained, they were all too eager to leave with me. Shadowing with even one full-grown man taxes my abilities to their limits, so Uresti had to hide in the darkened alley behind police headquarters while I shadowed back through the brick wall for Dominguez, but by the time I had both of them free Aguilar had arrived with changes of clothes and busfare for his friends.

They are already on their way south to Mexico, where new lives and new names wait for them. Like my new associate in the boilersuit and wrestling mask, Dominguez and Uresti were both born in California, and neither have left the country before. But I know they will adapt. They are hardly the first to have to leave the land of their birth and adopt new names in order to survive.

A dozen years behind the mask of the Wraith, and I've become too quick to make assumptions. Have I learned so much since the day Don Javier found me in the jungle that there is nothing left for me to be taught? Not hardly.

I had assumed the deaths by freezing to be the work of a demon of cold, though neither Don Mateo nor I had ever heard of any such creature before. Had I stopped and thought a bit more, might I have recognized the telltale signs of an untrained shifter-turned-specter, one whose touch bled heat away into the Unreal? And if I *had* recognized the signs, might some of those who died at the specter's touch still be alive today? Perhaps.

Too, I was all too quick to assume that a pachuco in a zoot suit was naturally guilty of any accusation. Like the "cold demon" I sought, the young delinquents were an invasion from without, a threat to the security of my city. But like poor Sarah Pennington, boys like Dominguez and Uresti were no invasion, but had been here all along.

I won't be around forever. And one day my patience may wear thin enough for me to storm the gates of the Guildhall and bring that monstrous building crashing down on the fat-cats' heads. When I am gone, there needs to be someone who can pick up where I left off. There must be a successor with the Sight capable of protecting this city against all threats, from without *and* from within.

Last night, Sepultura tangled with the Wraith. (Damn, I *do* refer to myself in third person, don't I?)

Today, assuming he makes our scheduled meeting at the cemetery, Roberto Aguilar will be properly introduced to Alistair Freeman.

And tonight, my successor's training will begin.

I may not be the daykeeper that Don Javier was, but with Don Mateo's help—and assuming that Aguilar is an apt pupil—I will make sure that the legacy of Xibalba does not end with me.

Charlotte will be here soon. I've not seen her since yesterday afternoon, and all she knows about the events of the night is what she might have gleaned from the morning papers. I will have to tell her that I banished an innocent girl to endless exile in unreality, all to safeguard a thankless city—but perhaps not right away. Let me pretend for a moment to be a simple writer of cheap fiction, an old man in fact as well as name, who can turn away from the night's horrors as simply as lifting his hands from his typewriter's keys. I know night will fall, and with it the need to take up the silver mask once more, but give me this one bright moment of sunshine for my own.

Can't I turn away for just an instant, just this once?

And somewhere past the edge of hearing, the wailing voice of Sarah Pennington calls out for help that will never arrive, joining the echoes of Cager Freeman's dying cries, and his father's pleas for mercy, and my sister Mindel shouting above the crackling flame, and all of the other countless voices crying out to be avenged . . .

. . . and I know that I have my answer.

☆　★　☆

Peter David is an author, comic book scribe, and screen and television writer, whose résumé includes over fifty novels (many of them *New York Times* bestsellers), episodes of such television series as *Babylon 5* and *Space Cases* (which he created with Bill Mumy), and a twelve-year run on the comic book series *The Incredible Hulk*. He is the cocreator and author of the bestselling *Star Trek: New Frontier* series for Pocket Books, and scripted issues of such comic titles as *Supergirl, Young Justice, Soulsearchers and Company, Aquaman, Spider-Man, Spider-Man 2099, X-Factor, Star Trek, Wolverine, The Phantom, Sachs & Violens*, and many more. Winner of an Eisner Award, as well as many other awards, David wrote the following tale with his wife, Kathleen.

Head Cases

PETER DAVID AND KATHLEEN DAVID

The musician stood on the curbside, gently strumming his guitar and nodding along with his own aimless tune. The young man sang equally aimless words that had the merit of rhyming without actually conveying any imagery or meaning. He liked that about his songs, believing that it meant they could be anything to anyone. His foot tapped along, half a beat behind. It was so disconcerting that people walking past him would trip slightly as his music put them out of synch.

"You suck," one guy muttered as he walked past.

"Thank you," said the musician cheerfully, as if a compliment had just been paid. He'd gotten used to it. Money was piling up in the guitar case that was open in front of him, and most of the people who dropped money in said the same thing: "For God's sake, get some lessons." His response continued to be "Thank you" in every case. No sense in pissing off the customers. The public knew what it wanted: It wanted him to improve and cease being painful to listen to. That was fine with him.

"I had a feeling," said an annoyed voice.

The musician's eyes opened. He knew what he was going to see. The knowing didn't make it any easier. If anything, it made it worse.

"I had a feeling you would be here," said the man who was facing him. He wore his blue pinstripe suit like a badge of honor.

"A feeling." The musician didn't sound impressed. He stopped playing, an action that promptly drew scattered applause from passersby, who were pleased that they could resume their strides without risking tripping over their own feet. "Did that feeling have anything to do with being tipped off by the cops?"

"I am a cop. Of course they tip me off."

"You're not a cop, Dad," he said with weary annoyance. "Working in the community PR department doesn't make you a cop. It's like saying the Mets equipment manager plays for them."

"Maybe he's not a player, but he's still part of the team. And the guys on my team look out for me."

"No, they look out for me. They spy on me. You're the one they ratted me out to."

"Look, Ari, you need to—"

"This is what I need to do, Dad," Ari said firmly. He held up the guitar. "I need to do what I feel like doing."

"And that's this? Playing guitar badly on street corners while people toss you pennies?"

"Dollars," Ari corrected him.

"As if that makes a difference."

"It does to me. That makes a difference, and this makes a difference." He held his guitar out toward his father. "This is my life . . ."

"You only started playing six months ago, for God's sake! This isn't your life, Ari. This is just the latest thing! And six months from now, it'll be something else!" He lowered his voice and said intensely, "There are things you can be doing. Should be doing."

"Like what? Like trying to convince neighborhood teens that Mister Policeman is their friend when the kids know that the cops would just as soon chuck them behind bars as look at them?"

His father ignored the jibe. He took a step closer and lowered his voice. "There was a bank robbery today just three blocks from here."

"Yeah, I thought I heard something going on. Sirens and everything. Sounded like a mess."

"You could have helped."

"I don't look good in nylons pulled over my face. Some people can make it work as a fashion statement, but—"

"I mean helped stop it! It was our kind of robbery, Ari! Someone who's invisible, they think. Or a mind wiper. Nobody remembers anything. One minute it's business as normal, and the next, all the cash drawers are empty."

Ari moaned. "I don't want this, Dad. You know that. I don't want any part of this . . ."

"The security camera recordings were all blank—"

"Dad, for God's sake, will you just—?"

And suddenly Ari was shoved to the ground. Before he even realized what was happening, someone had grabbed the guitar out of his hand. He had a brief glimpse of a scruffy-looking guy with ratty hair and even rattier coat. His father shouted angrily, made a grab for the guy, but the guy dodged away with the foot speed of a dancer and kept going. He started running.

His father made no effort to pursue him.

"Thanks, Dad," muttered Ari, still on the ground, and then, taking action before he had the opportunity to think better of it, he slammed his head on the sidewalk.

It hurt like hell, which was typical.

The instant his skull banged against the sidewalk, an earsplitting blast of sound erupted from all around. People staggered, clutching at their ears, but the target of the sound blast was the thief. He was blasted right off his feet, sent flying through the air to crash-land several feet down from where he'd been before. He lay there, looking stunned.

Ari staggered to his feet, the world swimming around him. His father was saying something to him, speaking with some urgency, but Ari couldn't hear him. He knew the ringing would subside; it always did.

Pushing his father aside, he moved quickly down the sidewalk, staggering as he did so. He shook it off and made it to the fallen guitar thief. He yanked the guitar away from him and gave him a swift kick in the gut. The thief moaned. "This isn't yours!" Ari told him angrily.

The thief glared up at him. "You can't play worth a damn."

His instinct was to say that he heard that a lot, but instead Ari said nothing. He could have called a cop or something, but he didn't even want to be bothered with it. Instead he slung his guitar over his shoulder, moved back through the various pedestrians who were trying to shake off the effects of the thunder blast, and scooped out the money from his guitar case. His father said nothing, but instead just stood there and watched as Ari shoved the guitar into the case, closed the lid, snapped it shut, and stalked away.

His father watched him go, shaking his head. The thief who had stolen the guitar staggered up to him and glared. "You owe me, Ted," he said. "You *so* owe me."

"We're trying to serve a greater good, Barry. Set my son on the right track."

Barry rubbed his midsection. "That's easy for you to say. You're not the one who got kicked. I was ready to arrest the little jerk for assaulting a police officer."

"Well, you *did* steal his guitar . . ."

"Because you asked me to, and it's not like I couldn't have busted him for vagrancy in the first place, and besides, stopping him from inflicting what he considers music on the public . . . that's serving and protecting, if you ask me." He winced once more.

"Sorry about that," said Ted, indicating the injury. "Need some aspirin . . . ?"

"Bite me," said Barry as he walked away, still rubbing his chest.

☆ ★ ☆

It was quiet at the DMZ that afternoon, except for Simon Wang's high-pitched shouting, which was attracting the amused attention of the other patrons scattered throughout the pub. They nodded toward him and muttered, "There he goes again" and "Ignore him; he thrives on attention." Simon didn't hear any of it, and wouldn't have cared if he had.

Simon hated the fact that his voice tended to go into upper registers when he was upset. He fought it as best he could, but it wasn't something over which he had a good deal of control. The stocky young Asian man was thudding the table repeatedly with his open hand, or paw as some would have called it because of its being covered with thick, dark bristling hair, as was much of the rest of his body. "You swore to me, Xander! You swore it was a sure thing! You told me it was a sure thing!"

The object of his wrath, Xander Abono, looked up at him with bleary, red-rimmed eyes. His age was indeterminate; sometimes he seemed Simon's age, sometimes younger, sometimes older. He was disheveled as always, wearing the only clothes he appeared to own: jeans, a dirty T-shirt with the Cleveland Cavaliers logo on it for reasons long forgotten if ever known, and a moth-eaten blue denim jacket. He took a slow drag on his bong, sighed contendedly, and then refocused on Hairbag. "I did?"

"Yes! You sat right there! You sat right there and you told me that it was going to be the Astros in four!"

"You mean in the World Series."

"Yes! I asked you for a World Series prediction, and you said, 'The Astros in four!'"

Xander squinted, looking inward rather than outward. "Yeah. Yeah, that sounds right. Okay."

"And I bet on that! I bet big!"

"Okay."

"And they lost!"

"Okay."

"No, man! Not okay! They were blown out! They lost in four straight!"

"Yeah."

Simon gaped at him. "Wait. You're saying that's the prediction you saw coming? Not that they were going to win in four straight, but that they were going to lose in four straight?"

"Looks like."

"Then why the hell didn't you say that?"

"I just kinda think losing is more interesting than winning."

Simon moaned and sank down onto a chair.

From behind the pub's bar, the bartender called over in her amused lilt, "Why do ye do this to yuirself, Hairbag? Why do ye keep asking him for predictions or to read peoples' minds for ye? *Look* at him, for the love of Christ!"

"He's the only seer I know, Selkie, and I don't remember asking you, and by the way, I hate that name."

"Christ?"

"*Hairbag!* I hate it when you call me Hairbag!"

"It's yuir superhero name."

"My hero name," he reminded her archly, "is Monkey King. Because I'm descended from the Monkey King. So if you're going to call me by a hero name, then call me Monkey King."

"And what'll ye do if I keep calling ye Hairbag? Throw poop at me?"

"Yeah, that joke just never gets old," he said sourly.

Xander leaned forward and growled in his husky voice, "She's got a little thing for you, y'know."

"Oh, like I'm supposed to rely on you now. Don't ever tell me anything again."

Xander put up his hands defensively. "Just saying. You don't have to be so cranky."

"I'm cranky because I lost two hundred bucks thanks to you."

"That and because you never get laid. Which brings me back to Selkie . . ."

"Shut up."

"Just sayin' . . ."

Xander shrugged and leaned back. He stroked the bong absently. "You'll be in a better mood when Vikki gets here."

"Vikki's not coming around today."

"Yeah, she is. First Ari's going to come in and mention her except it won't be by name, and then she'll come in."

"She never comes around during the week. Only on weekends. During the week"—Simon's hirsute face twisted in derision—"she's too busy in her perfect little superhero wife world."

"Not so perfect."

Simon stared at him, his eyes narrowing. "What's that supposed to mean? What do you know, Xander?"

Xander shrugged. "I thought you didn't want me to tell you anything again. Make up your mind."

"Right after you're done telling me this thing, don't tell me anything."

"Hey, guys."

Ari sauntered in. "What's going on?"

"Usual stuff," said Simon guardedly.

"Yeah? So basically you lost money because you misinterpreted something that Xander told you, and Xander's busting your chops about Selkie, and we're all snickering over the latest blog entry from Lonely Superwife."

"That's how much you know, we were not—" Simon sat up, his eyes widening, a look of glee spreading across his face. "You're going to mention her except not by name. Holy crap. Are you saying . . . ?"

"Am I saying what?"

"That Vikki is Lonely Superwife!"

Ari's face froze for a moment and then he forced a cool look. "What the hell are you talking about?"

"She is! And you knew!" he said accusatorily.

"Man, I have no idea . . ."

"You knew! All this time, you—"

With an angry whisper, Ari said, "Will you shut up?!" He yanked a chair over and sat so close to Simon that he was practically in his lap. "Look—"

"I'm right, aren't I?"

Ari fired a look at Xander. "You told him. You told him, didn't you?"

"Told him what?" said Xander, staring at him with glazed eyes.

Simon was ignoring him, focused instead on Ari. "The greatest blog in the world. It's the greatest blog in the world, and you know I love it, and you didn't tell me—?"

"Tell you what?"

Vikki Quikk, diminutive and chipper, her long red hair hanging in her face as it typically did, was leaning in toward them. She had been wearing mirrored sunglasses, but she had pushed them up so that they sat perched atop her head. Xander didn't even have to bother to say, "I told you so." He simply gestured with a sort of "tah dah!" flourish as a magician would.

"Hey, Vikki," Ari said, trying to sound a note of warning in his voice. "This is unexpected!"

"Eh." She shrugged and dropped onto an empty chair. "I happened to be in the neighborhood and I figured, why not take a break from errands and swing by and say hi."

Keeping his voice down, Simon nevertheless looked as if he were ready to jump out of his chair with excitement. *"You're* Lonely Superwife?"

Her usual expression of perkiness dissolved and she glared at Ari. He put up his hands defensively. "I didn't tell him!"

"How *could* you?"

"I didn't tell him!"

"I swore you to secrecy!"

He pointed at his own mouth. "Could you at least pretend that there are words coming out of here and maybe, y'know, listen?"

As if he hadn't spoken, Vikki turned to Simon. "Have you told anyone else?"

"When would I have? He just told me."

"*I didn't tell you!*"

"You didn't *not* tell me."

"That sentence doesn't even make any sense, dude!"

"Could we forget about who told who what"—Simon shifted his attention back to Vikki—"and get back to that you're Lonely Sup—"

"Shhhh! Will you pipe the hell down!?"

"If I talk any lower," he said, glancing around, "people are going to think we're planning to kill somebody."

"They may not be far wrong," she said pointedly.

Ari could not recall the last time he'd seen Simon look so chipper. "So Nicky Quikk—Captain Quikk himself—is 'Major Clueless.' That is beautiful . . ."

"It's not beautiful!" Vikki moaned and put her face in her hands. "I am the worst wife in the world. I should never have . . . dammit!" She slapped her palm on the table. "I should have known this would happen. I should have known!"

"You did know," Simon said, trying to sound sympathetic and only partly succeeding. He put a paw atop her hand. "It was a cry for help."

"If you don't let go of me, it won't be the only cry for help around here."

Slowly he removed his paw from her hand. "Gotcha."

At that moment, an elegant, well-attired woman swept in through the door as if she were expecting a round of applause for her arrival. When she received no response at all, she shrugged and headed over to a corner table. She was wearing a huge, broad-brimmed hat that looked as if she'd mugged someone from the Easter Parade for it, and a pair of sunglasses that she did not remove even though it was much darker in the pub than it was outside. Ari looked closely and saw that, yes, the top of the bonnet was undulating slightly.

Then something slapped him on the arm. It was Simon, pulling his attention back to Vikki. Vikki hadn't noticed; she seemed to be looking more into herself than at any of them.

"It was just . . ." She ran her fingers through her hair. "It just . . . it seemed like a good idea at the time."

"All ideas seem good at the time," said Xander. His head was propped up on his hand, his eyes half lidded.

"You have to understand what it was like, being one of Nicky's—"

"Groupies?" said Simon.

"We were *not* groupies!" Vikki said defensively. "We were his fan club!"

"The Quikkies."

"I hate that name."

"And I hate your husband."

"*Simon!*"

Simon didn't back down. "There. I said it. Vikki, your husband's a prick. Captain Prick. He was a prick back in high school when he walked around like he was Mister Wonderful."

"Simon—"

"He was a prick when he enjoyed giving me crap about my fur, and he was a prick when he acted like just because he was the fastest thing on the football field, the world owed him a living."

"You don't know him, Simon."

"If I didn't know him from high school, Viks, I'd know him from what you've been writing about him."

"That's not really him," she said defensively and not at all convincingly. "It's just . . . I get mad at him sometimes because . . ." She looked away. "I'm like a selfish doctor's wife, y'know? He belongs to the world, and I know he loves me, but he has to be other places, and sometimes I get so lonely, and I say stuff I shouldn't. But when I get in front of that keyboard . . . you know what it's like? It's like that old Disney cartoon with Goofy, who's this normal guy until he gets into his car and then he goes nuts. That's me. Goofy."

"You're not selfish," Simon assured her.

"Yes, I am. I mean, you don't know what it was like. Being the president of the Captain Quikk fan club, and when he set eyes on me at QuikkCon 1, it was just . . ." She sighed. "It was like lightning striking. Which, y'know, figures, I guess. And then a whirlwind courtship, which, y'know, also figures. He's just a tough guy to resist."

"Yeah, I noticed that when he was repeatedly shoving my head in a toilet."

"Simon, it was high school!" She sighed. "You've got to let it go!"

"It was last Saturday."

"Oh." She shifted uncomfortably in her seat. "Well . . . that wasn't right. It doesn't sound like him. Did you say something to him?"

"I complimented him on his hair."

"That's it?"

"That's it."

"Well . . . I'm sorry. I don't know what to say."

"You always know what to say on your blog." Simon grinned lopsidedly and began to quote: " 'Major Clueless did his husbandly duty with his typical brisk, passionless efficiency. His mind is on anything but me. I'm starting to wish *he* was on anything but me.'"

"Stop it!" She whapped him on the shoulder, her face flushing with embarrassment.

Xander spoke up. "He's the world's fastest human, kid. What did you expect?"

"Nothing. I don't expect anything from anybody, okay? Look"—she rubbed the bridge of her nose—"you gotta promise me you won't tell. Anybody. Not anybody, Simon, I mean it."

"On my ancestors, I swear," he said solemnly.

"Thanks. And look . . . I feel bad about the whole toilet thing. How about I get you a refill." She nodded toward his nearly empty mug of beer.

"That'd be great, thanks."

She smiled wanly and headed over to the bar. The moment she

did, Ari leaned in toward Simon and said sarcastically, "You complimented him on his hair?"

"Well—"

"Dude! *You told him Vikki was a good beard!*"

"Technically . . ."

"That's not technically! That's word for word!"

"All right, that's word for word." Even though Vikki could not hear them, he still lowered his voice and said, "How could she not know?"

"First of all, you don't know for sure that he's in the closet. Second, it's not your business if he is. And third, who cares if he is in this day and age?"

"*He* cares! He cares and he's using Vikki to cover it because he can't deal with the idea 'cause it doesn't fit in with this whole macho image he's built up for himself, and since I care about Vikki, that makes it my business. And oh, by the way, *you* care about her, too. "

"Yeah. Yeah, I do," said Ari softly.

"So what are we going to do about it?"

"Do?"

"Yes. Do." Without thinking about it, Simon was picking fleas out of his hair. "We have to do something about it."

"You could try throwing crap at him."

"Yeah, that joke just never gets old. That's only the fourth time I've heard it today; twice in the last hour."

Xander chuckled. "It always makes me laugh." Simon growled low and bared his teeth.

"Sometimes we don't do anything about stuff, Simon," Ari said. "In fact, most of the time, we don't."

"Then what's the point, man? What's the point in having powers? What's the point in being us if we can't solve problems?"

"Because it's not our problem, man. It's Vikki's. And if she decides to do something about it, then she does something about it, and we're there for her to pick up the pieces, and it's all good. And if she decides she just wants to, y'know, be what she is, then that's all good, too. Besides,"—he continued over the protests Simon was clearly about to make—"she's got the blog going. She's pushing the whole situation. You know that sooner or later her husband's going to figure it out. Captain Quikk may be slow, but he's not *that* slow. She's keeping that blog to build up her own nerve to confront him, and she's gotta do that on her own schedule. If we come sweeping in, then it's like we're saying she can't handle it. It's insulting. Just because you want to help someone, it don't mean they need it or would welcome it."

"So are you saying," demanded Simon, "that we shouldn't ever mix in?"

"Yes! Well . . . no. I . . . yeah, there are times to mix in. Times to get involved."

"And how do we know?"

"Because we just do! We know when we should get involved!"

And Xander said in that slow, ponderous way he sometimes had, "Do we?"

"Yeah! We do!"

"Do we?" he said again, and this time his gaze shifted toward the woman with the sunglasses. The waitress had just brought her a glass containing a clear liquid that she was now sipping and savoring.

Ari let out a low sigh and said, "Yeah. Yeah, we do. Gimme a minute." He got up, picked up the sunglasses that Vikki had left on the table, and put them on as he walked over to the woman.

He stood in front of her. She knew perfectly well he was standing there but made no effort to acknowledge him. With a grunt of annoyance, Ari said, "Hey, Zola."

Zola affected the air of someone who had been thoroughly startled. Her hand fluttered to her throat. "Ari! Darling! How lovely to see you again!"

"Yeah. Lovely."

"Sit, sit, darling." With her toe, she pushed the chair out across from her. He stared at it for a moment as if he expected the chair to pop out spikes that would gut him like a trout. Then, slowly, he sat.

"I was *just* thinking about you, darling." She spoke with that soft Greek accent that she always seemed to amp up whenever Ari was there. She held up the glass. "Would you like a sip of my ouzo?"

"You realize you're the only person they stock that stuff for, right?"

"How could I not be flattered that they would make all that effort for me?"

"Yeah, whatever." He rapped on the table, a nervous habit of his when he knew something should be said but was reluctant to say it.

Zola reached over and placed her hand atop his. It caused his heart to skip a beat. "Your hand's ice cold," he said.

"Yes, I know," she said playfully. "All of me is. That's what you always loved about our time together, wasn't it? Warming me up?"

"Yeah." He was feeling increasingly uncomfortable.

She propped her chin on her hand and said lazily, "Remind me why we gave all that up?"

"Because there's only so much danger I want to have in a relationship. I only want the normal amount. The yelling, the screaming, the threats, the tears . . ."

"The make-up sex?"

"Make-up sex that doesn't have the potential for killing me, yeah."

"Oh, you." She gestured dismissively. "You worry too much."

"I worry just enough. Zola, you have to give it back."

"Give what back, darling?"

"The money."

The edges of her mouth curled ever so slightly. "What money?"

"The bank robbery today. I know it was you."

"Me?" She gasped. "I'm amazed you would think that. I hear it was someone who could become invisible."

"There's no such thing as someone who can turn invisible," he said dismissively. "If there was, they wouldn't be able to see because if they could bend light around themselves, then it wouldn't get to their eyes. It'd be like wearing a blindfold."

"And you'd know all about that, wouldn't you," she said. He couldn't see her eyes, but he had a feeling she'd winked at him.

Ari refused to let himself get distracted. "The people in the bank not remembering anything. The tapes blank. That's because you looked into their eyes and they became instantly paralyzed, and you looked straight into the camera and paralyzed the guard in the security room who was monitoring it. Then you just went in and erased the tape—"

"Magnetized it, actually," she said. "Same result."

"And then walked out with the money. When everyone came around, they didn't even realize what had happened."

"How masterful of me."

"You need to return it."

She shrugged her elegant shoulders. "Why?"

"Because it was a robbery. Because it was wrong. And it's not like you need the money."

"That's true," she sighed. "I *am* stinking rich. Still . . . money can't buy everything, now, can it. Or . . . *can* it?"

She reached over and placed her hand upon his again.

Behind his reflective glasses, he closed his eyes in pain. "You've gotta be kidding me."

"Ari, darrrrh-ling—"

"*That's* what this is about? Hooking up with me again?"

"Well, *someone* is sorely full of himself. Couldn't it be that I was simply bored and decided to shake things up a bit and see the result?"

"Zola . . . come on! You're dangerous! And you're, y'know, an ancient evil! Greek warriors made a point of killing people like you!"

"Are you endorsing racism now, darling?"

He moaned. "Zola—"

"Fine, fine, fine," she said in annoyance. "The police will find a nice package waiting for them on their doorstep. It will be there by six this evening. Will that make you happy, Ari?"

"What's the catch?"

"No catch. No strings. No—"

A snake suddenly stuck its head out from under her hat. Thin and black, it hissed at him, its tongue whipping out. Zola reached up in annoyance and slapped at it. "Stop it. Behave." The snake cast one final resentful glance at Ari and withdrew.

"No strings," she repeated, sounding wistful. "Consider it . . . a magnanimous gesture."

She still hadn't removed her hand from his. He noticed it was starting to get warmer.

Ari rolled his eyes. "Pick you up at seven."

"Seven-thirty."

"You were going to add half an hour to it no matter what time I said, weren't you."

Her thin green lips spread even wider. "No one knows me the way you do, darling."

"Yeah. I wonder why that is."

He got up and returned to the other table. Vikki had returned with her drink for Simon, who was nursing it more than he was drinking it. He looked questioningly at Ari. "'S'up?"

"Nothing. Nothing's up."

"You're lying," said Vikki. "I can always tell when you're lying."

"Yeah, his lips are moving," said Simon.

"Okay, fine. I have a . . . thing . . . tonight."

"A thing. You mean like a date thing? With . . ." Vikki's eyes widened. "With *Zola*?"

Across the way, Zola raised her glass of ouzo to her in a mocking salute.

"Could'ja keep your voice down, please?" said Ari pleadingly.

Simon grinned. "Dude. Back to living life on the edge, huh?"

"It's just . . . y'know . . . dinner or something. I'm thanking her."

"For what?"

"Because she's doing the right thing."

"What right thing?"

"It doesn't matter. The specifics don't matter. It's just this thing she's doing, and it's right, and I figured that I'd do the right thing and thank her for it."

"She doesn't want your thanks," said Vikki. "She wants . . . y'know . . ."

"Yeah. I know."

"And you're okay with that?"

"I don't know, Vik. I don't know what I'm okay with. All I know for sure is that I'm trying to figure all that out and I'm still not nearly there."

"When do you think you're going to be?"

"C'mon, Vik, it's not like I can put it into Mapquest and get an ETA. It is what it is."

"There you are!"

No one had seen Captain Quikk enter the DMZ. No one ever did. He was simply not there, and then he was. Ari noted that Quikk was in his hero pose, his arms akimbo, his mouth in a broad grin. "Greetings, all!" he called out. The response was half-hearted waves followed by everyone going right back to their drinks. "Darling! I was looking all over town for you!"

"Yeah?" said Simon. "How long did that take?"

"Thirty-seven seconds, but I had a lot on my mind. Come on, Vikki. We have a photo op!"

"A photo op?" she echoed.

"That's right! I just saved a jumper from falling to certain death! There's photographers galore! So I figured, what could be better than some nice big pictures of me next to my best girl!"

"What indeed?" said Ari.

"Okay, well, sure," said Vikki.

"Vikki," Simon began to say, "I—there's something we need to discuss." He was glaring up at Captain Quikk and Ari noticed a warning look in the Captain's eyes. Ari had a feeling that he knew what Simon was going to say, and he further had a feeling that the Captain also knew.

"Can it wait, Simon? I think"—she squeezed Quikk's hand—"the Captain needs me right now."

Simon hesitated for what seemed an age. When he spoke, he was glaring at Ari but addressing Vikki. "Yeah. Sure. Wouldn't want to, y'know . . . get in between you guys."

"Oh, you'd never do something like that, Simon," said Vikki. "I know you better than th—"

"Time to go," said Captain Quikk, and just like that, he was gone. So was she. The only trace left was a surge of air that blew napkins all over the place. Selkie muttered a curse in her native tongue and started cleaning them up.

"Tell me he gets his," said Simon.

"I'm sure that somehow he—"

"Not you, man," Simon interrupted Ari. He was now looking at Xander. "Tell me. Tell me he gets his."

Slowly Xander nodded.

"I mean that he gets his in this life, not the next one. And this—I dunno—this particular reality instead of some other dimension or something. That that guy, right there"—he pointed toward the door—"who just left with Vikki . . . that it doesn't end well for him. And that it doesn't end well in my lifetime and I get to see it."

"You're responsible for it," said Xander.

Simon grinned. "Out-freaking-standing." He picked up his beer.

"You don't want to know the details?"

"Don't need to, dude. Let it be a surprise. Sometimes just knowing is enough, y'know?"

"Like knowing what's right?" said Ari.

"Whatever." He sighed. "Women. They mess with your head."

"Everyone messes with your head. That's what friends are for: to help you keep it on straight."

Zola stopped by the table. She was wavering slightly; apparently she'd had a bit more ouzo than was typical for her. "Make it seven forty-five, all right, darling? Give me another fifteen minutes to be at my best," she said to Ari.

"Yeah, okay." Ari was suddenly very intent on staring down into his glass. He realized he'd neglected to return the sunglasses to Vikki, and then decided that it was a fortunate memory lapse.

"Simon"—she smiled sweetly at him—"I couldn't help but listen in before. I think you handled that ghastly speedster with admirable restraint."

"Thanks, Zola."

She ruffled his fur. "Honestly, I thought you were just going to throw feces at him." And she sashayed out the door.

"Yeah," sighed Simon, "that joke just never gets old."

Joseph Mallozzi is best known as writer and executive producer of the *Stargate SG-1*, *Stargate: Atlantis*, and *Stargate Universe* television series. Other television credits include *Big Wolf on Campus*, *Student Bodies*, and *The Busy World of Richard Scarry*, among many others. He also runs a science fiction and fantasy book-of-the-month discussion group on his blog (http://josephmallozzi.wordpress.com), which invites genre authors to participate in group Q & A sessions. A veteran of numerous teleplays, this is his first ever work of straight prose. I am supremely confident that the universe would be a poorer place if it proved to be his last.

Downfall

Joseph Mallozzi

He was pummeling the fourth one into submission, raining a barrage of bare-fisted blows down on the combat suit's delightfully malleable helm, when he realized that a large section of the bank's west wall had collapsed, allowing onlookers an unobstructed view of the proceedings. From their vantage across the street, he reasoned, any cell phone videos would prove spotty at best. Still, the optics were bad and he couldn't chance a fresh YouTube fiasco. His publicist would have another meltdown and that would mean one more round of morning show apologies and children's hospital visits. The very thought made him ill.

Abandoning his long-unconscious opponent, he threw a look to the remaining three as they crawled out from under the rubble. In their diamond-thread virinium-reinforced battle armor, they were more than a match for any hero. But, unfortunately for them, he wasn't just any hero. He was The Imperial, "Vanguard of Justice," "The People's Protector," and the only reason they were still standing was because he'd been holding back, toying with them, partly out of a desire to deliver a powerful lesson (*Stay in school, kids! Don't rob banks!*) and partly in the hope that an extended skirmish would help snap him out of his present funk, an inexplicable lassitude that had descended on him that morning like some ponderous blanket sodden with ennui and the lingering odor of last night's chicken shawarma. However, six minutes into the fray and some considerable structural damage later, he still wasn't feeling any better. That fact, coupled with their ever-growing audience, simply curdled his already sour mood. As much as he would have enjoyed the cathartic release of an elaborate beatdown, he knew that present circumstances would not allow it. Time to wrap things up.

His adversaries seemed to come to the same conclusion and simultaneously launched into action. One spearheaded the attack, vaulting over the information desk and coming in with a driving double-legged strike, while the other two moved to close. They may as well have been moving in slow motion. The Imperial pivoted, rolling the lead blow off one shoulder, and followed through, clapping his hand around a booted ankle and swinging his opponent round, sweeping the area clear of obstructions: a deposit station, some promotional displays, and one of the other battle-suited thugs. Their helms connected with a resounding clang, and a piece of someone's faceplate ricocheted off a teller's window, nicking a silver dollar-sized chip out of the thick plastic surface.

The first attacker went cartwheeling across the room, obliterating an enormous placard depicting a happy couple and an equally happy malamute taking possession of their first home. The other simply folded in on himself, buckling to a cross-legged sitting position, head bowed, looking as though he'd grown suddenly weary of the skirmish and decided on a meditative interlude. *You guys go ahead. I'll sit this one out.*

The last one demonstrated an impressive burst of speed, covering the distance between where he'd been standing and the exit in less than half a second. But The Imperial was already there, intercepting him with an outstretched hand that stopped him dead, collapsed his chest plate, and broke almost every one of his ribs. Then, before gravity could lay claim, the Vanguard of Justice swept him up and slammed him down, one-handed, in a thunderous finishing move that shattered the concrete floor, shook the building, and, more important, set the bystanders buzzing. *Upload THAT, bitches!*

He opted for the more theatrical exit through the hole in the west wall, striding over the debris to take full advantage of the photo op presented by the local press who had finally arrived on the scene. Shouts were raised. Photos snapped. The Imperial acknowledged his many fans with a wave and his trademark self-effacing grin. A quick scan of the crowd revealed Eliana Herrera, KDVB Action News reporter and host of the top-rated Herrera's Heroes, desperately trying to draw his attention. She was one of his favorites: smart, syndicated, and a spitfire in the bedroom. Acknowledging her with a nod that let her know she'd just landed herself an exclusive, he started toward her.

At which point the nausea struck. He held up, his stomach roiling, his head swimming with the enormity of what he was experiencing. He was feeling sick. Sick! How the hell was that possible? His enhanced constitution ensured this sort of thing didn't happen. He'd never had so much as a cold in his life. His body metabolized alcohol as fast as he could down it. And yet, here he was, in full view of his adoring public, suddenly as queasy and lightheaded as a post-prom princess.

Nightly News segment be damned. He couldn't let them see him like this.

Without so much as a parting sound byte, he abruptly spun on his heels, away from a surprised Eliana Herrera, took a running start and jumped, clearing a row of parked cars and a high-end chocolate shop before initiating his jet boots and shooting skyward. Up and away.

Two seconds later, he passed out.

On the other side of town, having concluded their high school presentation on the joys of abstinence, the cybernetic duo known as Twin Atomica powered up their nuclear cores and took flight. They left St. Ignatius at 10:03 a.m., headed west toward their Inner Sanctum Headquarters in Little Italy.

While an unconscious Imperial streaked north at a little under the speed of sound.

Their paths crossed approximately two and a half miles over Midtown.

The ensuing explosion and fallout forced the evacuation of twelve city blocks.

☆　★　☆

Their walk along the foot trails of the arboretum took them all the way around Lancaster Lake, by the bird sanctuary, then circling back past the school and the rec center still under construction. Remy stayed close, occasionally straying to sniff a suspicious bush or mark his territory, but the second they passed the tree line bordering Miller Park, he was off, tearing across the open field toward the playground. By the time a breathless Marshall caught up, the black lab was sprawled on his back, basking in the attention of a group of children.

"Bad dog," scolded Marshall in a face-saving gesture that convinced no one. "Get over here." His bad dog responded by scrambling up and bounding off, much to the delight of the kids who hooted, hollered, and gave chase.

"Now you're never getting him back," offered Jennifer Hollins from one of the park benches where she sat alongside some of the other neighborhood parents. In her faded blue jeans and halter top, the pretty, raven-haired former model was the unabashed standard for the term "hot mommy" as it applied in most erotic fiction. Her husband, by contrast, a former shortstop for the local Triple-A affiliate whose one and only call-up to the majors was cut short by a line-drive nut shot that had made ESPN's Not Top 10 Plays of that year, was the quintessential lout. How he'd managed to land her was a mystery that had haunted the town for years.

"If I go back home without Remy, I'll be the one sleeping in the doghouse," Marshall informed her, watching the merry pursuit.

"You and Allison coming Saturday?" asked single father Ramesh Dosanjh, the only male in the group. "I hear Tony is bringing his new girlfriend." Recently-divorced Tony Salazar was reputed to be dating a stripper from Sweet and Sassy, a gentlemen's club in nearby Fielding County, positively scandalizing the local community. Durham Falls hadn't been rocked this hard since that time Mrs. Obershon, the town librarian, had had her secret *Hustler* subscription inadvertently delivered to her place of work.

"We'll be there," Marshall assured him. "Here's hoping she brings her tassels."

Jennifer threw him a look of mock disapproval. He smiled and watched Remy fake out the fast-closing kids, feinting left then darting right. Devon, Marcie Krutzen's eldest, pounced and came up short, hitting the ground face-first. A sharp gasp from one of the mothers and, as if on cue, all the parents rose as one. But Devon was quickly back on his feet, spitting up grass and resuming the chase undaunted. Relieved, the adults exchanged smiles and headshakes, retaking their seats, catastrophe averted.

And suddenly, Marshall felt acutely self-conscious standing there, the outsider in their midst playing at fatherhood, doting over his four-legged fur baby while they good-naturedly humored his paternal affection. Mid-thirties, married, yet childless. Did they ever wonder? Did they even care? Or was he simply allowing his own self-doubt to fuel paranoid imaginings of them, gathered at the local Starbucks, speculating about the relative strength of his swimmers over macchiatos and carrot cake? He tried to dismiss the thought but, once considered, it ate at him like some shameful secret.

In truth, the decision to not have children had been a mutual one, a logical and ultimately difficult sacrifice, and yet, while he had been able to make peace with the situation, he wasn't so sure about Allison. It wasn't anything she ever said or did but more the notable omissions—her increasing disinterest in neighborhood get-togethers, her self-imposed exile from family events. Doubtless his wife already had an excuse in mind for why she wouldn't be able to attend the Dosanjh barbecue.

"Remy!" he snapped. The tone of his voice instantly commanded the lab's attention, let it know he was no longer kidding around. Remy trotted over, tail down, chastened. Marshall gave the dog a pat on the head. "Time to go, buddy." Buoyed, Remy bounded off again, this time toward the boxwood-lined sidewalk of Sumac Avenue. Marshall followed.

"See you Saturday!" Ramesh called after him.

"See you then." And they headed home.

Marshall spotted the black SUV in the driveway as he turned down Spruce Crescent. Black, tinted windows, government plates. They may as well have landed a helicopter on his front lawn. As he approached, he was suddenly seized by the urge to turn and retrace his steps, wait out the day at the park, and come back after dinner once they'd left. But he knew they weren't going anywhere.

They met him as he made his way up the walk, two of them in dark suits and standard-issue shades. And it wasn't even sunny. They flashed their badges and invited Marshall inside, into his own home. They needed to talk to him.

☆   ★   ☆

They introduced themselves as Agents McNeil and Bryerson. McNeil was the talker. Slim and youthful, he struck Marshall as atypically warm for a fed, almost amiable in his approach. Bryerson, on the other hand, was more of what Marshall had come to expect from the bureau. A buzz-cut bruiser with a sour disposition, he kept his shades on.

A clearly concerned Allison set down the coffee tray and biscuits, then excused herself and headed upstairs without so much as a backward glance. Marshall watched her go. She was no doubt dreading the prospect of another move, and the thought of putting her through the process yet again filled him with a deep regret that instantly gave way to anger. It wasn't fair. They should have been free and clear. What now?

McNeil waited until he heard the bedroom door click shut before starting: "Mr. Mayhew, do you know why we're here?"

Ten years ago, that question would have garnered the type of smart-ass response that usually resulted in an interrogation room beating. But, of course, a lot had changed in ten years. For one, his clothing was no longer fashioned from oscillating molecular fabric, meaning it could tear and stain. So, instead, he asked: "Where's Agent Palmer? I usually deal with him."

"Agent Palmer passed away in May," McNeil informed him. "Heart attack."

"Oh." Marshall was genuinely dismayed. "I'm sorry to hear."

"Are you?" Bryerson sneered from where he sat, arms crossed, seemingly defying Marshall to contradict him.

"Yeah, I am," said Marshall. "He was a good man."

McNeil dropped his gaze and adjusted his cuffs. "Yes, he was." And then, right back to business: "I assume you heard about what happened to The Imperial."

"Sure," said Marshall. It would have been impossible to miss the lead news story going on three days running.

"Were you sorry to hear about that too?" challenged Bryerson.

"No," Marshall responded truthfully. "Not really. He was an asshole." And, when all was said and done, and all personal animosity set aside, that pretty much summed him up, although "petty," "spiteful," and—as Marshall had discovered firsthand— "incredibly vindictive" would've done in a pinch. Whereas other heroes tended to simply crash the party and arrest you, only resorting to violence when absolutely necessary, The Imperial seemed to derive sadistic pleasure in punishing offenders. He never just hauled you in. He had to humiliate you first, whether it was a bitch-slapping, a literal ass-kicking, or his patented "forced freefall" that had reduced even the chronically stoic Dr. Disastro to tears. All things being equal, a primetime takedown by the buffoonish Captain Spectacular at his grandstanding best would have been preferable to the self-proclaimed People's Protector who, amusingly enough, ended up needing some legal protection of his own the time Ray Mephistopheles brought that civil suit against him.

"Sounds like motive," noted Bryerson.

That remark won him a bemused look from Marshall. The Imperial was a heavy hitter. He'd thrown down with the likes of Star Father Celestio and Shatterdam. To suggest that Marshall could have had a hand in taking him out was beyond ridiculous. It was downright flattering.

"Marshall, we're not accusing you of anything," McNeil was quick to clarify, sparing his partner the briefest of glances. "We're here because we think you can help us find out who killed him."

Marshall eyed them uncertainly. He'd had his suspicions, but never expected to have them officially confirmed. He elected to play it coy. "Killed him? They said it was an accident."

"Yeah," said McNeil. "That is what they said. But we know better, don't we? The Imperial was damn near invincible. It would've taken a hell of a lot more than that midair collision to take him out. He was compromised." McNeil threw Marshall a meaningful look, waiting for him to ask. He didn't. So the fed went ahead and answered him anyway. "A spectral analysis detected traces of ferenium-17 on his remains."

"Ferenium-17?" Marshall was stunned. Although Planetary Judicial Enforcement had officially denied its existence, the criminal underworld had long held that the fabled element did, in fact, exist. According to those in the know who had heard from those with an intimate knowledge who had been informed by reliable sources, ferenium-17 was a low-level radioactive mineral, extraterrestrial in origin, that, while reputedly harmless to humans, was rumored to have devastating effects on certain ultracapable individuals. No specifics on what, exactly, those devastating effects could be, but speculation ranged from mild disorientation to molecular degradation.

"You've heard of it," said McNeil. It was more a statement of fact than a question.

Marshall nodded.

"Not many individuals have the knowledge or the resources to get their hands on ferenium-17," McNeil continued. "In fact, I'd say there are only four we know of. One is busy serving ninety-eighty consecutive life terms on terrorism-related charges at Bathgate. Another quit the planet last year after getting his ass kicked by the Confederacy of Justice. Another was presumed killed in the explosion that destroyed that particle accelerator last fall. And the fourth . . . well, the fourth is someone you know."

"Someone I used to know," Marshall corrected him, well aware of where this was going. "A long time ago."

Agent Bryerson leaned in, forearms on knees, cocked his head and smiled. He reminded Marshall of that cartoon shark from the Freshwater Tuna commercial. "Yeah, well—we're going to need you to reconnect. Help us out, right?"

"And why would I want to do that?" But, of course, Marshall already knew the answer.

"Because," Agent McNeil reminded him, "the terms of your conditional release require you to."

Marshall sat back and had a shortbread cookie. Allison was in luck. It looked like they wouldn't be making the Dosanjh barbecue after all.

☆　★　☆

He stopped by the hospital on his way to the airport and found his mother up in her room, rereading one of her favorite Maeve Binchys while Joanie, her nurse, sat at the foot of the bed, wrapping presents. The plump Filipina spotted him first. "Emma, look who is here!" she announced, setting aside the red and gold Chinese-themed gift boxes his mother had no doubt picked up from the stationery shop in the facility's main lobby. "It's Marshall!"

His mother patiently finished the passage she was reading, bookmarked the spot, and set her well-worn copy of *The Glass Lake* aside before greeting him with a "Hello, sweetheart." Then quickly over to Joanie—"That one's for Jeffrey, the weekend intern," indicating one of the boxes. "Better mark it now or you'll mix them up."

"I come back and finish these later. You spend time with your son." Joanie hopped up, grinned, and cocked her head back toward the bed. "Maybe she can tell you about the handsome man who came to visit her last week. Very distinguished looking."

Marshall threw his mother an amused look. She frowned back, clearly annoyed, and dismissed the suggestion with a flick of her wrist. "He had the wrong room. He was looking for Mrs. Henry in D wing."

"Then I hope you got his number before he left." And with that, Joanie was out the door.

His mother gave a sad shake of her head. "Poor girl. Her husband has the shingles, you know. She's here all day taking care of me, then goes home at night and takes care of him. What a life." Then, as if suddenly realizing: "Where's Allison?"

Allison, he informed her, was at work. No, they hadn't argued. No, nothing was wrong. He was alone because he was heading out of town for a few days and wanted to make sure he got to see her before he left. This seemed to satisfy his mother, who, as a rule, was predisposed to worst-case scenarios, reading domestic strife into the most innocuous things: a missed appointment, a passing comment, that well-worn copy of *Chicken Soup for the Soul* Allison had been carrying around with her the last time they'd come to visit.

Of course, Marshall had to remind himself that past experience excused a lot. His mother had raised him as a single parent with little in the way of an education or vocational training, her days spent booking discount getaways at a local travel agency, her nights devoted to editing the letters section of what she termed "a saucy gentleman's rag." And yet, despite the long odds and even longer hours, she'd always found the time to be there for him. Like the time fellow third-grader Melanie Fincher broke his heart. Or the day his abilities first manifested themselves in the heat of an after-school bullying incident.

The events that led up to his being cornered that afternoon were lost to memory, but Marshall distinctly recalled the sensation of overwhelming terror that had swept over him like a pre-op anesthetic, rooting him where he stood, the moment Wally Briggs strode up to him that fateful day. His friends, of course, had bolted at the first sign of trouble, abandoning him to the not so tender mercies of the playground Fates, they who judged so harshly upon the weak, the overweight, and the awkwardly named. In retrospect, Marshall couldn't really blame them. But at the time, doubled over by a shot to the solar plexus, his head firmly nestled between Wally's bicep and forearm, he did blame them. He blamed them a lot. And as he dropped to one knee in a misguided attempt at passive resistance, and Wally countered the move by shifting his weight and tightening his grip, permitting himself a far more effective choke hold, Marshall had felt another sensation suddenly sweep through him—hotter, sharper, more intense than mere fear. It was the devastating awareness of his own utter humiliation. And that turned out to be the trigger. He felt his face flush; the back of his head prickle. Then, the next thing he knew, he was sitting on the grass, fighting to catch his breath while, almost twenty feet away, Wally Briggs lay on his back, clutching his leg and howling in pain. They were the only two in the schoolyard. Confused and more than a little terrified, he ended up running the entire sixteen blocks home.

Later that night, Wally's father had come calling. He angrily informed his mother that Wally's ankle was badly twisted, Marshall was responsible, and what the hell was she going to do about it?! What she did was launch into a stunning, expletive-ridden tirade that Marshall had never before and, thankfully, never again, borne witness to, capped by the promise that Wally could expect much worse if he ever bothered her son again. Mr. Briggs, an ogre of a man at well over six feet and built like one of those Saturday matinee wrestlers Marshall used to watch on TV, simply wilted under the verbal onslaught meted out by this four foot eight, one hundred and five pound she-devil, and quietly slunk away.

After which he and his mother had "the talk." She informed him that he was special, possessed of certain abilities that set him apart from his fellow classmates and that, over time, these abilities would begin to manifest themselves with greater frequency. Exactly how, however, was impossible to predict. One day, he might be a little faster; another, a little stronger. The thing to remember, she told him, was not to be afraid, but to accept these talents as something uniquely his, and, most important of all, to keep them a closely guarded secret.

Despite his curiosity about his newfound abilities and her willingness to discuss them, there was one mystery she seemed unable (as it turned out, unwilling) to solve for him: Why? Why him? Why was he different? This particular question seemed to cause her great consternation and, after repeated queries, she finally settled on the answer she would offer from then on: It was a gift. And for all intents and purposes, that settled the matter.

Until many years later when a high school biology lesson changed everything.

"What's with the presents?" asked Marshall, picking up one of the gift boxes and giving it a cursory once-over. It smelled of jasmine and sandalwood. "It's too early for Christmas."

"Well, I might not be around for Christmas," she informed him with a trace of whimsy, getting up and putting on her slippers.

"Mom, you just had a physical. Your PSA levels were fine. Aside from your hip, the doctor said you're in perfect health."

"That doesn't mean anything," she countered. "You remember Mr. Rosenfeld from across the hall? He passed away last week."

"Yeah, I heard. He was kayaking in New Zealand when it happened."

"That's my point. You never know." She moved the boxes off the bed, carefully aligning them on the windowsill. "That's why you should seize the opportunities when they present themselves. If you wait too long, it may be too late."

"Too late? Too late for what?"

She sighed wearily and suddenly changed tack, turning to face him. "There comes a time in everyone's life when they finally stop to take stock. And they ask themselves, What have I accomplished? How will I be remembered? What do I leave behind?" She offered a melancholy smile. "And I look at you and I have my answers."

"It could have gone the other way," he felt the need to remind her. "I could still be in prison, or worse."

"Is that what's stopping you?" she asked. "The fear that your children may follow in your footsteps?"

He stared at her. *What the hell brought this on?*, he wanted to ask. Instead, in an attempt to curtail further discussion he went with: "It's more than that. It's different for me, Mom. You know it is."

"Yes," she agreed, "it is different because you'll provide a stable home for your children. You'll be there for them." She lay a hand on his cheek, a gesture reminiscent of bygone heart-to-hearts and, in that instant, he was eight again and alarmingly unsure of himself. "Marshall, you didn't make bad decisions because you were faster or stronger than other people. You made bad decisions because your father was a deadbeat who wasn't there for you growing up, and your mother, God help me, tried her best but ended up failing you as well."

It was a rare admission of failure, and it troubled him greatly. "Mom, you didn't fail me. Don't ever—"

She sensed his unease and cut him off. "There's no reason you can't start a family. Not anymore. Just . . . talk to Allison when you get back. Will you do that?"

"Okay," he acquiesced, much to her obvious delight. "When I get back." And, in the back of his mind, for the first time and only to himself, he acknowledged the uncertainty of the coming days. *IF I come back.*

☆ ★ ☆

They had to wait for some connecting passengers returning from a Caribbean cruise and ended up leaving the gate forty-five minutes late. Fortunately, the bureau had demonstrated uncharacteristic largesse by booking him in business class so that by the time they finally touched down in Fortune City, he was three scotches and a couple of Chardonnays past caring. He caught a cab to the hotel, where a message from Agent Bryerson awaited. "He requested you call when you get in," the woman at the front desk politely informed him.

Marshall headed up to his room, unpacked, ordered a surprisingly good bison burger from room service, and then, after checking in with Allison and assuring her that, yes, he was being careful and that, no, he hadn't forgotten to pack his shaving gel (he actually had but didn't want to admit it because she'd made a point of reminding him twice before he left), he decided to walk the five blocks, through the old neighborhood, to Vinny's Tavern, picking up some shaving gel along the way.

The place was still there, right next door to a nail salon that had once been a wig shop and another wig shop before that. And it hadn't changed much in eight years, still boasting its original artwork: boxing prints, a stuffed moose head, and the wall-mounted samurai sword bequeathed to Vinny by one-time regular Wakizashi who, tragically, lost his life, not in honorable battle but under the wheels of the crosstown 364 bus. The establishment's venerable owner, however, was nowhere to be seen. Instead, a paunchy fellow with a salt-and-pepper walrus mustache ambled over to Marshall's table and greeted him with a raspy "What'll you have?"

"Draft. Whatever's on tap. Hey, Vinny around?"

Walrus fixed him with a pitying look, the sort you might give a child who'd just buried his pet frog. "No, Vinny ain't around. Vinny's dead."

It was devastating news and, in the back of his mind, a small, irrational part of Marshall claimed a Heisenbergesque responsibility. If he hadn't come back, Vinny would still be alive and well and just as he'd left him, serving up drinks to the likes of Demolition, The Blue Basilisk, and Damian Fortune. "What happened to him?"

"The Purple Lamprey happened to him. Vinny tried to break up a fight between him and Ray Mephistopheles, ended up catching a neuro-blast for his troubles. Three days later, they took him off life support. I bought the place from Francine, his widow, a couple of years back. Kept the name outta respect, y'know?" Walrus looked him over, trying to place the face. "You once a regular?"

"Once," conceded Marshall, wishing he could get that drink.

"What'd you go by?"

He hesitated, reluctant to say, as though doing so would bring it all back. But the fact was he'd brought it all back the second he'd stepped off that plane. "Downfall," Marshall told him.

A couple of seconds of careful consideration, and then Walrus's face lit up. "Shit, yeah. I remember you. You used to run with Princess Arcana and The Plague Zombies. What happened to you?"

"Prison. Prison happened to me. Hey, can I get that drink now?"

"Sure, sure," chuckled an oblivious Walrus, shaking his head and ambling off. "Downfall. Shit. I've got to get you to sign something."

The place was empty save for a bunch of college boys out celebrating a big sporting win and a businessman passed out in a booth at the back. A far cry from the old days when Vinny's was "the" gathering place for the city's underworld elite and ordinary, an egalitarian refuge from the perils and uncertainties of the cape and cowl daily grind where the law steered clear, adepts rubbed shoulders with amateurs, and all were welcome regardless of gender, social status, or planet of origin.

Marshall sighed out his disappointment. In all likelihood, this was a waste of time. Still, he was on the bureau's clock and it was kind of late to be launching a blind search for old friends and co-conspirators. He'd probably be better served taking the night off and starting fresh in the morning. So decided, he eased back and helped himself to the complimentary bowl of salty snacks, fishing out the lone pretzel amid the sea of predominantly stale cashews. He smiled inwardly and held it aloft, its shape vaguely reminiscent of a double helix.

Basic genetics. Dominant alleles. His mother's refusal to discuss the father who'd abandoned him. Over the course of a high school biology lesson, the seemingly unrelated pieces had coalesced to form a theory of revelatory significance. His mother was right. In many ways his newfound abilities *had* been a gift, one determined by hereditary predisposition, passed on to him by a man he never knew. He truly was, it turned out, his father's son.

Of course, that had only opened the door to a host of other questions, questions he never dared put to her. So, instead, he watched the news reports, read the papers, and formed his own theories based on indicators such as like abilities, physical similarities, timeline opportunities, and his mother's frustratingly all-too-subtle reactions to the numerous costumed heroes who would grace the evening news and Leno's couch. Dynamix was a possibility because he was quick and his eyes were green, while Star Drive was an early scratch because it turned out he was just a regular human whose powers were derived from a form-fitting exosuit. Nantech seemed an interesting candidate because he was strong *and* fast and, according to an interview in *People* magazine, shared Marshall's affinity for Hawaiian pizza and extra-thick chocolate shakes, while DataStorm seemed less likely because he was rumored to be Asian and then actually turned out to be a Caucasian woman with a voice calibrator built into her helmet mic. Ansible, Zero-G, Paradrive, and Moon Shift were definite maybes. Major Singularity, Neuromatik, Hyperjump, and Dionysus Jackson were not.

He kept a running list in a dedicated notebook that he continually updated and revised, adding names, striking others, rearranging the prospects in order of likelihood. But eventually, the speculation became less important to him as other aspects of his life began to intrude and command his attention. Girls, school, friends, and, of course, girls. He lost his notebook on a school trip to the Grand Canyon and never bothered replacing it. In the end, he never stopped wondering. He just stopped caring.

Marshall popped the pretzel into his mouth, effectively snuffing the memories.

It turned out to be a relaxing couple of hours. He knocked back a couple of drafts while watching a late college game on the tavern's big screen, politely turned down an offer from a tipsy cougar out celebrating a friend's engagement, and even signed the back of a Budweiser poster for Walrus: "To Jermaine, Keep the dream alive.

Your pal, Downfall." It was just after midnight, as he was finishing up what he'd planned on being his last beer, when he heard someone call his name. Assuming he'd misheard because whoever it was couldn't possibly be addressing him, Marshall didn't even bother acknowledging the speaker. But the second "Marsh!", emphatic, almost indignant, made him turn.

And the sight that greeted him when he did was a prospect so bizarre, so altogether wrong, that it took Marshall several seconds to convince himself that he hadn't lost his mind and that, yes, it was Terry Langan standing there, fists on hips, grinning at him like he'd just cracked the sentinel system to the real Fort Knox beneath the Lincoln Memorial. Clean shaven, roughly twenty pounds lighter, and sporting a stylish tan leather jacket over a white cotton dress shirt and black slacks, he looked, thought an amazed Marshall, much better in death than he had ever looked in life.

☆ ★ ☆

They caught each other up over several rounds, Marshall filling Terry in on the monotony of prison life and his eventual return to freedom, conveniently leaving out the details of his conditional release, suburban do-over, and the terms of his all-expenses-paid trip to the old neighborhood, while Terry enlightened Marshall on just how the hell he was still alive given that the last time Marshall had seen him, Terry and his associates were being buried under several tons of debris.

"Force-shield generator," his old friend explained, knocking back a shot of Tennessee whiskey and grimacing. "Part of the Professor's bag of tricks. He activated it in the nick of time; saved the whole damn crew." He sighed contentedly, sank back in his chair, resting his clasped hands on his chest, and sniffed. "It was crazy. One second we were as good as dead and the next . . ." The very memory made him shake his head in dazed disbelief. "Nobody said a word. Nobody even moved. That shield was eggshell thin and so clear we could make out every piece of fucking rubble hanging over our heads. Took him a while but, eventually, the Professor was able to expand the field and get us out."

"Ha!" Marshall clapped a hand on his long-thought-lost friend's shoulder. He would have gotten up and hugged him but for fear that in his inebriated state, the all-too-tricky maneuver would land him face-first on the suspiciously sticky floor. Instead, he smiled, knocked back his shot, and marveled at the twists and turns that typified his alternately dazzling and disheartening once-profession.

He and Terry had met as hired muscle for an anthropoid dandy who went by Python, a colorful if not altogether noteworthy miscreant with an affinity for bowler hats and the works of W. H. Auden. As fellow first-timers, they had been given the relatively straightforward task of taking up position at the bank's back emergency exit to ensure no one went in or out while the heist was in progress. They acquitted themselves nicely, looking their nonchalant best as they manned their post, casually chatting about the state of officiating in professional sports, a recent political scandal, and whether or not Vin Diesel should ever make another movie. And then, the alarm went off. Too late, both realized that, while doing a bang-up job of keeping an eye out for enterers and exiters, they'd done a comparatively poorer job of keeping track of time and were thus late for their own getaway. By the time they scrambled around the corner, the Crown Vic was long gone.

To their credit, they didn't panic, simply strolling by the crime scene as curious observers, then catching a bus back to the hideout. Or close to it anyway, because, by the time they got there, police were already on the scene and the entire block had been cordoned off. And so, instead of prison, they ended up celebrating their not-exactly-good-but-not-altogether-bad luck in a manner that would become tradition: over shots of J.D. at Vinny's.

Over time, they became fast friends, henching for the likes of MaNYEik, Dragoon, and the sullen Firewire before he found God and renounced his sinful ways to become a Baptist minister in Charlotte. Eventually, however, Marshall grew tired of playing second banana to megalomaniacs and Machiavells whose best laid schemes were, all too often, uncredited rehashes of old movie plots—hijacking a treasury plane, launching a solar-powered satellite weapon, threatening Silicon Valley with a massive double earthquake, perfecting a subspecies of flying piranha—so when the opportunity presented itself, he seized it, parlaying his deep-seated dissatisfaction and a modest poker win into a step up in the criminal underworld, adopting the Downfall persona and striking out on his own. To arguable success. He and Terry lost touch after that, occasionally reconnecting at Vinny's or on a joint op like the U.N. takedown. But it was never quite the same after Marshall went solo.

"You were damn lucky," said Marshall.

"We came out of that rubble expecting to go another round, probably get our asses handed to us, but by the time we saw daylight again, the heroes were long gone."

"Yeah, they were busy ferrying everyone clear of the potential blast zone," Marshall recalled. He himself had been one of their charges, a helpless sack of flesh, alert to his circumstances yet helpless to react, his motor functions short-circuited by Nantech's miniature invaders. His last ride as Downfall.

"Right. So the Professor initiated the oscillator's self-destruct and we cleared out. When that thing blew—"

"Wait a minute," Marshall interrupted. "Bedlam triggered the self-destruct?"

"Oh, yeah," Terry responded matter-of-factly, as if explosions vaporized everything within a two-mile radius of secret Mojave labs all the time. "If you think about it, it was genius." Clearly, Marshall was having a hard time thinking about it, so Terry elucidated: "The Professor was done. The heroes were going to get their hands on his oscillator anyway. Eventually, they'd have taken it apart, reverse-engineered their own version, and then some mental midget like QuickThink would've claimed he'd invented it like he did the Volcanizer or the Weather Accelerator. The Professor figured he'd rather start from scratch than let that little prick cop himself another Nobel Prize in Physics. So we all started over. As far as anyone knows, Professor Bedlam and his Agents of Chaos are dead."

"So you guys took yourselves out of the game?" The whole scenario struck Marshall as altogether bizarre. And most un-Terry-like.

"Didn't say we were out of the game." Terry leaned in conspiratorially, looked around to make sure the businessman was still passed out in that booth at the back, and lowered his voice. "Professor Bedlam and the Agents of Chaos may be history, but Brainstorm and his Cerebellum Squad are alive and kicking."

"Cerebellum Squad?"

Terry waved off the implied criticism. "Look, all I know is we're off the radar and these new outfits are killer. Did you ever try on one of those Chaos suits?

Marshall had to admit he hadn't.

"They weren't particularly well insulated. And they never got the boots right. They were always too tight around the toes."

"So, Brainstorm and the Cerebellum Squad," said Marshall, still far from convinced.

"We hit a few banks. Run protection on a drug shipment or two. Nothing flashy, but enough to keep us in coin and the Professor in plutonium and weapons-grade rividium."

It all sounded unnecessarily complicated, but Marshall saw no point in arguing the logic. Whatever strange turn his life had taken certainly seemed to agree with Terry, who looked better than he had in years.

"So how long you been out?" asked Terry.

"Not long."

An awkward lull in the conversation as Terry deliberated and then, almost reluctantly: "Hey, if you want, I can talk to the Professor, see if I can get you in with us."

"No, I'm not looking for work."

Terry was palpably relieved.

"I'm looking for Adam Virtue."

"Adam?" Terry jerked his head back and squinted, his telltale way of letting you know he was genuinely perplexed and/or thought you were nuts. "Geez, it's been a while. Why do you want to look

him up for? The old-timer hasn't had anything going on in years."
And then, suddenly intrigued: "Has he?"

"I don't know," said Marshall. "But, like I said, I'm not looking
for a job. I just want to say hi."

Terry seemed to find it a strange request, frowning down into
his lap and taking a few seconds to think about it. Long enough for
Walrus to deliver their next round. Whatever internal battle raged
within him was immediately decided at the sight of those amber
shots. "All right," he announced, suddenly upbeat. "I'll ask around,
see if I can track him down for you." He raised a glass. "To crimes
past."

"And scores future."

☆　★　☆

He was aswim in darkness, a thick, torpid presence that pressed
up against him, obstructing sight and sound. He shifted and felt it
recede, its soft black essence drawing back slightly and then, suddenly, solidifying. Six inches to either side and directly above. He
became aware of his own heartbeat, its quickening thrum pulsing
in his ears, the tips of his fingers. He tried to cry out, let them know
he was still alive, but his parched throat could manage little more
than a strangled gasp.

A shuddering thud as the first shovelful of earth struck his coffin, dirt and dust filtering through the shifting slats to sprinkle his
exposed face and neck. Full panic snapped him out of his paralytic
stupor. He struggled wildly. Sounds filtered down to him through
the mounting barrier of soil and mud. Traffic. Voices. The flush
of some distant toilet. He fought to get air to his oxygen-deprived
lungs, the tangible darkness closing in on him once again. And, as
he thrashed and kicked and struggled to give voice to his terror,
he became aware of two things. One: the walls of his coffin had
magically dissolved away and he was able to breathe freely once
again. And, two: the burial earth on his face tasted a lot like chipotle
barbecue.

He opened his eyes. The first sight to greet his resurrection was that of Agent Bryerson looming over him, casually munching from a bag of Olde Southern Hand Cut Chips. "He's alive after all!" he said, looking vaguely disappointed. From the bathroom at the end of the hall came the sound of a faucet running.

"What time is it?" Marshall propped himself up on his elbows and searched the room for the bedside clock he could have sworn had been sitting on the dresser the night before. Nauseous, disoriented, and thoroughly dehydrated, he hadn't felt quite this crap since that time he caught a Juno Jones disruptor shock full in the face. Of course on that occasion, sweet unconsciousness had been his savior. No such luck this time.

"Ten-fifteen," announced Agent McNeil as he stepped out of the bathroom and shot his cuffs.

"You were supposed to contact us when you got in," said Bryerson. "We left you a message."

"I didn't get it."

"Bull shit." Byrerson pronounced it as two separate words.

McNeil raised his hand in a calming gesture. Bryerson responded by sucking his teeth, a mannerism Marshall had always assumed proprietary to Jamaicans and white rappers. The big man crushed the chip bag in his meaty fist and tossed it in the general direction of the trash basket. It sailed wide and disappeared behind the desk.

"So what happened last night?" asked McNeil.

"I went to Vinny's Tavern, a gathering place for the local riffraff back in my time. Ended up meeting someone who might be able to get me a line on Virtue."

"Oh yeah? Who?" Bryerson wanted to know.

Marshall hesitated. The code of the underworld dictated he be circumspect when discussing former associates, especially a former associate he'd once considered a friend, and, in particular, a former associate and friend who was now, for all intents and purposes, officially dead. He wished he'd had the opportunity to prep a suitable cover story, but he'd been caught flatfooted and quickly realized there was no way he was going to spin his way out of this one.

"Withholding information could be considered a breech of your parole," McNeil prompted.

"Terry Langan," Marshall fessed up, hoping that as a relatively small fish in a pretty big barracuda pond, the details of his career profile wouldn't warrant too hard a look. "He works backup, hired muscle for some of the low-level players, but says he can tap some of his connections for me."

"And how likely is that, you figure?" asked McNeil.

Marshall shrugged. He honestly had no idea. The feds exchanged looks. Bryerson rolled his eyes, lost interest, and directed his attention to the minibar, squatting down to root through its contents.

"I gave him my number here at the hotel," said Marshall. "He said he'd be in touch as soon as he had something."

McNeil sighed. "Well, we can't just sit around, hoping he calls. Virtue is dangerous."

"Assuming he was responsible for what happened to The Imperial." Annoyed, Marshall got up, grabbed the open can of cola sitting amid the ruins of last night's dinner, and downed the cloying, lukewarm remnants, slaking his unearthly thirst.

McNeil fished a briefcase out from behind a chair and set it down on the desk. "Process of elimination makes him the most likely candidate."

"Fuck process of elimination." Marshall surprised himself with his own anger. He paused, softened. "Like I've been saying, Virtue's been out of the game longer than I have. Besides, he never had a beef with The Imperial. If he'd go after anyone, it'd be Captain Spectacular. Juno Jones, maybe."

"Then all you got to do is prove he's innocent and clear him." Bryerson, hunkered down in front of the minibar, pocketed minibottles of Chivas and Tanqueray. He briefly considered the Bailey's Irish Cream before slotting it back. "You'll actually be doing him a favor."

McNeil unsnapped and opened the briefcase, angling it to face Marshall so he could see the lone, black leather belt sitting within. "This is for you."

"And I didn't get you anything," quipped Marshall. McNeil's expression was inscrutable. Marshall stepped in and picked up the belt. Grooved striping and burnished silver buckle aside, it was wholly unremarkable.

"The buckle houses a solid-state radiation module capable of detecting trace amounts and residue," McNeil informed him. "It's been specifically calibrated to sniff out ferenium-17, which has a half-life of about two weeks."

"If Virtue's our guy, then we got him." This from Bryerson, who, having cleaned out the minibar to his satisfaction, straightened, both knees popping in protest.

"And if he isn't and we don't?" asked Marshall.

Bryerson shrugged, cocked his head, and offered his shark grin. "Then we'll thank you for your service to this great nation and hope that we never have to lay eyes on you again."

☆　★　☆

After impressing upon him the time-sensitive nature of the investigation, they left him to hit the streets and reconnect. Instead, Marshall went right back to bed. But he couldn't sleep and ended up spending several hours watching CNN's coverage of the mayhem in Atlanta. Early Wednesday morning, law enforcement officials backed by local heroes, including Georgia's favorite son, Johnny Victory, had descended on The Indigo Club in the city's Five Point district, igniting a firestorm that had transformed the downtown core into Battleground Zero. So far, damage estimates were in the hundreds of millions, with eighty-six confirmed dead and over two hundred missing, including Johnny Victory. Newly elected mayor Anthony Williams, who had campaigned on a tough-on-crime platform and authorized the ill-advised raid on the nightclub "notorious for catering to the city's criminal elements," had already tendered his resignation in a hastily convened press conference. Although order had been more or less restored with the arrival of Captain Spectacular and his Confederacy of Justice, open skirmishes were still being reported in isolated pockets of the city.

As he watched a live feed of Amnesty and The Silver Gryphon take down Flashback on the grounds of the Georgia Institute of Technology, Marshall couldn't help but wonder how a similar scenario would have played out on his old stomping grounds. Probably not all that differently, he eventually concluded. Nobody liked to have their downtime crashed, least of all volatile psychos like Shatterdam and The Purple Lamprey. Throw in The Imperial's reckless disregard for collateral damage and you'd have been lucky to have a building standing once the dust settled. Fortunately, the authorities in Fortune City had always had the good sense to steer clear. In his day, Vinny's, and a few places like it, were considered off-limits in the life-or-death battles waged by the costumed narcissists and their hangers-on, undeclared sanctuaries where the rules no longer applied, and every so often, it hadn't been uncommon to see the odd hero having a drink at the bar or holding a civilized conversation with someone whose headquarters he'd trashed only hours earlier.

The recollection of those days stirred a melancholy longing, something he found altogether baffling given that they'd been, for the most part, truly miserable times. Blaming the previous night's excesses, Marshall showered, dressed, and headed out for some fresh air.

Rather than pick up his spirits, however, the walkabout had the opposite effect. It was all somewhat surreal, like wandering a dreamworld cobbled together from fragmented pieces of memory, his surroundings familiar yet disquietingly incongruous. The Parkview Shopping Center, once a bustling hangout for highschoolers and determined shopaholics, was all but deserted, its high-end shops long gone, now little more than a collection of dollar stores and knickknack emporiums. The Win Wah Buffet had also disappeared, along with its room-temperature chicken balls and uninspired shrimp toast. Gone too was the Odessa Video run by the stoic Russian couple, the woodfire pizza place that was always running out of pepperoni, and the mailing depot that doubled as a doggy daycare because half the staff used to bring their pets in to work with them.

Some things had survived, transformed by time, while others had remained surprisingly unchanged. The Italian deli on Main Street for one. And even though he had never been a fan of the food back in the day, Marshall nevertheless grabbed a table at the adjoining café and enjoyed a sandwich and an espresso, finding comfort in the familiarity of the place.

Partway through the late lunch, his cell phone rang. It was Allison calling to check up on him. And she sounded unusually upbeat. Between booking their Hawaiian getaway and testing out new desserts for the Dosanjh barbecue, she was beginning to prep the house for the arrival of her parents, who would be coming in for a ten-day visit sometime next month. Marshall told her not to worry, that he was being careful, and that, hopefully, he'd be back before week's end.

It was only after he hung up that he was struck by her puzzling change of heart regarding the barbecue. On its own, it seemed trivial, but married to his mother's recent unsolicited advice . . . well, if he didn't know better, he'd suspect that they were in collusion. A few seconds of considered reflection and then it dawned on him that, in fact, he *didn't* know any better.

He paid for his meal and headed back to the hotel, his mind racing, reviewing past visits, past conversations, ferreting out incongruities, inconsistencies, correlations, and connections. The tumblers turned, aligned, and a potential conspiracy locked in place. Well, it would certainly explain a few things.

"Hey!"

He glanced up, reverie interrupted, to find Terry standing outside the hotel entrance. His old friend, styling in a black bomber jacket and jeans, grinned and jerked his thumb back to indicate the electric blue mustang parked across the street. "Let's go for a ride."

☆　★　☆

Terry sat behind the wheel, singing falsetto accompaniment to a pop tune while a detached Marshall took in the passing scenery from the passenger-side window. As the warbling vocals of Destiny Lewis singing "Gangbang Gravy" faded out, Terry turned off the radio and threw his former accomplice a sideways glance. "You okay?"

"Sure."

"Still hungover?"

"No." They passed through Chinatown, its faux-pagoda store-fronts and stone dragon-flanked entranceways timeworn and in disrepair, the once vibrant community now reduced to less than a third of its former glory by the defections of those who had abandoned their immigrant roots for a better life in the suburbs. "Can't believe how much has changed since I left."

"Well, it has been eight years."

"I know. Still—coming back and seeing things so different. It's . . ."

"Sad? Strange?"

"Yeah," said Marshall.

"I get it," said Terry. "You're feeling kinda disconnected."

"I know, it's silly—"

"No, it's not. It's like . . . everything you knew moved on without you and what used to be familiar is suddenly unfamiliar, hell, even a little scary."

"That's pretty much it," Marshall conceded, impressed by Terry's surprising empathy.

Terry nodded knowingly. "It's like watching that Brady Bunch reunion movie."

Marshall sized him up, uncertain as to whether he was kidding or not. And realized he wasn't. "Uh, yeah. Kind of like that."

Terry redirected his attention back to the road and gave a sad shake of his head. "Man, Greg got old."

In fact, it had all gotten old for Marshall some time ago, and being back reminded him of just how much he too had changed. And all it had taken was the love and support of a good woman, a willingness on his part to walk away, and, of course, those five years in prison.

Less than six months after she moved in with him, Allison stumbled across the Downfall uniform concealed behind the false wall of his closet. He came home one afternoon to find it draped over the couch, Allison seated right beside it, leafing through the latest issue of *Nefaria Weekly* with its coverage of the Decimator/ Princess Arcana wedding. "What's that?" he managed lamely. She threw him a look that extinguished any hope of escape, and the next thing he knew, he was fielding a barrage of questions. Yes, he was the ultracriminal responsible for crashing the Governor's Diamond Ball last spring. Yes, he'd been involved in that massive assault on L.A.W. headquarters. No, he had nothing to do with the break-in at the Metropolitan Museum timed to coincide with the Crown Prince of Brunei's Gold Shoe Exhibition. That was Deadfall.

She asked, he answered, she pressed, and he gave it all up: his atypical childhood, his secret identity, even his sole foray into team iniquity with the short-lived criminal cartel Pandemonium that eventually disbanded because people kept confusing them with the popular kids' band Pandamonium. In truth, it was an enormous relief to finally come clean, and after a while he required no prompting. Over the course of those six hours, Allison learned everything about his double life as Downfall, and, to his surprise, Marshall even discovered a little something about himself as well. Yes, more often than not crime did pay, and of course the camaraderie was an important part of it, but, when all was said and done, it was far simpler than that. He enjoyed being Downfall because it fed his ego. He had to admit, there was an undeniable rush that came with knowing he had fans, supporters who followed his criminal exploits with a fervor usually reserved for professional athletes and film celebrities. There was no greater satisfaction than seeing his name outrank the likes of middleweight heroes like Counterforce and Zero-G in the latest Google search rankings, or surfing the multitude of online communities dedicated to his alternate persona. Yes, it was ego that drove Downfall, but it was humility that killed him.

Humbled by Allison's willingness to forgive, he promised to change and immediately set out to make good on his word— trashing the uniform, cutting ties with his former cohorts, and enrolling in a web design program at the local community college. Downfall was done.

For about eight months, after which his funds dried up and the lure of a one-time-only score proved too much for him to resist. With the help of two associates, Ember and Blow-Out, he succeeded in tracking down the bio-signature of his Downfall uniform and rescued it from the local landfill, then joined Professor Bedlam and his Agents of Chaos in a multimillion-dollar extortion plot that, had it succeeded, would have set him up for life. Unfortunately, it all went sideways and he ended up in prison, doomed to reflect upon that last unlucky roll of the dice.

Allison didn't attend his trial, nor did she answer any of his letters, and after his first year in prison, he gave up hope of ever seeing her again. And so, when she eventually did pay him a surprise visit during that second year of incarceration, he was shocked, to say the least. She revealed that as much as she wanted to, she was unable to move on because she still loved him and, more importantly, still believed in him. Whether he believed in himself was another matter entirely.

And suddenly, Marshall did believe, and he attacked the remainder of his sentence with single-minded purpose, not once straying from his new role of model prisoner. After three years, his determination paid off with an offer of conditional release—provided he was willing to play ball with the authorities. Weary of his solitary existence and anxious to prove himself, he'd been more than willing.

"We're here," Terry announced.

Marshall frowned. "We are?"

"Yep." The parking lot wasn't that full. They were able to find a spot right in front of the Science Center entrance.

☆ ★ ☆

The entrance hall was alive with the recorded gibbers, chitters, squawks, and caterwauls of the animal kingdom. Upon catching sight of their approach, the redheaded teen at the reception desk

quickly wrapped up his phone conversation, clicking off and greeting them with an annoyingly chirpy "It's a great day to learn. Welcome to Science World. This month's exhibits include Dinosaur
Dynasty, a treat for children of all ages—"

"We're here to see someone," Terry cut to the chase. Then,
glancing down at the receptionist's name tag, added, "Dirk." He
smiled amiably—or attempted a close approximation thereof.
"We're looking for Muriel."

"Muriel is finishing the two-twenty Gideon Sundback Zippermania tour. It'll be wrapping up shortly in the blue room."

"Thanks." Terry started through the turnstiles. They locked,
catching him mid-thigh and doubling him over. He grunted something that sounded like "Ngraw!", then straightened and shot a
look back at Dirk, who cheerily inquired, "Will that be one ticket
or two?"

Marshall pulled out his wallet. "Two."

"No, no." Terry waved Marshall back. "This one's on me. Two
tickets."

Dirk rang them up. "Two tickets, eighteen dollars each. That'll
be thirty-six dollars in total."

"Thirty-six dollars!" cried Terry, clutching the lone fiver he
had fished out of his pocket. "For thirty-six dollars, those dinosaurs
better do a song and dance!"

"Actually, they do," Dirk blandly assured him.

"Well, I don't care! I'm still not paying that."

"It's all right." Marshall stepped up. "I've got it."

He paid and they proceeded into the boisterous main hall, passing a Parasites of the Human Body display and stopping to check
out the Robot Zoo exhibit en route to parking themselves outside
the blue room where Terry glowered, still bristling over the exorbi-
tant entrance fee and, to a lesser extent, his failed attempt to draw
the attention of the mechanical lemur. This, Marshall couldn't help
but note, was the same guy who had never thought twice about
dropping five to six hundred dollars a night visiting Fortune City's
upscale strip clubs. Marshall reminded him of the fact, but it did

little to mollify his old friend, who indignantly countered, "Strippers are real, Marsh. Dinosaurs aren't."

He was tempted to call him on it, but ultimately decided to give his buddy a pass. After all, he had come through for him. According to Terry, he had asked around, exhausted his sources, and apparently come up empty. So far as anyone knew, Adam Virtue had disappeared six years ago; vanished without a trace. Some heard he was dead; others that he had moved to British Columbia, where he was enjoying a tranquil retirement in a senior community euphemistically referred to as "God's Waiting Room." Still others suspected that he was in hiding, biding his time as he tried to reassemble his surviving Terror Syndicate teammates for one final shot at infamy. But it all amounted to little more than groundless conjecture. He had pretty much given up when, late that morning, he received a phone call from an unidentified woman who wanted to know his reason for asking after Virtue. Terry hedged, explained he was acting as a go-between for an interested third party, and then, when pressed, fearful she was going to hang up on him, offered up Marshall's name—to which she'd responded by hanging up on him. About an hour later, she phoned back and provided him with a time, a place, and a name.

The double doors to the blue room swung open and the Zippermania tour let out: schoolchildren, an elderly couple, a group of German tourists, and, bringing up the rear, a mid-fortyish, heavyset, bespectacled woman sporting the Science World navy blue suit and a name tag that identified her as MANAGER: MURIEL HENRY.

"Muriel!" called Terry as if hailing down a long-lost relative. "Hey!"

She stopped and threw him a suspicious look, trying to place the face.

"Terry Langan. We talked this morning."

She coolly shifted her gaze to Marshall and asked, "You are . . . ?"

"Marshall. I'm an old friend of—"

"Of course." She beamed, her aloofness evaporating. "Adam's looking forward to seeing you. This way."

They followed her through a door marked EMPLOYEES ONLY, down a narrow, carpeted hallway to another door with a keycode, through that door and down a flight of stairs to a bleak, gray, wide concrete corridor and up to a steel-reinforced door with a biometric lock. She pressed her meaty thumb against the pad. A corresponding click and the door swung open into a room that could have passed for a posh studio lounge, complete with sleek leather couches, kitchenette, and bar.

She led them in. "Adam will be with you shortly. In the meantime, make yourselves at home."

Terry already was, taking up position behind the bar and fixing himself a drink. Marshall, for his part, was far more interested in the collection of framed pictures adorning the far wall. They offered a timeline of Virtue's life: a teenage Adam at the state science fair being presented with the first-prize trophy by then governor Edmund G. Brown, a young and up-and-coming Virtue and his coworkers outside the head offices of military subcontractor Farrow-Marshall, Virtue and the rest of the Los Alamos research team meeting President Lyndon B. Johnson, Virtue as head of military R&D meeting with President Richard Nixon, a rare group shot of the Terror Syndicate, Donald Rumsfeld presenting Virtue with the Secretary of Defense Medal for Outstanding Public Service, Virtue being presented with the NASA Distinguished Service Medal by President Ronald Reagan, Virtue receiving the Presidential Citizens Medal from President Bill Clinton, Virtue the former national hero being led into court for his arraignment, Virtue on the steps of the courthouse addressing the press following his sentencing. Of course, house arrest barely slowed him down and, while Doc Arcanum may have ceased to exist, Adam Virtue continued to operate, quietly supplying the underworld high-rollers with everything from plasma gauntlets to cloaking technology until a heart attack finally succeeded in doing what the heroes and authorities could not: end Virtue's criminal career.

"So, uh, what's the deal here?" asked Marshall, finally giving voice to the question he'd been nursing since the parking lot.

Muriel smiled, the crow's feet around her bright green eyes deepening. "The bulk of the funding to build the Science Center came from private donations—and one investor in particular. In fact, if not for Adam's continued financial backing, the center would have closed down ages ago. He's been a great supporter of efforts to promote science education in developing minds."

"That right?" mused Terry, not even bothering to look over as he took a sip of his cocktail, frowned, and added an extra shot of bourbon.

Muriel ignored him. "About five years ago, we were looking to complete some major renovations. Again, as he'd done so many times in the past, Adam stepped up. Over the years, he's helped us immeasurably and never asked for anything in return. This time, when he did ask, we were more than happy to accommodate his small request."

"Small request?" Terry swung around the bar, cocktail in hand, and dropped himself onto one of the comfy-looking leather couches. "This place is nicer than my apartment."

"Adam greatly values his privacy." She threw Terry a look that could've melted the ice cubes in his highball glass. "I trust you won't do anything to jeopardize it."

Terry put his feet up on the ottoman and hit the remote, turning on the wall-mounted flat screen. Then, realizing she was referring to him, he furrowed his brow and shrugged, clearly annoyed. "Who am I going to talk to?"

Muriel's sour look turned cherry sweet as she swung her gaze back to Marshall. "It was nice meeting you, Marshall."

Terry watched her go, then sniffed and redirected his focus to the TV. "What a bitch."

Marshall barely registered the remark, focused as he was on a rare group shot of the Terror Syndicate. He guessed it was probably taken sometime in the mid-seventies, just before its members went their separate ways. On the left stood Funkmaster Fly, formerly The Groovinator, and, later, Crunk Daddy, who eventually tired of his life of crime and turned himself in. He repaid his debt to society through the many years of community service that ended up endearing him to various inner-city leaders, stoking his successful run for a seat on the Detroit city council and, in time, the mayor's office, where his two terms as The Motor City Maverick won him the love of his constituents, national attention, and a later career as a political pundit. Beside him stood The Gargantuan, six hundred pounds of corpulent fury, who fell on hard times after the team's breakup and, following a series of arrests, briefly made a name for himself on the competitive eating circuit before being felled by a massive coronary in Bridgetown. To his left, arms folded across her iron and leather yoroi and sneering defiantly at the camera, stood Onna Buegeisha, who was reputed to have once fought Commander Liberty to a bare-knuckle draw. From what Marshall had heard, she was now managing a ladies-only bar in Oakland. Beside her and front and center stood the man himself, Doc Arcanum, a.k.a. Adam Virtue, his face concealed behind a first-generation virinium helm, looking surprisingly buff in his form-fitting midnight black exosuit. To his other side and practically leaning up against him was another masked teammate, the pixyish Silver Sylph, whose secret identity allowed her to fade into obscurity soon after The Terror Syndicate called it quits. To her left stood The Antagonist, the lovable rogue who achieved celebrity heights as "the villain no jury could convict." He parlayed his charm and good looks into a small screen career, winning accolades for his performance as Matt Marvelous on the critically acclaimed HBO underworld series *Sinners & Saints*. Finally, standing on the very right and just a little off on his own was the aptly named Discord, another mystery behind his mask and cowl, whose rumored falling out with Doc Arcanum was said to have precipitated the team's dissolution.

"Would you look at this," muttered Terry. On-screen, CNN was showing aerial footage of the devastation in Atlanta. A rolling scroll at the bottom of the screen updated the grim statistics: 127 dead, 143 missing. "The fuck were they thinking kicking that hornet's nest?" Quick cuts to various on-the-street interviews:

"If Mayor Williams thinks he can just up and walk away from

this mess, he's got another thing coming. The man ought to stand trial for mass murder."

"The mayor was doing what he was elected to do: keep our streets safe from these costumed psychopaths. He's not the criminal. They are!"

"Calling in the heroes caused things to escalate. They just made a bad situation worse."

As if to underscore the point, the on-screen image switched to footage of Amazon Grace taking on Lady Draconia in aerial combat—buzzing each other like furious wasps, sweeping, circling, seeking an opening. Draconia loosening a double salvo from her arm cannons, dousing her opponent in a sustained stream of white-hot plasma. Grace, hovering in place, the bright blueness of her protective force shield deepening to a rich indigo, patiently biding her time. The intensity of the assault flickering and failing. Grace, dropping the shield and closing quickly, connecting with a thunderous right cross that sends Draconia streaking down to street level, where she collides with an antiquated five-story brick building, blowing out the entire first floor and every window in the place. The building teetering uncertainly, then lazily pitching forward to strike a facing skyscraper, remaining propped up against it like some hapless drunkard, vomiting the contents of its posh studio apartments onto the street below.

"That's what you call a right fuckup." Terry crunched down on a piece of ice. "Couldn't leave well enough alone. Had to go and flex their goddamn muscles; make a show of it. Bunch of self-righteous assholes, the lot of 'em."

Hypocritical bastards would have been more fitting, thought Marshall. Always playing to the media, their public acts of altruism little more than a bullshit patina glossing over the ugly truths—alcoholism, malignant narcissism, anger management issues. Their slightest charities aggrandized, their failings easily forgiven and forgotten, inculpable colossi towering over their lessers, imposing themselves and shattering lives with a casual indifference born of self-affected ambition.

Suddenly, a click and hiss from somewhere behind him. Marshall spun around and watched as the far wall shuddered, retracted slightly, then slid aside with a sustained whoosh, revealing the not-so-secret hidden lab he'd been expecting, its modest confines packed full of high-tech gak. And, amid the impressive display of blinky light units and state-of-the-art weaponry stood the man himself, Adam Virtue, his once disheveled salt-and-pepper mop now a sleekly styled silver, his frame a little slighter, his face a little gaunter, but his eyes as bright and full of life as the day Marshall had first met him, some thirteen years ago, at one of Trudy McIntyre's (a.k.a. Princess Arcana, a.k.a. Mrs. Decimator) monthly poker nights.

The memories of that evening came back to him. The way Virtue's entry hushed the raucous gathering. The way his casual demeanor and folksy presence had quickly put them all at ease. The way he'd gone all in with pocket aces and lost it all. Alas, while Adam's social skills were proficient, his poker skills were severely wanting, and by night's end he owed Marshall two thousand dollars. "No problem," Marshall had told him. "Pay me back whenever." As if to affirm the confidence placed in him, Adam suggested Marshall give him a lift back home, where, in lieu of cash, he would be free to choose something from among the numerous items in his "workshop."

Marshall remembered being struck by the shocking normality of that modest little bungalow in the upper-class suburban neighborhood. Not that he'd presumed some hidden lair built into an inconspicuous cave or a foreboding mansion more in keeping with the legendary persona, but at the very least a well-tended garden or a roof that didn't look like it was in desperate need of a reshingling. Virtue walked in and set his keys and wallet down on a shelf beside—Marshall couldn't help but notice—a blinking ankle monitor. "I'm going to go make us some coffee," he said, disappearing into the kitchen. "Why don't you head down to the basement and pick something out."

The basement held a "mad professor's garage sale" assortment of weapons, accessories, and formidable-looking god-knows-whats. It was nothing short of overwhelming. "How're we doing?" asked Virtue when he finally came down carrying two coffee mugs.

"I was thinking of this." Marshall held up a pair of virinium-lined gloves, the most modest item he could find. "If that's all right with you."

Virtue tut-tutted and set down the coffees, walking by him and wading into the mass clutter. "No, no. You can do better that that. Hmmmm. Let's see . . . How about this?"

"This" was a jet black exosuit that, Virtue explained, was fashioned of first-generation virinium polymer less than a tenth of a centimeter thick, bulletproof and resistant to temperatures in excess of 2800 degrees Fahrenheit yet possessed of ultraflexible second-skin technology. A smart chip, centered in the crown of the cowl, fed power to a multitude of transistors within the suit attuned to the approximately six hundred muscles in the human body, providing the boost that would amplify his already extranormal strength, speed, and dexterity tenfold. Its cost far exceeded the two thousand owed, but Adam was more than happy to suggest an arrangement. Marshall could have the suit and apply the two grand against its purchase price, then pay off the balance by working for him. And thus, Downfall was born.

He could have paid off that original suit in a year, but there was always something—an added accessory, some sort of upgrade—that kept him in Virtue's employ. Eventually, they stopped keeping count and Marshall continued working with him, not because he owed him, but because Adam was his friend. They formed a bond so strong that, in the beginning, Marshall had even considered the possibility that Adam was his long-lost father come to secretly make amends. But, in the end, it turned out to be mere wishful thinking on his part as he quickly learned that, while gifted with above-average intelligence, Adam Virtue was just an average man, possessed of no extranormal powers. And even though, in his heart, he knew it had been a reach, having his theory quashed proved shockingly disappointing at the time.

And now, suddenly, seeing his old friend again and knowing he had come back to betray his trust filled Marshall with an ineffable sadness.

"I was wondering how long it would take you to find me." Adam threw his arms wide and welcomed his former protégé with a hug. Then, noticing: "And who's this?"

Marshall glanced back at Terry, standing awkwardly behind them, drink in hand, anxiously awaiting his introduction.

"Terry Langan," said Marshall. "An old friend."

"Pleased to meet you, Terry."

"Pleasure's mine, sir—uh, Mr. Virtue."

Virtue gave them a wink and cocked his head back toward the hidden room. "Come on. I've got something to show you."

They followed him back into the lab, where he took up position behind a computer adjacent to a floor-to-ceiling circular containment field emitting a low, soothing hum. It was roughly two feet in diameter, its walls an impenetrable shimmering pearl. Adam input a sequence and hit a switch. The shield powered down, its opaque walls dropping to reveal the prize concealed within: a full-body exoskin hovering in place. Marshall felt his neck prickle, a thousand tiny centipedes creeping up his spine.

"It's for you," said Virtue, confirming Marshall's darkest fear. "Welcome home."

☆   ★   ☆

"Holy shit!" marveled Terry, stepping in for a closer look but maintaining a respectful distance all the same. A sustained, reverential gaze and then again, almost a whisper: "Holy shit!"

"It's a microthin, shifting-state, liquid nanite construct," Adam explained, barely able to conceal his pride. "State-of-the-art, second-skin technology offers unsurpassed strength, speed, and agility. Thrusters in the boots deliver limited hovering ability. Once manually activated, the smart chip in the trigger arm band initiates a neural link to all active in-suit systems, including impulse-command wrist-mounted persuaders—"

"I can't."

Adam's mouth fell open in muted shock. It was Terry who spoke up: "You're kidding, right?"

An uncomfortable silence and then Adam found his voice: "If you're worried about the cost—and it is significant—we can work out a deal—"

"No," Marshall was quick to respond. "No deal."

A twitch of his silvered eyebrows, and Adam dropped his gaze, twisting his mouth up into a half frown. Several seconds of considered contemplation, and then: "All right." He glanced up, brightening. "Consider it a gift."

Terry uttered his third "Holy shit" of the afternoon.

"I can't accept."

"What?!" Terry's outrage at Marshall's response was surpassed only by Marshall's outrage at Terry's outrage at his response.

"Terry, why don't you go wait in the lounge," Marshall suggested, trying very hard to keep his anger in check. "Do me a favor, huh?"

Terry vacillated, throwing the exosuit a longing look and then, picking up on Marshall's palpable frustration, nodded. "Sure, sure." And happily complied.

"I don't understand," said Adam, his voice edged with uncertainty. He looked lost, like a child denied some life-altering trifle.

"I'm done with Downfall."

This seemed to strike Adam as altogether confounding. He looked at Marshall, uncomprehending, brow furrowed, as if trying to work something out in his head. "I realize you don't want to take a chance of ending up back behind bars, but this suit's impulse defense systems can detect molecular-level threats. They'll lock down, vent, and seal you off from any airborne attack. If you're worried about Nantech—"

"I'm not worried about Nantech. I just—" Marshall sighed and found himself unconsciously fingering his belt, *the* belt. He'd put it on before leaving his hotel room, not on the off chance he'd cross paths with Virtue, but because it looked good with his jeans. No fucking prescience. Just dumb luck, a spur-of-the-moment decision that had unwittingly completed his betrayal. "I just don't want to do it anymore." He was already thinking about where he would dump the belt. Somewhere far away from both the Science Center and his hotel, possibly a bin in some alleyway or in the dense forest on the city's outskirts. "I have a new life now, one that doesn't involve any of this." He swept his arm wide to indicate the veritable treasure trove of high-tech toys: lasers and rocket boots and plasma cannons and frost grenades. "I don't want to hide anymore. I don't want to put the people I care about at risk. I don't want to spend my nights worrying about whether I'll be able to get the suit on before they can kick in my door and get to me. I left it all behind years ago."

Adam's voice was barely a whisper. "Don't you ever miss it?"

"Sure. But not enough to risk everything I have."

"And what do you have?"

"A wife who loves me, who I won't disappoint." And then, almost as an afterthought: "Peace of mind."

Adam managed a weak smile and nodded. Marshall wasn't sure whether it was understanding or acquiescence. "So you're definitely out?"

"Yeah."

Virtue's eyes narrowed. Fists in pockets, he threw Marshall a searching look, clearly confused. "Then . . . why did you come back?"

To meet the terms of my conditional release? To track you down? To betray our friendship? "Because I wanted to see you." Which was partially true. "I never got the chance to visit you in the hospital."

Adam conceded the point with a shrug and a faint smile. "I never got the chance to visit you in prison."

"Yeah, well, I guess we were both kind of busy."

That managed to elicit a chuckle from the old man. But his good humor was short-lived. "So I was wrong to think you were coming back for this." His tone was almost accusing. "It never even crossed your mind? Even with The Imperial out of the way?"

Inwardly, Marshall reeled at the dangerous and unexpected turn in the conversation. "What the hell does The Imperial have to do with it?" he snapped.

Adam hesitated, threw a look at the exosuit, and then seemed to think better of it. "Nothing. Nothing at all." He seemed suddenly bitter.

Time to go. For both their sakes. "I'm sorry," was all he could think to say before turning and heading back into the lounge. There, he found Terry at the bar, fixing himself another drink. "We're going," he told him.

"Can I finish my drink?"

"We're going," Marshall repeated, not even breaking stride as he headed out into the corridor without so much as a parting glance for his former mentor.

☆   ★   ☆

The drive back to the hotel was a quiet one. Terry sensed something was up but knew better than to ask. He kept the radio off and his mouth shut, not even bothering to question Marshall's actions when, halfway through the ride, he suddenly stripped off his belt, snapped off the buckle, and tossed them both out the passenger-side window.

"Thanks for everything, Ter," said Marshall when they finally pulled up to the hotel. He gave his old friend a parting shoulder pat, then got out of the car and headed inside.

He was in the process of packing when the phone rang. He briefly considered ignoring it but ultimately figured he would have to answer for his actions sooner or later and so snapped it up on the sixth ring. "Hello?"

"Marshall?" He recognized Agent McNeil's voice.

"Yeah, listen—"

"Nice work." Marshall fell silent, felt himself go numb. His mind scrambled and fell on the possibility that they'd had him followed. "Marshall, you there?"

"Yeah."

"We've confirmed trace elements of ferenium-17 in his lab."

"How?" Marshall cursed himself for not acting on his first instinct to dump the belt somewhere out in the middle of nowhere. Then again, if they'd been following him, it wouldn't have really mattered. They'd have found it regardless. *If*, he suddenly realized, they'd found it because their recovering the belt would have been dependent upon their seeing him dump it, which, in turn, would have made clear his intention to back out of their deal. And yet, the tone of McNeil's voice gave no hint that the feds were pissed. He was being played. "You don't have the belt."

"We don't need it. The data is instantly transferred through wireless networks. Virtue's our guy." Marshall dropped the phone and stumbled back. The back of his left leg caught the edge of the bed and he dropped down to a sitting position. He heard McNeil's voice, distant and tinny: "We're sending a car by to pick you up. Marshall? Marshall, you there?"

☆ ★ ☆

Walking away was no longer an option. Armed with the certainty of Virtue's involvement in the death of The Imperial, the feds were prepared to move against him and so, for Marshall, it came down to one of two choices: either lead them to the lab, or refuse and allow them to put the squeeze on Terry, who he'd helpfully offered up earlier that morning. Not much of a choice at all. At the very least, Marshall reasoned, he could minimize the damage already done by ensuring a peaceful resolution to the situation.

He sighed audibly, shifted in his seat, and threw a look out the window at the emptying parking lot. Night was falling. Inside the Science Center, federal agents led by McNeil were moving into position, at first blush just another bunch of paying customers milling about as closing time neared, nothing at all to worry about had you, say, glimpsed them on a security monitor. Once satisfied that the area was secure, they would signal Marshall, who would make his way into the building and lead them to the basement lab. McNeil had been adamant. Marshall was not to communicate with Virtue.

He was not to involve himself in the takedown. He was not to take any action that risked compromising the operation. Simply put, his job was to lead them to the lab; nothing more, unless called upon.

Bryerson, seated beside him in the driver's seat of the double-parked SUV, assured him that what he was about to do was the best thing for all involved, especially Virtue. Rather than quell Marshall's mounting anxiety, his words merely served to drive home the magnitude of his treachery.

"Relax," said Bryerson, his fingers drumming out a silent piano concerto atop the steering wheel. "Tomorrow morning, you'll be back home and this'll all be over."

"No," said Marshall. "It'll never be over. Not for me. This was a huge mistake."

Bryerson's voice was steady. "You're helping us take down a murderer."

"I'm betraying a friend—"

"A murderer—"

"—who always looked out for me—"

"—killed a fucking hero—"

"—even after all these years—"

"—poisoned him—"

"—and even though I turned my back on him—"

"—robbing not only this city, but this planet—"

"—he never stopped looking out for me."

"—of one of its biggest defenders."

"He did it for me! The Imperial—"

"The Imperial—"

"Deserved to die!"

There, he'd finally said it. And shut Byerson up in the process. The big man eyed him doubtfully and then, very calmly: "No. No, he didn't. Just because he was an asshole doesn't mean—"

"Let me tell you something, Agent Bryerson. I didn't hate The Imperial because he was an asshole. I hated him because he ruined my life."

Bryerson sighed. "You ruined your own life."

Marshall responded with a derisive snort. "Yeah, I fucked up. I made some bad decisions. And I paid for them. I did my time. I had a right to a fresh start. But he wouldn't let me."

The fed threw him a quizzical look. "What do you mean he wouldn't let you?"

"After all those times he'd kicked my ass, it was Nantech who brought me in for the last time. Fifty-something, alcoholic Nantech was the one who taught me my final lesson, and that pissed him off. Pissed him off so much that he wouldn't let me go. Every time I moved to a new neighborhood, he'd track me down and make damn sure that everyone in town knew who I was; who I'd been. Every time I tried to start over, he'd show up and destroy everything I'd built. Town after town after fucking town. You can't even begin to imagine what it was like."

"No," Bryerson coolly conceded. "No, I can't."

Marshall took a deep breath, released. When he spoke again, his voice was calmer: "Even though the law said I'd earned a clean slate, he wouldn't let it go. And because he wouldn't let it go, I had to suffer—along with everyone I cared about—on edge every second of every day, afraid to let my guard down, relax, make friends, get a fucking library card knowing I probably won't be around to use it."

"Did you report him?"

"Of course I reported him." Marshall was spent, resigned. "But what the hell was anyone going to do about it? He was The fucking Imperial." He shrugged. "Sure, they were sympathetic. They paid for my relocation. And the next one. And the one after that."

"Hunh." Bryerson shifted back in his seat and stared out at the darkening sky.

"It's impossible to set down roots, start a family, knowing that sooner or later, that other shoe's going to drop and it'll all come undone."

A solemn silence settled between them. Bryerson sucked his teeth, considered, then popped the glove compartment. He pulled out the two bottles he'd taken from the hotel minibar, dangled them in front of Marshall's face, Chivas and Tanqueray. Marshall took the Chivas.

"To the future," said Bryerson.

They unscrewed the caps, toasted, and knocked back their contents. The whiskey was warm and comforting.

A sweep of headlights suddenly intruded on the moment. Bryerson uttered a breathless "Shit" at the sight of the three black town cars pulling up. Dark-suited men and women hopped out and were met by two of the plainclothed federal agents stationed outside the Science Center entrance.

"Go! Go! Go!" whispered Bryerson, then opened the door and stepped out to greet the new arrivals with a cordial "What's the problem here?"

Marshall slipped out of the SUV and started toward the entrance. "NSA!" he heard someone bark. "We're going to have to ask you to stand down."

"You can even ask nicely, but that don't mean we will," countered Bryerson.

Marshall risked a glance back, saw the NSA talker speed-dial his cell phone and hold it out to Bryerson. "Well, how about if your boss asks nicely?" Bryerson hesitated, then took the phone. "Hey, you!" called Mr. NSA, spotting Marshall as he reached the doors. "Stop right there!" Marshall ignored him and kept right on going, through the entrance and into the building. "Hey!"

Once inside, he picked up the pace, hopping the turnstile and crossing the main hall where the last of the Science Center staff were being corralled and ushered toward the back exit. He was met by McNeil, who wanted to know: "What the hell is going on out there?"

"They said they were NSA."

McNeil reacted, snapping his fingers and motioning a couple of his men over to the entrance, presumably to run interference. Then, quickly over to Marshall: "Let's go!"

The door marked EMPLOYEES ONLY was locked. McNeil shouldered it open and, guns drawn, they swept in and down the narrow, carpeted hallway to the second door with the keycode. McNeil pulled Marshall aside, allowing one of his men to step up and deliver a flurry of well-placed kicks to the frame. On the fifth blow, the door splintered and gave. And then they were flying down the stairs to the bleak, gray, wide concrete corridor. They hurried up to the steel-reinforced door with the biometric lock. Again, Marshall was motioned away. He backed off, halfway between the door and the stairwell, and watched as one of the agents pressed a brick of plastique up against the lock. McNeil waved the remote. "Clear the area."

"Hold it right there!"

They froze. A half-dozen NSA agents charged down the stairs. Mr. Cellphone waved his identification. "Agent Rose, NSA. We're ordering you to stand down." The NSA agents muscled their way in to take up position directly in front of the door, forcing McNeil and his men farther back down the opposite end of the corridor. "We're taking over this investigation."

"The hell you are." McNeil was livid.

"Feel free to check in with Agent Bryerson upstairs. You're in no position to argue."

A tense standoff. "What the hell is going on?" McNeil demanded to know.

"We're here to deal with a threat to national security."

Marshall stood by, helpless, a mere spectator to the proceedings. He threw a glance up the stairs, briefly considered heading back up and slipping away, then decided against it. He needed to see how things played out, had to ensure Virtue's peaceful surrender. And as he considered the many ways it could go sideways, his gaze trailed back down and fell on a lone shoe, a black pump, peeking out from beneath the stairwell behind him.

"Bullshit," he heard McNeil say. And then, a dawning realization. "No. You're here to protect your asset."

Marshall ignored them and slowly drew near the stairwell, glimpsed a pool of blood, then a stockinged foot.

"That's it, isn't it?" he heard McNeil say. "He's still your guy."

"You're done here."

But McNeil wasn't quite done. "Virtue was too valuable, so rather than cut him loose, your people just looked the other way. You didn't give a damn what he did on his off-hours so long as he played ball with you. And now you're here to rein him in before this turns into a public clusterfuck."

Around the corner, tucked beneath the stairwell, lay the body of Muriel Henry. Her eyes were wide, her neck angled awkwardly. Her right hand was a gory mess. The thumb was missing. The thumb! Marshall heard Rose say, "Good night, Agent McNeil."

"Wait!" shouted Marshall, spinning around and starting toward them. "Wait!"

They all turned, their looks a mixture of annoyance and confusion. Rose opened his mouth to say something—

At which point the door they were standing in front of blew out with such force it took out the surrounding concrete frame, pulping Rose and three of his associates against the far wall, knocking everyone else off their feet, and bringing sections of the structure down on top of them.

Marshall blinked, found himself flat on his back, ears ringing, eyes stinging from the smoke and drifting particulates. Disoriented by the concussive burst, he could barely make out the figure calmly striding down the corridor toward him. The ringing in his ears faded to an utter silence that, had he been thinking straight, would have positively terrified him. Pushing himself up with one arm, he used the back of the other hand to wipe away the tears. The scene snapped into focus and he watched the new Downfall suit, in all its glossy jet glory, stride past. It moved deliberately up the stairs and was gone. At which point the silence suddenly gave way to an onrush of sounds: the spit and sizzle of damaged circuitry, distant alarms, his own labored breathing.

Marshall pulled himself up and stumbled down the corridor, over the broken bodies and severed limbs to where McNeill lay, staring up at the ceiling, wild-eyed, swallowing quick shallow breaths. Marshall hunkered down beside him. "Hey." His voice broke. "Hey." Steadier this time. McNeil met his gaze, looked through him and away. He was bleeding profusely from a leg wound. As Marshall tore off his shirtsleeve and applied a tourniquet, sounds carried down to them from the cavernous main hall. Shouts and gunfire, followed by staccato barrage of heavy ordnance. More shouts raised, less authoritative, frightened. Another barrage and then a sickening hush. "You're going to be okay," Marshall tried to reassure him. But McNeil was barely there.

Marshall rose, a mounting fury fueling his determination to finally step up and sever the links to his former life once and for all. He stumbled over the rubble and into the lounge, intent on finding something, anything, he could use from among the storehouse of weapons.

What he found, instead, was Adam Virtue lying facedown on the floor of his own lab.

Marshall went to him, gently turned him over. His mentor looked shockingly old, tired. His face and neck were bruised, his eyes unfocused at first. Then, a dawning recognition alighted. "Marshall."

"What happened?"

"I'm sorry."

"Adam—"

"I was selfish. A coward."

"What are you talking about?"

"I wasn't there for you, and I've spent so long trying to make up for that mistake. I'm sorry I let you down."

"Adam, you've never let me down. You were like a father to me."

The old man's whispered response gave way to a convulsion, and then he was still. The life had finally left those bright blue eyes. And as Marshall sat there, cradling Adam's head in his lap, those last words hung in the air: "I am."

☆ ★ ☆

The mezzanine level was a ruin of blood-spattered debris and littered corpses, the plaintive cries of the injured and dying punctuated by the sounds emanating from the robot zoo exhibit. A blackbird's whistle. The call of a stag. A hole had been blasted through the ceiling, a still-smoking crater that peered out into open night. And, accompanying the view, the staccato beat of a helicopter, the rattle and boom of heavy ordnance. Marshall hefted up the weapon he was holding, right hand gripping the stock, left hand supporting the weighty pulse barrel, and made for the stairwell that would take him up.

He kicked open the door and stepped out onto the roof. Overhead, the Apache circled a hovering Downfall and loosened a brain-shaking fifty-round burst from its 30-millimeter M230 chain gun. The high-energy penetrators tut-tut-tutted against the impenetrable suit, barely forcing it back a foot or two from its wavering mark. Marshall leapt back under protective cover as the rain of red-hot shell casings clattered down around him. Then, another fifty-round burst, again barely fazing its intended target. The Apache swung round and wide. Downfall rotated effortlessly in place, tracking the copter as it pulled back, hung in the air, then fired off one of its Hydras. Marshall ducked away from the open doorway. The 70-millimeter rocket impacted with an explosive force that shook the building, followed by the whistle and tag of high-velocity fragments.

He hazarded a peek. Downfall, who had apparently shrugged off the rocket attack with no ill effects, raised his arm. A multi-barreled bracelet shifted and formed, solidifying as wrist-mounted persuaders. Marshall jumped back out onto the roof, swung his weapon high and fired. The bolt of blue energy erupted with a punch and sizzle, sailing wide. Downfall fired off his persuader, but the copter was already on the move, banking and sweeping as the ordnance missed its mark. Downfall revolved in midair, tracking his target as it came round.

Marshall steadied himself, took careful aim, and fired. The punch, sizzle, and this time, a direct hit. Downfall hung in the air, back arched in a tortured pose as the blue energy played over him, then plummeted and struck the roof with a sickening thud.

Past experience told Marshall to leave nothing to chance. He closed the distance between them quickly, cranking the charge on the weapon and leveling it at his target. Downfall was struggling to rise, the ebb and flow of the suit's suddenly unstable molecular structure shifting liquid-like across his exposed chest and back, revealing islands of vulnerable flesh. Marshall pulled the trigger. The weapon clicked and died with a protesting whine. *Shit*.

Downfall turned—and took a two-armed swing of the heavy stalk off his protected temple, a mere glancing blow that caused him to stumble back in surprise. Marshall cursed his instincts, followed up with a barrel strike to the more vulnerable unprotected chest area. *Too slow*. Downfall intercepted the blow, twisted the weapon out of his grasp, and delivered a backhand sweep that would have caved in his skull had Marshall not had the presence of mind to duck. Marshall followed through with a mid-core punch. The suit's free-flowing construct shifted, absorbing part of the impact. Marshall felt his hand break, the fourth and fifth knuckles shocking numb, but the second and third knuckle scoring flesh and winning an unmistakable and satisfying rib fracture, staggering his opponent. Marshall sprang back and spun around to deliver a roundhouse kick to the injured area. He was inhumanly quick, but no match for Downfall, who caught his ankle, swung him wide, then let go, sending him skittering across the rooftop to crash against the brick perimeter abutment.

Downfall advanced, the smart chip in his suit already adjusting to the attack on its neural network, the active nanite shield's unstable pattern shifting back to uniformity. Marshall knew it was now or never. He jumped up to meet his advancing opponent, springing forward with superhuman speed, ducking another blow and coming in with an open-hand, closed-fingered strike designed to end it there and then, pierce the chest wall and penetrate the heart. Instead, the blow was deflected with almost casual indifference, snapping his left wrist in the process and catching his lower jaw with a glancing blow that broke it as well. Marshall staggered back, had his foot catch the abutment, and toppled. Almost over— but Downfall saved him, grabbing him by the collar and snapping him back, swinging him around, away from the drop, up close, then delivering a restrained headbutt that broke his nose, fractured the occipital bone below his left eye, and brought him to the precipice of consciousness. His knees gave out and he collapsed.

He was beyond exhausted, his body spent, his mind scrambling to maintain focus as Downfall stepped up to loom over him, triumphant. *The king is dead. Long live the king.* Marshall tasted blood and spat. In his weakened state, he barely managed it. The spittle dribbled out the side of his mouth and ran down his cheek. He tried to lift his head, but even that proved a task too Herculean for his present state. And so, he waited.

Downfall gave a shake of his head, reached up with his right hand, and triggered the remote on his arm band, dialing back the suit. It swept away like a black tide, retreating to just above his shoulders to reveal a smiling Terry Langan. "Hey, Marsh," he greeted him. "What's up?"

Marshall was surprised. Honest to God he was. And if he'd been up to it, he certainly would have expressed his dismay at the shocking turn of events. But he wasn't, so instead, he settled for a disgusted grunt.

Terry shook his head. "What a difference eight years makes, huh, buddy? Bet you kind of regret not taking Virtue up on his offer now." Terry paused, as if awaiting some sort of response, then continued: "Some of us aren't as lucky as you, Marsh. We don't get everything handed to us. We have to seize our opportunities, make our own future, you know what I'm saying?"

Fuck it. Ignoring the overwhelming pain, Marshall pushed himself up to a sitting position.

"New suit, new name," said Terry matter-of-factly. "I'm considering going with . . . Munition. What do you think?"

Marshall gathered himself, looked up at his former friend, and, despite the state of his jaw, managed: "Munishuns."

"What was that?"

"Munishuns," Marshall repeated. "Ith plural ya thtupid fuck."

"Is it?" Terry frowned, considered, then shrugged. "Well, fuck it. Who's gonna correct me?"

A crack of gunfire interrupted their conversation. Both men glanced over as—

A shadowed form stepped out of the doorway and slowly advanced on them, arm extended, gun in hand, the other hand supporting his shooting wrist. Agent Bryerson stepped into the light.

Terry smirked and went for the arm band, but Marshall had already calculated the move, expending his last reserves to lunge forward and slap his broken hand over the trigger. Terry tried to pry him off, but Marshall's hold was a superhuman death grip. Another gunshot. Another whistled miss. Bryerson quickly closing the distance.

Marshall never saw the blow that shattered his left clavicle and forced him to release his hold. As he fell back he heard the third shot, saw Terry reach for the arm band and then suddenly pause as if reconsidering. A look of deep concern fell over him as he reached up and cupped his chin. He pulled his hand back. It came away slick and sticky. The fourth shot blew through one cheek and out the other, shattering teeth and bone. Marshall saw his old friend teeter and drop out of sight.

Dizzy and disoriented, he watched Bryerson step into view and casually empty his clip into his target. Then, he turned and addressed Marshall. But Marshall couldn't hear him. All was silence as the darkness crept in on him, closing out all but a tunnel to his former reality, growing tighter and dimmer. Bryerson, at the other end of that tunnel, yelling something at him.

And in a sudden moment of clarity, Marshall marveled at their ingenuity. If only his cluttered mind had caught it earlier: that group shot of The Terror Syndicate, the pixyish Silver Sylph practically leaning up against her teammate Doc Arcanum, Virtue's endless benevolence. His whole life, the answers had been there all along. He'd simply been asking the wrong questions. And he thought of Allison and how different things could have been and how he would have loved to start over with her one more time, really start over. And then the darkness claimed him.

☆　★　☆

Contusions, abrasions, multiple lacerations, concussion, occipital bone fracture, shattered left clavicle, compound wrist fracture, multiple rib fractures, dislocated right shoulder, punctured lung, right elbow fracture, multiple fractures to both hands, fractured jaw, fractured nose, rotator cuff tear, ankle strain, groin pull, and a partial tear of the left ACL. All in all, he got off lucky. By the time they wheeled him into the OR, his bones had already started to reknit, much to the amazement of the medical staff, who were then forced to rebreak and set the radius and ulna of both forearms.

He was in terrible pain through those initial twenty-four hours as his advanced regenerative abilities kicked in to repair the damaged muscles, patches of scar tissue fibers taking form overnight and guaranteeing a less than restful sleep. By morning, however, his body was breaking down the scar tissue, restoring muscular alignment, and he was feeling well enough to go for a short walk—down the hall to Room 217 to pay McNeil a visit—only to be intercepted by a cantankerous nurse and ushered back to bed. When he tried again later that day, slipping out during what seemed like a quiet enough moment, she was waiting for him. After that, a large intern of Samoan descent stationed outside his room ensured there would be no third attempt.

The following day, he was discharged. While waiting for Allison to pick him up, he took another stroll down to 217. This time, he encountered no obstacles and managed to complete the journey, finding a recuperating and spirited McNeil in the company of his fiancée, a pretty blonde who had just landed herself a position at a boutique East Coast law firm. According to McNeil, he had already requested a transfer and, once well enough, would be making the move. Marshall sat with them for a while and then, at the appointed time, wished them all the best and excused himself. "See you at the wedding then?" McNeil asked him.

"Sure," said Marshall, holding up at the doorway and throwing them a wink. "See you then."

By the time he got downstairs, Allison was already there. "Waiting long?" he asked as he made his uncertain approach. Her response was a long, drawn-out sigh of unmistakable relief. She fell into his arms. They held each other wordlessly until they began to draw curious looks from passersby. Then, Allison said, "Let's go home."

Months passed. His mother was given a clean bill of health and moved into a place twelve blocks away. "Close enough," as Allison was fond of saying. They settled in. She was promoted, joined several weekend charity drives. He landed a job with the local branch of a major pharmaceutical company and finally got that library card he'd been putting off. In early February, Allison announced she was pregnant. Time passed. They were happy.

Finally, that spring, while in the area on company business, Marshall drove the forty miles out to pay Agent Bryerson a visit.

"What's this?" asked the stone-faced bruiser when Marshall presented him with the gift-wrapped bottle.

"An overdue thank-you present," said Marshall.

Bryerson sized up the bottle, gave a satisfied nod, and set it down on his desk. "Yep," he said. "I save your life, you get me a bottle of wine. Sounds about right."

"A great bottle of wine," Marshall clarified.

"No doubt," said Bryerson, throwing him his shark grin. He motioned toward the doorway. "Come on. Let's go do this and then you can take me to lunch."

It was a request Marshall had made months ago and Bryerson was happy to accommodate. No rush. Even though the case was closed, its evidentiary material wasn't going anywhere. It would be drawing the scrutiny of investigators and eggheads for some time to come.

Bryerson led him to a room at the end of a long corridor, unlocked the door, and waved him in. The halogen lights flickered to life, casting their ice-blue illumination down on the facts and figures of the investigation. "The Downfall suit isn't here, of course," Bryerson informed him.

"Didn't think it would be," Marshall said as he scanned the various photos and documents laid out in front of him.

"The army hired that little brainiac, QuickThink—you know him—?"

"Yeah, I know him."

"—to reverse-engineer the suit. He thinks he can have special forces outfitted by middle of next year."

But Marshall's mind was elsewhere. He'd already spotted what he'd come for—confirmation sitting on a table at the back of the room. He approached it, pointed. "This how the ferenium-17 was delivered?"

"Yeah. They figure it was dusted on a copy of his own book he was asked to sign. The return address was bogus, but he never got around to sending it anyway. I mean, isn't that a kick in the pants. No special bullet or elaborate trap. It was just sent regular mail."

Marshall picked up the box and studied its Chinese motif—a gold dragon embossed on a crimson red backdrop. Incredibly, after so many months, it still held the scent of jasmine and sandalwood.

A two-time winner of the British Fantasy Award, Mark Chadbourn is the critically acclaimed author of sixteen novels and one nonfiction book, including the Age of Misrule series of *World's End*, *Darkest Hour*, and *Always Forever*, and the Swords of Albion series that begins with *The Silver Skull*. A former journalist, he is now a screenwriter for BBC television drama. In the world of comic books, Mark is the author of *Hellboy: The Ice Wolves*, a novel-length tale of Mike Mignolia's famous creation. Whether his imagination takes him to the distant past or peels back the curtain on the darkness lurking in our present reality, Mark always presents us with strong, accessible characters dealing with supernatural horrors, the invasion of the numinous on the everyday.

By My Works
You Shall Know Me

MARK CHADBOURN

One hour after the body had been buried in an unmarked grave, he set fire to the box of memories on the roof and prepared to greet the dawn with something approaching hope.

When the embers of his past had cooled, he was ready to take the steps down into the penthouse, where he could finally remove the mask. Every muscle burned, and blood still leaked from the knife wound in his side.

Only a shadow was reflected in the mirror in the lounge, bisected by the lightning strike that cracked the glass from top to bottom. Black, tight-fitting body armor, nano-engineered to absorb all light so he could ghost across the surface of life, a shimmer of dark against a darker world.

Nox, the name he had chosen for himself when he had been

reborn. In mythology, Nox was a she, but as the personification of the night, it was too fitting to pass up. It was only later he realized Nox gave birth to sleep and death, fate and blame.

Stripping off his mask, he thought briefly of how haunted his face appeared. But what did he expect from a man who had just killed the person closest to him? As his eyes glistened, his acute vision saw it like a flare at sea; a distress call.

Locating the medical supplies, he sprawled in a chair while he tended to his wounds, looking out the picture window over San Francisco at its darkest, in that hour before dawn. Soon it would be waking; soon he would be sleeping.

Once he'd stanched the blood flow, he began the digital recording, his nightly ritual, a confessional and a chance to make sense of what his life had become. One day he would have to play all the recordings back, review his experiences. But why would he want to do that? Living through them once was enough.

"October tenth. It was cold out there tonight." He paused in the flood of devastating images. "Everything's changed. There's no longer a need for Nox, for this secret life. For everything I've been doing this past year. My enemy is dead. The architect of all my misery, all this city's suffering. Killed by my hand, buried where he'll never be discovered. I didn't plan it that way, of course I didn't. It was the last ending I wanted. But what happened was inevitable. I know that now. All those seemingly unconnected strands drawing together. If only I'd been able to see it at the start. I remember . . ."

☆　★　☆

Waking.

"Matt?" Her hand closed on his.

As he surfaced from the depths of his head, he opened his eyes to painfully bright illumination. "Owww!"

"Dim the lights!"

Daniel, his best friend. His savior? Yes, of course—it would have to have been Daniel. And Rose. God, he'd put her through so much.

"How are you feeling?" The concern in Daniel's voice had an edge of excitement.

As his thoughts settled, Matt understood the reason for Daniel's exuberance. "Finally got an experiment that can talk back?" The words trailed away when he realized he could see so clearly in the hospital room's gloom, it was as though it were flooded with sunlight. Daniel, with his faintly baffled expression and untamed blond hair sticking out at angles like a clichéd mad scientist. Rose, never a cliché, her hair sapphire blue today, her eyes glistening with tears that flared in his acute vision; a beacon of hope.

"Hey," he said gently. She gave a pale smile that did little to hide the pain that lay between them. "I feel . . . great?"

The explosion. The shock wave and heat. He looked down at his hands, the skin flawless.

"Phenomenal healing is just one small part of it," Daniel said. "I'd never have gotten here if not for Roger Penrose. He was right: brains are hypercomputers. The Quantum Mind gives massive scope for reapplication of function."

"How bad was I?"

"Third-degree burns over eighty percent of your body. And a metal spike rammed through your skull, puncturing both hemispheres of the brain. But mechanics really don't matter, just like Penrose said. Consciousness is created and maintained on the quantum level."

"So, I'm okay now?"

"Well . . . there may be some side effects."

"Looks like my decision to invest in your research was the right one after all."

"And there was me thinking you were just helping out an old friend," Daniel responded wryly. "It's self-interest all the way with you, Matthew."

Rose leaned in so that he could smell her perfume, so rich and powerful it was intoxicating; all of his senses had been magnified. "I'm glad you're okay, Matt. We thought we'd lost you that first night."

"I'm sorry." The tremor in his voice gave away the depth of his feelings. "What I put you through—"

"Later," she said. "We'll talk later."

They never did.

☆ ★ ☆

"Side effects? Just one or two. Like my mind shutting down completely when the first rays of the sun hit me. In return, I get super night vision and magnified senses, optimum strength when I need it, and a healing capacity a thousand times better than anyone else's. Superhuman abilities. Anyone would want it. But . . . would I have lost so much if I'd been a typical guy, just muddling through, trying to survive without thinking of the consequences of my actions? Maybe that's the way the world works at the quantum level—the more good you do, the more shit rains down on your head. There are patterns all over the place, but most of the time you're too close up to see them for what they are.

"Before Daniel's process, I was never a good guy, not really. I didn't see that at the time, but everybody thinks they're the hero of their own particular story. The only superpower I had back then was making money, and I pursued it relentlessly. Nothing, nobody, stood in my way. It was all legal, sure. But moral? Part of my new existence . . . part of my curse . . . is that I can now look back at who I was with new eyes. The joke at the time was that nobody gets to be a billionaire by being a saint. Funny. But I had my army of creative accountants and business managers to shield me from the harsh glare of judgment, and I set about buying up, and stripping down, with a relish that increased with every extra dollar. Jobs were discarded. Lives discarded. People. They were *assets*. Desks and chairs and computer servers.

"When I was setting out, I bought out the company owned by Rose's father. It was a way to win her over, some kind of pathetic peacock display. The company was her father's life's work, and I gave it a lifeline. Everybody loved me. Then when I was too busy to pay it any attention, some drone in the accounting department shut it down and sold it off. Everybody thought it was my direct order. Rose's father killed himself. She never forgave me.

"Then, as the recession bit, I became a hate figure all over, not just in Rose's house. That's when I got caught in the bomb blast at the company I was closing down in Modesto. Some guy who'd lost everything wanted to take out the big supervillain. And he never knew how close he came to doing it. Nobody knew.

"Daniel's Quantum Mind process gave me a chance to be someone different. I cashed in everything, retreated to this penthouse, cut off ties with everyone who knew me, except Rose and Daniel, and thought about what I wanted to do with my second chance. But maybe I really was cursed, like the Flying Dutchman or something, and all I gained was just a chance to cause misery on a greater scale.

"Right at the start, there was still a chance of breaking the pattern. I didn't have to be a hero. I could have made the most of my permanent night shift, while the world went on with its business just around the corner of my life.

"All I had to do was turn away when I saw the writing on the wall. Ignore the mystery. Cut the threads that held the pattern together. Refuse to keep . . ."

☆   ★   ☆

Running.

Choking smoke filled the pitch-black corridors of the medical research facility at UCSF. Rescue workers stumbled blindly around the fringes of the blast, but Matt moved through it with clear purpose. He saw in bright, unwavering detail, felt the shifting air currents, selected and processed distant sounds that others would have lost in the confusion. His brain regulated oxygen, adrenaline, and a host of other processes with an efficiency far beyond that of even the greatest athlete.

His memory recalled the route to Daniel's suite of labs with perfect clarity. The center of the blast had been somewhere near there, according to Daniel's garbled message left on his phone.

As he reveled in his abilities, he recalled Daniel's long, dense explanation about quantum coherence in the ion channels of the brain, and Godel's theorem, and how the brain really wasn't a computer like the mechanistic biologists said. "It's not algorithm-based, you see," Daniel had said, not realizing he'd left Matt behind long ago. "It has abilities far beyond any computer. And now I think I can manipulate it at the quantum level to magnify those abilities. Imagine what we could do."

Imagine what we could do.

Another blast. Chunks of concrete and burning pieces of shrapnel hurtled toward him. Matt avoided them as if they were moving in syrup. He didn't even feel his heart beating fast. Everything was still. No stress, no confusion; golden, perfect.

Feeling her way along the wall, a woman staggered from the billowing smoke, crying and coughing at once. Matt paused to guide her down a branching corridor, which he knew was the quickest route away from the disaster zone.

The area around Daniel's labs was devastated. Fires raged out of control around a dense pile of fallen masonry. Staggering around in the half-light, Daniel tore at the wreckage.

"Are you crazy? You need to get out of here. I can show—" Matt began as he tried to lead his friend away.

Daniel threw him off. "No! You've got to help Rose."

"Rose? What's she doing here?" His incomprehension was washed away by a rising tide of anxiety as he looked around what remained of the research facility.

Thrusting Daniel to one side, he threw himself into the worst area, letting the clarity fall on him. As irrelevant sounds and sights faded, he quickly processed what remained. A murmur. Fingernails scraping weakly against a door hidden behind the debris. Hints that would have been missed for hours by any other rescuers.

Futilely, Daniel attempted to lift a steel roof beam barring the door. Calmly, Matt eased him away. When he gripped the beam, his abilities optimized in an instant. On past experience, he wouldn't be able to maintain it for long, but as he felt the beam shift, he knew it would be enough.

With an effort that exhausted all his strength, he threw the beam to one side and tore away the remaining chunks of masonry. Wrenching open the door, he found Rose, coughing from the smoke but unharmed. Sweeping her up in his arms, he raced through the corridors, with Daniel unable to keep up in the dark and the confusion. Matt could feel her eyes on him, sense her gratitude and a hint of the emotion that had existed before her father's death, and a notion began to form deep in the core of his enhanced Quantum Mind.

Finally he broke out into the night awash with the glare of the flashing lights from the emergency vehicles. He didn't move from her side until the paramedics told him she would be okay, and then, as Rose hurtled away in the back of the ambulance for observation, he was overcome with exhilaration.

"You couldn't have planned a better test of what I can do," Matt said. "She could have died in there. I saved her." He turned his attention from the disappearing lights to Daniel's puzzled expression. "What I did . . . that meant something. It was important. I can do it again."

"Save Rose?"

"Save *people!*"

Understanding, Daniel led him to one side. "You don't have to make up for your past life."

"Yes, I do. I was a bastard. This is my shot, Daniel. My chance to pay back for all I've taken."

Suddenly angry, Daniel jabbed an accusatory finger. "So instead of having your face all over the media for being such a financial parasite, you now want it up there so everyone can see what a great hero you are? With abilities you wouldn't have if I hadn't given them to you?"

Matt was stung by his friend's words, but put it down to the shock of his ordeal. "No, I don't want that. You can develop some kind of armor, something lightweight, that'll hide my identity."

"And then what?"

"And then I make a difference." Matt could see he still hadn't convinced Daniel, but there was plenty of time for that. His attention was drawn back to the devastation. "What happened here? An accident?"

"I don't think so."

The blast had come at sunset, when most people had gone home for the day. "So the motivation wasn't loss of life," Matt mused. "Then, what?"

While the emergency services still searched the devastation for survivors, he bribed his way into the security offices to examine the digital recordings from the cameras.

"Money still gets you everything," Daniel said with an uncomfortable note of bitterness.

"If you've got it, might as well put it to some good," Matt replied, adding with a regretful note, "Finally."

While the images sped by, Daniel ventured, "I think I know who did this. After word leaked out about your recovery, I started getting enquiries about the process. Anonymous at first."

Matt continued to scan through the recordings. "What did they want?"

"To own it. Completely. Take it out of the hands of everyone else, I guess, or use it just for themselves."

"And you said no."

"Yesterday they made the final offer. And the agent let slip a name. Mr. Styx."

"What kind of name is that?" Matt's words trailed away as he brought the scrolling images to a halt. Near the entrance to Daniel's research suite, a shadowy figure wearing a skull-shaped Halloween mask looked toward the camera. There was something knowing in that glance, almost a signature, as if the wearer were saying, *Here I am—the one you're looking for*. Arrogance, contempt, a hint of cruelty, all captured in the nuance of body language and that cold stare leveled directly into the lens.

"Styx?" Matt was drawn to the death's-head, the name ringing deep in the caverns of his mind.

"After that, the name was everywhere. Linked to a heist here, a murder there. Soon the cops were talking about a network of crime across the Bay area, all leading back to Mr. Styx. Gangs working to his design. Hitmen taking out important establishment figures who got in his way. Drugs and prostitution, people smuggling, illegal weapons. I became consumed with the questions. Where did Styx come from? How did he get so powerful, so quickly? And how had he found out about Daniel's Quantum Mind process? Sitting here now, the answers are obvious. Hindsight is a great thing.

"Rose made a fast recovery from the smoke she'd inhaled, but she wouldn't see me, refused all my phone calls, ignored my e-mails. Daniel told me to give her time. Maybe she'd get over what happened to her father.

"But I was distracted, as always, by the thrill of what I could now do. I'd gradually come to terms with my loss of the daylight world. I slept; I woke refreshed to the night; I accepted it as my own. Complaining furiously, Daniel finally agreed to provide me with the black body armor tailored to my precise requirements. I could travel around the darkest parts of the city, unseen until I made my move. Watching. Listening. Slowly building a picture of Mr. Styx. By that stage, I'd already decided it was personal. He attacked my friend, the woman I loved. He deserved to be brought down for that alone, never mind all the other awful things he was doing.

"But Styx was a brilliant strategist. He marshaled his growing army of criminals in a constantly shifting network so it was impossible to trace the lines through the structure. And he spread like a virus through the city. In the early days, his work was only visible in the Tenderloin, among the lowlifes, the hookers, and the drug dealers. Within weeks, I was finding evidence of his influence everywhere, from Pacific Heights to Russian Hill, from the Mission District to Fisherman's Wharf. His rapidly growing criminal activity must have earned him a fortune, because he'd bought himself influence in city politics and business, in the SFPD too. He'd made himself untouchable.

"His network kept his identity secret. I couldn't find out where he was based, so I couldn't get close to him. All I knew was that he was smart, cunning, and ruthless. Bodies of people who had failed him turned up everywhere.

"Daniel was worried I was getting in over my head. Even with all my enhanced abilities, I was vulnerable to a knife or a bullet. And as he so harshly pointed out, my moneyed life had left me too cosseted to deal with such a hard world. Give up, he kept urging. Leave Styx alone.

"But Daniel was always like that, ultraprotective ever since we were kids. We were both smart, but he was the really clever one; I was just practical. He used to get bullied a lot for his nerd style— Daniel was King of Nerds—and I'd step in to look after him. But he would never let me get in a fight. He'd take any level of abuse to keep the peace. Good-hearted. Yeah, not like me. Guess that's why I thought we went well together. I always believed Daniel felt the same, but since I'd gone through the process, he seemed to be losing patience with me rapidly.

"'You've got a messiah complex,' he told me. 'You thought you were the bad guy before and now you've turned one hundred and eighty degrees and you think only you can save everyone. But in the end, it's all about you. What's good for Matthew is good for the world, right?'

"Maybe he was just trying to rile me, and if that was right, it worked. Back at the penthouse I punched the mirror and it cracked in two. I left it there as a reminder. One day I'd show Daniel I was a better man than he thought.

"But even with his doubts, he still tried to help. 'Trust the enhanced Quantum Mind,' he said. 'It'll communicate with you in new and interesting ways. Sending clues through your unconscious. Guiding you in the right direction. Things might look like coincidences, but you need to pay heed to them. It's you, speaking to yourself. Situation normal, I guess.'

"Finally I decided on a name, taking my cue from Styx. He'd gone for a mythological connection, the river on the boundary of the underworld, which meant *hate* in Greek. I decided to call myself Nox. It was ironic, I said, but Daniel told me bluntly that I clearly thought I was some kind of mythological god. And that decision bound Styx and me together on a symbolic level. Just as Daniel had said: secret connections lying just beneath the surface.

"Once I had my code name I was ready to break up Styx's operations across the city. I made an impact quickly. Disrupting supply lines, tipping off the cops, or cracking heads—I did whatever was necessary. Every time my name was mentioned in the bulletins it was a validation that I was making up for my past self-obsessed life. I pretty much gave up my life as Matt. The penthouse was only nominally a home; stripped of just about anything personal, it became simply the place for my day-sleep; a bat's cave.

"I forced Styx to notice me. That's when it became personal for him too . . . and when everything started to fall apart. I began to notice cameras positioned around the city with infrared sensors to pick up body heat. He was looking for me. I got Daniel to modify the armor to minimize heat leakage, but within a few days the cameras were made more sensitive, fitted with motion sensors, image recognition. His operations shifted rapidly beyond my reach. I started to lose the game, and I didn't like it. I'd never lost anything before.

"Even if he tracked me down to the penthouse, he wouldn't be able to get inside. I had the best defenses money could buy. Not even Daniel was allowed to know how to bypass them. It was my sanctuary, my prison cell; the place where I could guarantee being safe and where Styx could never reach me.

"I worked harder to try to overcome his tech, but I couldn't shake the feeling that he was laughing at me. That he thought I was ineffectual. On more than one occasion I failed to bust up his works in progress. Once I got on the wrong end of a flamethrower; that left me needing hospital treatment, even with my healing skills. At that moment, Styx was only sending out messages to get out of his way, but sooner or later he'd step things up to take me out.

"I always knew he was a killer, but I didn't realize exactly how brutal until that day a week before Easter when he slaughtered an entire family—father, mother, two kids—in their home and left a taunting message for me in their blood. I was physically sick. For several nights, I never left the penthouse. Their deaths were on my conscience. Yeah, that's what Styx wanted me to think, but it didn't lessen the blow any.

"And they were only the first. Innocent people gunned down in the street, bludgeoned or stabbed in their homes . . . the body-count rising every time I did something that irritated Styx. It was destroying me. Did I walk away and give him free rein, knowing I had the power to stop him? Did I carry on and cause more deaths?

"That was the time when it stopped being a great adventure. Since then, every single day has felt like I was killing myself a bit more. Has it made me a wiser person? It's made me a sadder one.

"The conflict continued. Styx and me circling each other, a blow given here, another one received there, the stakes rising higher and higher with each death, until I hated him with every fiber of my being.

"Daniel pleaded with me to stop, before I lost my own life, or my sanity, which he was convinced was dwindling with each encounter. But I couldn't stop. It was clear to me I was the only one who could end Styx's reign. When I'd undergone Daniel's process, I'd been given a purpose in life. Fate? Who knows, but I was sure that Nox could only die when Styx did.

"And then I was flattened by a blow completely out of left field. One night, in the middle of an argument, Daniel admitted he'd been dating Rose. I think in my heart I knew, but it still felt like a betrayal. I didn't respond well, told him to get out. I loved her. I wanted a chance to prove I was different now. It wasn't fair. In the heat of the moment, I said some things that weren't very friendly, but I'll still never forget the look Daniel gave me at the door. Hard, contemptuous. I started to think that maybe that youthful friendship wasn't as clear-cut as I remembered.

"I tried to contact Rose, and I know that caused some tension between them, but then they both stopped taking my calls. I was on my own.

"I took all that frustration out on Styx's organization, carved a path right through the center of it. That was a step too far; I could no longer be tolerated. His net began to close around me. And then, I guess, he decided to give me one final warning to keep away. My last chance. Rose went missing. How did he know to go for Rose? Yeah, any smart person can see where this is going. I remember . . ."

☆　★　☆

Searching.

Even an enhanced Quantum Mind couldn't contain the cauldron of human emotions. In the Tenderloin, away from the lights, Nox emerged from the dark to break limbs and pulp the faces of Styx's dealers and strong-arm men, to interrogate the hookers and the runners, aware that his own night-clock was quickly running down. When the sun came up there would be nothing he could do; Styx would have won and he would be destroyed forever.

Amid the sound of sirens drawing nearer, the trail led to Nob Hill. He knew it had to be a trap, but it didn't matter; saving Rose's life was the only thing that concerned him.

At the hill's summit, a cable car stood motionless. In the dark interior, Nox saw Rose clearly, strung by chains, her arms outstretched across the width of the car, her head hanging down. She'd been badly beaten. Fighting a wave of raw emotion, he raced to help.

Ten feet away, he heard the loud clunk of the brake being disengaged automatically, and then the cable car began to roll backward down the hill, gathering speed.

His body chemistry altered in a fraction of a second, flooding his muscles with the power needed to propel himself across the remaining distance. His perception slowed time so that the world appeared to hang, and then he crashed against the side of the cable car and clawed his way inside as the velocity increased.

Styx had disabled the brake and the backup system. As Nox turned to free Rose, he was overpowered by the chemical stink of the explosives packing the car.

A grand gesture. San Francisco would never forget Styx after this.

"I'll get you out of here," Nox called. Rose jerked her head up, peered at him through bruised eyelids. It was the last thing he saw before he was blinded. Along California Street on either side, powerful torches flooded the interior of the cable car with a brilliant white light.

Styx knows all about me, he thought, clamping one hand across his eyes to protect his hypersensitive vision. *Of course he does.*

Without his sight, every other sense was instantly magnified. Ignoring the violent rocking of the cable car as it thundered down the hill, he concentrated on the scent of Rose's perfume, and the iron tang of blood droplets caught in the air currents, heard each exhalation as if it had been amplified a hundredfold. Hauling himself along the carriage, he reached her in an instant, and in a perfectly calibrated flood of adrenaline and oxygenated blood, tore the chains holding her. Weak from her ordeal, she fell into his arms.

"Don't worry," he whispered. *I can save you. I can make up for all the terrible things I've done.*

In that strange, timeless world, Nox moved with the certitude of a savior filled with a righteous fury that Rose would never be hurt again. Carrying her effortlessly, he hauled them both on to the cable car roof, effortlessly making thousands of microcalculations to balance perfectly against the conflicting motions. In his mind, he glowed like a star as he shifted rapidly along the roof, avoiding the glaring lights.

I can do anything, he thought. *No one can stop me.*

Farther down the hill, the cops had created an impromptu roadblock with their cars to stop the carriage's progress. Not even he would survive that impact. Instantaneously calculating the wind currents, he leapt from the roof, shifting his body subtly to accommodate Rose's weight. Landing like a cat, he immediately broke into a sprint. All around, Styx's foot soldiers bolted for cover.

They're scared of me, he thought with grim pleasure.

The deafening explosion blasted out windows for blocks and sent a fountain of orange and scarlet flame high into the air. As debris rained down, Nox sheltered in a doorway with Rose.

"Who are you?" she asked weakly.

He removed his mask so she could understand what he'd done for her. There was surprise and confusion, but the time for explanations would come later.

"Styx is going to keep coming for you to get at me," he said. "I'm not going to let you suffer any more. I have to end this one way or another. Where is he?"

She gave him directions to the place she'd been taken when they snatched her. Her concern for him was clear.

"Don't worry about me."

She read his thoughts. "It's over with Daniel. I broke it off. It was a stupid thing, a reaction to you and me and . . ." As her words trailed away, he understood why she had been made to suffer and his anger burned fiercely. But when he looked into her face, he saw every sacrifice he had made—the loss of his days, his isolation, his obsession—and the sacrifice he would undoubtedly have to make, would all be worthwhile.

☆ ★ ☆

"Once I'd made sure Rose was safe with the paramedics, I returned here, to the quiet of the penthouse, my sanctuary from the world. I figured Styx wasn't going to run to another hideout. He wanted me to find him, or he wouldn't have let Rose know his base. Over the months I'd been tracking him, I saw the intricacy of connections and the depth of his thinking. He had always been one step ahead of me, but that was coming to an end now that I knew the truth. He couldn't hide behind masks anymore, and it was easy to understand his motivations.

"But that very revelation had sent my own world spinning

off its axis, and I was no longer sure I could trust my reactions. I needed time to assimilate. In a secret compartment in the bedroom, there was the box containing the few remnants of my past life that I wanted to keep—photos, of Rose, and Daniel and me, diaries, the usual stuff. As I sifted through them, they gradually revealed themselves to me in a new light. That expression on Daniel's face after I'd hauled him away from the kids threatening to beat him up in the locker room—it didn't look like relief any more. He was clever, used to being at the top. How did he really feel about some dumbass coming along and making him seem like a loser?

"The three of us drinking champagne after I'd bought out Rose's dad's company. Was Daniel really looking with affection at San Francisco's hottest couple? Or was it yearning for the woman that the dumbass had snatched from him? Another blow in a life-time of blows. What was really going on in that supersmart head of his?

"I didn't want to believe it. I was who I was because of Daniel, on so many levels. He'd been the only person who stood by me during my single-minded, cold-hearted rise to the top of the financial ladder. He was always there for me, the best of friends, an anchor in the harshest of environments. The betrayal—if that's what it was— was almost too painful to bear.

"When had he used the process on himself? Before my accident, or was I the guinea pig? Either way, he clearly had not suffered from my debilitating loss of the daylight world. Maybe my disability was just a by-product of the rod tearing through both hemispheres of my brain.

"And the truth beyond the truth? However important Daniel was in my life, I couldn't let him hurt Rose anymore. She was good and decent and honest, and she didn't deserve either of us. But life, as I'd discovered early on, was all about the hard choices. If I didn't bring Daniel to justice, I'd be spending the rest of my nights trying to keep Rose alive, trying to stay alive myself; and could I ever outthink Styx? I'd been behind him pretty much every step of the way so far.

"It had to end tonight. Whatever it cost me, it had to be over. I remember . . ."

☆   ★   ☆

Creeping . . .

. . . through the shadows surrounding the seemingly derelict building on the edge of the Tenderloin. The moment Nox saw it he understood the irony: it was one his company had bought for redevelopment before the bottom fell out of the market. Daniel had hoped to build a new research center there, but he'd never been able to raise the cash from investors.

Styx undoubtedly already knew he was there. Traps would be laid, his death would be planned, unfolding, not like clockwork, but with the seemingly inexplicable patterns of the quantum world. Nox knew he and Styx were entangled, like Schrödinger's cat and its decaying atom, had always been that way, and their fates were just as inextricably linked. *Spooky action at a distance*, Einstein had called it, and he'd always said Daniel was smarter than Einstein. He couldn't outthink Styx, but he did have instinct, cunning, and brutality, traits that had served him so well in the financial world.

The power supply to the building went first. When the fires were started across the ground floor, Styx's men ran out into the night like rats, and as choking smoke filled the pitch-black upper floors, Nox searched the interior methodically and rapidly. He had no idea if the process had adapted Styx in exactly the same way, but the dark and the confusion were his own perfect world.

To the last he hoped he was mistaken and Daniel had no part in this; that he would be safe at home, and someone else would be waiting at the heart of the web. But on the top floor, with the flames already roaring up on every side and the air almost too hot to breathe, Nox saw there was no going back. Consumed by panic, Daniel searched frantically for a way out of the burning building. He wielded a hunting knife in a desperate manner that made him appear to be attacking ghosts, or as if he expected Nox to emerge suddenly from the billowing smoke.

Daniel couldn't see in the dark. There was the advantage.

Circling Daniel, he waited for his moment to attack, acutely aware of that intermittently slashing knife. But time was short, and soon the conflagration would prevent any exit. Nox lunged.

At the last, Daniel must have heard something, for he whirled and stabbed the knife into Nox's side. Reeling backward from the pain, Nox dropped his guard, and Daniel hacked and slashed in a frenzy, still not seeing who was there.

All the months of repressed anger rose up in Nox, and he returned the attack just as furiously.

"Why?" he yelled. "What did I ever do to you?" He pressed the black mask close to Daniel's face, and in the ruddy light now glowing through the shattered windows saw recognition flare in Styx's face, and then realization, and finally fear.

He couldn't give Daniel a chance to turn the tables again. His fists were like hammers. Bone cracked under his knuckles, and blood sizzled on the hot concrete floor. He told himself it was justice in action, but really it was just the old Matt, betrayed and frightened and alone. He knew in that moment that whatever the wonders of an enhanced Quantum Mind, it was still tethered to the person beneath; the flawed individual always fighting to escape the gravity of his own destiny.

He didn't know if he'd already beaten Daniel to death before the floor shattered beneath them and they plunged through the burning building. But by the time Daniel hit the ground, there was no life left in him.

Nox dragged the body outside and stood over it as the sirens rose up in the distance. Conflicting emotions threatened to tear him apart. He'd saved Rose, saved himself, but what had he lost? In the end, he decided to preserve his memory of Daniel. Carrying the body off into the night, he buried it in an unmarked grave so that Daniel would never be linked with Styx or his criminal activities. He couldn't forgive his old friend; nor could he forgive himself.

☆   ★   ☆

"And that was it, the end—of the person who had been at my side for all my life, of the threat that had brought so many deaths and so much suffering, of the pain that had been heaped upon Rose. As I sit here in the last of the night, I only feel numb. But at least there's hope of a fresh start. Yeah, yeah, a new dawn, right? Funny. With Styx gone, I can put away the suit, and the Nox identity, and all the inadvertent pain I caused along with it. Because without me, there wouldn't have been Styx. Quantum entanglement on a human scale. Only now I haven't got my best friend to explain all that stuff to me."

He paused in deep reflection for a moment and then switched off what he hoped would be the final recording. His eyes burning, he felt the sun coming up hard at his back. Quickly, he stripped off the costume and stored it away in the hidden compartment so there would be no sign of his secret self if anyone did break through his intricate defenses while he was out cold.

Then, with hope, and relief, and sadness, he laid himself down on the bed and went into a deep slumber the moment the first rays of the sun broke through the window.

☆　★　☆

Ten minutes later, Matt woke, stretched, felt typically refreshed. He strode to the picture window and looked out over San Francisco, enjoying the heat of the sun on his face. When he felt ready, he slumped into the chair at the desk and began the recording.

"One day I'm going to have to play back these recordings, review my experiences, but then who's got time for that. I've got an empire to build. October eleventh. A new day dawns. With any luck, the plans I put in place will have taken out that idiot Nox. If not the bomb in the cable car, then the electric net on the top floor of the old factory. He won't be interfering with my work anymore. And with a typical flourish, it should have gotten rid of Daniel Stride too so no one else can benefit from his wonderful process. I'm not a bad guy. I gave him a chance. But if he doesn't understand the value of money, what can I do? And Rose? I'll be sad to see her gone too, but if she doesn't want me . . ." A triumphant grin rose up as he realized how close he was to his dream.

"So I've lost the nights, which would have been the natural time for my business, but it's not been too much of an obstacle. The days are mine. This city is going to be mine, soon now. With Nox gone there is no one left to stand in the way of Styx. All hail me."

☆ ★ ☆

Marjorie M. Liu is an attorney, and the *New York Times* bestselling author of two ongoing series: Dirk & Steele, novels of paranormal romance, and the Hunter Kiss urban fantasy series. She has also written the novel *X-Men: Dark Mirror*, and, in the world of comic books, is the writer of *NYX: No Way Home*, *Black Widow*, *X-23*, and *Dark Wolverine* (with Daniel Way, for Marvel). Here, she turns her imagination loose on one of comic books' foundational archetypes, with brilliant and surprising results.

Call Her Savage

MARJORIE M. LIU

There were gods in the sea, but Namid had never prayed to them; nor to any holy spirit since she had buried the tin star. But she found herself on the cusp of religion as she plummeted fifty feet to the dark Pacific, a leather harness buckled around her torso and shoulders, secured to a thick hemp cable that snapped tight the moment she hit the cold rough waters; dangling like some gristly worm at the end of a long hook. The cable was not quite long enough to accommodate the weather; and when the dirigible heaved upward, caught by the first smashing gust of the oncoming storm, Namid was torn from the brine, swinging madly, naked toes skimming foam. She would have vomited had there been anything in her stomach; but she had emptied her gut days ago. Never an admirer of flying.

"You see it?" roared one of the lieutenants, boots securely locked within the iron braces of the hangar floor. Namid, on the ascending portion of her dizzying, madcap swing, managed to glimpse the young man leaning down, headfirst, into the fifty feet of air separating him from the churning sea. It was night, no moon. Low clouds. He was dressed in warm silver wool and leather, and wore search goggles over his eyes, crystal lenses lit like twin moons.

Namid wished to remind the young man that he was in a better position to see than she; but the dirigible dipped, plunging her back into the sea. The lieutenant shouted again, though the drone of the engines drowned his words. Namid, clinging to the cable as she kicked her legs, cast a wild glance around her.

Nothing. Impossible to see. The hull's exterior lights had been dimmed, and the waters were black. A wave slammed, rolling Namid upward with sickening speed—and then down, sucked under. She held her breath as the ocean buried her, listening to a brief muted roar in her ears. She gripped the cable with all her strength.

When she resurfaced, the lieutenant was still calling out to her. His voice had gone hoarse. He held a knife in his hand, serrated steel reflecting the soft phosphorus glow of the night paint smeared against the wall around the exposed hangar gears. He was not looking at her, but at the sky.

Namid twisted around the cable, searching—and discovered pinpricks of light, burning behind the clouds, growing larger, brighter. Rumbling shuddered the air, metallic groans broken with pops and low whistles that cut through her eardrums. She gritted her teeth and threw back her head. The lieutenant was staring at her again, his knife pressed to the cable. Namid fumbled to free her own blade, sheathed among the sealed packages strapped to her body.

One-way trip. She had understood that, even before leaving the mountains; before saying yes; before packing her guns and memories, and her father's chemicals.

"Go!" she screamed at him, cutting through the cable in one swipe, nearly breaking off the blade in her haste. The dirigible surged upward at the last moment, leaving her airborne. As she fell backward into the sea, swallowing a scream, she glimpsed that final surge of light through the clouds.

And then, nothing. Just down, down deep into the ocean. Her eyes squeezed shut. She lost her knife and did not care. All she could hear was her hammering heart, and another kind of pulse—longer, deeper, a single shock wave that boomed through her body like thunder. She clawed upward, lungs burning, and burst through the surface with a gasp.

The dirigible was trying to flee. It was a small airship, built for speed and the transport of politicians, intercontinental couriers—but not war. Silver as a bullet, and slender as one, engine-fired with some of the finest core crystals the skull engineers could produce; and still, it had no chance against the vessel plunging from the clouds: an iron maiden, bristling with the sharp mouths of canons, each one silhouetted like needles against the beacon lights shining from the hull. A monstrous thing, blotting out the sky as its belly rode overhead, radiating such heat from its exposed crystalline core that her face felt burned.

Namid heard the thrumming charge before the canons fired—felt the vibration in the water. Flinched, instinctively, at that first shot—blasted in rings of fire at the escaping dirigible, which was making a sharp ascent into the clouds. Shells tore through the silken sail, igniting hot gas. She stared, resigned and horrified, as a fireball erupted around the dirigible.

Reminded her of a man burning alive. Or a mass coffin in the oven, souls trapped inside. She imagined bodies tumbling, falling, swallowed by the sea.

Just as she was swallowed, moments later.

Hands grabbed her ankles, and yanked her under.

☆　★　☆

There had been experiments in her youth involving a pressure chamber, performed by a man on loan from the redcoats who had something to prove. The ocean brought back those memories: all that immense, inescapable strain, as though the sea wanted to squeeze her vital organs into pudding, or implode her eyes and brain.

Namid had no skill for water, having never been able to stand its weight against her body. The men had to drag her along, blind, like a child. One of them, only moments after slinging lead hooks through her harness and tugging her unbearably deep, guided her hand to her nose. He forced her to pinch her nostrils shut, and then held a tube against her mouth. Bubbles tickled her lips. She opened then, just enough, choking—swallowing ocean and air as her mouth clamped tight around the tube. The ache in her lungs eased, but little else.

After an interminable length of time—during which she suffered a slow-burning hysteria—the men holding her arms stopped swimming and the top of her head brushed a hard surface. The hooks were removed from her harness, and the air tube pulled from her grasping lips. The men shoved her up a long metal tube, and she kicked and clawed toward the light that burned through her closed eyelids. Strong hands grabbed the harness knotted around her body. She was hauled upward. Dragged from the ocean onto a warm steel floor.

A thick blanket was spread immediately over her body, tucked against her legs with immeasurable care. The cold had never bothered her, but nevertheless, Namid lay for a long moment, shuddering, focused on nothing but the air in her lungs and the pleasure of no longer enduring that unspeakable pressure. Aware, even with her eyes closed, of all the men packed into that small space around her. Every sound was amplified: the rasp of their breathing, the shuffle of boots, the hum of the crystals and the coal furnaces burning somewhere beneath her.

"Lady Marshal," said a quiet voice. "You, MacNamara."

Namid exhaled, going still. Suffocating again, but in a different way. Until, with all the grace and strength she could muster, she pushed herself to her knees. Strong quick fingers tugged the blanket higher upon her shoulders so that it would not slip, and she helped, clutching it to her as she tried to sit straight and strong.

The crew would talk. Best to make a good impression, what little was left.

But it was difficult. When she looked into the faces of those silent staring boys who were crammed around the hatch—hardly a man with real years among them—she was unprepared for the awe and fear in their eyes.

She did not feel fearsome. Just wet and cold, and tired. A woman old enough to be their mother, black silvered braids dripping seawater against skin the color of sun-dried walnuts. She had been pretty once, or so others had said, but she had not looked at herself in a reflecting glass for more than ten years. Namid could only guess that she had aged like her mother.

The sealskin parcels strapped to her body were heavy, as was her soaked clothing: rough cotton shirt and a man's trousers, clinging to her, perhaps indecently. Gold glinted above her left breast, hammered in the shape of a star. A new badge. The envoys from the fledgling American government had given it to her, right before she left the warm Pacifica coast of New China. She had almost tossed the badge into the sea, but at the last decided to wear it. It meant nothing to her—but to the aircrew, it had been legend. Part of a costume. A mask.

A sinewy brown hand appeared. Namid stared, taking in the thick cuff of scar tissue around that muscled wrist, and then allowed herself to be pulled to her feet. She glimpsed a dizzying blur of navy wool and gold stars before anchoring her gaze on handsome cheekbones, a shaved head. The man had a Chinese look about him—in his eyes, mostly—but something else, too. Mixed blood, like her. Namid searched his face with great care, finding wrinkles about his weathered eyes, and a touch of silver in the bristle around his jaw. She had been finding white in her own hair for five years, but had not thought much of it until now.

"Captain Shao." Namid tightened her grip on his hand, as he did hers, before letting go.

He inclined his head. "I apologize for our late arrival. The British have dropped mines throughout the Pacific. We had to alter course almost a dozen times before we found a safe route."

"The airship that brought me here," she began, and then stopped, unable to continue. Gone soft, when she could not even speak of the dead.

Captain Shao rubbed his scarred wrist. "My swimmers witnessed the attack. They're searching for jumpers who might have survived the explosion."

Namid thought again of that aircrew, young as this one, all earnest and red-blooded, most of them too nervous to look her in the eyes. "Beijing," she said hoarsely. "The Emperor."

Captain Shao hesitated. "Best if you come with me."

Namid gave him a sharp look. He issued a command. Boys scattered, returning to their duties, many with lingering, backward glances. She had not realized how many had come to see her until they dispersed. All of them, bursting with rumors and the damnable old stories. As she followed the captain down the corridor, every boy she passed—every single one—pressed his knuckles to his brow. None could have been older than sixteen.

"They've talked of nothing else since learning you'd be coming aboard," Captain Shao told her, gently patting one of those genuflecting boys on the head. The teen blushed, tearing his gaze from Namid, and stooped to pick up a brush and pot of night paint. He began streaking a fresh layer into the grooves set along the iron wall, and the immediate glow was cool as winter light.

She almost reached for the captain, but pressed her fist against her thigh. "They should know better. You're all in danger now. When I discovered who they had sent to meet me—"

"We're always in danger," Captain Shao interrupted, glancing at her over his shoulder with eyes that were far harder than the soft, pleasant tone of his voice. "But I do believe they think you're worth it."

"They're only children."

"My men," he corrected sternly. "Don't belittle them, *Marshal MacNamara*. Not when you know why there's no one else left to fight. Not when they admire you so. They need a hero. We all do."

The admonishment cut deeper than it should have. "Call me Namid. I stopped being a Marshal after the war."

"Did you?" Captain Shao gave her a faintly mocking smile, glancing down at the gold star pinned to her shirt. "I don't think the world has quite caught up with your resignation."

He turned before she could think of an appropriate response—though there was none. Stories had been spun for years, becoming larger and more fantastic, turning her into a woman, a creature, that she could never hope to be. Legends were not flesh and blood. And she was no hero.

The corridor twisted. Steam exhaled from small valves, and when Captain Shao led Namid past a narrow iron stairwell, she felt a wave of suffocating heat rush upward over her body. Engine room. Voices shouted below, accompanied by the mournful wail of a fiddle; and then, in countermelody, the lilt of a penny whistle. Some Gaelic tune, the likes of which she had often heard in Albany.

Namid raised her brow. "You play music in the core?"

"It increases engine efficiency," Captain Shao replied, peering down. She followed his gaze and glimpsed fragments of immense crystal shards, part of a whole crown embedded in an iron cradle that left its roots exposed to the ocean itself: a natural, necessary coolant. "The more complex the tune, the better. Musicians have become quite sought after by the military, though each core seems to respond differently. Mine prefers strings, but I know one commander who can only make fifty knots accompanied by a harmonica."

Captain Shao opened another narrow iron door, revealing a small cabin: bed crisply made, papers stacked neatly on a small desk bolted to the floor. Fresh night paint had been spread over grooves in the wall, casting a cool luminous glow throughout the crunched space. Not much decoration: just a small ink painting of a sparrow hidden among cherry blossoms, and a golden locket that hung from a hook. Namid felt like stooping when she entered, and straightened with caution, half expecting her head to brush against the ceiling. The air smelled humid, metallic—like blood mixed with gear grease and sweat.

Captain Shao squeezed inside, shutting the door securely behind him. He set the lock, and she was glad. For the first time in weeks she felt safe, though it was strange being together in such a tight space. Reminded her of things she wanted to forget.

Namid stared at the locket. "This is your cabin."

"I won't have you bunking with the crew," he replied, and then hesitated, studying her. Namid met his gaze, remaining steady, unruffled. She might have spent the past decade lost in the mountains, but she remembered what it felt like to be judged.

"You have something unpleasant in your eyes," she said.

"This is a suicide mission," he replied bluntly. "*Your* suicide."

"Such a pessimist." Namid turned from him and began removing the sealskin packages strapped to her body. At least ten, of varying sizes. Beneath her bare feet the floor was warm and unsteady. When she stood in one place for too long, vibrations from the crystal core rattled her bones. She unwrapped her boots—still dry—and sat on the edge of the hard bed, turning them upside down, one after the other. She carefully shook out other small parcels, which made faint sloshing sounds when she held them up to her ear. Satisfied that the contents were still whole, she set them aside and tugged on her boots.

"How long have you been captain?" she asked quietly, not looking at him as she smoothed her hands over the tall worn leather; poking her fingers through a bullet hole or two.

He was silent a moment. "Several years. After the Brits were rousted from the Colonies, we were ordered into the South Pacific to work with the Chinese and their fleet. I received my command at the beginning of the Opium conflict."

"You would die for your men," she said, unfolding another parcel.

Captain Shao pushed away from the door. "Who are *you* dying for?"

Namid smiled bitterly, pulling free her gun. "I believe that would be your sister, Tom."

There was no such thing as one truth, but so far as the witnesses were concerned—and those who wrote down their stories, and couriered them across the sea to the East Americas and the Pacifica regions of New China—it seemed that some years back, British sailors had vandalized a temple in Kowloon, killing a monk, and then, after getting drunk, raged through a local village with guns blazing, taking turns with the young women and murdering men in cold blood. It was not the first time such violence had occurred, but unlike previous encounters (resulting, with one exception, in quick beheadings) Qing authorities were summarily denied access to the sailors. Who, with a great deal of sobriety, were set immediately to sea by their superior officers and ferried to India on a fast ship. Given that one of the criminals happened to be the bastard son of a duke, this was not entirely surprising.

Ties, however, had long been strained between China and England. Not that anyone should have been surprised about *that*, either. Namid might have been living in the mountains, but she still heard from the trappers, Cheyenne, and Chinese gold miners who occasionally visited her home. The English, she had been told, had finally found a way to take revenge on the Chinese for trading with the colonists during the war for independence; and it was a wickedness that had taken even her breath away.

Using the exclusive trade rights of the British East India Company, England had saturated Chinese markets with opium. So slowly, so insidiously, the imperial trade authorities had not realized the danger. Not until two million were turned into addicts. And then two million had become ten million.

Efforts to halt the import of drugs would have eventually led to war, but it was said by some that the Kowloon murders were the final straw. The Emperor ordered all British sea ships seized and their cargos burned. Dirigibles were shot down, torpedoed with cunning gunpowder kites and blazing missiles.

And the British, in turn, declared war.

But even the risk of China falling to England would not have been enough to bring Namid down from the mountain. No matter how much the fledgling American government—and the Chinese officials from the Pacifica court—begged.

Until the rumors changed everything.

☆   ★   ☆

It took three days for the submersible to reach the southern China coast. Twice they encountered mines, and both times swimmers—Scots-Irish colony lads and former Chinese pearl divers—had to be sent out to cut the nets with their bare hands and weight the explosives with iron balls to sink them to the bottom of the sea. No other way around. The British war machine was thorough.

"The Emperor has already relocated his children and most of his wives to the Chinese colonies on the Pacific coast," Captain Shao said on their last evening together, drinking oolong tea and snacking on dumplings that the cook had made specially for Namid. For the most part, Shao had avoided her until now; and she had obliged by keeping her own distance, mingling with him only at meals, or the few concerts she had attended in the engine room, sitting quietly in the corner while the boys played twisty jigs to the humming crystal core.

"South, in the gold country," he went on, "though I've heard rumors that his oldest sons will be journeying deeper inland to live with the Navajo. The Brits never could keep up with the natives, and the Emperor wants his heirs to learn about survival in case they must return to fight for their kingdom. He thinks his family has gone soft."

"Everyone saying yes to you all the time will do that," Namid told him absently, studying the last of the Imperial military reports that he had saved for her, some of the complicated characters scribbled in obvious haste on rough sheets of raw silk. "The iron maiden that destroyed my transport could have hit, in three days, any part of New China territory. It might be there now. Our air defense is strong, but all it would take is one good strike."

He looked at her as he did only when they were alone: with thoughtfulness, a glimmer of warmth, and a sadness that Namid could hardly tolerate. "Fears of air attacks aren't why you were called back. *Or* why you agreed."

"The envoys told me stories," she admitted, touching the revolver holstered to her hip. No need for a weapon on the submersible, but its weight helped her think. That, and the crew enjoyed seeing it. She had used a rifle during the war, and it was her firearm of choice, but the revolver was a recent invention and Namid found that she liked having the ability to shoot rounds in quick succession. Not that she had been aiming at much of anything but fir trees for the last decade; though occasionally, some men had thought to visit her mountain home in the hopes of murder and reputation.

"Stories," Captain Shao echoed flatly.

She gave him a hard look. "They told me things that no one could have made up."

"A trap, then."

"No." Namid stroked the revolver, and then her thigh; feeling the puckered scars beneath the clothing she had borrowed from one of the crew. "Not this time. They know I'm alone and not a threat. Not anymore."

Captain Shao made a small sound. Namid looked at him sharply, but he made no effort to hide the faint amusement darting against his mouth.

"Queen of the Starlight Six," he said quietly. "Most feared band of riders on the continent. I heard once from a captured British sailor that mothers still tell children stories about you, to scare them into being good."

Namid shrugged. "They also say I'm ten feet tall, a Cheyenne princess who can change into a wolf. *And* that my eyes are capable of looking into a man's soul and burning it free of his bones. Which, apparently, is what I did to an entire army of Brits off the Atlantica coast, leaving corpses that were little more than ash."

"Well," Captain Shao replied, "you always terrified *me*."

"That was your sister," Namid shot back, looking again at the golden locket hanging on his wall; and then him, searching for Maude in his face. "I was the quiet one."

He rubbed his face and leaned back in the chair with his eyes closed. Their knees brushed, and for a moment she was a child again, sitting on the swing her father had built, and that all the children fought and made bets over, simply because it could go higher and faster than any other. A swing built for a child who possessed similar strengths of speed and power.

"Quiet, but savage," he murmured. "That's what Maude would say. Nor are those stories far wrong. If you'll recall, I was part of the unit brought in to dig the graves."

Namid shuffled his papers into a neat pile, unwilling to remember. "We arrive tonight?"

"You know we do."

"Your orders are to wait for a day, and then go."

"With or without you."

"It will be without me." Namid finally looked him in the eye. "You'll wait for a messenger who will tell you whether or not I succeeded."

Captain Shao stared for a moment, and then leaned forward—so quickly, with such menace, her hand flew to her gun. She moved faster than he did, and suffered a vision before he stilled: her weapon raised at his head, trigger pulled, with blood and brain and bone; and the aching silence, the terrible silence, suffocating the roar of the shot. She could taste the gunpowder on her tongue, and feel the burn of the recoil in her shoulder.

But it was not real. Not yet. Not ever. Namid forced herself to relax, even as Captain Shao stared from her eyes to her hand, still pressed to the revolver at her hip.

"They all said you were dead," he murmured stiffly, as though he could hardly force the words past his lips. "And if not dead, then ruined. No one could imagine another reason for you to abandon your responsibilities. Not when you had so much power. Not when someone like you was needed in the rebuilding."

"Someone like me," she whispered, unable to move her hand. "I was a killer."

Captain Shao shook his head, but that was instinct, in the same way she had reached for her gun—and she listened for reassurance and heard none—watched his eyes and saw only his memories: of blood, and bone, and the gristle of decay under days of hot sun. No denying truth. No denying how much she had done in the name of others and herself.

"It was not your fault," he said.

"My time was over," she replied, wishing he would understand, ashamed that she wanted him to. Just a little truth between childhood friends. Something the rest of the world would never comprehend.

But there was no opportunity. A bell chimed, and a sharp whine cut through the hull. The engine quieted, signaling the beginning of a steady drift. Three days, and now they were done.

"Well," Captain Shao said softly, still watching her with that grim, unbearable sadness.

"I know," Namid replied, and finally forced her hand away from the gun.

☆ ★ ☆

A boat was waiting for her when she broke through the surface of the ocean. A small craft, little more than a slab of wood laden down with fishing nets and fat cormorants squatting inside bamboo cages; so flimsy, a two-mast junk would have sunk it with merely a swipe. Namid said nothing, though. It was night, and she could see the stars. She had almost forgotten what they looked like.

Captain Shao joined the swimmers who guided her from the submersible. It was against protocol for him to leave his vessel, but none of the boys who saw her off made mention of their commanding officer abandoning them, if only temporarily. They said good-bye in the same way they had said hello—with silence, and respect, and fear. Namid thought she might allow herself to miss them, but only because she could not abide the thought that their deaths would mean losing one of the few people who remembered her in pigtails.

Her belongings were strapped to her body, wrapped again in

sealskin, along with a set of dry clothes. Captain Shao, who had stripped down to a special suit made of shark hide, pushed her out of the water into the boat; helped, from within, by its sole occupant: a young Chinese woman. Her hair was shorn so close to her scalp that even in the darkness Namid could see the cuts and bruises in her skin, and a deep red welt, nearly a scar, that covered her throat. Her movements were slow and pained. Captain Shao frowned, giving her a hard, thoughtful look.

Namid leaned over the edge of the boat, gripping his forearm tight as she could. He tore his gaze from the other woman and did the same, his knuckles white, seawater streaming down his face. Beyond the harsh rasp of their breathing and the lap of waves against the boat, she heard distant booms, one after the other, raining down into her bones.

She tried to release his arm, but he held on, pulling himself so close the boat tipped dangerously sideways.

"No mercy," he whispered. "Don't you dare."

Namid forced herself to smile, though it was faint, grim, and felt like death. "Stay safe, Tom."

His jaw tightened with displeasure, and something else, too much like desperation for comfort. Namid jammed her hip against the edge of the boat and reached down, ready to pry his fingers off her arm. His grip was beginning to hurt, and his men were staring.

But he let go before she touched him. Let go, as though burned, and pushed away from the boat—and her. He treaded water, holding her gaze, and she did not look away, or blink. Just held on, in the only way she knew how: with memory, and heart, and the certain knowledge that distance was always safer.

The Chinese woman began rowing. Namid raised her hand. Captain Shao did not. He stared a moment longer, and then dove. His men followed him in silence. Swallowed, as though their flesh was made of sea and shadow. She knew better than to watch for them, but found herself doing so anyway.

"Are you ready?" asked the other woman softly. She sounded as though she was from the Mainland south, perhaps even Kowloon, which spoke a different Chinese dialect entirely; though her tone was educated, even refined. Namid was accustomed to Mandarin, having been born to a Cheyenne mother in the territory of New China, but she had spent most of her adult life out east in the Colonial Americas, speaking English. Sometimes she still had trouble with the various accents of the native Chinese (and the Europeans, as well), though enough gold miners had come around the mountain over the past ten years to give her practice.

The woman's breathing turned ragged, accompanied by a faint whistling grunt every time she pulled at the oars. Her movements were awkward. Blood seeped from the deep welt in her neck. Namid scooted forward, and without asking, placed her hands on the slender wooden grips. Cormorants clucked, shifting their wings, and in the distance, low crashing booms still rumbled. Familiar, even after ten years.

"You're injured," Namid said, as the other woman leaned slowly away from the oars. "The Emperor should not have sent you."

The woman touched her throat, and then her shaved, nicked scalp; a flick of a delicate wrist, so that her frayed black sleeve fell down a fine-boned arm. Namid would have thought her a Buddhist nun had it not been for the fine weave of her dark clothing, as well as the look in her eyes, wild and hard. "I was uninjured in the beginning. Nor was I meant to meet you here. Everyone . . . everyone else . . . was captured. I was the only one who escaped." She swallowed heavily, looking at the birds, the ocean, anywhere but at Namid. "You are not what I expected."

"I am Namid MacNamara," she replied, because she had never found a better answer to that statement, not even after hearing it for most of her life. No one was ever who he or she was supposed to be; not even Namid could say for certain that she knew herself completely. Truth rested only in action; the rest was mystery.

"I am Xiao Shen Cheng," said the woman, after a brief hesitation.

Namid was focused on the horizon, where a faint orange glow had appeared. As such, it took longer than it should have to recognize the name. But when she did, everything stopped—everything—and the boat began to drift. She stared at the woman, letting it sink in; and suffered disbelief, and dread.

"You came too late," whispered the Empress, rubbing her pale hand against bloodshot eyes. "My husband is dead."

Namid forced herself to breathe. "How?"

Shen Cheng gave her a disdainful look. "It was a sustained effort. We fought well. But the Emperor had sent our crystal skull away with the children, and the remaining core was not powerful enough to feed the lines. When the Juggarnauts came, we could only slow them."

Namid sat back, struck with a chill. Juggarnauts. She had heard that name from the envoys—heard it for the first time in a decade—and then again in the imperial court on the Pacifica coast; from the mouths of the silver bullet aircrew, and on the submersible, whispered when the boys would see her coming. No one ever thought she could hear them, but that was the curse and the gift of being who she was. Only Captain Shao had refrained from speaking of those skull-enhanced men and women—but that was because he was also Tom, and shared the pain.

Behind them, below, in her bones, Namid heard a low oppressive groan, a rumble that rose from the sea through the bottom of the boat. A despairing sound; and the answering swell that lifted them was unnatural and stomach-roiling. Something brewing in the water. More than one submersible. A battle.

Namid tightened her grip on the oars, prepared to row again—and found herself staring down the barrel of a ruby-studded revolver. British design, new and gleaming.

Shen Cheng closed her eyes and pulled the trigger. Namid had already begun to move, reaching out to knock aside the weapon, but the deafening blast skimmed her left arm and sent the Empress recoiling backward over the edge of the boat. She bobbed to the surface immediately, gasping for air, arms thrashing the water. Not much of a swimmer, either.

Namid did not jump in after the drowning Empress. She took

a deep breath, rolling through the pain and rush of blood to her head. Ten years on the mountain. Quiet, peaceful. She would have died an old woman, with no one the wiser. A good meal for the scavengers.

She picked up the British revolver, testing its weight in her hand. "Where are the Juggarnauts?"

Namid was not entirely certain the woman would hear—or care—but that bruised, battered face turned toward her, and a skinny hand managed to latch on to the edge of the boat. Below them, the waters swelled again, as though from the passage of a large body. Namid thought of Shao, and Maude, and the rest of her old crew, and balanced the revolver across her forearm, aiming it at the woman's head.

"Tell me where they are," she said again.

Shen Cheng shook her head, though the corner of her gaze lingered on the glittering gold star pinned to Namid's chest. Despair flickered through her face.

"I know the stories," she whispered. "You are savage. You will kill me if I tell you."

"I've killed for less," Namid agreed, and slammed the revolver butt on the woman's fingers. She howled, flailing. Namid placed the weapon on the floor of the boat and picked up the oars. She started rowing. The Empress, sobbing, tried to follow; but it was like watching a log thrash.

"They tortured me!" she screamed at Namid, her voice choking on seawater. "I had no choice!"

Namid did not stop.

☆   ★   ☆

It was an accident, or so her father had always said. A Scottish engineer, an adventurer, who had studied with the skull masters in China before traveling across the Pacific to the imperial colonies— a vast network of villages and cities that had been thriving for almost a century before England sent its first ships of men to hack a new civilization on the frontier of the far eastern continental tip.

By the time her father had arrived in New China, the Pacifica court and its alliance with the western native tribes was well known, but only by accident; the Chinese Empire had done its best to keep its colonies secret. Too many precious resources at stake: not just gold, but rich and verdant farmland, the likes of which did not exist in Asia.

Her father, who had become a favorite of the old Emperor, was allowed frequent access to the crystal skull that powered the Pacifica court, and formed the root strain of its crystalline harvests. Only fifteen skulls had been found throughout the world—four of them were in Chinese possession—though rumor had it that many were yet to be discovered in the jungles of the far south. Expeditions were regularly sent—usually ending in bloody conflicts—but only one had thus far been found, and that by the new Americans themselves, raising their current possession to two—the other having been given to the new colonies when they were still under British rule.

No one knew quite for certain how the skulls worked, only that some Mohammedan king of the Holy Lands had discovered three in the sands of an oasis: blocks of perfect crystal carved in the shape of human skulls, the likes of which no artisan had ever yet been able to duplicate.

Rather than declare the skulls a simple curiosity, the king had devoted himself to hours spent staring into those translucent eyes—one after the other, in patient succession. This, according to legend, went on for several years until, quite abruptly, the king suffered a massive stroke that left him blind and speech-impaired, but functional enough to declare that he had discovered the secrets to the skulls.

An overly ambitious statement. Two hundred years later, engineers were still learning what powers the skulls possessed—though it was widely known that an electrical current flowing through a skull into a special mineral bed was enough to instigate the growth of crystals that could be used to power the armadas, towns, even entire cities. Beyond that particular commonality, however, each skull was different. Some provided visions. Some made others go insane.

And some, as her father had discovered, changed the very essence of a human being.

☆   ★   ☆

Namid found the shore far sooner than expected. She dragged the boat onto the beach, but did not bother hiding it. Just stood in rock and sand, staring at the ocean as she stripped off her wet clothes and dressed in dry trousers and a shirt. The rest of her belongings were unwrapped quickly: revolver, two knives, her special bullets, and last, the vials of chemicals her father had prepared during the colonial war, and left to her upon his murder.

She loaded her gun very carefully. Then, with equal care, pinned the gold badge to her shirt, tracing her fingers along the points of the star. Warmth filled her, and then cold, sensations accompanied by memories.

We need you, voices whispered. *No one else but you.*

We will die if you cannot turn them back. All of us, our freedom, lost. Shut your heart to the blood, shut your ears to the screams. You were born to no other purpose. You are exceptional only in death.

Namid began walking to the rhythm of those old words, spoken in many different ways by many different people, though the message had always been the same. Even her mother's people, the Cheyenne, had told her future in blood, but that was to be admired, and not feared. She had been touched by some great power, which the First People claimed to be from the stars, and so the stars were in her name, and as an adult, she had worn a star upon her breast in the service and protection of others; first in peace, and then in war.

The terrain was not far different from the estuaries and tangled forests that could be found on the coastlines of New China and the Colonial Americas. She smelled the sea and the spice of firs growing tangled on rocky outcrops. Listened to the booms and thunder of some not-so-distant battle. If the Chinese military realized the Emperor was dead, then they might have already surrendered. She hoped not. She hoped that the fire staining the horizon was the

British burning, and had a feeling she would be finding out for herself, soon enough. Shen Cheng had not been a strong rower. She had been sent from someplace near—and someone would be waiting for her to return. She could take a fine guess who.

But not long after Namid abandoned the boat, she heard sounds that did not belong: shouts, the clunk of steel and wood. Familiar noises, which sent her running. She was careful, and kept the revolver in her hand. Felt herself slipping back into the old days, except now she was alone, and the burden was hers. Hers, knowing that it was the others in her crew who had always been the real heroes. So very human, with no power to protect themselves, driven only by courage and grit, and honor.

She missed them.

Shouts grew louder, frantic, cut with hoarse cries. Namid burst onto a rocky beach and found herself facing boys, boys crawling from the sea, boys wearing air-filled ties made of sheep gut. She recognized all those faces, but there were so few, less than a quarter of their former numbers dragging free of the waves.

Namid ran to them. Several cried her name, pointing. The rest let out a ragged cheer, and their smiles—those smiles of relief when they saw her—cut and burned, and twisted her heart. *As if now*, those smiles said, *everything will be all right.*

She grabbed the arm of the nearest boy, who was limping heavily across the rocks. Blood ran down his leg. He was pale, blond, just a scrap of a lad, but he was dragging a sealskin pouch behind him in a white-knuckled grip.

"Captain Shao," she said, running her hand over his face to push his sea-soaked hair out of his eyes.

The boy coughed raggedly into his palm. "Left 'fore him. He gave me 'is papers, he did, f'safekeepin'."

"Bastards cracked the crystal core," added another boy, drawing near. "Had to jump before we sank too deep. Cap'n promised he'd follow."

Namid gritted her teeth, briefly searching the faces around her.

No sign of her friend. He was out of her hands. She holstered her weapon and slung her arm around the waist of another child who was close to falling on his knees. Coughs wracked his chest.

"Come on," she said, and caught the eye of a sturdy red-haired lad who seemed to be doing better than the others. "Go, pass the word. Everyone needs to hurry. Something worse than redcoats might be close."

His reaction was an infinitesimal flinch, but he gave her a sharp nod and ran down the beach, grabbing the boys who were already out of the water and steering them back to the waves to help the ones still struggling. Namid dragged the child in her arms as far as the brush, and then left him to go back for others. She kept count, as best she could, still searching for their captain.

She saw the red-haired boy again. "Your name."

"Samuel," he said breathlessly, still looking over his shoulder at the darkened sea. No one else was there. No one she could see.

"Samuel," she said, grabbing his chin and forcing him to look at her. "Weapons?"

"No'm," he replied, blinking hard. "Just fists."

Namid let go of his face and patted his shoulder. "Good. Find other sensible lads who can lead, and then break yourselves up into small groups. Scatter, but head for the hills. You'll be able to hide better there."

"But," Samuel began, stopping himself almost as quickly, before continuing, "You're not coming with us?"

Namid hesitated. "I'll be making sure no one follows."

"We can fight."

"You can live." She unsheathed one of her knives and pressed it into his hand. "The others need you. So do I."

Samuel swallowed hard, but again gave her that sharp nod, as though it was his way of steeling himself. Namid watched him as he ran toward the others, and then turned away from the ocean, away and away, where her friend was not emerging from the waters. She faced the hills and the scrub, and listened to the distant sounds of airships and gunpowder bombs, imagining the scent of smoke, finally, in the air. Her skin prickled, a focused chill that rode from her scalp down the back of her neck.

Namid pulled out her revolver. Behind her, one of the boys shouted. She turned, glimpsing a hulking figure looming from the shadows at the edge of the beach, moving in perfect silence. He was monstrous, a giant, more than eight feet tall and built like the side of a rock-hewn mountain. His fists were clad in iron, as was his chest, and he held a sword in his hands that could slice any of those boys in half with hardly a touch. Scalps hung from his belt, long black braids looped and tangled, still dripping with blood.

"Run!" she screamed, and dove through them as they scattered, throwing herself toward the giant. He grinned when he saw her and took swipes at the escaping boys, his sword whistling through the air. Namid skidded to a stop and fired her revolver. The bullet hit his bicep, but he laughed at the wound and shook his head.

"Queen of the fookin' riders," he bellowed. "Bullets dinnae hurt me, lass."

Namid holstered her gun and withdrew her knife. Took another running leap, dodging under his sword, feeling a shift in her body as she moved—blood surging, burning, boiling in her veins. Red shadows gathered in her vision, and her heart pounded so hard she could taste her pulse at the back of her throat. Taste that, and more.

She slashed at his thighs, cutting deep, hacking and stabbing every part of him that she could. Taking her time, playing up his amusement. His muscles were grotesquely shaped, distended beneath skin pocked with old burns and scars—a man who had been unnaturally grown over years of deliberate exposure to crystal light. Namid remembered others like him. Monsters, made: rapists and murderers, freed from prisons to be fed to the skull engineers and their experiments. Few usually survived. This one smelled like an outhouse, and his laugh was careless; arrogant and cruel.

Until, quite suddenly, he made a choking sound.

Namid darted away as his knees buckled. He fell face-first onto the sand, but not before she saw his hands clutching his throat, his tongue so swollen it protruded from his mouth. His eyes bulged. Namid could not imagine what he had looked like before the engineers had changed him, nor did she care. She watched the man choke to death. Poisoned by her bullet.

Footsteps behind her. Namid turned, glimpsing a pale face.

And got shot in the chest.

The blast was deafening, and so was the pain. Namid rocked backward onto the sand. She tried to reach for her revolver, but a knife stabbed through her palm. Namid glanced down and saw a hole in her chest the size of her fist. Blood bubbled from her mouth. She vomited blood.

Then stopped moving at all.

☆ ★ ☆

Namid drifted. No dreams. Just darkness pricked with moments of desperate sorrow and a terrible aching homesickness for a life lost so long ago it might as well have been something she never had.

Until, finally, she remembered her body—her body, which she did still have—and opened her eyes.

Overhead, stars. Namid twitched her fingers, and then her feet. No restraints. The hole in her chest had healed, though scar tissue remained; one more to add to all the others that covered her body. She knew without looking that her revolver was gone—her hip felt too light. The bullets and the chemical vial had been removed from her pockets, as well. One knife remained sheathed against her thigh.

Her mouth tasted like raw meat. She smelled wood smoke, and listened to a fire crackling. A woman hummed, a low familiar tune that sent Namid back to a time when she remembered how to smile.

She swallowed hard. "Hello, Maude."

The woman stopped humming. "I knew you would come."

Namid sat up slowly, drinking in the person who had once been her greatest friend. Analyzing the deep wrinkles, and the sagging flesh around her waist and jaw. Maude had been beautiful, her brown hair sleek and fine, and her eyes bright. But the years had not been kind. Everything had dulled. Golden skin looked like stone. Her hair was gray.

Maude touched her face self-consciously, almost withering beneath Namid's stare. "You look the same, except for the silver in your hair. But I . . . I think there were side effects to what was done to me."

Namid thought of her father, unwittingly exposing his body and seed. Her pregnant mother, who had spent time with him during his experiments. "You made that choice."

Maude smiled bitterly. "I was jealous. But you knew that, in the end. I was only human, and wanted what you had."

Namid closed her eyes, heart aching; so much raging inside her, she was afraid to speak. "Did it give you peace? Handing yourself over to the redcoat engineers for their experiments? Were you satisfied after you came back and killed the others?"

"I didn't—" she began, but Namid surged to her feet, the knife somehow in her hand.

"You led those monsters to us while we slept," she snarled, and threw the blade at Maude's face.

The woman caught the knife out of the air and spun away through the sand. She was quick—quicker than Namid remembered—and rammed her hard in the shoulder, sending them both into the fire. The knife slid against Namid's side, but it was the flames that made her howl, and she rolled sideways as her hair and clothing burned. Maude did not scream, but darted away, smoking, reaching for the revolver that Namid suddenly saw in the sand.

"I heard about your father's work. But you didn't have this the last time we met," she whispered, picking up the weapon, just as Namid put out the flames on her body. "I watched from the ridge while you ripped out the throats of the Juggarnauts who killed your crew. You used your bare hands. You were . . ."

"Savage," she hissed, trembling. "I had good reason to be."

Maude gave her a sad smile. "I dream of it every night. You chase me, and I run. Ten years running from you, when all I ever did before was run with you, toward you, after you."

She raised the revolver with its poisoned bullets and aimed it at Namid's stomach. She did not fire, though. Just studied her, with that sadness deepening in her eyes. "Why didn't you ever come looking? I expected it. I expected you at every corner, with your hands at my throat."

But Namid said nothing. Nothing she *could* say, though the words bottled inside hurt worse than the burns along her back and scalp. Ten years thinking of that night, and nights before that, nights and battles and all of them together, like family. Namid had hated the redcoats, but she had been unprepared to hate a friend—and that was a cut that had never healed right.

On their left, a branch snapped. Maude glanced away, just for a moment. Namid lunged.

No mercy. She slammed her fist into the other woman's face, and then hit her again, with all her strength. Bone smashed. Maude cried out, trying to bring the revolver back around to fire. Namid grabbed her wrist and broke it with one swift twist. The revolver fell. And just like that, Maude stopped fighting.

"I'm here," Namid whispered, staring into her eyes, "with my hands at your throat."

"Finally," Maude breathed.

☆　★　☆

When Namid was done—and Maude was truly, irrevocably, dead—she sat down by the fire and found Captain Shao crouched on the other side of the flames. He was nearly naked, soaked; a deep scratch ran down the length of his side. But he was alive. Staring at the poisoned remains that had once been his sister.

"I'm sorry," she said to him, too weary and heartsick to feel anything but shame at seeing him again; shame, that he should witness her covered in the blood of the only family he had left. Anger simmered in her gut, too—and despair.

"It had to be this way," he said quietly, also without emotion. "But if she had seen me again . . ."

He stopped himself, and said nothing more for a very long

time. Namid lay down on the sand, holding her revolver close. Just before dying, Maude had told her that no other Juggernauts were close. The rest had remained in Shanghai, working with the British to overrun what remained of the Emperor's southern seat. The Chinese military still fought, but not for long. They were running out of hope.

Light was creeping into the horizon when finally, softly, Captain Shao said, "I understand now why you left."

"I doubt that," she whispered, but pushed herself up and rubbed her face. "Your men are safe. As many as could be saved. We should find them."

His eyes glittered, reflecting the dying firelight. "We have no submersible. And there is a war raging."

Namid studied the revolver in her hands. She had found the vial of poison nearby. More bullets could be made. "I suppose that's true."

A sad smile touched his mouth, so much like his sister's that Namid's eyes burned with tears. "And I suppose it might also be true that the only way for us to survive is to fight."

Namid sighed. Captain Shao whispered, "Can you be what they need?"

"What people love in war, they hate in peace," she said quietly. "But yes, I can be what they need."

Captain Shao stood and walked to her. He did not look at his sister's body, but held out his hand to Namid.

"Lady Marshal," he said. "You, MacNamara."

"Yes," she said again, and took his hand.

☆ ★ ☆

Ian McDonald is the acclaimed science fiction author of such works as *The Dervish House, Brasyl, River of Gods, Cyberabad Days, Desolation Road, King of Morning, Queen of Day, Out on Blue Six, Chaga,* and *Kirinya.* He has won the Hugo Award, Philip K. Dick Award, and the BSFA Award, has been nominated for the Quill Award and the Warwick Prize for Writing, and has been nominated several times for the Hugo and Arthur C. Clarke Awards. *Asimov's Science Fiction* called him "one of the most interesting and accomplished science fiction writers of this latter-day era. Indeed, maybe the most interesting and accomplished." Need more be said?

Tonight We Fly

Ian McDonald

It's the particular metallic rattle of the football slamming the garage door that is like a nail driven into Chester Barnes's forehead. Slap badoom, slap badoom: that he can cope with. His hearing has adjusted to that long habituation of foot to ball to wall. Slap baclang. With a resonating twang of internal springs in the door mechanism. Slap baclang buzz. Behind his head where he can't see it. But the biggest torment is that he never knows when it is going to happen. A rhythm, a regular beat, you can adjust to that: the random slam of ball kicked hard into garage door is always a surprise, a jolt you can never prepare for.

The bang of ball against door is so loud it rattles the bay window. Chester Barnes throws down his paper and is on his feet, standing tiptoe in his slippers to try to catch sight of the perpetrators through the overgrown privet. Another rattling bang, the loudest yet. A ragged cheer from the street. Chester is out the front door in a thought.

"Right, you little buggers, I had enough of that. You've been told umpteen times; look at that garage door, the bottom's all bowed in, the paint's flaking off. You're nothing but vandals. I know your parents, though what kind of parents they are letting you play on the street like urchins I don't know. This is a residential area!"

The oldest boy cradles the football in his arm. The other boys stand red-faced and embarrassed. The girl is about to cry.

"I know you!" Chester Barnes shouts and slams the door.

"Chester, they're nine years old," the woman's voice calls from the kitchen. "And the wee one, she's only six."

"I don't care." Back in the living room again, Chester Barnes watches the five children slink shamefacedly down the street and around the corner. The little girl is in tears. "This is a quiet street for quiet people." He settles in his chair and picks up his paper.

Doreen has balanced the tea tray on the top of her walker and pushes the whole panjandrum into the living. Chester leaps to assist, sweeping up the precarious tray and setting it down on the old brass Benares table.

"Now you know I don't want you doing that, it could fall as easily as anything, you could get scalded."

"Well, then you'd just have to save me, wouldn't you?"

There is tea, and a fondant fancy and a German biscuit.

"Those chocolate things are nice," Chester says. "Where did you get them?"

"Lidl," Doreen says. "They've a lot of good stuff. Very good for jam. You never think of Germans having a penchant for jam. Is it in again?"

"What?"

"You know. The ad. I can see the paper, you've left it open at the classifieds."

"It's in again."

"What does it say this time?"

"Dr. Nightshade to Captain Miracle."

"And?"

"That's all."

"Are you going to reply?"

"With what? It's nothing. I'll bet you it's not even him. It's kids, something like that. Or fans. Stick on the telly, we're missing *Countdown*."

"Oh, I don't know, I don't like that new girl. It hasn't been the same since Carol left."

"It hasn't been the same since Richard Whiteley died," Chester says. They watch *Countdown*. Chester's longest word score is a seven. Doreen has two eights, and gets the numbers games and today's Countdown Conundrum. Doreen gets up to go and read in the backyard, as she doesn't like *Deal or No Deal*. "It's just a glorified guessing game," she says. *Not for me it's not*, Chester Barnes says. As she advances her walking frame through the living room door, she calls back to Chester, "Oh, I almost forgot. Head like a seive. The community nurse is coming round tomorrow."

"Again?"

"Again."

"Well, I hope it's after *Deal or No Deal*."

Doreen closes the door after her. When the creak of her walking frame has disappeared down the hall, Chester Barnes picks up the newspaper again. *Dr. Nightshade to Captain Miracle*. A rising racket on the screen distracts him. Noel Edmonds is whipping the audience up into a frenzy behind a contestant reluctant to choose between the sealed prize boxes.

"Twenty-seven, pick number twenty-seven, you blithering idiot!" he shouts at the screen. "It's got the ten pounds in it! Are you blind? No, not box twelve! That's got the fifty thousand! Oh for God's sake, woman!"

☆　★　☆

Nurse Aine is short and plump and has very glossy black hair and very caked makeup. She can't be more than twenty-two. She radiates the rude self-confidence of the medical.

"You're not Nurse Morag," Chester Barnes says.

"No flies on you, Chester."

"Nurse Morag calls me Mr. Barnes. Where is she anyway?"

"Nurse Morag has moved on to Sydenham, Belmont, and Glenmachan. I'll be your district nurse from now on. Now, how are we, Mr. Barnes? Fair enough fettle? Are you taking your half aspirin?"

"And my glass of red wine. Sometimes more than a glass."

"Bit of a secret binge drinker, are we, Mr. Barnes?"

"Miss, I have many secrets, but alcohol dependency is not one of them."

Nurse Aine is busy in her bag pulling on gloves, unwrapping a syringe, fitting a needle. She readies a dosing bottle, pierces the seal.

"If you'd just roll your wee sleeve up there, Ches . . . Mr. Barnes."

"What's this about?" Chester says suspiciously.

"Nasty wee summer flu going around."

"I don't want it. I don't get the flu."

"Well, with a dose of this you certainly won't."

"Wait, Miss, you don't understand."

Plump Nurse Aine's latex hands are quick and strong. She has Chester's arm in a grip, and the needle is coming down. She checks.

"Oh. I'm having a wee bit of a problem finding a vein. Chester, you've obviously no career as a heroin addict."

"Miss, I don't—"

Nurse Aine comes in again, determination set on her red lips. "Let's try it again. You may feel a little prick."

"Miss, I won't . . ."

"Oh. Wow." Nurse Aine sits back.

"What is it?" Chester asks.

She holds up the syringe. The needle is bent into a horseshoe.

"I've heard of hard arteries . . . I can honestly say I've never seen anything like this before. Mr. Barnes—"

The living room door opens. The walker's rubber toes enter first, then Doreen's low slippers.

"Suppositories," Doreen says. "My husband gets all his medication by suppository."

"It's not in my case notes," Nurse Aine protests.

"My husband is a special case."

The rattle of the letter box disturbs Nurse Aine's departure.

"There's your paper, Chester." She hands him the *Telegraph* as the paperboy nonchalantly swings his leg over the fence to Number 27 next door. Chester waves it after her as she goes down the path—daintily for her size, Chester thinks—to her small green Peugeot 305.

"Mr. Barnes!" he calls. But the kids are hovering around the garage door again, casting glances at him, trying to block the football from his view with their bodies.

In the living room Doreen sits on the unused seat beside Chester's big armchair in the window bay rather than her wing-back chair with the booster cushion by the door.

"Yes?"

"Nothing."

"You're hovering."

"I am not hovering, I'm perching. So is it in?"

"Is what in?"

"Don't come that with me, Chester Barnes. Turn to the small ads right now."

They flip through the pages together. Their fingers race each other down the columns and sections, stop simultaneously on bold print.

Dr. Nightshade to Captain Miracle. Ormeau Park.

"Ormeau Park. He's close. Where do you think he is?"

"I heard Spain, on the Costa, with the rest of them."

"What do you think he wants?"

"I don't know."

"Chester, I'm concerned."

"I'll look after you, don't you ever worry. Nothing will ever harm you."

Doreen lays her hand on her husband's.

"If only you could do that."

Then with a slap baclang! like a steel avalanche descending into Haypark Avenue, the first goal hits the metal garage door.

☆   ★   ☆

Old men wake easily in the night. A bulge of the bladder, the creak of something that might be an intruder, the gurgle of water in the pipes, a night plane, the lumber of a big slow truck making deliveries to Tesco, the sudden start of a dream, or a nightmare, or that edge-of-sleep-plummet into nothingness that is much too much like death. Anything at all, and they're awake and staring at the ceiling. And no amount of lying and turning and punching up the pillow to try to make it comfortable or flicking the blankets in under your feet will send you off again. Doreen sleeps sound as a child, her mouth open, her eyes crinkled up in a private, slumbering smile. Every insomniac knows the rule that a partner steals the sleep from you.

Chester waddles out to the toilet and pisses, long and appreciatively. Still a good pressure there. On the landing he looks up through the skylight. He never puts the main light on because if anything is guaranteed to banish all hope of sleep it is harsh centralized lighting. Beyond the yellow city glow stand the brighter stars. A constellation of fast lights crosses the rectangle of night. Chester Barnes holds his breath, thrilled by a wonder he feared he had forgotten.

"Away, avaunt!" he breathes. "Plays hell with City Airport Air Traffic Control, my arse. They always were bloody jealous dogs." Then he hears the high rumble of jets. A lesser wonder.

A wave of warmth and laundry-fresh fabric conditioner spills over him as he opens the hot-press. Socks, shirts—Doreen still irons his underwear. Chester thinks that one of the greatest tokens of love anyone can show. Sheets, towels. To the top shelf, where everything is piled along the front because Doreen can't reach any higher. Chester takes down the shoe box. Inside are the press clippings, yellowed and redolent of age and laundry, and the comics.

Chester lifts the comic out, then sets it back, replaces the lid. A confidential, matey tap.

The Bushmills bottle is at the back of the kitchen cabinet for the same reason that the top-shelf laundry is at the front. Not that Doreen would object; it's that it would be too easy, over *Deal or No Deal*, or the documentaries he likes on the History Channel. Chester Barnes still has an image, still has pride. When he opens the mock leather lid of the Dansette record player, the smell of old vinyls and glues and plastics whirls him back through years and decades. It's a dreadful tinny box and he can't find a decent replacement for the stylus, but it's like valve sound. The 45s only sound right on it. He takes them out of the shelf of the old radiogram, stacks them up on the ling spindle, settles back into his chair with the Bush and the comic. Always the dread, as the latch moves in, that more than one disc will fall at once. The Dansette doesn't fail him tonight. Billie Holiday. "God Bless the Child." Except the ones who bang that bloody ball off the bloody garage door. No. God bless the child and God bless you, Lady Day. He opens the comic. *Captain Miracle, issue 17*.

The setup is rubbish; the writer never was any good. It's the one with Dr. Nightshade's Malevolent Meteor Machine, and the usual superhero dilemma: save the girl or save the city from destruction. The true hero must do both, in a method that surprises but is consistent, different enough from last month's installment, and return all the balls in play to their original triangle on the table. Nothing must change in the world of comic book superheroes, unlike real superheroes.

So, Captain Miracle, decide. The woman you love, or two million people in Belfast.

Cobblers. There weren't even that many people in the whole of the North. Chester Barnes smiles. Good panels of Captain Miracle flying into the meteor storm plunging down through the upper atmosphere haloed in plasma. Kick two into each other, send a third into the Irish Sea just off Dublin where it swamps Blackrock (*It's PR*, the Northern Ireland Office management team had said), fry one with laser vision, swing one by its tail, get underneath the big one bearing down on the city (the artist was an American, no idea about what Belfast looked like: a shipyard and the City Hall surrounded by miles of thatched cottages) and struggle and strain until the people in the streets were pointing and staring, before heaving it on his shoulders back up into orbit again. And of course, leaving one last, unseen straggler to bear down on innocent Belfast, before grabbing it and booting it back into orbit as sweet as any drop goal at Ravenhill.

"I'd've been good at rugby," Chester Barnes says. "Ach, too good. It would've been no game at all."

Then screaming fist-forward back down to Dr. Nightshade's Castle of Evil, which was based on the real Tandragee Castle where they made the potato crisps, which Chester Barnes always found stranger than any Northern Ireland superhero comic. Intercepting the deadly grav-beam with which Dr. Nightshade had hauled the meteors from the sky and with which, on full intensity, he would collapse his hapless prisoner into a black hole. Pushing the ray back, back, with both his hands, until grav-beam projector, power unit, control room and the abominable Dr. Nightshade himself all collapsed into eternal oblivion. Until he extricated himself in the next episode.

I've got you, Doreen. Soaring up from the singularity, his love in his arms.

"Away, avaunt," Chester Barnes whispers. Dean Martin now; good old Dino.

They're PR material, the NIO Department for Nonconventional Individuals had insisted. He has every issue of Captain Miracle, from Number 1 in 1972 to the final issue in 1979.

It's not really making any difference, is it, Chester? But it couldn't, that was always understood. Now Chester lifts out the press cuttings. Robbers thwarted. Passengers rescued from sinking car ferries. Fires put out. Car bombs lifted and hurled into Belfast Lough. It was always impressive when they exploded in midair, until people started putting claims in about damage to roofs. Freed hostages.

Masked villain apprehended: *Supervillain for our Superhero?* Here he could make a difference. Here were things a hero could do. Against politics, against sectarianism, against murders and no warning bombs and incendiaries slipped into pockets of clothes on racks, there is nothing super to be done.

It's four-thirty. The stack of singles has played out. The bottle of Bush is half-empty. Chester Barnes refills the shoe box and climbs the stairs. Beyond the skylight there's a glimmer of dawn.

☆　★　☆

Together they paw over the *Belfast Telegraph*, so eager they tear the sheets. Forefingers race each other down the small ads.

"What's it under?" Doreen asks.

"Prayers and novenas," Chester Barnes says.

Their digits arrive simultaneously on the message. In bold: **Dr. Nightshade to Captain Miracle. Ormeau Park. Tonight . . .**

"Does that dot dot dot mean there's something more?" Doreen asks. "Maybe the rest of it's in the late edition."

"Him pay for two small ads?" Chester Barnes says. "That wouldn't be like him."

"Tonight, then."

"Yes."

"Are you going to go?"

"Of course not."

There's a pounding all along the right side of Chester Barnes's head, from behind his eye to just above his ear, a steady pulsing beat, a painful throb. A headache. He never gets headaches, unless they're tension headaches. Then he realizes that his brain is thumping in time to the thudding of the ball, that ball, that bloody ball off the garage door. Slap baclang. He had been so intent on the message from his former nemesis that he hadn't noticed the little voices outside, the cries, the ringing smack of football on the pavement.

"Bloody kids!" Chester Barnes shouts, sitting bolt upright, trying to scrub the hammering out of his head. "Will they never, ever, never go away and leave me in peace?"

And now Doreen is saying that she's worried, what's it all about, why has he come back and what does he want with Chester, are they safe? But all Chester can hear is the slap baclang of the ball and then a different noise, a change in tone of the voices, alarm, fear. He rises from his seat and turns around as the football comes looping in through the front window in a smash and shower of shards, great spears hanging from the frame, fangs of glass poking up from the sash, splinters flying around him and Doreen as he covers her. No flying glass, from a window or a blast, could ever harm him. Chester seizes the ball and storms out onto the street where the children still stand, frozen in horror. They are very small. But months and years of the rage and frustration of a man able to do anything but allowed to do nothing bursts inside him like a boil.

"You little bastards, you could have hurt my wife, all that flying glass, do you ever think of anyone but yourselves? Of course not, it's the way your parents bring you up; you're all selfish bastards, no sense of gratitude for anything, it's all me me me." The children stand shaking with fear. Chester Barnes throws the ball into the air. He throws it far and hard. It loops so high it is almost out of sight, but as it drops down he looks at it, looks at it long and hard, like he looks at the boxes on *Deal or No Deal*, looks with all his power. The football explodes in a deafening boom. Scraps of vinyl rain down, but the children are already running and every door on Haypark Avenue is open and the people staring.

"Selfish, the lot of you!" Chester Barnes shouts. "None of you ever said thanks, not one. Ever."

Then he slams the door and goes in to sit on his glass-strewn chair and pretends to watch *Countdown*.

☆　★　☆

Officer Ruth Delargy is very fresh and smart and every inch the majesty of the law in her crisp white shirt and cap that shades her eyes and makes her remote, authoritative, just. She is the community officer from Ballynafeigh PSNI Station. She sits in the living room of Number 27 in Doreen's chair, but Chester thinks it better not to complain. The glass has been swept up, the window patched with cardboard and parcel tape. The glazer can't make it until the end of the week. Three of his Poles have suddenly announced they've had enough of Northern Ireland and are going home.

"The situation, Mr. Barnes, is that where children are concerned, we have no option but to investigate. It's a statutory duty. Now, from what I've heard this isn't the first time you've had issues with the McAusland children."

"Is that what they're called? McAusland?"

"Yes, Mr. Barnes. Do you not know your neighbors?"

"Did they bring the complaint?"

"I can't tell you that, Mr. Barnes, under the Data Protection Act. It is the sort of thing we would try to resolve at a community level through a mediated meeting between yourself and the McAuslands, and we wouldn't want to invoke anything as heavy-handed as an Anti-Social Behaviour Order . . ."

"An ASBO? You'd try and give me an ASBO?"

"Like I said, Mr. Barnes, we wouldn't want to be that heavy-handed. That would be using a sledgehammer to crack a nut. Now, I'm prepared to overlook the criminal damage to the football, but I do think it would be good if I arranged a series of meetings with the McAuslands: I've seen this kind of thing before, and you'll be amazed how much better relationships are when people get to know each other."

Chester Barnes sits back in his chair.

"Do you think they can get to know me?"

Officer Ruth frowns.

"I don't know what you mean."

"It's just that some people, well, you think you know them but you don't know anything at all. It's just that some people, well, they're not like you know. They're different. They have their own rules. You see, it so happens that I know you. We've met before. It was a long time ago, you were very small, maybe four, five. It was Christmas. Now, they always say that Christmases blur into each other, but you might remember this one. You were in town with your parents, they took you to the Santa's grotto, it was a good one, in the old Robb's department store. It's not there anymore, it was destroyed by incendiaries, back when they were doing a lot of that sort of thing. But they always had a very good Christmas grotto. You went on a ride first: Santa's Super Sleigh. It didn't actually go anywhere, it was set of seats that went up and down while the walls rolled past, and there were stuffed reindeer in the front bobbing up and down so you felt you were on a journey. You were on it when the firebombs went off. Do you remember? I'm sure you don't remember all the details, you were very small and it must have been a terrible trauma for you. You got separated from the rest of your family, somehow, you slipped in under the mechanism and got trapped there. There was smoke everywhere, the fire had really caught. Then someone came through the fire. Someone pulled you out from burning reindeer, someone took you in his arms and flew you out through the flames, down the stairwell. Someone flew you to safety, Officer Delargy. There was a hero there for you. And maybe I'm wrong, maybe it's just vanity, but I like to think that because someone did right that day, that's the reason you're doing right today. And that's more than I could hope, because we don't have children, me and Doreen, it's part of the whole super thing, apparently, but if someone does right because right was done to them, that's as much children as I can hope for. So, I appreciate that there are rules, there have to be, but maybe you also appreciate now that the rules are different for some people."

He watches her drive off when she has finished with her notes. The police are in Skodas now. They used to be in Rovers, but that was when Rovers were good cars and Skodas were joke cars. *These claims, well, they're so outlandish I don't think anyone could really believe them*, Community Officer Delargy had said before closing her electronic notebook. It will be quiet again. He can carry on in his life of everyday unsuperness.

"That was a bit naughty," Doreen says, entering now that her rightful chair is hers again. A Tesco bag swings from the handles of her walker.

"What?"

"Pulling rank like that."

"I did remember her. It was real, it happened. And I think at the end she may have remembered me."

"Chester, it was over thirty years ago."

"What's in the bag?"

"A present."

"For me?"

"Who else would it be for? Not that you deserve it; that was a horrid thing to do, you bad old goat. Here you are anyway."

In the bag is a brown paper parcel tied with string. The rule with Doreen's presents has always been no peeping. Chester does not break it now, but it does smells of fabric conditioner, and the package is soft, springy to his touch. He tears open a corner. Crimson and gold spill out.

"I thought I'd thrown this out years ago."

"You did. I threw it back in. Oh, I know I was so very afraid, every time you went out, and I know that's why you got rid of it, but I couldn't. I couldn't. It needed a damn good wash, and I'm afraid some of the stretch has gone. Go on. You have to go. You have to find out."

Chester Barnes holds the paper parcel in his hands.

"I won't leave you, Dor. I won't ever do that."

☆   ★   ☆

He thinks he may have strained something scrambling over the wall. A twinge in the lower back. Stupid stupid stupid, with just a thought he could have been over it, quicker and less conspicuously than climbing up the moss-smooth stone. Chester Barnes pauses, stretches, one side then the other. Even superheroes need to warm up. He's only a stone's throw from the main road, the yellow street light glows through the tree branches, and the traffic is a constant rumble, but the Ormeau Park seems far away from the concerns of Haypark Avenue. The night is warm and the flowering shrubs release a tremendous sweetness. Shaking out the muscle cramp, stepping out boldly along the deserted path, he feels hugely alive. Every breath empowers. Here is a secret heart in the city and tonight he is connected to it as he hasn't felt in years. With the merest flicker of his powers, he can steer clear of the dog shit as well.

"So, Captain Miracle!" a voice booms from a rhododendron clump. Chester Barnes stops dead. For all his powers, he's a little shocked.

"You know I can see right into that rhododendron," he says.

"You know, would you ever, once, let me finish?" says a peevish, cigarette-thick voice from inside the shrubbery. "Just let me say it. So, Captain Miracle! Tonight!"

"Tonight what, old enemy?"

"Tonight . . . we fly!"

Dr. Nightshade, evil genius, Pasha of Crime, Tsar of Wrongdoing, steps from the rhododendron. He wears his purple cape and leotard; the Facility Belt has been let out at the waist and the mask sags over one eye. Chester doesn't remember him so short.

"So you made it then, Chester."

"Well, Sean, you made it hard to refuse."

"Good to see you anyway," says Dr. Nightshade. He extends a gloved hand. Chester Barnes takes and shakes it warily. "I don't want to seem an ingrate, but I did kind of make an effort." He indicates his costume. Chester Barnes steps back. With his two hands he takes his cardigan and tears it open. Golden yellow on scarlet shines forth: a glowing letter M.

"Give me two minutes." Chester Barnes steps into the bushes. Dr. Nightshade averts his gaze. In less than the advertised time he steps back, a hero in scarlet and gold, creased at knee and elbow, loose across the chest and tight across the belly. Chester tugs at the cape.

"I could never get this bloody thing to sit right."

"I never bothered," Dr. Nightshade says. "Pain in the hoop, capes. Shall we, er?" He nods down the empty path. They walk together, hero and villain.

"It feels rather odd," Chester says, tugging decorously at his crotch. "What if someone sees us?"

"I don't know, it feels kind of free to me," says Dr. Nightshade. "A bit mad and wild. And there's much worse goes on in this park after dark."

They stroll through the trees to the high point overlooking the football pitches. The grounds are closed up, someone has left a light on in the pavilion. Beyond the dark circle of the Ormeau Park, Belfast shines. Aircraft lights pass overhead.

"There's no one else understands, you know," Dr. Nightshade says.

"What about all those alumnus groups, the online forums, Heroes Reunited, all that?"

"Ach, who could be arsed with that? It's all bloody talk, and a few wankers like to hog the forum. And anyway, it's our thing, you know? A Belfast thing."

"No heroes or villains here," Chester says. "Only politics. I thought you went to Spain after you got out?"

"It was good until everyone started moving there and, well, to be honest, it's expensive now. The pound's weak as piss against the euro and I'll let you into a wee supervillain secret: I was never that well off, thanks to you. Those Criminal Asset Recovery boys; that's a real superpower. It's just, well, in the end, you understand more than anyone else."

Traffic curves along the Ormeau Embankment. The river smells strongly tonight. The night smells merely strong. Chester Barnes looks up to the few stars bold enough to challenge Belfast's amber airglow.

"Do you ever?" Chester asks. "Have you ever?"

"Oh no. It doesn't seem right. You?"

"No, never. But tonight . . ."

"Let's see if we still can. One last time," says Dr. Nightshade, suddenly fierce and passionate. "Just to show we bloody can!"

"Because we bloody can, yes!" shouts Chester Barnes. "Who's

like us? Who can do what we can do? They're all too busy on their iPods to look up when they hear something go over their heads, too bloody busy texting to look up when they see a flash of light up there in the sun. Come on, we'll not get another chance." He punches a fist at the stars, then runs after it, down the hill, pell mell, headlong, in golden boots over the dew-wet grass.

"Hey, wait for me, you bastard!" cries Dr. Nightshade and runs after his enemy, the only one who can ever understand him, but Captain Miracle is ahead and drawing away and Dr. Nightshade is panting, heaving, the breath shuddering in his chest. He stops on the center spot of the football pitch, leaning on his thighs, fighting down nausea. Captain Miracle is far ahead, almost at the Ravenhill Road gates. Then he hears a strange cry and a peal of laughter, ringing out over the traffic and looks up to see a streak of gold and crimson arc up into the sky. The curve of light bends back over him, dips with a supersonic roar, then turns and climbs toward the lower stars with a faint, half-heard shout: "Away! Avaunt!"

☆ ★ ☆

Bill Willingham is the multiple award-winning author of the DC Vertigo title *Fables*, itself the recipient of fourteen coveted Eisner Awards to date. His *Jack of Fables*, created with Matthew Sturges (whose work opens this anthology), was chosen by *Time* magazine as number 5 in their Top 10 Graphic Novels of 2007. His first *Fables* prose novel, *Peter and Max*, was released in 2009, the same year that his comic book, *Fables: War and Pieces*, was nominated for the first Hugo Award for Best Graphic Story. One of the most popular comics writers of the current time, he delivers a massive novella that forms an entire super-pantheon in and of itself, a brilliant comics continuity out of whole cloth that is the perfect end piece for this anthology.

A to Z in the Ultimate Big Company Superhero Universe (Villains Too)

BILL WILLINGHAM

A is for Achilles
Hero of Old

It was bitter cold up in the hills above Lamia, where Major Kyle Stewart and Manolis Siantas had retreated following the operation. They'd been cut off from the other Greek resistance fighters, those fierce and wild andartes, along with their British SOE advisors, and were thus unable to make it to the designated rendezvous point for extraction. The backup plan was for every fighter to fade into the surrounding wilderness on his own or in small groups, which is precisely what the two soldiers, one Greek and one Canadian, had done.

"Did we do it, Major?" Manolis asked. His halting breath puffed staggered semaphores of vapor into the dark November air.

"Splendidly," Kyle said. He replaced the dying Turkish cigarette in the other man's mouth and lit the new one for him. One of Manolis's hands was gone completely, along with most of that arm.

The other hand was too torn up to matter much by comparison. In the retreat he'd caught part of a German 88 shell burst. "Operation *Harling* was an overwhelming success. The Gorgopotamos railway bridge is but a memory, the occupying forces are confounded, and the German supply trains are already backed up twenty or thirty to a side, sitting ducks for the next Allied air strike. The Greek Resistance has well and truly announced its existence to the world. Be proud, my friend."

"Die proud, you mean."

"Nonsense. You're going to be fine. I'm going to get you to a medic, once we've rested here for an hour or two."

"I don't think so. I appreciate the encouraging lie, but we both know I'll be crossing the river tonight. Don't forget to put a coin under my tongue, so I can pay the ferryman. Don't be stingy, either, trying to get by with one of your joeys. I expect a full quid at least. Maybe I'll get one of the better seats."

Manolis died an hour later, and Kyle granted his last request, grinning through his tears at his friend's superstitions.

Little time had passed after that before Kyle thought he could just make out a ghostly figure standing over Manolis's body. A trick of the cold, the mist, and my lack of sleep, he thought. Or did I fall to sleep at last and this is a dream?

Then Kyle imagined he could see a semitransparent duplicate of Manolis rise up from his own body and join the first ghostly figure. They walked off together, down the hillside.

Kyle shouldered his weapon and followed.

"Dream or no, I'll be damned if I'm going to abandon a comrade in the field," he muttered.

Kyle shadowed the two ghosts for an hour or more, down the rocky defile and then into a deep and twisting dry gorge that eventually opened up onto the expanse of a great river valley. Ink-black waters flowed sluggishly in the river, the opposite shore of which he couldn't make out in the night's gloom. He knew the territory well enough to be certain that this wasn't some uncharted tributary of the strategically vital Sperkheios River, the one they'd fought at earlier in the day. It couldn't be. This one was too big and in the wrong place.

Considering the weird circumstances under which he'd arrived, he realized this had to be the River Styx, though his rational mind still resisted the knowledge. Kyle was well versed in his classical mythology.

There was a long wooden rowboat pulled up to the pebbled bank, with a cloaked figure beside it. The two ghosts approached the boat, whereupon the first guide faded. Manolis spit Kyle's two-quid coin into the ferryman's hand. He took his place in the boat as the ferryman pulled hard on the oars, sending the craft out onto the silent waters. Kyle followed, walking down to the river's edge, watching his friend for as long as he could, until they'd rowed out of sight.

In ancient times the hero Achilles had bathed in these waters. His mother was the sea nymph Thetis, lovely beyond description, beloved of both Zeus and Poseidon. But the gods forced her to marry a mortal, as otherwise her son was prophesied to be stronger than the both of them combined. Thetis dipped Achilles into the River Styx as a newborn. Holding her son by one heel when putting him in the water, she made the child's entire body, except the heel, immortal and invulnerable.

Impossible dream or not, Kyle was never one to pass up a golden opportunity. He wouldn't make the same mistake Thetis had. He dropped his weapon and stripped. When he was entirely naked, he took a short run and dove into the coal-dark Styx, immersing himself completely. No heel, or any other part of him, remained untouched by the water.

The Styx hit him like the strike of an angry god's hammer against the anvil of his heart. He shuddered and thrashed in its terrible, haunted depths, pained and horrified beyond the limits of mortal imagination. When he was at long last able to drag himself out onto the embankment, he cried and mewled for uncountable days.

Some months after that a miracle warrior, mighty and unstoppable, appeared in besieged Stalingrad, and the German forces quaked at his fury. Then he was seen at Tripoli, and perhaps at Kasserine Pass, and possibly at a hundred other battles. Reports became confused and unreliable in the superman's wake.

Kyle Stewart had entered the Second World War as a Canadian expatriate member of Hugh Dalton's Special Operations Executive, part of the so-called Ministry of Ungentlemanly Warfare. He was determined to do his part in following Churchill's instructions to "set Europe ablaze." He returned from the war as an immortal and invulnerable champion of justice and "what is right" in the civilized world. He called himself Achilles, after the first champion born of the Styx's miraculous, if dreadful, transformations.

He was the first, but in short time new heroes and dire villains, each blessed with extraordinary powers, began to make themselves known in this suddenly alien and disordered world. A new age had begun.

B is for Bad Moon
Distant and Cold

Peryon Hark, disgraced black prince of the Magnificent Krona Clan, the famous Battle Moons of Saturn, hung sulky and alone in space, pondering the many defeats in his notorious career and what he might do to revenge himself against his various tormentors. For thirty long years he'd drifted here, banished to far Earth orbit, healing from his last engagement against the assembled heroes of the ridiculous Fidelity League.

His features were dour, saturnine. The globe of his face, or his body—the two being one and the same—was pockmarked with craters large and small. Countless meteors, ever capricious and suicidal, had touched him often over the vast ages of his life.

Slowly, incrementally, cold passion yielded to colder calculation, and a new plan began to occur to him. Hark moved out of his sullen orbit, shedding velocity as he altered trajectory, just a small nudge here and a gentle tweak there, causing himself to fall inward once again, toward the great blue sphere of his desire.

His destiny was to one day rule the Earth and everyone on it. Of that he was still certain.

His mass had diminished to an embarrassing state during his exile. At the moment he was barely larger than a modest suburban family dwelling. There were no thralls out here to feed him with their accumulated joys and fears, dreams and worries. That would change, once he came within range of the Earth and its easily susceptible populations. He'd grow large and formidable again soon enough. But for now, he considered, his lack of size was an advantage. The bigger he was, the easier for one or more of the world's too many costumed do-gooders to spot. He tightened his orbit and shed more speed.

Few noticed the Bad Moon rising in the night sky over Liberty, Pennsylvania. Of those who did, none recalled their superhero history enough to recognize the odd phenomenon as a threat. This was a world of almost daily strange occurrences, after all.

C is for Cryptera

And the Esteemed Doctor Sable

At most only a handful of people in the world knew that the celebrated Emil Sable, MD, PhD, Nobel Prize winner, among sundry and numerous other achievements and awards, was once also the infamous Professor Hell. Unfortunately for Emil and his comfortable new life, Bad Moon happened to be one of the few.

Emil.

"What the hell?"

Exactly. Put down your book and come outside, good doctor. I want to speak to you more intimately, but despite my subtracted stature, I'm still too big to fit inside your apartment.

"Who—?"

You know who I am. It hasn't been that long, all things considered. Now rush to obey me. My wrath hasn't dissipated over the years. Nor has my patience improved. I'm in the alley behind your building.

Emil did as he was commanded. Whatever courage he'd had in life was long spent in his adventurous youth. He crept into the alley behind his downtown Liberty apartment building, glancing this way and that for any sign that he might be observed by some unfortunate street tramp or overly curious bystander. He was famous now, outside of the old mask. Easily recognizable, at least by those that matter in the world. He had to be especially careful.

Don't worry, Professor Hell. I've spread a bit of my moondust all about. No one will come back here. No one will stumble across our clandestine assignation.

Around the last corner, where the trash Dumpsters were clustered like a modern Stonehenge of rust and dented steel, there was Bad Moon in all of his past glory and fearsomeness. The bright sphere of his body floated a few feet off the pavement, filling the alley.

"Good to see you again, Professor Hell." Bad Moon spoke verbally this time. His teeth were yellow, chipped and jagged. They were canted at every angle, like bits of exposed rubble in the debris of a recently bombed temple.

"Good evening, Pery," Emil said.

"When did I ever invite you to use my given name?" Bad Moon thundered back at him. "And then you have the audacity to shorten it, as if we're old friends?"

"Forgive me, Prince Hark," Emil said. "I didn't mean to— Look," he began again, "I'm not sure what you want."

"I should think that would be obvious, Professor. I intend to gather the old Cryptera together again—those of us still alive at least. We've so many dark and fretful deeds to do. It's long past time to be back about our business."

"I can't!"

"Oh?"

"Please understand, dread prince. I'm no longer Professor Hell. Not for many years. I've served my time, entered the witness protection program. They gave me a new face. A new identity."

"Yes, I can see now that you've had some work done. It's difficult to tell, what with how similar all of you humans look."

"I use my powers, my spellcraft, strictly in public service now. I've changed, even as I've helped to change the world for the better. Retired. Reformed." Emil tried not to tremble openly, failing more completely than he realized. "I'm respected. Honored. I can't go back to cloaks and masks, and skulking about in dank alleys."

"Isn't that nice?" Bad Moon smiled a wicked smile and then, pursing his lips, blew a puff of moondust into Emil's unprotected face. When the thick ochre cloud had dissipated, Emil remained, standing before the dishonored Battle Moon, stiff of form, but suddenly quite pliant of mind.

"Here's what you're going to do, Emil. Forget the old cloak and mask, if that's what you really want. But, openly or not, you're going to visit each of our surviving old comrades in arms. You're going to reform the Cryptera, inviting in new members, such as may seem useful to our designs. I'll give you a supply of moondust, to aid you in recruiting whosoever you need to. Use it sparingly, though. Don't overdo it and dull those inventive criminal minds we want to exploit."

"Of course, Prince Hark," Emil said.

"And here's an important detail. From now on you're the group's public face. Its only master. No one will ever know that I'm back in the world and secretly behind the scenes, pulling your strings. This old devil moon can learn a few new tricks."

"A wise precaution."

"Now, here's what we're going to do."

They talked long into the deepening night, and no one observed or overhead them.

D is for Dormouse
A Champion Most Able

Here's a fun fact: The average adult male lion, in the prime of his vigor, can reach speeds of up to fifty miles per hour, whereas the average adult human female, in the prime of her vigor . . . cannot.

I could feel the beast's stinking, heavy breath, blowing hot like a blacksmith's bellows on my all too vulnerable backside. He was close! Do something now, girl! Anything!

I zigged, while he zagged (lucky for me), and he shot past me like a tawny furred rocket. That maneuver bought me maybe a second at most. He put the breaks on at a snap, plowing up massive divots in Strangeface's manicured lawn. I kicked out with everything I had, aiming for his huge dangling ball sack. I missed, impacting the big cat's upper rear leg haunch instead. Solid muscle and bone. That got his attention nicely enough, but didn't seem to hurt him one wee bit.

Oh well.

I ran for it again, in the opposite direction this time, going the wrong way, but I didn't have much choice. He finished scrambling in the turf, got all four of his feet under him, and followed, still as fast as—well, as fast as a charging lion. (Sorry, that's all I had. No deft wordsmith, me.)

Of course Mr. Angry Tabby can't sustain such speeds for very long. Short bursts only. He gets tired quick, whereas I don't get tired at all.

Not ever.

Well, at least not until I want to.

That's my one bona fide superpower. More about that later. I'm a bit busy just now!

The wide grassy yard was surrounded by a tall stone wall—the one I'd just come over in my efforts to break into Strangeface's current lair. I ran back for that wall now, frantically wondering if I'd make it in time, and then if I could climb it fast enough to escape the lion on my ass. (Pardon me. I only cuss when I'm scared.)

I'd had lots of time to climb the outside of the wall, coming in. I wouldn't have more than a second to go back the other way. I ran. He followed. I was still at my all-time top possible speed. He'd started to slow, just a smidgeon.

Good news, bad news. I made it to the wall ahead of the lion, but not nearly far enough ahead of him to climb out of claws' reach. So I changed plans on the fly and dropped, tucked and rolled instead, pushing off the wall at the last instant, so that I was suddenly going back the other way again, right under the cat. He stepped on me a bit as he stumbled over me, and that hurt quite well enough. He was a big one. But he didn't have time to actually rake me with his giant claws, so that's one for me. Oh, and also he didn't stop fast enough to avoid hitting the wall with his big face.

Hard.

I didn't waste a moment watching him do the crazy, drunken, "I just ran full speed into a wall" stagger, or note with satisfaction the stars and tweetie birds circling his head. I didn't need to pause to catch my breath. Instead I dashed away from there just as fast as my feet could carry me.

This time I was pointed back in the right direction again, straight toward Strangeface's inner fortress. I made it with ease, found the nearest door, and immediately discovered the next problem. It was big, thick, reinforced, and locked. And here I was with no superstrength. No laser-beam eyes. Nada. As I mentioned before, my one power is not getting tired. But that doesn't help a relatively wee girl kick in a solid door. Outside of bad genre TV, that just isn't possible. So I pulled out my tools and started working the lock.

In hindsight, maybe I should have tried going back over the wall, while the guardian kitty was still out of action. I'm a great climber. I aced our brickiating class back at Superhero School. Okay, the actual class name was Urban Brachiating, but everyone called it *brick*iating. Get it? Not funny? Fine. You go graduate top of your class from Mount Pelion and then feel free to critique me all you like. The point is, I'm much better at climbing, jumping, and bounding over rooftops than I ever was at lock picking. I was ever only so-so in Forced Entry class.

I worked the lock.

In the meantime papa lion had recovered enough to start toward me again. I spared a glance just long enough to see him loping this way with his noble face twisted in a look of profound ouch and regret. And maybe there was a touch of "Now it's personal, little lady!" in there as well, or am I anthropomorphizing?

Don't look at the lion! Work the lock, girl!

Of course, right at that moment two more lions came bounding around the building, headed my way. These were females. More to the point, they were clearly as rested as I still was, so no advantage for me this time.

I worked the lock.

Bam! The last tumbler fell, the door popped open, right in the nick, and I scooted inside, with just enough time to slam the door in three disappointed feline faces.

I began to search the place, and here's the odd thing: lots of technology in evidence—no supervillain's lair would be complete without it—but no robots. Not a one. But Strangeface is all about the tin men. That's his thing. Even the big cats in the courtyard were real, not robocats, or cyborgs, or whatever. Weird, huh?

Eventually I found Strangeface in some sort of inner sanctum slash laboratory.

"You're trespassing," he said, not bothering to look up from whatever it was he was working on.

I'd intended to ask him about the dearth of robots first, but instead found myself blurting out, "Lions? Seriously? You actually attacked me with lions?"

"I didn't attack you with anything. You're the one breaking and entering, remember?"

"Yeah, okay, but—who in the hell uses lions in the courtyard? Did you suddenly wake up this morning and decide to become some old-time Saturday morning serial villain?" That's when I realized I was already too late. He had his teleportation belt on, as usual. I expected that. But it takes time to power up. My plan was to jump him and thump him before it could activate. Except that I could see it was already ready to go. Green lights clear across the control surface. Did he know in advance I'd be coming? If so, how? My understanding is that the belt isn't the kind of thing one keeps powered up at all times, just in case. Never mind the incredible cost, which is bad enough, but one wrong move—one accidental bump against the furniture—and zowie! You could disappear to anywhere. Deep inside the middle of the Earth. Fifty miles above it. Atoms randomly scattered. Anywhere at all.

"I happen to like the animals," he said. "I've always wanted some, so finally I decided to indulge myself. If not now, when?" He finally deigned to look up at me. I forced myself not to flinch away from the crazy quilt of his massively scarred face. A lab accident? Probably. But Razorheart swears the guy had a falling out once with Max the Knife, who went to work on the poor old guy with his favorite swiftblade.

"Besides, my usual guardians are all busy elsewhere," he added.

Damn. I'd come prepared to fight robots. I'd even borrowed one of Saint George's area-effect nullifiers. My plan for the day was to take a crowbar to millions of dollars worth of suddenly inanimate plastic and metal, and basically hit Strangeface where it really hurts—his wallet.

"Good-bye, child," he said. "I'd stay for the traditional battle, but I'm late for an important meeting." Then he touched his belt and was gone. Not even a wink of light.

Foiled again.

I spent some time snooping around the place, looking for clues, a diary, a hastily scrawled note near the telephone, or a dropped matchbook. No luck. Then, just for spite, I spent a couple of hours smashing stuff. Some of the machinery did look expensive, after all. But my heart wasn't in it. Then I called Animal Control about the lions and went home.

I'd been up for days, tracking Strangeface to his latest in a long line of hideouts, and then doing the actual assault. I still wasn't tired, but if I didn't let myself get that way soon, I'd be working up a big debt. Better to take care of it now and not have to be out of commission for a month or more.

I entered my apartment through the secret passage, stripped, and locked away my costume and equipment. I spent an hour typing after-action notes on the secure computer and sent them off to the usual folks: Achilles, Saint George, Doc Jerusalem, and anyone else in our business who might be better than I at figuring out what Strangeface was up to. Then I ate a bowl of Cheerios and went to bed. As soon as I lie down I opened the mental gates and let all of the deferred fatigue wash over me.

I'd be asleep for a long time. Days at least. But eventually the snoozing Dormouse will wake up again to this mad tea party that is our life, our world. And then we'll see what we see.

E is for Eleanor

She Loves the Knight

Eleanor Eastman, three-time Pulitzer Prize–winning star reporter for the *Liberty Crier*, was lovely in the way that supermodels and Hollywood celebrities could only hope to be. She was blonde, unblemished, full of lips, curved but sleek, refined and graceful. Her smile could light a ballroom. Her erudition charmed the rich and powerful, from Washington to Beijing. Her writing, sparse, unadorned, and merciless, could bring down a mighty potentate. Every man wanted her, but all knew by now that her heart belonged to one man alone. It was the romance of the century. On second thought, better make that plural—the romance of this century as well as the one recently retired.

Saint George, the gleaming Rocket Knight, came out of the sky, settling slowly onto the building's rooftop helicopter pad. His boot jets cut out just in time so as not to scorch the pad's concrete-over-steel surface. Eleanor was there waiting for him.

"You called?" Saint George said—rather, the electronic speakers on either side of his helmet said. He was covered head-to-toe by his powered armor, painted green and gold, shined bright. No part of the man within was exposed.

"You look different," she said. Clipped tone. Almost dismissive. She was in a mood again.

"No, I look the same. The suit looks different. I'm always modifying it. Improving it. I added new point defense modules since the last time I saw you."

"And how would I know that?" she said.

"Excuse me?"

"You said, and I quote, 'No, I look the same,' but how would I know? I've never actually seen the man under the suit. I wonder what the world would say if they knew our famous love affair was a sham? Strictly platonic at best, an entire fabrication if we're really going to be candid."

"Oh, so it's this again," he said.

"My God! Don't you dare take that tone with me!"

"It's not a tone, Eleanor. It's just the speakers. I have to sacrifice some of the subtleties of voice quality in exchange for durability of the equipment. I get in a lot of battles, after all."

"Sometimes you're so sweet and attentive, and—what's the word I'm looking for? Flirtatious! You're positively flirtatious, really pouring on the charm. And I begin to think you're sincere and that you really do want this to go somewhere. But then the next time I see you, you're so goddamn aloof I could scream. So which is it? Do you just get off on the mind games, toying with the one woman anyone else would be happy to be with, or do we actually have something?"

"It's complicated."

"Not anymore, because this time I want a simple answer. I think I've earned it, waiting so many years for you to shit or get off the pot. Are you scared to reveal yourself to me because I'm a journalist? Because of what happened to Sergeant Liberty? Remember, it wasn't anyone at the *Crier* who burned him, it was those fuckers at the *Post*! We're not all alike. Some of us actually have standards."

"That's not it at all."

"Then what?"

Saint George didn't answer for a long moment. He looked out over the downtown Liberty skyline, huddled along the riverfront. There was a giant billboard on the rooftop directly across the way that read, PLEASE COME BACK, SERGEANT LIBERTY. PLEASE FORGIVE US.

After a while he said, "Have you ever considered the sole reason you're attracted to me might be because I'm the one man you can't have with a snap of your fingers?"

"How dare you!"

"It's a common psychological condition," he said. "There's even a name for it, though it escapes me at the moment. You disdain what you have, or can have, and only place value on what's unavailable."

She opened her purse and took out a pack of cigarettes, but her hand was shaking too violently when she tried to shake one cigarette from the pack, causing a number of them to spill out all over the rooftop. She crumpled the empty pack and started to toss it away, then thought better of it and put the crumpled ball back into her purse.

"How can you do this?" she said, once some measure of composure had been restored. "How can you be so incredibly cold, after the way you've treated me so many other times?"

"When you called you said you had some vital information for me. Was this it?"

She felt like screaming then, but didn't want to give him the satisfaction of seeing her entirely lose control. So she turned away instead, walking back toward the building's small heliport lobby in a controlled stomp. Without turning back to face him, she said, "I received an anonymous tip that something big was going to happen in Liberty, in the next day or two. Something cataclysmic. The caller insisted on speaking to me because he knew I'd be able to get the word out to the superhero community, me being your special sweetheart and all." The door into the glassed-in waiting vestibule was on a sensor, opening and closing automatically, robbing Eleanor of the ability to slam it behind her.

Saint George rose from the rooftops on a flair of boot jets, quickly disappearing into the crystal blue sky.

F is for Fast Johnny
Always First to the Fight

Three days later, when the Public Safety Building in Liberty blew up, Fast Johnny was in Morocco, clearing out a newly discovered nest of the Demon League. Before the rubble had finished falling to the ground, Fast Johnny had arrived on the scene. Most of the delay was due to the thirteen long seconds it took for his earpiece, a gift from Underman, to decide this was news that merited his immediate notification.

G is for Gunslinger
Marksman Extraordinaire

The gutted hulk of the Public Safety Building continued to burn. A dark column of smoke marched defiantly into the sky. Bits of ash and burning debris drifted down from the sky. A blue and scarlet blur whipped and danced all around the destroyed building, sometimes disappearing into it for a second or two, after which it would emerge again, carrying someone out to safety.

"He has to slow down every time he brings a survivor out," Professor Hell said, from one of the undamaged buildings across the way. "That's when you take the shot."

"Don't tell me my business," Gunslinger said.

"But you don't even have your gun out yet."

Gunslinger took his attention off the blurred image of Fast Johnny across the street and fixed his cold gray eyes on Professor Hell. "I appreciate you giving me this opportunity, Professor. I sincerely do. I haven't had a real challenge to my abilities since—well, since never. But if I can take down Fast Johnny while he's in motion, that would be the shot of a lifetime. Only don't tell me my business. Back off, shut up, and let me work."

"Don't you forget who's boss, kid. I was in the original Cryptera, taking on the biggest, baddest heroes of the day, while you were still in diapers." Emil hated trying to talk tough. He was no good at it. Everything he said came out sounding like an absurd cliché from B-movie gangster flicks. But he felt he needed to constantly reinforce his dominance over these people. Every one was a powerful and wild creature of anarchy and chaos. This new generation of supervillains wasn't like the previous one. They couldn't always be relied upon to act in their own best interest. Absolute dominance was his only hope of controlling them. He thought about using some of Hark's moondust on the kid, but he didn't want to do it in front of the others. He didn't want them to realize how most of them had been convinced to accept his leadership. Plus, he didn't know how the enthrallment of moondust might affect Gunslinger's incredible marksmanship.

"Go right ahead and be the boss," Gunslinger said. "Boss anyone you like. You told me who to shoot and that's what bosses do. But telling me how to go about it won't work, because you don't know how to do what I know how to do. Make sense? Go bother one of the others. Tell them the rest of your ingenious plan. Make all the noise you want. I won't be distracted as long as you don't talk to me."

What to do? Was this an act of insubordination, and if so, was it worth dealing with? Would the others think he was weak if he let it drop? What would Bad Moon do in the same situation, or expect him to do? Certainly, he could destroy the boy with a single spoken word. Since being forced back into the life, he'd made certain to always have just such an emergency spell at the ready. But he needed the kid. The plan required him. It was essential that they take out Fast Johnny first. His impossible speed made him the most deadly of the heroes. And Bad Moon in his wisdom had determined that Gunslinger—this puppy who couldn't even shave yet—was the only way to make sure of the speedster.

"Then get it done," Emil said, leaving it at that, while leaving his place beside Gunslinger at the fourth-floor window. He walked deeper back into the commandeered office space, where the others were gathered, affecting a calm he didn't feel.

"So, since the kid brought it up, what is the rest of the plan?" Max said. He was idly tossing his nearly invisible swiftblade from hand to hand. There were faint traces of red on the blade. Max had been the one to single-handedly remove the office's former occupants. There was still the smell of blood and dead secretary in the air.

"Once Fast Johnny is down, the rest is relatively simple," Emil said. He was wearing the old mask, the cloak, and the slouch-brimmed hat. If he had to be Professor Hell again, he was going to go all the way. Maybe then, if this went bad, he could claim it had to have been someone else posing as him. "We lure all of the other heroes to Liberty and kill them."

"That's it? That's your plan?" It was Strangeface speaking this time.

"In broad strokes, yes," Emil said. "That's always the plan."

"You're insane," Strangeface said. "It's never worked before. It's insanity to suppose it'll work now." Strangeface was one of the few surviving members of the old Cryptera. It was true they'd tried to destroy the world's superheroes en masse many times before, always without success. And that was back when there was still only a relative handful of them.

"In the past we didn't have the cooperation of The Ordinary Man," Emil said.

"Are you shitting me?" Max said.

"He's really on board?" Dirty Bomb said. She'd managed to reincorporate her body sometime in the past few minutes, while

Emil's attention had been on Gunslinger. Truth be told, she was still a bit misty around the edges.

"The Ordinary Man should be arriving on the six o'clock commuter express from Philadelphia any minute now," Emil said, with no small degree of pride. "In fact, someone should probably head out to pick him up. Someone who can pass as human," he added, looking at Thunderhead. "I promised him we'd meet him at the train." The others couldn't entirely hide their newfound admiration.

That was the moment when Gunslinger drew and fired his pistol in one smooth motion. One shot. Then he holstered it again. Everyone in the room saw it except Emil, who was facing the wrong way.

Outside, the single 230-grain bullet traveled toward Fast Johnny at a paltry 885 feet per second. However, Fast Johnny was traveling toward the bullet at a more respectable 54,000 feet per second, having just put on a burst of speed after depositing the latest bomb blast survivor with the emergency medical technicians. When the bullet impacted the man, both velocities combined to release a truly impressive amount of energy inside an enclosed space—that being the hero's chest cavity.

Fast Johnny vanished in a red mist.

H is for Holocaust
Heroes Beware

Building by building, the downtown area of Liberty blew up in a fiery holocaust, each consecutive explosion greater than the last. Just as she'd done with the Public Safety Building, Dirty Bomb moved from one structure to the next, exploding herself into atoms, waiting for her body to reform, and then doing it again. Civilians died by the thousands.

"I'm beginning to get the impression she reincorporates in a random spot after each explosion," Visionary said. "I don't think she has control over it. But that isn't the disadvantage one might assume at first. It makes it impossible to anticipate where she'll appear next. Three times in a row now, by the time I've spotted her, she's already detonating herself again. Frustrating, to say the least." He stood on a low rooftop nearly a mile outside of the bleeding and burning downtown area. Dormouse crouched near him. They were both in the shade of a billboard that read: "Sergeant Liberty Come Home. We're Sorry."

"Perhaps if you get closer," Dormouse said.

"Wouldn't help," Visionary said. "That would just narrow my focus even further. I need the perspective of this distance to give me even a slight chance of catching her. Why are you here, anyway? The big guns are on the way. This isn't going to be the sort of fight you could survive. No offense, but it's out of your league."

"Believe me, I know it. But I was already here last night, tracking down a lead. When I woke yesterday I took a look at the reports from my mousetraps. It's what I always do when I wake up, to see what's happened while I was out of commission. One of the mousetraps in Liberty had caught a partial picture of one of Strangeface's robots. I figured this must be where he'd sent them all, so this was the most likely place to find him."

"You have every city under surveillance by your electronic bugs?"

"Hardly. As inexpensive as they may be individually, I'm a girl on a budget. But I served my internship year here, after graduating from Pelion. Pissed me off at the time, let me tell you. I was top of my class. Valedictorian. And yet the Kyron sentences me to a year in Liberty? What did I ever do to him?"

"Not overly fond of the place?"

"Who could be, after what they did to Sergeant Liberty? I did my job though. Exactly three hundred and sixty-five days of first-rate superhero work. Saved lives. Cats out of trees. The whole package. In my time here I brought in the Ling Brothers, broke up the Jolly Rogers, and even survived a throwdown with Thunderhead once. Then, when I was reprieved, I moved on and never looked back. Well—except that I check in through my mousetraps from time to time. I still have some here, left over from back then. The little things are designed to be hard to spot, and randomly change location, making them not quite as easy to recover as they are to deploy. A few always get left behind. And even three years later, some of my guys here still work."

"Here they come," Visionary said.

Saint George flew in from the west, fast, like a launched missile. In the sky over Liberty he rendezvoused with Doc Jerusalem in her chariot of fire.

"Achilles and Underman are in the chariot with her," Visionary said. "Must have picked them up on the way."

"How can you tell?" Dormouse said, shading her eyes from the stab of brightness overhead. "I can't see a thing." Visionary didn't answer. Instead his attention shot back toward the center of town. A brief smile flitted across his face.

"There she is," he said. His eyes flashed bright blue for an instant. "Got her!"

"Dirty Bomb?"

"Yep. I froze her in place, right in front of Anthony's Café. Couldn't be certain of killing her with Red. If she can recover from blowing herself to bits, maybe she could recover from being disintegrated by an outside force. Why take the chance? Had to zap her with Blue instead."

"You would have killed her?" Dormouse said.

"Of course."

"But we don't do that."

"Open your eyes, Miss," he said. "This isn't going to be police work today. This time someone started a war. Different rules. Better make yourself scarce now. It's about to get rough."

There were no further explosions, but the heart of Liberty continued to burn.

I is for Imaginary

A Friend in Need

Like a swarm of gnats off an animal's carcass, a sparkling cloud rose up from the burning heart of the town, into the sky. Then the twinkling motes began to disperse over the city. Hundreds of them moved toward the newly arrived heroes, resolving themselves into individual shapes as they came closer.

"Here comes Strangeface's robot army," Saint George broadcast to the others. The robots were giants and they were miniatures. Some were shaped like men. Some looked like featureless small metal boxes or shiny baseballs. They floated on invisible suspensor fields, or shot forward on plumes of fire, mimicking Saint George's own rocket jets. Most bristled with weapons, and all were incased in a carapace of mirror-bright chrome.

"I'll take them," Saint George said. He pointed his laser finger at the approaching figures and slowly fanned a bright red pencil-thin beam back and forth through their ranks. Pieces of metal bodies began to rain down from the sky.

On the ground, giant tracked monsters rumbled along the streets, mowing down people wherever they went with their canons and machine guns and grenade launchers. Strangeface's amplified voice boomed from every vehicle. "Attention, heroes! The time for ultimate sacrifice has come upon you at last! All you have to do is kill yourselves and we stop killing civilians! That's your only choice! Those are the only terms we'll accept! Do you have what it takes to give the last full measure of devotion? Are you true heroes after all? Kill yourselves and we stop killing civilians!" The message repeated continuously. It was also simultaneously broadcast from every TV and radio in town.

Achilles leapt down from Jerusalem's chariot, still suspended in the sky. He advanced toward one of the tracked robot tanks and began tearing it apart, ignoring the bullets and bombs that shot at him or exploded around him.

Achilles wore his own piece of shining steel armor, a single protective brace around one ankle. Most of the ground robots concentrated their fire there, not realizing it was a simple but effective trick, designed to distract and divert an enemy's efforts and attention. It had worked for fifty years. To this day no one knew that this Achilles had no special weakness to exploit.

Other heroes began to arrive. The new generation, with names like Xenoboy, Razorheart, and Wonder Child.

A convoy of black vans roared into the city, and then pulled up at the edges of the rapidly expanding battle zone. Armed federal agents helped a thin young man out of one of the vehicles. It was immediately clear the man wasn't cooperating.

"Take me back!" he shouted. "I'm no superhero, you idiots! I tell you I can't help in a fight! Only afterward!"

"This is a special situation, Mr. Faust!" one of the agents said. "We need your imaginary men! As many as you can conjure!"

Fagan Faust was known in public as The Imaginary Friend, and he was indeed a proven friend to the entire civilized world. His Zero Men had created many public works that fed and housed thousands. They worked tirelessly, after earthquake or flood, or any other sort of disaster or national emergency, and in peaceful times turned wastelands into parks, deserts into farmlands, slums into palaces. But Fagan Faust was something of a dedicated coward.

"Don't you get it? I can't use my imaginary men in a fight, because I can't imagine myself in a fight! I couldn't conjure a single one under these conditions if my life depended on it! Take me out of here!"

And, with utmost reluctance, they did.

J is for Jerusalem
Legend in Song and Deed

Jenny Green was better known as Doc Jerusalem, champion of England's green and pleasant land. She took up her bow of burning gold and shot the arrows of desire into one deadly machine after another. She never missed, and each robot so struck died instantly. On her hip the Sleeping Sword began to stir in its sheath, waking to the din of battle, aching to once more be in her hand, where it wouldn't sleep again until the struggle was ended.

K is for Kyron
In the Black Tower

The black tower floated stately and serenely, suspended on its four powerful gravity subtraction engines, high above the forested valley below. It was over southern Minnesota today, drifting east toward the Wisconsin Dells. This was the Mount Pelion School, the most elite, prestigious, expensive superhero training academy in the planet's history. Pelion had been in continuous operation since it was actually located in a cave on the original Mount Pelion, when Jason and Heracles were numbered among its original student body.

High up on one of its smooth obsidian flanks a hanger door was open, to let the natural daylight flood the large chamber. Owen Dixon, the current Kyron of the school, operated the remote control of an electronic winch with one hand, slowly and carefully lowering himself into the strange vessel directly underneath him. It was a robotic horse's body, missing a head, built on a scale to match a knight's heavy warhorse of old—a copper-colored metal Clydesdale or Percheron. With small touches on the control, Owen continued lowering himself in his cradle, until the burn-scarred stumps of his missing legs dangled just over the robot's cockpit, located where the missing head would be, were this an actual steed. Then he thumbed the switch that caused the three direct-interface cables to rise up from the cockpit and attach themselves to him. He winced only slightly as the long needles inserted themselves. When that was done, he disengaged the cradle straps and settled his body the remaining few inches with arm strength alone. He engaged the locks and tightened the harness belts. Then he began systems tests. The horse's powerful legs responded to his mental commands. The jump jets flashed green-for-go in his mind's eye. One by one, various weapons systems reported themselves as loaded, armed, and ready. He walked forward a few tentative steps. Heavy metal hooves boomed a watch bell's dull toll against the metal floor. Moving over to a rack against the near wall, he began to take up the helmet and additional pieces of armor that would protect his exposed upper torso, arms, and head.

"Kye Owen, would you like to tell me what you're doing?"

Owen turned, and the robot horse body turned with him, becoming more a part of him with every second. Melvin Agerholm, the only currently living Kye emeritus of the school, was standing in the smaller open doorway leading back into the tower's greater depths.

"Good morning, Kye Agerholm," Owen said. "I'm just on my way out."

"To do what?"

"Isn't that obvious?" Owen gestured to the large flat-screen TV mounted on one wall. It showed live news coverage of the battle in Liberty. At the moment the camera was following a wild-eyed young man, dressed all in red, madly cutting down one person after another with what may have been a knife. It was hard to be certain, as his weapon hand moved too swiftly to follow. Then another man in a cape landed next to the knife-wielder, was clearly about to strike him, but suddenly looked pained, weak, and confused. The knife hand moved in a blur. There was a spray of crimson and then the caped man fell headless to the ground.

"I'm going to Liberty, to help," Owen said.

"No you don't," Melvin said. There were liver spots visible on the pleated folds of his neck. "You aren't in the superhero business anymore. Those days ended when Gravesmith took your legs. You're a teacher now. Your job is to create new heroes to take up the mantle."

"But with this battle wagon—" Owen began.

"Which isn't yours. It's school property, created at great expense to help you train your students. Period. School's not in session now, so you've no business fiddling with it. Park it back in its stall, Owen, and stand down. I see a number of your former students are already in Liberty, doing what you've so ably educated them to do. Let that be enough."

Owen moved a few steps toward one of the shuttles parked in the hanger—the heavy one, big enough to carry him and his borrowed robot half to Liberty in a matter of minutes.

"Leave now and I'll convene an emergency meeting of the board," Melvin said. "You'll be dismissed within the hour."

The two men, equally stubborn and willful, stared at each other as the black tower drifted silently through untroubled skies.

L is for Liberty
Man of the Hour

Only five short years ago, Liberty, Pennsylvania, was the safest of all major American cities in which to live, work, and raise a family, because Sergeant Liberty, its beloved hometown champion and protector, kept it so.

Then Sergeant Liberty fought the (now infamous) duel with his arch nemesis King Ogre, and everything changed suddenly and, it seems, irrevocably.

Everyone knows the details. It was a long and terrible battle, ending only when Sergeant Liberty finally threw his foe down from the top of the Codex Tower's revolving restaurant. King Ogre went to the morgue. Liberty went to the hospital.

In the emergency room, dedicated doctors worked tirelessly to save him. Of course, they had to cut away his mask. The wounds to his face and head were too severe. And of course, the entire incident was recorded by the treatment room's cameras. It was strict hospital policy to record all medical procedures for educational and insurance purposes. But it wasn't policy for one of the hospital's many employees (the specific offender was never discovered) to isolate a few key frames of that recording and sell the pictures to the *Liberty Post*.

Before he was out of the critical care ward, while he was still in a medically induced coma, the *Post* had identified Sergeant Liberty as none other than one Joseph Armstrong Wilcox, a contractor specializing in decorative stonework for new home construction. Afterward they never adequately explained, nor unconditionally apologized for, their decision to publish. One reporter described it as "more of a case of no one deciding not to publish." Within a day of the news hitting the streets (Saturday morning bulldog edition) Joe's wife and three children had been slaughtered in their Cedar Valley neighborhood home. The killers were never found. It was widely known that Sergeant Liberty had many enemies, most of whom were certainly the sort to carry a grudge and have the will to act on it in so brutal a fashion.

When he'd recovered, of course, Joe Wilcox left Liberty, never to return. Nor was Sergeant Liberty ever seen again.

M is for Max

Master of the Blade

There was a pause in the battle for a moment and The Ordinary Man couldn't help himself. He was standing next to Max the Knife and he had to ask. "You know the song is '*Mack* the Knife,' right? Not Max."

"Yeah, so? My name happens to be Max."

"Okay, but some part of you has to realize it's dumb to use one of your real names as part of your trade name. And it's even dumber, because that isn't actually the name in the song."

"You'd best let it drop," Strangeface interrupted. "Max doesn't like to be corrected."

N is for Nightfall
The Avenging Shade

Describe it? Okay, it was a mess, a complete clusterfuck, and getting worse every minute. Achilles and Doc Jerusalem were doing well enough, I suppose, but overwhelmed by all those killer robots. No wonder Strangeface had been so inactive for so long. The whole time he must have been building a new robot army, only this time it numbered in the thousands—maybe even the tens of thousands. How could he do it? Who was bankrolling him? And why weren't we watching him more closely? I have to admit, we really dropped the ball there.

Some of the new kids were doing well too. Xenoboy was tearing hell through the steel mob, like an atomic-powered buzz saw, leaving shrapnel in his wake. Captain Yesterday showed up and blasted away with her ray gun. And that new girl, Wonder Child, was incredible. She was evacuating and rescuing bystanders right and left, sometimes snatching them right out of the bad guys' clutches. You could barely see her, she was so fast.

And speaking of fast, where the hell was Fast Johnny? I heard a report over the system that he was on his way, but he certainly wasn't there by the time I'd arrived. I don't think he ever showed up. That can't be good news.

Anyway, we were doing pretty good against the robot troops, but no one was getting past them into the ranks of the actual villains, who were all huddled together, making sure they stayed close to one guy in the middle. I decided to head that way and see why— you know, spread some darkness, amp up the spooky, and see if I could scare some of them away. I certainly wasn't doing any good against the damned robots. They weren't human and couldn't be frightened. It was a big stalemate. They couldn't harm me, since all their bullets and laser beams passed right through me, but I couldn't do fuck all to them either.

So I went after the leaders.

Boy was that a mistake.

No sooner did I get within spitting distance than I started to feel weird—decidedly unghostly. And that's when I knew I'd screwed the pooch something awful. Suddenly I was grounded, solid, alive, and very normal again. Do you know what happened? The guy with them was The Ordinary Man! I didn't recognize him until it was too late. Before I could say "oops," some kid with a normal handgun shot me right between the eyes.

Dead before my body hit the ground.

So, that brings us to this. What do you say, you Spirits of Vengeance? Do I get another one of your phantom resurrections? Who makes that decision? You? The entire Steering Committee? Or is this something the full voting body has to weigh in on? Am I still your ghost with the most?

O is for Ordinary
The Power Taker

No one could safely approach the members of the New Cryptera as long as The Ordinary Man was among them. If they stepped inside the area covered by his "bubble of normalcy," their extraordinary powers vanished, even while he still allowed his new partners in crime to keep theirs. He'd learned how to be quite selective with his gift. When Visionary shot at them from miles away with his array of deadly glances, those effects stopped short at the barrier. Only ordinary phenomena were allowed in his vicinity, unless he was the one to grant an exception.

"We're doing great!" Professor Hell said. "No one can harm any of us!"

"But I'm still losing robots at a terrible rate," Strangeface said. "And none of the heroes are suiciding like they're supposed to." The broadcasts instructing the heroes to kill themselves continued without letup.

"You'll be compensated for the losses," Professor Hell said.

"And the capes will do what they must, once they fully realize their cause is hopeless. Continue killing the innocent and they'll have to relent. Or we'll eventually succeed in killing them ourselves. Either way we win."

Thunderhead wandered here and there, outside of The Ordinary Man's zone of safety. He'd never been one to cower behind someone else's skirts. Emil watched him blast Xenoboy with a bolt of lightning from the dark tangle of roiling cloud that permanently obscured his head—or maybe existed in place of his head—no one seemed to know for certain. Xenoboy wasn't down for long, though. He shrugged off the attack and returned to the fight. Emil uttered the word that would make Xenoboy's flesh melt off his body, but nothing happened. Damn, he thought. What's his weakness?

Suddenly Underman was among them, striking out right and left. Max went down, followed by Gunslinger, who fell in such a way that Emil knew at once that he was dead. His neck was clearly broken. His head lay at an odd angle to the rest of his body.

"He's still got his powers!" Emil called out to The Ordinary Man. "Do something!"

"I can't!" The Ordinary Man said. "I'm not sure what's wrong!"

"Nothing's wrong," Underman said. "I just don't happen to have any superpowers for you to cancel. This strength is perfectly normal for where I come from. Ordinary, I guess you'd say."

Underman struck again, and The Ordinary Man went out like a light.

P is for Pretender
The Consummate Faker

Lawrence Nash, The Great Pretender, pointed his finger at a woman trying to crawl away on a broken leg. "Pow," he said, and the woman died from a gunshot wound.

"Pow," he said again, and a man thirty feet away fell.

He brought his other hand up to join the first and swept a small cluster of people huddling under a half-collapsed bus stop shelter. "Rat-a-tat-tat-tat," he said, and three of them fell to machine-gun fire. He swept his pretend tommy gun back the other way, and the remaining two died alongside them.

"Trench broom!" he said. "The Chicago typewriter!"

Lawrence was having the time of his life. If Professor Hell wanted him to kill harmless civilians, then he was tickled to do it. Privately he thought their big plan was idiotic, but that didn't worry him. When the time came, and the tide of battle turned, as it inevitably would, Lawrence would simply imagine himself at the controls of a sleek personal rocket ship—just like Captain Yesterday's—and make his escape.

Enough simple gunplay, though. Time for something bigger, grander, and more imaginative.

Lawrence saw a news truck down the street and pretended he had a portable missile launcher on his shoulders—one of those things they kill tanks with. "Woosh!" he said and the news truck exploded up into the air. Bodies flew out of it. About half of them were still alive when they came down. One of the survivors was blonde and pretty.

"Hey, do you know who that is?" Lawrence looked around for someone to tell, but everyone near him was dead. Damn. What's the use of spotting the world's most famous news personality if no one was there to witness it? He walked over to get her autograph.

Q is for Questing Beast
The Magician's Last Scheme

Emil was scared again. While The Ordinary Man was awake and active, he'd felt terrific, untouchable, and had begun to think of himself as the dreaded Professor Hell again. But now he was once more acutely aware of all of the dangerous superheroes in the immediate vicinity and his many vulnerabilities.

Don't lose your nerve, Doctor. We can still win this.

It was Bad Moon's voice in his head again.

"Where have you been? You were supposed to be guiding me!"

I couldn't reach you as long as you huddled within The Ordinary Man's sphere of influence. He didn't know I was involved and so didn't allow for my mental communications to flow into you. A simple oversight on our part, corrected now.

"Corrected only because The Ordinary Man is out of action! Maybe dead! We're in serious trouble without him!"

Not at all. You've enough power to win the day all on your own, provided you keep your wits about you. First, send the others out, looking for targets. No need to stay together now. Command them to die, if necessary, as long as they take an opponent with them.

"And if we all die in the doing of it, then who's left to rule this world we've sacrificed ourselves to conquer?"

Me.

"You? Alone!"

Surely a man as intelligent as you had to realize that was the heart of my plan all along, Doctor. All that matters is that I survive to step in, once the carnage of this day has run its course. Now go and sow destruction among your enemies. Use those amazing powers. Impress me.

Emil tried to convince himself that the fugitive prince of the Battle Moons was right. He was smart and powerful. He could indeed triumph today, even without The Ordinary Man. First he would take a cue from Hark and find a way for others to do the fighting for him from now on. He brought out a handful of Hark's moondust from his pocket and threw it toward Thunderhead, the closest team member to him.

"Kill them all!" he shouted. "All of the heroes! Nothing else matters!"

Then he reached deep inside of his own mind and gathered up all of the magic spells waiting there—every dark and deadly possibility—and bound them into a single container, to which he added claws, fangs, a feral, predatory nature, and unquenchable hunger, and threw in a few poisoned barbs, just for good measure. He spoke a word of conjuration and the creature stood before him, ready to do his bidding. He thought of it as his personal questing beast and placed the images of his many opponents into the thing's mind.

"Go get 'em," Emil said.

And it did.

R is for Razorheart

The Bionic Marine

Malcolm Westmore lost both of his hands in Afghanistan, fighting for his country. His country was grateful and replaced his hands with advanced bionic versions that included a retractable set of indestructible razor-sharp blades that he could deploy from the tips of his metal fingers. These blades cost more than the price of an aircraft carrier and could cut through any known substance.

Malcolm had sliced at least fifty robots to ribbons today and was looking for something more interesting to cut when he spied an old villain called Professor Hell stumbling toward him through the smoke and ash and general fog of war.

"You'll do," Malcolm said.

Emil saw Malcolm, the superhero who called himself Razorheart, at about the same time and yawped in surprise and fear. He'd spent all of his magic constructing the questing beast and had nothing left to save himself. But he did still have half a pocketful of Hark's moondust. He threw every bit of it into Malcolm's face. Then he looked around for something to order the frightening hero to do. He could barely make out Saint George a block down to the right.

"Kill Saint George," Emil ordered. "Open him like a can of sardines and then gut whoever you find inside." Emil didn't pause to see if Razorheart would obey, but just hurried on his way, quickly disappearing into the ash cloud that engulfed the entire riverside area.

Malcolm stood silent and still for a time, wondering at the strange sense of disorientation and numbness that had come over him. Then he slowly began to remember how much he hated Saint George. He hated Saint George with all of his heart and mind and oft-troubled soul. He began to walk down the street. Then he began to run.

Saint George saw Eleanor Eastman, the great but impossible love of his life, lying in the street. She was injured and bleeding. He quickly finished tearing apart the killer robot he was holding and flew to her side. He didn't see The Great Pretender approaching her from one direction, nor Razorheart approaching from another. All of his attention was on Eleanor. He picked her up, oh so gently, in powered arms that could lift a battle tank and throw it half the length of a football field.

"I've got you," he said.

That's when Razorheart sank all ten of his deadly blades deep into Saint George's unprotected back. No less than twelve different independent defense systems in the Rocket Knight's armor recognized Razorheart as a friend and ally, and so did nothing to stop him, not realizing the possible threat until it was much too late. The armor plating on the Gold and Green Knight's back pealed away like tissue paper, as did several of the major power lines running underneath it. Both major power plants suffered catastrophic failure. Saint George froze into place, Eleanor still in his arms.

"Going to kill you now," Malcolm Westmore said. But he didn't get the chance.

The Great Pretender was understandably upset. He'd nearly reached the pretty reporter to get her autograph—and maybe her phone number—when that armored oaf Saint George came swooping in ahead of him.

Jackass, Lawrence thought. He pretended he was at the gunner's station of an army tank, its big gun trained on the Rocket

Knight. But then he recalled that Saint George had survived tank shells before. He saw it on the very news show that the pretty reporter girl appeared on from time to time. So instead he pretended to be at the controls of a missile launcher—the huge stationary artillery kind. But a strange thing happened before he could fire. One of Saint George's goody-goody friends came along and started to gut him like a fish.

Interesting, he thought. He considered holding off, just to see what happened next, but the eagerness to fire his missile won him over. He aimed his pretend weapon at the Liberty Crier News Building, which loomed high above them, and pulled the lever. There was a gigantic explosion, bigger than Lawrence could ever have hoped for, and then the entire structure—all thirty floors of it—began to fall. It came tumbling down on Saint George, on the pretty woman he still held in his frozen arms, and on the other fellow. What was his name again?

Too late, Lawrence realized he'd fired too big a weapon from too close a range. It seemed the massive building was coming down on him too.

Yikes! he thought.

Acting quickly, he pretended he was encased in a suit of armor exactly like Saint George's, only before the bladed guy damaged it.

Nothing happened. He felt no protection around him.

Yikes indeed.

Sometimes the power didn't work if he couldn't accurately imagine, or understand, the thing he was trying to pretend into existence. That's why he mostly pretended at small arms in the general course of his frequent killing sprees. He knew those weapons quite well. Silly to let myself get carried away with grand ideas, he thought.

The collapsing rubble was nearly on him. He had no time left, and the only thing he could quickly think of was a giant version of one of his mother's old metal mixing bowls covering him.

Did I get it in time? That was his last thought as a section of wall came crashing down on him.

S is for Saint George
The World's Greatest Knight

Saint George watched Eleanor Eastman slowly transition back to consciousness.

"Don't try to move," he said. "There's an awful lot of rubble over us and it's not stable. Plus, I think one of your legs may be broken."

"What happened?" she managed to croak out. Her mouth was full of dust and grit. Saint George was lying close to her. They were in a small cavity, dim and dusty, but lit by one of his undamaged floodlights.

"Building collapse," he said. "My emergency power systems kicked in just as everything came crashing down on us. I was able to blast some of it away and get you tucked under me, but—well, you can see the result. Not too bad, all things considered."

"How long have we been down here?" she said.

"Couple of hours. They know we're here and have already started digging up above. Slow going, though. Have to be careful not to cause a secondary collapse."

"How do you know all this?"

"I've got pretty sophisticated sensors. I had time to do a thorough internal scan on you too, while waiting for you to wake up. No major internal injuries, you'll be happy to know. You'll be fine, Eleanor. Some pain, but mostly you'll be bored, waiting for them to dig us out. I'm working on a way to get a water tube over to you, so no worries on that front."

That's when Eleanor realized the giant steel girder pinning Saint George had also entirely crushed both his upper legs. They were as flat as pounded tin.

"Your legs were severed!"

"No, I'm okay."

"You have to be in terrible pain!"

"Calm down, sweetie. I'm fine."

She looked hard at him for a long time, and he could see the calculation and journalist's curiosity begin to supplant her momentary panic. He could almost see each fact fall into place for her.

Finally she said, "So that's your secret. That's why you never let me see the man inside the armor. There was never a man to see. You're a robot, aren't you?"

"Yeah, you got me. You finally figured it out. I was one of Strangeface's killer robots, but there was a short circuit during a mission into Romania. Luckily some magical gypsies found me and, since they couldn't repair me mechanically, they placed a human soul and self-awareness inside me. I became sentient, independent, learned to repair and improve myself, and thus a superhero was born."

"Seriously?"

"No, of course not, you gullible twit. I'm not a robot. I'm really just a guy in here, like I always told you. Only I'm not quite the guy you imagined, and—"

"And what?"

"Here come the big national secrets I was never allowed to reveal."

"And what?! Spill!"

"And I'm not alone in here."

"What do you mean? Not alone?"

"Saint George was never a superhero, or a robot, or a man in a suit of powered armor. Saint George is the name of a very advanced battleship—the ship I happen to serve in, along with about forty other crewmen. I'm not even the captain. He mostly runs the combat operations center. I'm one of four officers who stand a rotating watch at the con. That's military lingo for the main driver's seat."

Eleanor could think of nothing to say, and so said nothing.

"Okay," he said. "I see I've surprised you pretty thoroughly, so I might as well go all the way. You're about to see some hatches open here and there and a bunch of crewmen come out. They need to do some external repair work, investigate this cavity a bit more to make sure it doesn't decide to come crashing down after all, and run that water line over to you that I promised."

Hatches did begin to open. Small doors popped up, all over the exterior of Saint George's body. Tiny men and women crawled out of the various hatchways.

"I also need to send a medical team through any small passageways they might find, to see if Razorheart is still alive. He ended up about thirty feet away from us to the west-southwest, and six feet lower. We aren't receiving any life signs from him, but that could be due to all sorts of things. The nature of the material separating us. Interference from embedded power lines. Anything at all, really. Better to check and make certain."

The miniature men and women were scrambling all over the surface of Saint George by this time, pulling power lines into place, working with small diagnostic computers, and performing other complex and indecipherable duties.

"Anything you want to ask me, Eleanor?"

She considered for a moment and then said, "Who are you people?"

"Creatures of myth and legend," Saint George said. At least that's what the voice said that came out of one of his still-functioning speakers. "In our own tongue we're the Yerremorden, which means 'the wrathful people.' Another proper name would be the Pinnan-shee, which roughly translates as 'bottle faeries,' but that mostly applies now to those of us in the military service, in general, and those of us who crew these battleships, in particular."

"Some bottle," she said.

"Indeed. Basically any time you heard about sprites, or brownies, or little people in general, they were probably talking about us, whether they knew it or not."

"So you're not magical folks in little pointed hats with bells?"

"Some of us still dress in traditional costume, especially during festival days and such. But, no, not so much anymore. We moved on. You big folks made lots of technological and scientific advances over the years, and so have we."

Some of the little soldiers had run the water line over to Eleanor by this time. She took a few sips from it, coughed up some dirt and phlegm, and then sipped some more. When she spoke again, her voice was considerably less strained and frog-like.

"And, in the past," she said, "when you acted so attentive and caring, that was when you were the one on duty, running the ship."

"I knew you'd figure it out. By the way, my name's Awan. And even though I couldn't quite find the way to explain it to you—military secrets and all—I was really, genuinely crazy about you. Always have been, since that first time we met, during the Korean nuclear incident. I'd come out now and wave hello to you, so you could finally get that look at me you always wanted, but I can't leave my post."

"And then, when you acted so cold and aloof at times, that was because someone else was on duty." She didn't ask it as a question.

"Right. Mostly it was Lieutenant Commander Jerob on those occasions. He can be quite the jerk. A real tool. And then sometimes Lieutenant Carnovan had to be overtly standoffish to you too, but only because he's already married to a woman in the crew, and she gets hugely, insanely jealous of you. I can hardly blame her of course, but—"

"Hold on. I think I'm going to be sick."

And she was, but all of Saint George's crew still outside the ship were able to scramble to safety in time.

After a while she said, "I was right about one thing. You really were just playing mind games all along, since nothing could ever have come from your pretense at romance between us."

"Well, that's not entirely true. I've been petitioning the Admiralty and the Ministry of—well, I shouldn't tell you their name—for use of one of the new full-encounter suits. It's not a battleship like Saint George. It's more of an artificial man that can pass as human, on any inspection short of a really invasive medical workup, and it's fully functional. And best of all, it needs only a single driver, so it really would be an intimate occasion just between the two of us. It was always my intention to find some way to follow up on my—uhm, advances."

That's when Eleanor first screamed, and she did it for a long time.

Two hours later, when she was calm again, and had been for a while, and when they could begin to hear sounds of the rescue efforts from above, she said, "When we get out of here, I don't want to ever see you again. Any of you."

"Fair enough," Saint George (or, more properly, Awan) said. "But at least in the time remaining can I talk to you about the possibilities of keeping all of this secret?"

T is for Thunderhead
A Most Frightening Sight

As far as I could tell, I was the last villain standing. Most were dead or captured. Professor Hell had disappeared and shortly thereafter I saw Strangeface activate his teleporter belt and disappear too, in a more literal way.

For a while I'd watched Achilles battle a giant wolf-like beast, but one with saber fangs and a tail that had long spikes sticking out from it. All sorts of bizarre things happened around them as they fought. The ground erupted in localized earthquakes and upheavals of molten magma. A fall of meteors rained down on them for about ten minutes, but none of them hit the beast, and the ones that hit Achilles would knock him down sure enough, but he'd always get right back up again. Then Achilles burned for a long time, but when the flames finally died, all they had done was to leave him naked, but still unharmed. Finally Doc Jerusalem joined in and beheaded the creature with a single stroke of her sword. That was something to see.

That's about when I started seriously looking for a way to leave the area. Discretion wasn't possible—not when one looks as alien as I do, with nothing but a churning dark cloud where you'd expect to find a head—so I had no doubts I'd have to fight my way out, to one extent or another.

I picked a direction that seemed to promise the fewest

obstacles—both living and inanimate—and started out. Almost immediately I spotted Underman up ahead and blasted him with a lightning bolt. Underman went down. I didn't pause to see if he was dead or not. I adjusted direction and continued on.

Unstable Boy was next. He landed in front of me and demanded my immediate surrender. His eyes were glowing. I knew he was about to start shooting those miniature radioactive glowy-globe things at me—or worse yet, cause them to grow directly inside of me and start eating their way out—so I shot him quick with a bolt at extremely close range. The thunderclap was deafening. This time I knew I'd killed the guy, because there were at least three separate pieces of him staining the ground in front of me. I ran for it while everyone nearby was still moaning and holding his ears.

Before I could get very far, this new girl I'd never seen before landed in front of me, just like Unstable Boy had done. Why's everyone on their side able to fly these days? I didn't wait. I zapped her instantly.

But she wasn't harmed at all. Sure, she had tears in her eyes, but they were already there when she'd landed.

"He was my boyfriend," she said, and then the tears really began to flow. She was sort of cute. Skinny, and probably too young. No more than sixteen or seventeen. Cute costume too. Dark blue. Pleated skirt. Petite cape. She was going for sort of a retro look, I guessed.

She picked me up in one hand and threw me into the sky.

In a minute or two, when I didn't slow down at all, I realized she'd actually thrown me into space.

I'm not kidding.

At first I was scared to death. Then I was overcome with awe. You'd have to see what I see to understand. Then (who knows how much later?) the awe remained in full force, but also I began to get bored. Apparently you can feel both things at once.

Now I'm stuck up here in some sort of erratic low orbit. I see continents and blue oceans sliding by under me, repeating about every thirty minutes.

Before this, I had no idea I wouldn't die without oxygen, or air pressure, or whatever else folks usually need, but which isn't available in space. I wonder how long I can last up here.

I wonder if I'll burn up on reentry someday when my orbit starts to decay.

U is for Underman
The King Down Below

In ancient days, while the supercontinent of Pangaea was just starting its tumultuous breakup, the three smaller continents of Hyperborea, Lemuria, and Atlantis suffered the cataclysms that sank them beneath the waves. But they were great civilizations all, allied even then, and advanced in every form of science and sorcery. And so they survived for the most part. Over the ages they adapted and transformed themselves, that they might flourish in their deep and watery homes.

Today the earth isn't a world of vast continents, inhabited by diverse cultures. Rather it is that, but hardly just that. Why not describe a python as a creature with two eyes? Such a description would be accurate, as far as it went, but hardly comprehensive. Now open your eyes and look at our earth in another way. It's actually a water planet, filled with marvelously advanced and venerable civilizations, that happens to also have scattered incidents of dry land, which are peopled with primitive tribes of barbarian hominids, genetically and structurally similar (and perhaps related in fact) to their decidedly superior undersea cousins.

It's a matter of perspective.

If the envoys of vast galactic civilizations were to decide to contact the people of Earth (as they have), they'd ignore the relatively primitive land dwellers and proceed directly to the political centers of the cities under the seas (as they have). Want to know who runs the world? It's not your American president, or the so-called United Nations. It was never an emperor, caesar, tsar, pharaoh, or overly ambitious Macedonian conqueror. Small potatoes, all. It's the King of the Seven Seas who rules the world. It always has been, for longer than human beings have existed. They've just never seen the point of educating the surface dwellers to that fact. Why bother?

For the past twenty-odd years Warrender Norris was the reigning King of Kings, ruling over the seven united undersea kingdoms (which is what gives us the tradition of the seven seas, although there are certainly many more, depending on how one decides to divide and categorize them), and their combined three thousand cities, towns, and smaller settlements.

King Warren, as he liked to be called, preferring the diminutive that made his given name sound more like that of a surface dweller, was a half-breed, a miracle baby or a scientific oddity, depending on your mood, disposition, and politics. His mother was the previous reigning Queen, while his biological father, one James Norris, was a North Alaskan salmon fisherman. She'd suffered catastrophic engine failure of her personal subscooter while out on a private jaunt one day. There was an explosion (possibly due to sabotage, but that's a tale for another time). James was there to fish her unconscious body out of the drink, not knowing she was in no danger of drowning. Sparks flew. There was a short affair, followed by a long scandal.

Warren was born, illegitimate, to the Queen, shockingly pink of skin, clearly favoring his father. The cuckolded King of Kings went off to work out his shame and anger through his customary pursuits of war. There was always a breakaway province or two that needed a good scolding. The King died in battle, leaving Warren, bastard though he was, the only possible heir.

He was well loved. He was despised. In a civilization comprising more than a billion souls, you can take your pick. Politics was the sole industry of Atlantis Under, the current Royal Capital (ever since Umul the 38th moved it from Harruhold, because he thought the waters there were too warm for his delicate constitution), and intrigue was its chief manufactured product. Many were the dukes, counts, satraps, princes, and lesser kings who plotted against their liege lord.

Early in Warren's reign a particularly inventive scheme was hatched.

"He loves the surface dwellers too much," Preatus whispered to Ban, his friend and closest companion at court. Ban was the famous Deep Blue Prince of Rymehold Below.

"He's fascinated by them, to be sure," Ban said. "But love? That's something of a stretch. He was raised here, among his mother's people, cut off entirely from his father and the dryskins. It's only natural he'd be curious about the other half of his heritage."

As was often the case, Warren had his head firmly embedded in the viewing bubble, ignoring the boring matters of court, spying here and there throughout the surface world.

"He's taken no wife and has produced no heir, legitimate or otherwise," Preatus said. "If he were to suffer some unfortunate accident, the thousand-millennia Roor line would finally die with him. At long last a new dynasty would have to be selected. Your house is noble and you're immensely popular."

"I'm without ambitions," Ban said.

"Liar." Preatus said it with a familiar smile and a tone devoid of authentic accusation. Ban let his fingers brush across his signet ring, but didn't activate the illegal destroyer beam concealed within it. "Our king will be in the bubble all day. We won't be missed here. Swim with me awhile and let's talk further."

And they did.

Months later Ban requested a private audience with the young King, which was granted immediately, because Warren had always admired the legendary deep lord, hero of so many old battles. Warren was only slightly put out to see that Preatus, the furtive, gar-faced Baron of Gliss accompanied the Deep Blue Prince.

"With respect, sire, I can't help but notice your dilemma," Ban said. "And I'm grieved by your unhappiness. You long to visit the surface world, but you can't."

"By ancient tradition, our civilization has had no formal relations with the surface countries," Warren said. "I've already caused too much disruption to the realm by the simple fact of my existence. I can't further exacerbate the problem by being the first one to break that tradition. Perhaps my son, someday . . ." Warren let the statement trail off unfinished.

"Then don't visit in an official capacity," Preatus said. "Go informally instead. Or better yet, go anonymously."

"How?" Warren said.

"Those strange lands are overrun with their costumed heroes, each one an oddity possessed of bizarre powers and abilities," Ban said. "Why not become such a character? The differences in strength and speed and such will simply be accepted as your particular set of superpowers—if I understand their delightful vernacular correctly. No one will suspect that your seemingly unique and extraordinary abilities are natural to us and our kind. And in this guise you'll be able to learn firsthand about their world, while fighting for their causes. A young king should have adventures and military escapades, but unfortunately, our realm is too much at peace these tides. You govern too well."

Warren was still young then and susceptible to flattery from one of his heroes.

"But I can't simply abandon my responsibilities," Warren said.

"Then don't. Return as often as you need to. Many of those super characters are reputed to have their secret lairs and fortresses, where they retire sometimes to recuperate or enjoy their occasional need for solitude. Let this city be yours. I dare say, after so many ages to perfect it, most of the great engine of government swims along just fine on its own. I suspect you'll find that you're needed less often than you currently imagine."

"A man should have his adventures," Preatus said. "It's a vital part of what makes him into a man grown."

"All of the really memorable kings have them," Ban said. "The stronger metals are only refined in the cauldron. Go out and make yourself strong to better serve your kingdom. If you happen to sat-

isfy your own desire to learn more about the dryskins as a byproduct of such devotion, then so much the better." His smile was most sincere.

A week or so later Underman, the mysterious champion from the depths, made his debut, battling Korakan the Time Warrior (whose twenty-fourth-century weapons were still primitive stone knives and wooden clubs compared to Atlantean technology) in the streets of Seattle, defeating him soundly. No one knew that Underman's sleek and colorful costume was just a simplified version of the standard Atlantean military uniform. In time the Aquatic Ace was invited to become a member of the Fidelity League, where he served with distinction, twice as their leader, until they disbanded in the waning days of the '90s. Even after the League disbanded, Warren fought often at the sides of his friends Achilles, Doc Jerusalem, Saint George, and so many others, and had the time of his life doing so.

Down in Atlantis Under, the two conspirators had occasion to meet privately once in a while.

"Year after year the absurd Underman keeps failing to die," Preatus said.

"Patience, dear baron," Ban said. "He plays at a dangerous profession. Swims continuously in treacherous waters. The odds will catch up to him sooner or later. In the meantime, he never stays down here long enough to meet a girl with whom he might be inspired to continue the royal line. Our lives are long and our plan is intact, so all is well. We'll prevail in the end."

And so they did, but that again is a tale for another time.

V is for Visionary
Whose Eyes Brightly Glow

With the battle largely over, and time to really concentrate, Visionary turned his remarkable sight to other matters. He'd gotten a good look at Professor Hell a few times during the day, and was concerned at what he'd seen. The man had a lot of conversations when no one was around to hear him. True, he could have been talking into a communicator of some sort, but Visionary hadn't spotted one. What he had done was take up lip reading of late. He wasn't very good at it yet, but he had a skilled instructor and was making weekly progress. He was almost certain he'd caught Professor Hell repeating one frightening name over and over again.

When he wasn't distracted by city-engulfing battles, when he was really able to concentrate his powers, Visionary could track the progress of a single mote of dust in a hurricane, ten thousand miles distant. He could look past worlds and stars and galaxies, to the worlds and stars and galaxies beyond them. Given enough effort, he could look through the Earth entire and see what was on the other side.

He started looking here and there for a moon where there shouldn't be one.

W is for Wonder Child
Mightier Than the Rest

After throwing Thunderhead into space in a fit of pique, she remembered her real responsibilities and went back to saving innocents. There were more than two dozen dying, crumbling, burning buildings that needed clearing. She could still hear too many cries for help. So she flew and she lifted and she never stopped until all were safe or confirmed as being beyond her aid.

Afterward, when she was looking about for some other way to be of use, Visionary came up to her.

"I wonder if you could do me a small favor," he said.

X is for Xenoboy
He Tries His Best

Strange visitor from an alien planet, he came to Earth with amazing powers. Raised from a young age by foster parents—his mother, Laura, and his other mother, Anne—our world became his adopted home.

He could fly, but not as fast or as far as Wonder Child. He was strong, but once again, not as strong as she. He was tough, but not completely invulnerable like Achilles. And his senses weren't quite as acute as Underman's hearing or Visionary's incredible sight.

But not one of those heroes could interrogate a stone, talk poetry with a pond, or have a meaningful conversation with a tree. So he had that going for him.

He'd spent the day destroying robots, putting out fires, and holding up collapsing buildings long enough for emergency workers to finish the evacuations. When the Brandon Tower, burning from the middle floors upward, looked like it was going to finally collapse, and trapped people started jumping from its uppermost floors, Xenoboy flew to the rescue. He caught seven before they hit the ground. Of course every one of those seven died from the terrible impact with his harder-than-steel arms.

"Have to work on that," he said to no one.

Y is for Yesterday
Old Time Hero of Tomorrow

Captain Yesterday, of the Galactic Space Rangers (which so far included only her, but it's early days yet).

She wore a red metal helmet with a golden fin on its crown. Her hair was long and glossy black, hanging in a ponytail out of the back of her helmet. Her eyes were hidden behind green shaded goggles. Her skin was pale, her lips crimson. She wore a brown leather jacket, with twin rows of golden buttons. Twin red straps formed an X over her chest. She had khaki jodhpurs, knee-high red leather jackboots, and red leather gauntlets. There was an art deco ray gun on her hip, and a Buck Rogers spaceship at her beck and call.

Just about the time she'd run out of robots to burn out of the sky, she received a transmission over her cosmotron wrist radio.

"Can you rendezvous with Wonder Child up in space?" Visionary asked. "I'm not certain what's going on, but she seems to be having some trouble up there." Captain Yesterday was strapped in and ready to launch before he'd finished his request. Her trusty and ever loyal ship was named *Avenging Star*. Together they blasted off for adventure.

Following Visionary's radioed directions, Captain Yesterday and her *Avenging Star* homed in on a bright speck that became a round yellow dot, which became a small moon. Small is a relative term. It had grown as big as a bustling rural town, having fed often and abundantly off the fears, hopes, and desires of an unwary populace.

Moving closer still, she saw the young girl called Wonder Child pushing the moon deep into space, away from the Earth.

Help me, the rogue satellite sent directly into her mind. *I'm being moonnapped!*

"I don't think so," she said into her radio, not knowing, and not much caring, if he could receive her broadcast.

Eyes the size of soccer fields turned to her, pleadingly. *I insist! I command you to do what's right!* A mouth the size of any given Main Street attempted a sad frown of despair, but only managed to show rage and frustration. *This creature has no jurisdiction over me! Especially out in space!*

"I do," Captain Yesterday said. It was true. She'd recently completed work on her Outer Space Patrol Code and Ranger Manifesto, granting herself all of the jurisdiction she'd ever need.

Wonder Child broke off from pushing the big Bad Moon farther into the void and flew toward the *Avenging Star*, signaling silently, and a bit frantically, that she wanted to come aboard. When she emerged from the airlock, her expression showed abject misery and defeat. Her face and costume were powdered with yellow moondust, but it seemed to have no affect on her.

"I tried to push Bad Moon into the sun, to end his depraved life of crime for all time," Wonder Child said. "But I couldn't bring myself to do it. No matter how evil he may be, I can't kill a sentient being in cold blood."

"Don't worry, Child," Captain Yesterday said. Her smile was both jaunty and confidence-inspiring. "No one needs to force a sweet child like you to become a killer." She punched a bright button on the control panel, loading one of her planet-buster torpedoes into *Avenging Star*'s firing tube number one.

Z is for Zero Men
Custodians of Death and Sorrow

When it was all over, Fagan Faust returned to Liberty. His Zero Men moved in, in great numbers, to evacuate the injured, remove the bodies, and begin the cleanup. They swarmed over everything. When more were needed, they appeared, each one a duplicate of the others, strong, handsome, dashing, all-American—everything that Faust wasn't. When all that they could do had been done, they faded away, retreating back into Fagan Faust's oft-troubled but fertile imagination, vanishing once more into the nothingness they always were.

About the Editor

A 2010/2009/2008/2007 Hugo Award nominee, 2008 Philip K. Dick Award nominee, 2009/2007 Chesley Award nominee, and 2006 World Fantasy Award nominee, Lou Anders is the editorial director of Prometheus Books' science fiction and fantasy imprint Pyr, as well as the editor of the anthologies *Swords & Dark Magic* (coedited with Jonathan Strahan, Eos, June 2010), *Fast Forward 2* (Pyr, October 2008), *Sideways in Crime* (Solaris, June 2008), *Fast Forward 1* (Pyr, February 2007), *FutureShocks* (Roc, January 2006), *Projections: Science Fiction in Literature & Film* (MonkeyBrain, December 2004), *Live Without a Net* (Roc, 2003), and *Outside the Box* (Wildside Press, 2001). In 2000, he served as the Executive Editor of Bookface.com, and before that he worked as the Los Angeles Liaison for Titan Publishing Group. He is the author of *The Making of Star Trek: First Contact* (Titan Books, 1996), and has published over 500 articles in such magazines as *The Believer*, *Publishers Weekly*, *Dreamwatch*, *DeathRay*, *free inquiry*, *Star Trek Monthly*, *Star Wars Monthly*, *Babylon 5 Magazine*, *Sci Fi Universe*, *Doctor Who Magazine*, and *Manga Max*. His articles and stories have been translated into Danish, Greek, German, Italian, and French. Visit him online at www.louanders.com.